Alice

Tom can't decide if Alice is good or evil. She terrifies the local village lads, is related to two of the most evil witch clans (the Malkins and the Deanes) and has been known to use dark magic. But she was trained as a witch against her will and has helped Tom out of some tight spots. She seems to be a loyal friend, but can she be trusted?

Mam

Tom's mam has always known he would become the Spook's apprentice. She calls him her 'gift to the County'. A loving mother and an expert on plants, medicine and childbirth, Mam has always been a little different. Her origins in Greece remain a mystery. In fact, there are quite a few mysterious things about Mam . . .

THE WARDSTONE CHRONICLES

THE SPOOK'S BATTLE

JOSEPH DELANEY

Illustrated by David Wyatt

RED FOX

THE SPOOK'S BATTLE
A RED FOX BOOK 978 1 782 95248 0

First published in Great Britain by The Bodley Head,
an imprint of Random House Children's Publishers UK
A Random House Group Company
Bodley Head edition published 2007
First Red Fox edition published 2008
This edition published 2014

1 3 5 7 9 10 8 6 4 2

Text copyright © Joseph Delaney, 2007
Cover illustration copyright © Talexi Taini, 2009
Interior illustrations copyright © David Wyatt, 200

The right of Joseph Delaney to be identified as the author
of this work has been asserted in accordance with the
Copyright, Designs and Patents Act 1988.

Set in 10.5/16.5pt Palatino by Falcon Oast Graphic Art Ltd.

Red Fox Books are published by Random House Children's Publishers UK,
61–63 Uxbridge Road, London W5 5SA

www.randomhousechildrens.co.uk
www.totallyrandombooks.co.uk
www.randomhouse.co.uk

Addresses for companies within The Random House Group Limited
can be found at: www.randomhouse.co.uk/offices.htm

THE RANDOM HOUSE GROUP Limited Reg. No. 954009

A CIP catalogue record for this book is available from the British Library.

Printed and bound in Great Britain by CPI Group (UK) Ltd, Croydon, CR0 4YY

for Marie

THE HIGHEST POINT IN THE COUNTY
IS MARKED BY MYSTERY.
IT IS SAID THAT A MAN DIED THERE IN A
GREAT STORM, WHILE BINDING AN EVIL
THAT THREATENED THE WHOLE WORLD.
THEN THE ICE CAME AGAIN, AND WHEN IT
RETREATED, EVEN THE SHAPES OF THE
HILLS AND THE NAMES OF THE TOWNS
IN THE VALLEYS CHANGED.
NOW, AT THAT HIGHEST POINT ON
THE FELLS, NO TRACE REMAINS OF WHAT
WAS DONE SO LONG AGO,
BUT ITS NAME HAS ENDURED.
THEY CALL IT –

THE WARDSTONE.

CHAPTER 1
A VISITOR FROM PENDLE

The witch was chasing me through the dark wood, getting nearer and nearer by the second.

I ran fast, frantic to escape, weaving desperately, with branches whipping into my face and brambles clutching at my weary legs. The breath rasped harshly in my throat as I drove myself harder and harder towards the edge of the wood. Beyond that lay the slope leading up to the Spook's western garden. If only I could reach that refuge, I'd be safe!

I wasn't defenceless. In my right hand I gripped my rowan staff, which was particularly effective against witches; in my left was my silver chain, coiled about my wrist, ready for throwing. But would I get even

1

half a chance to use either? For the chain I needed a gap between us, but already the witch was close at my heels.

Suddenly the footsteps behind me ceased. Had she given up? I ran on, the waning moon now visible through the leaf canopy above, silver-dappling the ground at my feet. The trees were thinning. I'd almost reached the edge of the wood.

Then, just as I passed the last tree, she appeared from nowhere and ran at me from the left, her teeth gleaming in the moonlight, her arms outstretched as if ready to claw out my eyes. Still running, veering away, I flicked my left wrist and cracked the chain to send it hurtling towards her. For a moment I thought I had her, but she swerved suddenly and the chain fell harmlessly onto the grass. The next moment she thudded into me, knocking the staff from my hand.

I hit the ground so hard that all the breath was driven from my body, and in an instant she was on me, her weight bearing down on me. I struggled for a moment, but I was winded and exhausted and she was very strong. She sat on my chest and pinned my arms down on either side of my head. Then she leaned forward so that our faces were almost touching, and her hair was like a black shroud touching my cheeks and blotting out the stars. Her breath was on my face but it wasn't rank like that of a blood- or bone-witch. It was sweet like spring flowers.

'Got you now, Tom, I have!' Alice exclaimed triumphantly. 'Ain't good enough, that. You'll need to do better in Pendle!'

With that, she gave a laugh and rolled off me, and I sat up, still fighting for breath. After a few moments I found the strength to walk across and collect my staff and silver chain. Although she was the niece of a witch, Alice was my friend and had saved me more than once during the past year. Tonight I'd been practising my survival skills, Alice playing the part of a witch seeking my life. I should have been grateful but I felt annoyed. It was the third night in a row that she'd got the better of me.

As I started to walk up the slope towards the Spook's

western garden, Alice ran to my side and matched me step for step.

'No need to sulk, Tom!' she said softly. 'It's a nice mild summer's night. Let's make the best of it while we can. Be on our travels soon, we will, and we'll both be wishing we were back here.'

Alice was right. I'd be fourteen at the beginning of August and I'd been the Spook's apprentice for over a year now. Although we'd faced many serious dangers together, something even worse was looming. For some time the Spook had been hearing reports that the threat from the Pendle witches was growing; he'd told me that we'd soon be travelling there to try and deal with it. But there were dozens of witches and maybe hundreds of their supporters, and I couldn't see how we could triumph against such odds. After all, there were only three of us: the Spook, Alice and me.

'I'm not sulking,' I said.

'Yes you are. Your chin's almost touching the grass.'

We walked on in silence until we entered the garden and saw the Spook's house through the trees.

'Ain't said anything yet about when we're off to Pendle, has he?' Alice asked.

'Not a thing.'

'Haven't you asked? Don't find nothing out without asking!'

'Course I've asked him,' I told Alice. 'He just taps the side of his nose and tells me that I'll find out in good time. My guess is that he's waiting for something but I don't know what.'

'Well, I just wish he'd get on with it. The waiting's making me nervous.'

'Really?' I said. 'I'm in no rush to leave and I didn't think you'd want to go back there.'

'I don't. It's a bad place, Pendle, and it's a big place too – a whole district with villages and hamlets and big, ugly Pendle Hill right at its centre. I've got a lot of evil family there I'd sooner forget about. But if we've got to go, I'd like to get it over and done with. I can hardly sleep at night now worrying about it.'

When we entered the kitchen, the Spook was sitting at the table writing in his notebook, a candle flickering at his side. He glanced up but didn't say anything because he was too busy concentrating. We sat ourselves down on two stools, which we drew close to the hearth. As it was summer, the fire was small, but it still sent a comforting warm glow up into our faces.

At last my master snapped his notebook shut and looked up. 'Who won tonight?' he asked.

'Alice,' I said, hanging my head.

'That's three nights in a row the girl's got the better of you, lad. You're going to have to do better than that. A lot better. First thing in the morning, before breakfast, I'll see you in the western garden. It's extra practice for you.'

I groaned inside. In the garden was a wooden post which was used as a target. If the practice didn't go well, my master would keep me at it for a long time and breakfast would be delayed.

I set off for the garden just after dawn but the Spook was already there waiting for me.

'Well, lad, what kept you?' he chided. 'Doesn't take

that long to rub the sleep out of your eyes!'

I still felt tired but I tried my best to smile and look bright and alert. Then, with my silver chain coiled over my left hand, I took careful aim at the post.

Soon I was feeling a lot better. For the one hundredth time since starting, I flicked my wrist and the chain cracked sharply as it unfurled, soaring through the air and glittering brightly in the morning sunshine to fall in a perfect widdershins spiral about the practice post.

Until a week earlier, the best I'd been able to achieve from eight feet was an average of nine successful throws out of ten attempts. But now, suddenly, the long months of practice had finally paid off. When the chain was coiled about the post for the hundredth time that morning, I hadn't missed even once!

I tried not to smile, I really did, but the sides of my mouth began to twitch upwards, and within moments a wide grin split my face. I saw the Spook shaking his head, but try as I might, I couldn't get the grin under control.

'Don't get above yourself, lad!' he warned, striding towards me through the grass. 'I hope you're not getting complacent. Pride comes before a fall, as many have found to their cost. And as I've often told you before, a witch won't stand still while you make your throw! From what the girl told me about last night, you've a long way to go yet. Right, let's try some throws on the run!'

For the next hour I was made to cast at the post while on the move. Sometimes sprinting, sometimes jogging, running towards it, away from it, casting forwards, obliquely or back over my shoulder, I did it all, working hard but growing hungrier by the minute. I missed the post lots of times but I also had a few spectacular successes. The Spook was finally satisfied and we moved on to something he'd only introduced me to a few weeks earlier.

He handed me his staff and led me to the dead tree we used for target practice. I pressed the lever to release the hidden blade in the staff and then spent the next fifteen minutes or so treating the rotten trunk as if it were an enemy threatening my life. Time and time again I drove the blade into it until my arms grew heavy and tired. The most recent trick my master had taught me was to hold the staff casually in my right hand before quickly transferring it to my stronger left and stabbing it hard into the tree. There was a knack to it. You sort of flicked it from one hand to the other.

When I showed signs of weariness, the Spook clicked his tongue. 'Come on, lad, let's see you do it again. One day it might just save your life!'

This time I did it almost perfectly: the Spook nodded and led us back through the trees for a hard-earned breakfast.

Ten minutes later Alice had joined us and the three of us were seated at the large oak table in the kitchen, tucking into a big breakfast of ham and eggs cooked by the Spook's pet boggart. The boggart had lots of jobs to do around the house in Chipenden: cooking, making the fires and washing the pots as well as guarding the house and gardens. It wasn't a bad cook but it sometimes reacted to what was happening in the house, and if it was feeling angry or moody, then you could expect an unappetizing meal. Well, the boggart was certainly in a good mood that morning because I remember thinking it was one of the best breakfasts it had ever cooked.

We ate in silence, but as I was mopping up the last bit of yellow yolk with a large slice of buttered bread, the Spook pushed back his chair and stood up. He paced backwards and forwards across the flags in front of the hearth, then came to a halt facing the table and stared straight at me.

'I'm expecting a visitor later today, lad,' he said. 'We've a lot to discuss, so once he's arrived and you've met him, I'd like time to talk to him in private. I think it's about time you went home, back to your brother's farm, to collect those trunks that your mam left you. I think it's best to bring them back here to Chipenden, where you can search through them thoroughly. We may well find things in there that'll prove useful on our trip to Pendle. We're going to need all the help we can get.'

My dad had died last winter and left the farm to Jack, my eldest brother. But after Dad's death we'd discovered something very unusual in his will.

Mam had a special room in our home farm. It was just under the attic and she always kept it locked. This room had been left to me, together with the trunks and boxes it contained, and the will stated that I could go there any time I wanted. This had upset my brother Jack and his wife Ellie. My job as an apprentice to the Spook worried them. They feared that I might bring something from the dark back to the house. Not that I blamed them; that was exactly what had happened the previous spring, and all their lives had been in danger.

But it was Mam's wish that I inherit the room and its contents, and before she went away she'd made sure that both Ellie and Jack accepted the situation. She'd returned to her own land, Greece, to fight the rising power of the dark there. It made me sad to think that I might never see her again, and I suppose that's why I'd kept putting off going to look in the trunks. Although I was curious to find out what they contained, I couldn't face the thought of seeing the farmhouse again, empty of both Mam and Dad.

'Yes, I'll do that,' I told my master. 'But who's your visitor?'

'A friend of mine,' said the Spook. 'He's lived in Pendle for years and he'll be invaluable in helping with what we need to do there.'

I was astonished. My master kept his distance from people, and because he dealt with ghosts, ghasts, boggarts and witches, they certainly kept their distance from him! I'd never imagined for a moment that he knew somebody whom he regarded as a 'friend'!

'Close your mouth, lad, or you'll start collecting flies!' he said. 'Oh, and you'll be taking young Alice with you. I'll have lots of things to discuss and I'd like both of you out from under my feet.'

'But Jack won't want a visit from Alice as well,' I protested.

It wasn't that I didn't want Alice to come with me. I'd be glad of her company on the journey. It was just that Jack and Alice didn't exactly get on. He knew that she was the niece of a witch and he didn't want her near his family.

'Use your initiative, lad. Once you've hired a horse and cart, she can wait outside the farm boundary while you load up the trunks. And I'll expect you back here as soon as possible. Now, time's short – I can't spare more than half an hour for your lessons today so let's get started.'

I followed the Spook out to the western garden and was soon seated on the bench there, my notebook open and pen at the ready. It was a nice warm morning. The sheep bleated in the distance and the fells ahead were bathed in bright sunshine, dappled by small cloud shadows chasing each other towards the east.

The first year of my apprenticeship had largely been devoted to the study of boggarts; the topic for this year was witches.

'Right, lad,' said the Spook, starting to pace up and down as he spoke. 'As you know, a witch can't sniff us out because we're both seventh sons of seventh sons. But that only applies to what we call "long-sniffing". So write that down. It's your first heading. Long-sniffing is sniffing out the approach of danger in advance, just as Bony Lizzie sniffed out that mob from Chipenden that burned down her house. A witch can't sniff us out that way, so that gives us the element of surprise.

'But it's "short-sniffing" that we must beware of, so write that down too and underline it for emphasis. Up relatively close, a witch can find out a lot about us and knows in an instant our weaknesses and strengths. And the nearer you are to a witch, the more she finds out. So always keep your distance, lad. Never let a witch get nearer to you than the length of your rowan staff. Allowing her to come close holds other dangers too – be especially careful not to let a witch breathe into your face. Her breath can sap both your will and your strength. Grown men have been known to faint away on the spot!'

'I remember Bony Lizzie's foul breath,' I told him. 'It was more animal than human. More like that of a cat or a dog!'

'Aye, it was that, lad. Because, as we know, Lizzie used bone-magic and sometimes fed from human flesh or drank human blood.'

Bony Lizzie, Alice's aunt, wasn't dead. She was imprisoned in a pit in the Spook's eastern garden. It was cruel but it had to be done. The Spook didn't hold with burning witches, so he kept the County safe by locking them in a pit.

'But not all witches have the foul breath of those who dabble in bone- and blood-magic,' my master continued. 'A witch who only uses familiar-magic might have breath that's as fragrant as May blossoms. So beware, for in that sweetness lies great danger. Such a witch has the power of "fascination" – write that word down too, lad. Just as a stoat can freeze a rabbit in its tracks while it moves closer, so some witches can dupe a man. They can make him complacent and happy, totally unaware of danger until it's far too late.

'And that's very closely allied to another power of some witches. We call it "glamour" – so get that word down as well. A witch can make herself appear to be something she's not. She can seem younger and more beautiful than she really is. Using that deceitful power, she can create an aura – projecting a false image – and we should always be on our guard. Because once glamour has attracted a man, it's the beginning of fascination and a gradual eroding of his free will. Using those tools, a witch can bind him to her will so that he believes her every lie and sees only what she wishes him to see.

'And glamour and fascination are a serious threat to us too. Being a seventh son of a seventh son won't help one bit. So beware! I suppose you still think I've been harsh where Alice is concerned. But I did it for the best, lad. I've always feared that, one day, she might use those powers to control you—'

'No,' I interrupted. 'That's not fair. I like Alice – not because she's bewitched me but because she's turned out all right and been a good friend to me. To both of us! Before Mam left she told me she had faith in Alice and that's good enough for me.'

The Spook nodded and there was a sadness in his expression. 'Your mam may well be right. Time will tell, but just be on your guard – that's all I ask. Even a strong man can succumb to the wiles of a pretty girl with pointy shoes. As I know from experience. And now write up what I've just told you about witches.'

The Spook sat down on the bench beside me and was silent while I wrote it all down in my notebook. After I'd finished, I had a question for him.

'When we go to Pendle, are there any special dangers we face from the witch covens? Anything I've not heard about so far?'

The Spook stood up and began to pace backwards and forwards again, deep in thought. 'Pendle district is riddled with witches – there might well be things I've never come up against myself. We'll have to be flexible and ready to learn. But I think the biggest problem we face is their sheer numbers. Witches often bicker and argue, but when they do agree and meet together with a common purpose, their strength is greatly increased. Aye – we must beware that. You see, that's right at the heart of the threat we face – that the witch clans might unite.

'And here's something else for your notebook – you need to get the terminology correct. A "coven" is the term for thirteen witches gathering to combine their strength in some ceremony that evokes the powers of the dark. But the larger family of witches is commonly called a "clan". And a clan includes their menfolk and children, as well as family members who don't directly practise dark magic.'

The Spook waited patiently until I'd finished writing before continuing the lesson. 'Basically, as I've told you before, there are three main witch clans in Pendle – the Malkins, the Deanes and the Mouldheels – and the first is the worst of all. All of them row and bicker but the Malkins and the Deanes have got closer over the years. They have intermarried – your friend Alice is the result of just such a union. Her mother was a Malkin and her father a Deane, but the good news there is that neither of them was a practising witch. On the other hand, both parents died young, and as you know, she was given into the care of Bony Lizzie. The training she received there is something she'll always struggle to overcome, and the danger in taking her back to Pendle is that she might revert to type and rejoin one of the clans.'

Again I was about to object but my master stopped me with a gesture. 'Let's just hope that doesn't happen,' he continued, 'but if she *isn't* bent back towards the dark, her local knowledge is going to be very important: she will be of invaluable help to us and our work.

'Now, as for the third clan, the Mouldheels, they're much more mysterious. In addition to using blood- and bone-magic, they pride themselves on being skilled with mirrors. As I've told you before, I don't believe in prophecy, but it's said that the Mouldheels mainly use mirrors for scrying.'

'Scrying?' I asked. 'What's that?'

'Telling the future, lad. They say the mirrors show them what's going to happen. Now, the Mouldheels have mostly kept their distance from the other two clans, but recently I've heard that someone or something is keen for them to put aside that ancient enmity. And that's what we have to prevent. Because if the three clans unite and, more importantly, if they get three covens together, then who knows what evil they will launch upon the County? As you may remember, they did it once before, many years ago, and cursed me.'

'I remember you telling me,' I said. 'But I thought you didn't believe in their curse.'

'No, I like to think it was all nonsense but it still shook me up. Luckily the covens fell out soon after, before they could inflict more damage on the County. But this time there's something a little more sinister about what's happening in Pendle and that's what I need my visitor to confirm. We need to prepare ourselves mentally and physically for what could be a terrible battle – and then we need to get to Pendle before it's too late.

'Well, lad,' the Spook finished, shielding his eyes and glancing towards the sun, 'this lesson's gone on long enough so it's back to the house with you. You can spend the rest of the morning studying.'

I passed the remainder of the morning alone in the Spook's library. He still didn't trust Alice fully and she wasn't allowed in the library in case she read something she wasn't supposed to. Now that there were three of us living in the house, my master had finally opened up another of the downstairs rooms and it was currently used as a study. Alice was working there now, earning her keep by copying one of the Spook's books. Some of them were rare and he was always afraid that something might happen to them so he liked to have a copy just in case.

I was studying covens – how a group of thirteen witches came together for their rituals. I was reading a passage that described what happened when witches held special feasts, which were called 'sabbaths'.

Some covens celebrate sabbaths weekly; others each month, at the time of either the full moon or the new moon. Additionally there are four great sabbaths held when the power of darkness is at its greatest: 'Candlemas', 'Walpurgis Night', 'Lammas' and 'Halloween'. At these four dark feasts, covens may combine in worship.

I already knew about Walpurgis Night. It took place on 30 April, and years earlier three covens had gathered together at Pendle on that sabbath to curse the Spook. Well, we were now in the second week in July; I wondered when the next great sabbath was and began to search the page. I didn't get very far because at that moment something happened that I'd never experienced in the whole of my time in Chipenden.

Rap! Rap! Rap! Rap!

Someone was knocking on the back door! I couldn't believe it. Nobody came to the house. Visitors always went to the withy trees at the crossroads and rang the bell. To enter the gardens was to risk being torn to bits by the boggart that guarded the house and its perimeter. Who had knocked? Was it the 'friend' the Spook was expecting? And if so, how had he managed to reach the back door in one piece?

CHAPTER 2
THEFT AND KIDNAPPING

Curious, I returned my book to its place on the shelf and went downstairs. The Spook had already answered the door and was leading someone into the kitchen. When I saw him, my jaw dropped in surprise. He was a very big man, broad across the shoulders and at least two or three inches taller than the Spook. He had a friendly, honest face and looked to be in his late thirties, but the truly astonishing thing about him was that he was wearing a black cassock.

He was a priest!

'This is my apprentice, Tom Ward,' said the Spook with a smile.

'I'm very pleased to meet you, Tom,' said the priest,

holding out his hand. 'I'm Father Stocks. My parish is Downham, north of Pendle Hill.'

'I'm pleased to meet you too,' I said, shaking his hand.

'John has told me all about you in his letters,' Father Stocks said. 'It seems you've got yourself off to a very promising start—'

At that moment Alice came into the kitchen. She looked our visitor up and down with surprise in her eyes when she saw that he was a priest. In turn, Father Stocks glanced down at her pointy shoes and his eyebrows gave a slight twitch upwards.

'And this is young Alice,' said the Spook. 'Alice, say hello to Father Stocks.'

Alice nodded and gave the priest a little smile.

'I've heard a lot about you too, Alice,' he said. 'I believe you've family in Pendle—'

'Blood ties, that's all,' replied Alice with a fierce frown. 'My mam was a Malkin and my dad was a Deane. Ain't my fault where I was born. None of us choose our kin.'

'That's very true,' said the priest in a kindly voice. 'I'm sure the world would be a very different place if we could. But it's the way we live our lives that counts.'

Not much more was said after that. The priest was tired after his journey and it was clear that the Spook wanted us on our way to Jack's farm, so we made our preparations to leave. I didn't bother with my bag but just took my staff and a lump of cheese for us to eat on the journey.

The Spook walked us to the door. 'Here's what you'll need to hire the cart,' he said, handing me a small silver coin.

'How did Father Stocks manage to get past the boggart and cross the garden safely?' I asked as I put it into the pocket of my breeches.

The Spook smiled. 'He's crossed this garden many times before, lad, and the boggart knows him well. Father Stocks was once my apprentice. And a very successful one, I may add – he completed his time. But later he thought better of it and decided that the Church was his true vocation. He's a useful man to know – he has two trades at his fingertips: the priesthood and ours. Add that to his background knowledge of Pendle and we couldn't have a better ally.'

As we set off for my brother Jack's farm, the sun was shining, the birds were singing; it was a perfect summer afternoon. I had Alice for company and I was going home. Not only that: I was looking forward to seeing little Mary, Jack and his wife Ellie, who was expecting another baby. Mam had predicted that it would be the son that Jack had always wanted, someone to inherit the farm after he was dead. So I should have been happy. But as we drew closer to the farm, I couldn't shake off a feeling of sadness, which was slowly settling over me like a black cloud.

Dad was dead and there'd be no Mam to greet me. It was never going to feel like my real home again. That was the stark truth and I still hadn't fully come to terms with it.

'Penny for your thoughts,' Alice said with a smile.

I shrugged.

'Come on, cheer up, Tom. How many times do I have to tell you? We should make the best of it. Off to Pendle I reckon we'll be next week.'

'Sorry, Alice. I'm just thinking about Mam and Dad. Can't seem to get them out of my mind.'

Alice moved closer to my side and gave my hand an affectionate squeeze. 'It's hard, Tom, I know. But I'm sure you'll see your mam again one day. Anyway, aren't you looking forward to finding out what's in those trunks she's left you?'

'I'm curious, yes, I won't deny that . . .'

'This is a nice spot,' said Alice, pointing to the side of the path. 'I'm feeling peckish. Let's eat.'

We sat down on a grassy bank under the shade of a massive oak tree and shared out the cheese we'd brought for the journey. We were both hungry so we ate it all. I wasn't on spook's business so there was no need to fast. We could live off the land.

It was as if Alice had read my thoughts. 'I'll catch us

a couple of juicy rabbits at dusk,' she promised with a smile.

'That would be nice. You know, Alice,' I said, 'you've told me a lot about witches in general, but very little about Pendle and the witches who live *there*. Why's that? Reckon I'll need to know as much as possible if we're heading there.'

Alice frowned. 'I've lots of painful memories of that place. Don't like to talk about my family. Don't like to talk about Pendle much – the thought of going back there scares me.'

'It's funny,' I said, 'but Mr Gregory's never talked much about Pendle either. You'd think we'd have been discussing and planning what it's like and what we're going to do when we get there.'

'Always likes to play things close to his chest, he does. He must have some sort of plan. I'm sure he'll share it with us when the time's right. Imagine Old Gregory having a friend!' said Alice, changing the subject. 'A friend who's a priest as well!'

'What I can't understand is why someone would

give up being a spook to become a priest.'

Alice laughed at that. 'No stranger than Old Gregory being a priest and giving it up to become a spook!'

She was right – the Spook *had* been trained as a priest – and I laughed with her. But my opinion hadn't changed. As far as I could see, priests prayed and that was it. They didn't do anything directly to deal with the dark. They lacked the practical knowledge of our craft. It seemed to me that Father Stocks had taken a step in the wrong direction.

A little before dusk we stopped again and settled ourselves down in a hollow between two hills, close to the edge of a wood. The sky was clear, with the waning moon visible to the south-east. I busied myself making a fire while Alice went hunting for rabbits. Within an hour she was cooking them over the fire, the juice dribbling and hissing into the flames while my mouth watered.

I was still curious about Pendle, and despite Alice's reluctance to talk about her life there, I decided to try again.

'Come on, Alice,' I said. 'I know it's painful for you to talk about, but I do need to know more about Pendle . . .'

'I suppose so,' Alice said, peering at me over the flames. 'Best that you're prepared for the worst. Ain't a nice place to be. And everybody's scared. Whichever village you visit, you can see it in their faces. Can't blame 'em because the witches know almost everything that's going on. After dark, most ordinary folk turn the mirrors in their houses to the wall.'

'Why?' I asked.

'So they can't be spied on. Nobody trusts a mirror at night. Witches, specially the Mouldheels, use them to spy on folks. They love to use 'em for scrying and spying. In Pendle you never know who or what might suddenly peer out at you from a mirror. Remember old Mother Malkin? That should give you some idea of the sort of witch we'll be facing . . .'

The name Malkin sent a chill through my bones. Mother Malkin had been the most evil witch in the County and a year earlier, with Alice's help, I'd managed to destroy her. But not before she'd threatened the lives of Jack and his family.

'Even though she's gone now, in Pendle there's always someone else ready to step into the shoes of a dead witch,' Alice said grimly. 'And there are plenty of Malkins capable of that. Some of 'em live in Malkin Tower, which ain't a place to go anywhere near after dark. People who go missing in Pendle – that's where they mostly end up. There are tunnels, pits and dungeons under the tower, full of the bones of those they've murdered.'

'Why isn't something done?' I asked. 'What about the High Sheriff at Caster? Can't he do anything?'

'Sent justices and constables to Pendle before, he has. Lots of times. Not that it did much good. Mostly they hanged the wrong people. Old Hannah Fairborne was one. She was nearly eighty when they dragged her off to Caster in chains. Said she was a witch but that wasn't true. Still, she deserved to hang because she poisoned three of her nephews. Lots of that goes on in Pendle. It ain't a good place to be. And it ain't easy to sort things out there. That's why Old Gregory's left it so long.'

I nodded in agreement.

'I know more than most what it's like to live there,' Alice continued. 'There've been lots of unions between Malkins and Deanes, even though they're rivals. Truth is, the Malkins and Deanes hate the Mouldheels a lot more than they do each other. Life in Pendle is complicated. Lived there most of my life but still don't understand 'em.'

'Were you happy?' I asked. 'I mean, before you were looked after by Bony Lizzie . . . ?'

Alice grew silent and avoided my gaze and I realized that I shouldn't have asked. She'd never talked much about life with her parents or with Lizzie after they'd died.

'Don't remember life much before Lizzie,' she said at last. 'I mostly remember the rows. Me lying there in the darkness crying while my mam and dad fought like cat and dog. But sometimes they talked and laughed as well, so it wasn't all bad. That was the big difference afterwards. The silence. Lizzie didn't say much. More likely to give me a clout round the head than a kind word. Brooded a lot, she did. Gazed into the fire and muttered her spells. And if she weren't gawping into the flames, she'd be staring into a mirror. Sometimes I caught sight of things over her shoulder. Things that don't belong on this earth. Scared me, it did. Preferred Mam and Dad's fights to that.'

'Did you live in Malkin Tower?'

Alice shook her head. 'No. Only the Malkin coven and a few chosen helpers live in the tower itself. But I went there sometimes with my mam. Some of it's underground but I never went down there. They all live together in one big room and there was lots of arguing and screaming and smoke stinging your eyes. Being a Deane, my dad didn't visit the tower. He'd never have got out alive. We lived in a cottage near Roughlee, the village where most of the Deanes live. The Mouldheels live in Bareleigh and the rest of the Malkins in Goldshaw Booth. Mostly keep to their own territory, they do.'

After that Alice grew silent so I didn't press her

33

further. I could see that Pendle held a lot of painful memories for her – unspoken horrors that I could only guess at.

Jack's nearest neighbour, Mr Wilkinson, had a horse and cart and I knew he'd be only too happy to hire them out. No doubt he'd have one of his sons drive us so I wouldn't have to make a return journey later. I decided to call in at my brother's first to let him know what I intended to do with the trunks.

We made good time and came within sight of Jack's farm late in the afternoon of the following day. My first glance told me that something was badly wrong.

We'd approached from the north-east, skirting the edge of Hangman's Hill, and as we began our descent, I could see right away that there were no animals in the fields. Then, as I caught sight of the farmhouse, it got worse. The barn was a blackened ruin: it had been burned to the ground.

It never even crossed my mind to ask Alice to wait at the farm boundary. Something bad had happened and all I could think of was checking that Jack, Ellie and their daughter Mary were all right. By now the farm dogs should have been barking, but everything was silent.

As we hastened through the gate and across the yard, I saw that the back door of the farmhouse had been smashed in and was hanging from one hinge. I ran across, with Alice at my heels, a lump in my throat, afraid that something terrible had happened.

Once inside, I called Jack's and Ellie's names over and over again but received no answer. The house was unrecognizable as the home I'd been brought up in. All the kitchen drawers had been pulled out and there was cutlery and smashed crockery on the flags. The pots of herbs had been taken from the windowsill and thrown against the walls; there was soil in the sink. The brass candlestick had gone from the table and in its place were five empty bottles of elderberry wine from Mam's store in the cellar. But for me, the worst thing of all was Mam's rocking chair, which was in big jagged pieces, as if someone had taken an axe to it. It pained me to see that. It almost felt like they'd hurt Mam.

Upstairs, the bedrooms had been ransacked – clothes scattered across the beds and floors and every mirror smashed. But the scariest moment of all came when we reached Mam's special room. The door was closed but there was blood splattered across the wall next to it, and there were bloodstains on the floorboards too. Had Jack and his family been here when this happened?

I became filled with a terrible dread that someone had died here.

'Don't think the worst, Tom!' Alice said, gripping my arm. 'It may not be as bad as it seems . . .'

I didn't answer; just kept staring at the splatters of blood on the walls.

'Let's look inside your mam's room,' Alice suggested.

For a moment I looked at her, horrified. I couldn't believe that was all she could think about now.

'I think we should look inside,' she insisted.

Angrily I tried the door but it didn't yield. 'It's still

locked, Alice. I've got the only key. So nobody's been inside.'

'Trust me, Tom. Please . . .'

For safety, I kept the keys on a piece of string round my neck. There was a large key for the door and three smaller ones for the three largest trunks inside. In a moment I'd opened the door and stepped inside. Additionally I had a key made by the Spook's brother, Andrew, who's a locksmith, and it will open most locks without trouble.

I'd been wrong. Somebody *had* been in the room. It was completely empty. The three big trunks and the smaller chests had gone.

'How could they get into the room?' I asked, my voice echoing slightly. 'I have the only key . . .'

Alice shook her head. 'Remember the other thing your mam said: that nothing evil could enter here. Well, something evil's been here and that's for sure!'

I certainly did remember what Mam had said: it had been on my final visit to the farm when I saw her for the last time. She'd stood in this very room talking to

Alice and me and I remembered her words exactly:

Once locked, nothing evil can ever enter here. If you're brave and your soul is pure and good, this room is a redoubt, a fortress against the dark . . . Only use it when something so terrible pursues you that your very life and soul are at risk.

So what had happened? How had someone got inside and stolen the trunks that Mam had left me? What did they want them for? What use were they to somebody else?

After checking the attic, I locked the door to Mam's room again and we went downstairs and out into the yard. In a daze I walked across to what was left of the barn – just a few charred posts and fragments of wood amongst a pile of ashes.

'I can still smell the smoke,' I said. 'This happened recently.'

Alice nodded. 'It happened soon after dark, the day before yesterday,' she said, sniffing loudly at the tainted air.

Alice could sniff things out. She was usually right but now, looking at her face, I didn't like the expression there. She'd discovered something else. Something very bad. Maybe worse than what we'd already found.

'What is it, Alice?' I demanded.

'There's something else as well as smoke. A witch has been here. Maybe more than one—'

'A witch? Why would a witch come here?' I asked, my head whirling with what I'd seen.

'For the trunks, what else? There must be something inside 'em that they wanted badly.'

'But how would they find out about the trunks?'

'Mirrors, perhaps? Maybe they have powers beyond Pendle.'

'And what about Jack and Ellie? And the child? Where are they now?'

'My guess is that Jack tried to stop 'em. Big and strong, Jack is. Wouldn't have given up without a fight. Want to know what I think?' Alice asked, her eyes wide.

I nodded but was afraid to hear it.

'They couldn't go into that room themselves because your mam protected it against evil in some way. So they made Jack go in and fetch out the trunks for them. At first he put up a fight but when they threatened Ellie or little Mary, he had to do it.'

'But how could Jack have got in?' I cried. 'There's no sign of the door being forced, but I have the only key. And where are they? Where are they now?'

'They'll have taken your family with them. That's what it looks like.'

'Which way, Alice? Which way did they go?'

'Needed a horse and cart to carry the trunks. The three big trunks looked heavy. So they'd have kept to the roads mostly. We could follow and see . . .'

We ran to the end of the lane and followed the road south, walking fast. After about three miles we reached the crossroads. Alice pointed.

'They've gone north-east, Tom. It's just as I thought. They've gone to Pendle.'

'Then let's follow them,' I said, setting off at a run. I'd taken fewer than ten paces before Alice caught me, spinning me round by my arm.

'No, Tom, this ain't what to do. They'll be well on their

way already. By the time we get there they'll be hidden away, and there's lots of places to hide in Pendle. What hope would we have? No, we should go back and tell Old Gregory what's happened. He'll know what to do. And that Father Stocks will help too.'

I shook my head. I wasn't convinced.

'Tom, *think*!' Alice hissed, squeezing my arm until it hurt. 'First we should go back and talk to Jack's neighbours. Maybe they know something. And what about your other brothers? Shouldn't you send word to them about what's gone on? Surely they'd want to help. Then we should run for Chipenden and tell Old Gregory what's happened.'

'No, Alice. Even at speed, it's well over a day back to Chipenden. Then half a day or more to Pendle. By then anything might have happened to Jack and his family. We'd be too late to save them.'

'There's another way, but you may not like it,' Alice said, letting go of my arm and dropping her gaze to the ground.

'What do you mean?' I asked. I was impatient.

41

Time was running out for Jack and his family.

'You could go back to Chipenden and I could go on to Pendle alone—'

'No, Alice! I couldn't let you go alone. It's too dangerous.'

'It's more dangerous if we're together. If they catch us together, we'll both suffer. Imagine what they'd do to a spook's apprentice! A seventh son of a seventh son. They'd be fighting over your bones, for sure. Ain't nothing more certain than that! But if I was caught alone, I'd say that I'd just come back home to Pendle, wouldn't I? That I wanted to be back with my family again. And I'd have a better chance of finding out who's done this and where they're holding Jack and Ellie.'

My stomach was churning with anxiety, but gradually Alice's words started to get through to me. After all, she did know the place and would be able to travel through the Pendle district without arousing too much comment.

'It's still dangerous, Alice. And I thought you were afraid of going back.'

'I'm doing this for you, Tom. And your family. They don't deserve what's happened to them. I'll go to Pendle. Ain't nothing else for it now.' Alice came forward and took hold of my left hand. 'See you in Pendle, Tom,' she said softly. 'Get there just as soon as you can . . .'

'I will,' I assured her. 'As soon as you find anything out, go to Father Stocks's church at Downham. I'll be waiting there.'

With that, Alice nodded, turned and set off along the road to the north-east. I watched her for a few moments but she didn't look round. I turned and ran back towards Jack's farm.

CHAPTER 3
PRIORITIES

I called at the Wilkinsons' farm, which bordered Jack's land to the west. Dad had always preferred to keep a variety of livestock but our neighbours had gone over to cattle about five years earlier. The first thing I noticed now was a field full of sheep. Unless I was much mistaken, they were Jack's.

I found Mr Wilkinson repairing a fence in his south meadow. His forehead was bandaged.

'Good to see you, Tom!' he said, jumping up and rushing over. 'I'm so sorry about what's happened. I would have sent word if I could. I knew you were working somewhere up north but I'd no address. I sent a letter to your brother James yesterday. I asked him to come right away.'

James was my second oldest brother and worked as a blacksmith in Ormskirk, to the south-west of the County. It was almost surrounded by moss land and soggy marsh. Even if he got the letter tomorrow, it would take him a day or more to get here.

'Did you see what happened?' I asked.

Mr Wilkinson nodded. 'Aye, and I got this for my pains,' he said, pointing to his bandaged head. 'It happened soon after dark. I saw the fire and came across to help. At first I was relieved that it was only the barn burning and not the house. But when I got nearer, I smelled a rat because there were so many people milling about. As I'm your nearest neighbour, I was more than a little puzzled as to how they'd managed to get there before me. And I soon realized that no attempt was being made to save the barn; they were taking things out of the house and loading them up onto a cart. The only warning I got as I headed towards them was the sound of boots running up behind me. Before I could turn, I was hit hard on the head and went out like a light. When I came to, they'd gone. I looked inside the house but there was no sign of Jack or his family. Sorry I wasn't able to do more, Tom.'

'Thanks for coming across and trying to help, Mr Wilkinson,' I said. 'I'm really sorry you got hurt. But did you see any of their faces? Would you recognize them again?'

He shook his head. 'Didn't get a close enough look at any of 'em, but there was a woman near by, sat straight-backed on a black horse. A rare piece of horseflesh too – a thoroughbred like the ones they race during the big spring market in Topley. She was a fine-looking woman, large but very shapely, with a good thick head of black hair. She wasn't rushing around like the rest. I was still some distance away but I heard her call out what sounded like instructions. There was authority in her voice all right.

'After that blow to my head I was fit for nothing. The following morning I was still sick as a dog but I sent my eldest lad into Topley to report it to Ben Hindle, the constable there. He took a band of villagers with him the next day. They followed the trail north-east for about two hours and found an abandoned cart with one of its wheels broken. They had dogs with 'em and tracked the scent overland until it ended suddenly. Ben said he'd never seen anything like it. It was as if they had just vanished into thin air. So there was nothing for it but to call off the hunt and turn back. Anyway, Tom, why don't you come back to the house and get a bite to eat? You're more than welcome to stay with us for a few days until your brother James arrives.'

I shook my head. 'Thanks, Mr Wilkinson, but I'd better get back to Chipenden as fast as I can and tell my master what's happened. He'll know what to do.'

'Wouldn't it be better to wait for James?'

For a moment I hesitated, wondering what message to leave for James. One part of me didn't want to lead him into danger by telling him that we were heading for Pendle. At the same time he would want to help rescue Jack and his family. And we'd be heavily out-numbered. We'd need all the help we could get.

'Sorry, Mr Wilkinson, but I think it's best if I set off

straight away. When James arrives, would you mind telling him that I've gone ahead to Pendle with my master? You see, I'm pretty sure that those responsible for doing this come from there. Tell James to go directly to the church at Downham, in Pendle district. It's north of the hill. The priest there is called Father Stocks. He'll know where to find us.'

'I'll do that, Tom. Hope you find Jack and his family safe. In the meantime I'll keep an eye on the farm – his livestock and dogs are safe enough with me. Tell him that when you see him.'

I thanked Mr Wilkinson and set off back towards Chipenden. I was worried about Jack, Ellie and their child. Alice too. Her arguments had made sense. She'd persuaded me that the best thing was for her to go on alone. But she was scared and I suspected that, whatever she said, she'd be in grave danger.

I arrived back in Chipenden late the following morning, having spent part of the night in an old barn. Without ceremony I blurted out the bare bones of what had happened, begging the Spook to set off straight away for Pendle – we could talk on the road, I said, because every second we delayed increased the danger for my family. But he would have none of it and gestured towards a chair at the kitchen table.

'Sit yourself down, lad,' he told me. 'More haste, less speed! The journey will take us the best part of the afternoon and evening anyway, and it wouldn't be wise to enter Pendle during the hours of darkness.'

'What does it matter?' I protested. 'We'll be there for some time, won't we? We'll be spending lots of nights there anyway!'

'Aye, that's true enough, but the borders of Pendle are dangerous because they're watched and guarded at night by those who shun the sunlight. There's no hope of getting into a place like that unseen, but at least during the daylight hours we'll arrive with the breath still in our bodies.'

'Father Stocks could help us through,' I said, looking around for him. 'He knows Pendle well. He must know a way for us to get to Downham safely tonight.'

'Reckon he does, but he left shortly before you arrived. We've been talking it through and he's given me the final pieces of the jigsaw so that I can work out how to sort out the witches. But he's got a number of terrified parishioners at Downham and daren't leave them too long. Now, lad, start at the beginning and tell me everything again. Leave out no details. In the end it'll prove the better way than blundering off on the road without half a plan between us!'

I did as I was told, telling myself that, as usual, the Spook was probably right and this was the best way to help Jack, but as I finished my account, tears came into my eyes at the thought of what had happened. The Spook stared hard at me for a couple of seconds and then stood up. He began to pace back and forward across the flags before the kitchen hearth.

'I'm sorry for you, lad. It must be hard. Your dad dead, your mam gone away and now this. I know it's difficult, but you've got to keep your emotions in check. We need to think clearly now, with cool heads. That's the best way to help your family. The first thing I have

to ask is what you know about those trunks in your
mam's room. Is there anything you haven't told me?
Have you any idea at all what they might contain?'

'Mam used to keep the silver chain she gave me
inside the trunk nearest to the window,' I reminded
him, 'but I've no idea what else was inside. What Mam
told me was very mysterious. She said that I'd find
the answers to a lot of things that might have been
puzzling me. That her past and her future were inside
those trunks and I'd discover things about her that
she'd never even told Dad.'

'So you've no idea at all? Are you sure?'

I thought hard for a few moments. 'There might be
money inside one of the trunks.'

'Money? How much money?'

'I don't know. Mam used some of her own money
to buy the farm but I don't know how much there was
in the first place. There must have been something
left, though. Remember at the beginning of the winter, when I called home to collect the ten guineas Dad
owed you to pay for my apprenticeship? Well, Mam

went upstairs and got them from her room.'

The Spook nodded. 'So they could well have come for the money. But if the girl's right and witches *are* involved, I can't help thinking there must have been something else. And how did they know the trunks were there?'

'Alice thinks they may have been spying with mirrors.'

'Does she now! Father Stocks mentioned mirrors, but I can't see how they could have seen the trunks in a locked room. It doesn't make sense. There's something more sinister behind this.'

'Like what?'

'I don't know yet, lad. But as you have the only key, how did they get into the room without breaking the door? You say your mam protected the room in some way to keep out evil?'

'Yes, but Alice thinks they made Jack go in because they couldn't enter themselves. There was blood on the wall and the floor,' I said. 'I think they must have hurt Jack and made him go in and fetch out the chests –

though how the door was opened is still a mystery. Mam said that room was a refuge—'

I felt myself choke with emotion and the Spook came forward and patted my shoulder in reassurance. Then he waited silently until I'd got my voice under control.

'Come on, lad, tell me.'

'She said that, once it was locked, I could go in there and be safe from anything evil on the outside. That it was even better protected than your house. But I was only to use it when I was being pursued by something so terrible that my life and soul were at risk. She said that there was a price to pay for using it. That I was young and it would be all right but that *you* couldn't use it. And that if it ever became necessary, I had to tell you that . . .'

The Spook nodded thoughtfully and scratched at his beard. 'Well, lad, it gets more and more mysterious. I sense something deep here. Something I've never come across before. What we face is even more difficult now that innocent victims are involved, but we've no choice but to go ahead. We'll be setting off for Pendle within the hour – we can find somewhere to sleep on the way and arrive after dawn, when it's safer. I'll do all I can to help your family, but I have to tell you this: there's more at stake here than just their lives. As you know, I've decided to try and deal with the Pendle witches once and for all. And not a moment too soon – Father Stocks brought some very bad news. It seems that the rumours were true: the Malkins and the Deanes have already called a truce and moves are now afoot to get the Mouldheels to join 'em. So it's as bad as I feared. Do you know what happens on the first of August, less than two weeks from today?'

I shook my head. My birthday was on the third of that month. That was the only date in August with any significance for me.

'Well, lad, it's about time you did know. It's one of the feasts of the Old Gods. They call it "Lammas", and it's a time when witches' covens gather to worship and draw down power from the dark.'

'It's one of the main four sabbaths in the witches'

year, isn't it? I've read about them but I didn't know all the dates.'

'Well, you know the date of Lammas now. And from what Father Stocks has told me it seems that the Pendle witches are getting ready to attempt something especially dark and dangerous on that date. And the big danger is that the Mouldheels will join in and all three covens will be united, which will greatly increase their powers. It must be something big to draw them together like this. Father Stocks has never known so many attacks on graveyards – bones aplenty have been taken. The bad news about your brother and his family complicates things, but it's clear enough what our priorities are.

'We need to get into Pendle and meet up with Father Stocks at Downham. We need to stop the Mouldheels joining that unholy alliance and we need to find those who've been taken. If young Alice can help us with that, all well and good. Otherwise we'll have to go hunting ourselves.'

* * *

Our bags were packed and all we had to do was step out through the front door and lock it behind us. At last we'd be off to Pendle, and not a moment too soon. But now, to my dismay, the Spook sat down on a stool beside the kitchen table, took the whetstone from his bag and lifted his staff. There was a click as the retractable blade shot forward, followed by a grating sound as he began to sharpen its edge.

He looked up at me and sighed. He'd read the impatience and anxiety in my face. 'Look, lad, I know you're desperate to get on the road, and with good reason. But we have to do things properly and be ready for any eventuality. I've a bad feeling about this trip. So if at any time I tell you to run for it and use that special room of your mam's, will you do it?'

'What? And leave you behind?'

'Aye, that's exactly what I mean. Somebody has to continue our trade. I've never been one for praising my apprentices much. Praise can be bad for you. It can go to your head and give an inflated sense of worth so that you rest on your laurels. But I will say this.

Without doubt you've become what your mam once promised – you *are* the best apprentice I've ever had. I can't go on for ever so you might indeed be my *last* apprentice, the one I have to prepare to carry on my work in the County. If I do say the word, leave Pendle at once without either a question or a backward glance and take refuge in that room. Do you understand?'

I nodded.

'And if it's necessary, will you obey me?'

'Yes,' I said. 'I'll do it.'

At last the Spook was satisfied and there was a click as the blade retracted back into the staff. Carrying both our bags and my own staff, I followed the Spook outside and waited until he'd locked the door behind us. He paused for a moment, looked up at the house, then turned and smiled at me sadly.

'Right, lad, let's get on our way! We've delayed enough already!'

CHAPTER 4
EAST TO PENDLE

We travelled east from Chipenden, keeping to the southern edge of the Bowland Fells before curving away to cross the river Ribble's pleasant, tree-lined banks. I'd have hardly known it for the same wide tidal river that had run through Priestown but, once across, I began to feel more and more uneasy.

'Well, there it is, lad,' said the Spook, coming to a halt some distance from a stream that lay in our path. He pointed towards Pendle Hill, which had been growing steadily as we advanced towards it. 'Not a pretty sight, is it?'

I couldn't help agreeing. Although its shape reminded me of the Long Ridge, a local fell beyond the valley to the south of Chipenden, this was larger and more daunting. Above it was suspended a threatening bank of thick black clouds.

'Some say that it looks like a great beached whale,' said the Spook. 'Well, never having seen a whale myself, I can't be the judge of that. Others say it looks like an upturned boat. I can just about see that, but the comparison hardly does it justice. What do you think, lad?'

I studied the scene carefully. The light was beginning to fail but the hill itself seemed to radiate darkness. It had a brooding presence.

'It could almost be alive,' I said, choosing my words with care. 'It's as if there's something malevolent inside it and it's casting a spell over everything.'

'Couldn't have put it better myself, lad,' said the Spook, leaning on his staff and looking very thoughtful. 'But one thing's for sure: there's an unholy host of malevolent witches living within sight of it. Now, it'll be dark in half an hour and we'd be wise to stay this side of that stream until dawn. Then we can press on into Pendle.'

That we did, settling down in the shelter of a hedge. Half the width of a field separated us from the stream, but as I slipped down into sleep, I could hear it murmuring gently in the distance.

We were up at dawn and, without even a nibble of cheese to sustain us, quickly crossed the stream and pressed on towards Downham, a faint drizzle drifting into our faces. We were heading north, with Pendle Hill to our right, but we soon lost sight of it as we entered a dense wood of sycamore and ash.

'Here's something to note,' the Spook said, leading me across to a large oak tree. 'What do you make of that?'

There was a strange carving on the trunk. I peered at it closely:

'Is it meant to be a pair of scissors?' I asked.

'Aye,' said the Spook grimly. 'But they're not intended to cut cloth. That's a mark carved by Grimalkin, the witch assassin. Her trade is death and torture, and the Malkins send her out against their enemies. She's carved that as a warning. *Pendle is my territory*, she's saying. *Cross me and I'll snip away your flesh and your bone!*'

I shuddered and stepped away from the tree.

'Maybe I'll cross blades with her one day,' said the Spook. 'The world would certainly be a better place if she were dead. But although she's a ruthless killer, she lives by a code of honour – she would never use guile. She likes it best when the odds are against her, but once she's got the upper hand, watch out for those scissors!'

Shaking his head, the Spook led the way towards Downham. I'd learned a lot about Pendle in the last couple of days and I knew it was a dangerous place to be. No doubt there was worse to come.

* * *

The main village street meandered down the side of a steep hill. For reasons of his own, the Spook circled round to enter Downham from the north. Pendle Hill was directly ahead of us, dominating the village completely, filling half the sky with its brooding presence. Although it was already mid-morning and the drizzle had come to a halt, there wasn't a soul about.

'Where is everybody?' I asked the Spook.

'Hiding behind their curtains – where else, lad?' he said with a grim smile. 'No doubt minding everyone else's business but their own!'

'Will they tell the witches that we're here?' I asked, watching a lace curtain twitch to my left.

'I've brought us here by something of a serpentine way so as to avoid certain places where sight of us wouldn't go unreported. No doubt there'll be a few spies here anyway, but Downham is still the safest place in the whole district. That's why we're going to make it our base. For that we owe thanks to Father Stocks. He's been the parish priest here for over ten years and has done all he can to battle with the dark and keep it at a distance. But from what he tells me, even this village is now under threat. People are leaving. They're getting clear of Pendle altogether – some of them good families that have made this their home for generations.'

The small parish church was to the south of the village, just beyond a stream. It was set within a huge graveyard filled with rows and rows of tombstones of every conceivable shape and size. Many were horizontal, almost hidden by the long grass and weeds; others jutted out of the ground at any angle but the vertical, resembling rotting teeth. In all, this cemetery spoke of neglect, the headstones weather-beaten, their inscriptions faded or covered in lichen and moss.

'The graves could do with a bit of a tidy up,' observed the Spook. 'I'm surprised Father Stocks has allowed it to fall into neglect like this . . .'

The presbytery was a good-sized cottage set back under a dozen or so yew trees about a hundred yards beyond the church. We reached it by walking in single file along a narrow, overgrown path that snaked through the tombstones. When we arrived at the front door, the Spook rapped hard on it three times. After a few moments we heard the sound of heavy boots on flags; then a bolt was drawn back and the door opened. Father Stocks stood there, a look of astonishment on his face.

'Well, this is a surprise, John,' he said, relaxing his face into a smile. 'I wasn't expecting you until later in the week. Anyway, come in, the both of you, and make yourselves at home!'

We followed him through to the kitchen at the back of the house and he invited us to sit down. 'Have you eaten?' he asked as we each pulled a chair away from the table. 'What about you, young Tom? You look hungry enough to eat a horse!'

'I am hungry, Father,' I told him, glancing towards the Spook, 'but I'm not sure if we should be eating . . .'

The Spook always insists that we fast when working because it makes us less vulnerable to the power of the dark, so we usually make do with a nibble of County cheese to keep our strength up. A spook's life is not only scary, dangerous and lonely; it often means going hungry as well.

'It wouldn't do any harm to eat breakfast,' said the Spook, to my surprise. 'We need information before anything else and I was hoping, Father, that you'd be the man to get it for us. So we won't get much done ourselves until tomorrow. This could be the last square meal we eat for quite some time, so, yes please, I think we'll accept your kind invitation.'

'So be it!' exclaimed Father Stocks, his face lighting up. 'I'll be happy to help in any way I can, but let's cook first and talk while we eat. I'll make the three of us a hearty breakfast, but I might need a hand. Know how to cook sausages, young Tom?'

I was about to say 'Yes,' but the Spook shook his head at that and came to his feet. 'Nay, Father, don't let that lad o' mine near a frying pan! I've tasted his cooking before and my stomach's still not forgiven me!'

I smiled but didn't protest, and while the Spook was busy frying the sausages, Father Stocks got two other pans going – one sizzling away with thick rashers of bacon and slices of onion, the other struggling to contain a large cheese omelette, which was gradually turning a golden brown.

I sat at the table while they cooked, hungry but guilty at the same time. My mouth was watering at the smells wafting towards me but I couldn't stop worrying about Ellie, Jack and Mary, wondering if they were all right. They certainly wouldn't be getting a breakfast like this. I wondered how Alice was doing too. I'd been half expecting to find that she'd arrived at Downham with news. I hoped she hadn't run into trouble.

'Well, young Tom,' said Father Stocks, 'there's something you can do to help without damaging your master's stomach too much. Butter us some bread, and make it a big plateful!'

I did as I was told, and no sooner had I finished than three hot plates arrived at the table, each heaped with bacon, sausages and fried onion next to a big slice of omelette.

'Had a good journey here from Chipenden?' Father Stocks asked as we tucked into the food.

'I'm not complaining, but things have taken a turn for the worse since we last spoke,' answered the Spook.

While we ate, my master told Father Stocks about the raid on Jack's farm and the abduction of my brother and his family. He also mentioned that Alice had travelled on ahead to Pendle. By the time he'd finished the tale, we'd cleared our plates.

'I'm sorry to hear such news, Tom,' Father Stocks said, laying his hand on my shoulder. 'I'll remember them in my prayers . . .'

At those words an icy chill ran down my spine. He was talking as if they were already dead. In any case, what good were prayers? We'd delayed too long already and needed to start searching. I felt the heat in my face as I started to grow angry. Only politeness made me bite my tongue. Although my dad was dead now, I could still use the manners he'd taught me.

It was as if Father Stocks had read my mind. 'Don't you worry, Tom,' he said in a kindly voice. 'We'll put things to rights. Heaven helps those who help themselves – I'm a great believer in that. I'll do what I can, and maybe young Alice will arrive with news before the day's out.'

'I'd hoped that Alice might have called here already,' I said.

'So had I, lad. So had I,' said the Spook in a tone of voice that started the anger rising within me again. 'Let's hope she's not up to any mischief—'

'That's unfair after all she's done,' I protested. 'She's risking her life just by being here.'

'Aren't we all?' asked the Spook. 'Look, lad, I don't mean to be hard on the girl, but this will be just about the biggest temptation she's ever faced. I'm not sure it was a good idea letting her come here on her own. Our families play a big part in shaping what we become, and Alice's family are witches. If she ends up back with them, anything could happen!'

'From what you've told me about her, John, I think we can be optimistic,' said Father Stocks. 'We may not all have faith in God, but that shouldn't stop us having faith in people. Anyway, she's probably on her way here right now. I might bump into her on my travels,' said the priest.

Father Stocks suddenly grew in my estimation. He was right. The Spook should have more faith in Alice.

'I'll be off to see what I can find out,' the priest continued. 'There are still a few good folks in these parts who will want to help an innocent family. By nightfall I'll know where Jack and Ellie are being held, you mark my words. But first there's something else I can do to help.' He left the table and returned with a pen, a sheet of paper and a small bottle of ink. He pushed back the plates, uncorked the ink, dipped in the pen and began to sketch. After a few moments I realized that he was drawing a map.

'Well, Tom, no doubt you had a good look at your master's maps of this district before you set off – remembering to fold them properly afterwards of course!' Father Stocks said, smiling towards the Spook, then continuing to draw. 'But this little sketch might simplify things and help set a few locations into your mind.'

The drawing only took him a couple of minutes; he

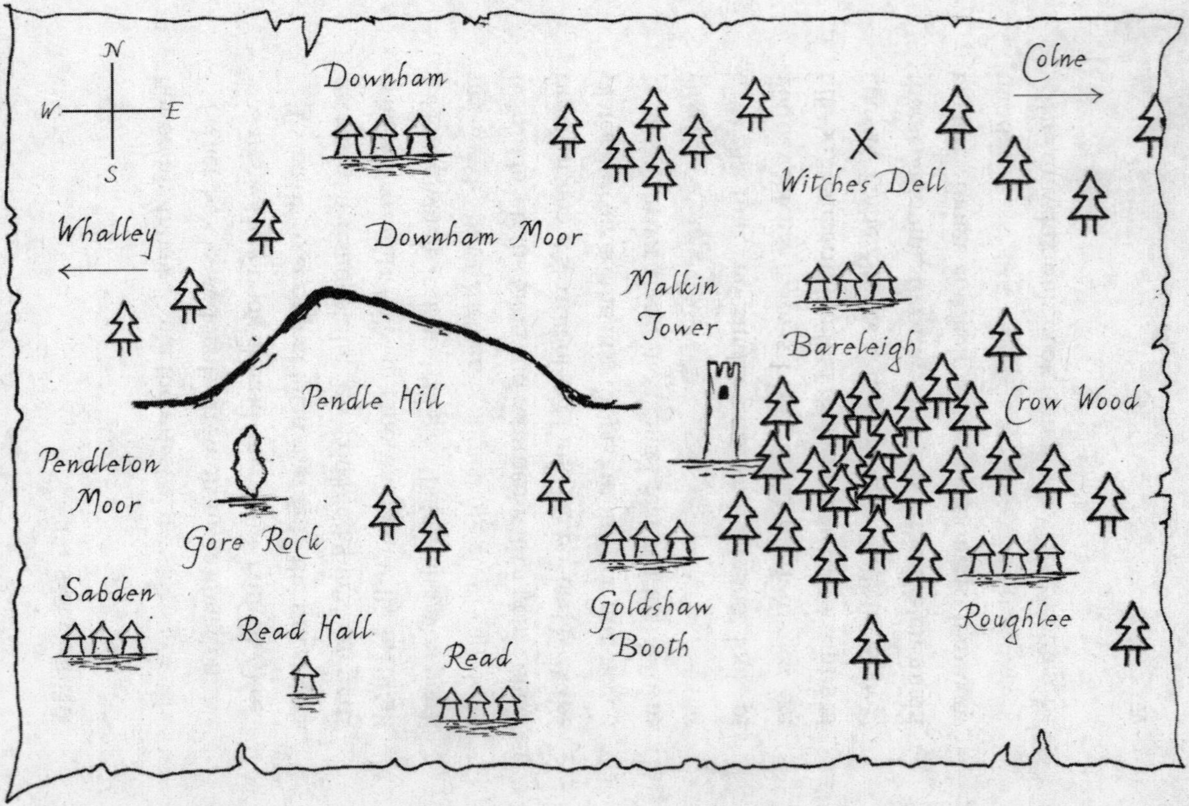
N
W
E
S
Downham
Colne
Witches Dell
Whalley
Downham Moor
Malkin
Tower
Bareleigh
Pendle Hill
Crow Wood
Pendleton
Moor
Gore Rock
Sabden
Goldshaw
Booth
Roughlee
Read Hall
Read

finished by adding in a few place names before pushing it across the table towards me.

'Can you follow it?' he asked.

After a couple of seconds I nodded. He'd sketched out the rough shape of Pendle Hill and the positions of the main villages.

'Downham, to the north of the hill, is the safest place in Pendle—' said the priest.

'I told the lad that on the way here,' the Spook interrupted, 'and it's all due to you, Father Stocks. We're grateful to have a relatively safe place to work from.'

'Nay, John, I couldn't sleep at night if I took all the credit for that. I've certainly done my best to keep the dark at a distance, but historically, as you well know, the danger has always been to the south-east of the hill. So travelling south from here, it's always safest to take the western route and keep the hill to your left. Of course, Gore Rock, marked there to the south-west, can be dangerous too. It's where witches sometimes carry out sacrifices. But can you see those three villages, Tom? Is my handwriting clear?'

'I think so,' I said and read them out to him just to be sure – 'Bareleigh', 'Roughlee' and 'Goldshaw Booth'. They were the villages that Alice had told me about. Each was home to a witch clan.

'That's right, Tom, and there, not too far from Goldshaw Booth, on the western edge of Crow Wood, is Malkin Tower. My own name for the area is the Devil's Triangle because that's where the devil's work is done. Somewhere within that triangle of villages is where we'll find your brother and his family, depending on which clan has taken him – of that I'm sure.'

'What's Witch Dell?' I asked, pointing to the place just north of Bareleigh, marked with a cross.

'Witch Dell?' asked the Spook, raising his eyebrows. 'That's a new one on me!'

'Once again, John, it's my own name for a danger spot. Things have changed for the worse since you were last here. That dell has become the refuge of a number of dead witches. Some have escaped from unhallowed graves; others have simply been taken there after death and abandoned by their families. They usually sleep during the daylight hours, burrowed down into the loam beneath the trees, but come out at night to hunt for the warm blood of living creatures. So when the sun goes down, even roosting birds aren't safe in that dell. It's certainly a place to keep well clear of and the locals do their best. Even so, a few poor souls still go missing each year. Two or three of the witches are very strong and travel miles from the dell each night. Others, fortunately, don't move more than a few paces from their lairs—'

'How many do you reckon there are?' asked the Spook.

Father Stocks frowned. 'A dozen at least. But as I said, only two or three have been seen outside the dell.'

'I should have come back sooner!' said the Spook, shaking his head. 'It should never have been allowed to get so bad. I fear I've failed in my duty—'

'Nonsense. You weren't to know. You're here now and that's all that matters,' Father Stocks replied. 'But yes, the situation is desperate – something has to be done before Lammas.'

'When you came to Chipenden,' said the Spook, 'I asked you a question but you never gave me a proper answer. So I'll ask you again. What do you think the covens are going to attempt at Lammas?'

Father Stocks pushed back his chair, came slowly to his feet and sighed. 'All right, I'll spit it out!' he said, raising his voice slightly. 'What is it that's brought two covens together and might just make a third join them? What could possibly make them put aside their ancient enmity? Most can't stand the sight of each other and have come together only once in the past thirty years—'

'Aye,' said the Spook with a grim smile. 'They came together to curse me!'

'That they did, John, but this time it's because the dark is growing in power, and I suspect that somebody or something is bringing them together. The gathering darkness will give them the opportunity to achieve something very dangerous and difficult. I think they're going to try to raise the Fiend himself!'

'I'd laugh, Father, if I thought you were joking,' the

Spook said, shaking his head gravely. 'I never taught you to believe in the Devil. Are you speaking with just your priest's hat on?'

'I wish I were, John. But as a spook and a priest, I believe they're going to attempt just that. Whether they can do it or not, who knows? But two covens believe it and the third one is being urged to join them in an attempt to try and raise the dark made flesh – the Devil himself. Some witches believe that when this world was first made, the Fiend walked amongst us. Now they're going to try and bring him back so that a new age of darkness can begin.'

I'd once talked to the Spook about the Devil. He told me that he'd begun to wonder if, after all, there was something behind all that we faced, something hidden deep within the dark. Something that grew stronger as the dark grew stronger. Well, Father Stocks certainly seemed to believe there was something in it.

A silence filled the room, and for a few moments both men were deep in thought.

Then Father Stocks stood up and set off without

further delay and we walked with him through the graveyard to the lych gate in front of the church. The clouds were clearing and the sun was warm on our backs.

'That sexton of yours could do with a strong word in his ear,' said the Spook bluntly. 'I've seen tidier church-yards . . .'

Father Stocks sighed. 'He left nearly a month ago. Went back to stay with family in Colne. It didn't come as any surprise though – I knew he was getting more and more nervous about tending the churchyard. Three graves have been robbed in the last eight weeks – that's the work of witches – so an untidy churchyard is the least of our worries.'

'Well, Father, while you're away I'll get my lad to tidy up here a bit anyway.'

We waved Father Stocks off and then the Spook turned to me. 'Well, you know how to use a scythe, lad, so let's make sure you don't lose what skill you have through lack of practice. You can tidy up that grave-yard. It should keep you busy until I return.'

'Where are you going?' I asked in surprise. 'I'd thought the idea was for us to stay in Downham while Father Stocks searches for my family?'

'It was, lad, but scared parishioners and grave-robbing suggests that the village is nowhere near as safe as I thought. I always like to find things out for myself, so while Father Stocks is away, I'll scratch about a bit and see what turns up. In the meantime, get your back into clearing the grass and weeds!'

CHAPTER 5
THE THREE SISTERS

I found the sexton's scythe in a shed at the side of the house, and after taking off my cloak and rolling up my shirt sleeves, I started to cut the grass and weeds as instructed. I began in the areas where the tombstones were horizontal because that was easier.

It was hard work, but I'd often used a scythe back home on the farm and I'd kept my hand in by cutting the grass in the Spook's garden, so I soon got into the swing of it. I could cope with being warm, but as mid-afternoon approached, the sun grew fierce and the heat and exertion started the sweat trickling down into my eyes. It seemed sensible to take a break and start again later.

There was a well behind the house and I wound up the bucket to find it full of water as cold and delicious as that from the felltop streams near Chipenden. After slaking my thirst I sat down, rested my back against the trunk of a yew tree and closed my eyes. Listening to the drone of insects, I soon became drowsy and at some point I must have fallen asleep because the next thing I remember was a dog barking somewhere in the distance. I opened my eyes to find that it was nearly evening and I still had more than half the graveyard to clear. Expecting the Spook or Father Stocks back at any moment, I immediately set to work again.

By the time the sun started to go down I'd just about finished the cutting. The grass needed collecting up but I decided that would keep until morning. My master and the priest still hadn't returned. I was on my way back to the house, just starting to worry, when I heard a faint noise beyond the low boundary wall to my left: a soft footfall in the grass.

'Well, you've certainly made a good job of that,' said

a girl's voice. 'Not been as tidy as that for many a long month!'

'Alice!' I cried, spinning round to face her.

But it *wasn't* Alice, even though her voice had sounded very similar. Standing on the other side of the low wall was a girl of about the same size, although perhaps a little older; and whereas Alice had brown eyes and black hair, this stranger had green eyes like my own, and pale hair that hung down over her shoulders. She was wearing a threadbare, pale-blue summer frock with raggedy sleeves and holes in the elbows.

'I'm not Alice but I know where she's to be found,' said the girl. 'She sent me to get you. Said you were to come right away. *Bring Tom to me*, she said. *I need help! Bring him right away*. Mind you, she didn't let on how fetching you were. A lot better looking than your old master!'

I felt myself blush. My instincts told me not to trust the girl. She was pleasant enough to look at and her eyes were large and bright, but there was something a little shifty about the way her mouth moved when she spoke.

'Where *is* Alice? Why couldn't she come with you?'

'She's not too far over yonder,' the girl said, gesturing roughly south. 'Ten minutes at the most, that's all it is. Couldn't come because she's got a bind on her—'

'A *bind*? What's that?' I asked.

'You a spook's apprentice and never heard of a spell of binding? That's shameful. Your master's not educating you right. Alice is spell-bound. They've got her on a short leash. Can't travel more than a hundred paces from where they cast it. Better than chains if it's done right. But I can get you close enough to see her—'

'Who did it?' I demanded. 'Who cast the spell?'

'Who else but the Mouldheels?' the girl replied. 'Think she's a traitorous little witch. They'll make her suffer for sure!'

'I'll go and get my staff,' I told her.

'There's no time for that. No time to waste. She's in serious trouble.'

'Wait here,' I told her firmly. 'I'll be back in a few minutes.'

That said, I ran across to the house, collected my staff, then sprinted back to where the girl was waiting and climbed over the wall to join her. I glanced towards her feet just in case she was wearing pointy shoes, but to my surprise her feet were bare. She saw me staring down at them and smiled. When she smiled, she looked really pretty.

'Don't need shoes in summer,' she said. 'Like to feel the warm grass under my feet and the cool breeze against my ankles. Anyway, they call me Mab – that's my name if you need it.'

She turned and set off at a fast pace, heading roughly south towards Pendle Hill. There was still some light in the sky to the west but very soon it would be completely dark. I didn't know the area and it would probably have been a good idea to bring a lantern. But my eyes work better in the dark than most people's, and after about ten minutes or so the waning moon came up from behind a bank of trees and cast a pale light over everything.

'How much further?' I asked.

'Ten minutes at the most,' Mab answered.

'You said that when we set off!' I protested.

'Did I? Must have been wrong then. Sometimes I get confused. When I'm walking, I go off into my own little world. Time just flies by . . .'

We were climbing onto the edge of the moor that skirted the north of Pendle Hill. It was at least another thirty minutes before we reached our destination – a small rounded knoll covered with trees and thick bushes on the edge of a wood; the great dark bulk of Pendle loomed up behind it.

'Up there in the trees,' she said, 'that's where we'll wait for Alice.'

I looked up into the darkness beneath the trees and felt uneasy. What if I were walking into some sort of trap? The girl seemed to know about spells. She might have used Alice's name to lure me here.

'Where is Alice now?' I asked suspiciously.

'Got her in a forester's cottage just back there in

the trees. Too dangerous for you to go closer at the moment. It's best if we wait up here until the time's right for you to see her.'

I wasn't happy with what Mab had suggested. Despite the danger, I wanted to see Alice straight away, but I decided to bide my time.

'You lead the way,' I told her, gripping my rowan staff tightly.

Mab gave a little smile and moved up into the cover of the trees. I followed cautiously, climbing up a twisting path through bushes and tangled brambles, alert for danger, my staff at the ready. I started to glimpse lights ahead and felt even more uneasy. Was there someone else waiting above?

At the very top of the hill there was a clearing with a number of tree stumps forming a rough oval. It looked as if the trees had been felled for the purpose of providing seats, and to my surprise, two girls were already seated waiting for us, each with a lantern at her feet. Neither one was Alice. Both appeared to be slightly younger. They stared towards me with wide, unblinking eyes.

'These are my younger sisters,' Mab said. 'The one on the left is Jennet, the other's called Beth, but I wouldn't bother too much about their names if I were you. They're twins and impossible to tell apart!'

I had to agree: they looked identical. Their hair was the same colour and length as Mab's but there the resemblance to their older sister ended. Both were very thin, with sharp, pinched faces and piercing eyes. Their mouths were hard, horizontal slits in their faces and their narrow noses were slightly hooked. They wore thin, threadbare dresses like Mab and their feet were also bare.

I gripped my staff harder. Mab's two sisters were still staring at me intently but there was absolutely no expression on their faces; no way to tell whether they were hostile or friendly.

'Sit yourself down, Tom, and take the weight off your feet,' Mab said, pointing to one of the tree stumps opposite her sisters. 'It might be some while before we can go to Alice.'

Warily I did so; Mab sat down on the stump to my

left. Nobody spoke and an odd silence seemed to settle over everything. To fill in the time, I counted the stumps. There were thirteen and it suddenly struck me that this could be a meeting place for a coven of witches.

No sooner had that disturbing thought entered my head than a bat swooped down into the clearing before flitting away through the branches to my left. Next a big moth appeared from nowhere and, rather than flying towards one of the lanterns, began to circle Jennet's head. Round and round it fluttered, as if her head were a candle-flame. She was still staring at me hard and I wondered if she'd even noticed the moth, which was getting closer and closer and seemed about to settle on her pointy nose.

Suddenly, to my astonishment, her mouth opened wide and her tongue flicked out, caught the moth and drew it in. Then for the first time her face became animated. She gave a broad smile, her mouth curving from ear to ear. Then she chewed quickly and swallowed down the moth with a big gulp.

'Was that good?' her sister Beth enquired, peering sideways at her.

Jennet nodded. 'Really juicy. Don't worry – you can have the next one.'

'Don't mind if I do,' said Beth. 'But what if another don't come?'

'In that case we'll play a game, and I'll let you choose what it is,' Jennet offered.

'Let's play Pin-spitting. I like that game.'

'That's because you always win. You know I can only spit pins on Friday. Wednesday today, it is. I only do feathers on Wednesdays, so it'll have to be something else.'

'What about Through a Hedge Backwards?' suggested Beth.

'Good game, that,' said Jennet. 'First to the bottom wins!'

To my astonishment, they both fell backwards from their tree stumps and did reverse rolls, spinning faster and faster until they disappeared into the bushes and brambles behind. For a few moments you could hear them crashing downwards with a great snapping and cracking of twigs, punctuated by shrieks of pain and bursts of hysterical laughter. Then there was silence, and somewhere close by I heard the cry of an owl. I looked up into the branches but could see no sign of it.

'Love that game, my sisters do!' Mab said with a smile. 'But they'll be licking their wounds tonight, just as sure as eggs rot!'

A few moments later the twins climbed back up the path. When they sat down opposite me again, I didn't know whether to laugh at the state of them or feel really sorry for the pain and discomfort they must be going through. Their threadbare dresses were torn – Jennet's left sleeve had been ripped off completely – and they were covered in cuts and scratches. Beth had a piece of bramble tangled up in her hair and there was a thin line of blood trickling down from her nose to her upper lip. But she didn't seem at all dismayed.

'I really enjoyed that! Let's play another game,' she suggested, licking away the blood. 'What about Truth or Dare? I like that too.'

'Fine with me. But make the boy go first . . .' Jennet said, squinting towards me.

'Truth, Dare, Kiss or Promise?' Beth demanded, staring right at me, a challenge in her voice. All three girls were watching me now and none of them were blinking.

'I don't want to play,' I said firmly.

'Be nice to my younger sisters,' Mab insisted. 'Go on, choose. It's only a game.'

'I don't know the rules,' I said. It was true. I'd never heard of the game. It sounded like a game that girls would play and I hadn't had any sisters. I didn't know much about girls' games.

'It's easy,' said Mab from my left. 'You just choose one of the four. Choose Truth and you have to answer a question truthfully. Choose Dare and you're set a task. Pick Kiss and you have to kiss who or what you're told to – there's no getting away from it. Promise is hardest of all. Have to make one, and bound by it, you are – maybe bound for ever!'

'No! I don't want to play,' I repeated.

'Don't be silly. Don't have any choice, do you? Can't leave this spot until we say so. You're rooted to it – hadn't you noticed?'

I'd been growing more and more annoyed. It seemed to me now that Mab had been playing some sort of game with me from the moment we'd first met at the graveyard. I didn't believe for one moment that we were going to rescue Alice. What a fool I'd been! Why had I followed her here?

When I tried to stand, though, nothing happened. It was as if all the strength had left my body. My arms fell uselessly to my sides and my rowan staff slipped from my grasp onto the grass and rolled away.

'You're better off without that nasty stick,' Mab said. 'You go first – it's time to choose one of the four. You'll play our game whether you want to or not. You'll play and you'll like it. So choose!'

By now I had no doubt at all that the three of them were witches. My staff was out of reach and I felt too weak to stand up. I wasn't afraid because somehow it seemed more like dreaming than waking, but I knew that I wasn't asleep and that I was in danger. So I took a slow, deep breath and thought carefully. Better to humour them for a bit. While they were concentrating on the game, I might find a way to get free.

But which one of the four options should I choose? 'Dare' could lead to some type of dangerous task that I might be forced to carry out. 'Promise' was full of risk. I'd made promises before that had got me into trouble. 'Kiss' seemed harmless. How could a kiss hurt you? But then I remembered that she'd said 'who or *what*' and I didn't like the sound of that at all. Even so, I almost chose that option, but then I decided on 'Truth' instead. I always tried to be honest and truthful. It was something that my dad had taught me. What harm could come from choosing that?

'Truth,' I said.

At my answer the girls all smiled broadly, as if it was exactly the option they'd wanted me to pick.

'Right!' said Mab triumphantly, turning to face me. 'Tell me this and be truthful. And you'd better, if you know what's good for you. Wouldn't do to cross us!

Which one of us do you like best?'

I looked at Mab in astonishment. I'd had no idea what kind of question I'd be asked but this was like a bolt from the blue. And it wasn't easy to answer. Whichever one I picked, the other two would be offended. And I wasn't even sure what the truth was. All three girls were scary and almost certainly witches. I didn't like any of them. So what else could I do? I told them the truth.

'I don't like any of you that much,' I said. 'I don't mean to be rude, but it's the truth you wanted and it's the plain truth I've given you . . .'

All three let out a simultaneous hiss of anger. 'That's not good enough,' Mab said, her voice low and dangerous. 'You have to choose one of us.'

'Then it's you, Mab. You were the one I saw first. So it might as well be you.'

I'd spoken instinctively, without thinking, but Mab smiled. It was a self-satisfied smile, as if she'd known she was going to be chosen all along.

'It's my turn now,' said Mab, turning away from me

to face her sisters. 'I'll take Kiss!'

'Then kiss Tom!' Jennet exclaimed. 'Kiss him now and make him yours for ever!'

At that, Mab stood up and walked across to face me directly. She leaned down and put a hand on each of my shoulders. 'Look up at me!' she commanded.

I felt weak. All my willpower seemed to have deserted me. I did as I was told: I looked up into her green eyes and her face came closer to mine. Her face was pretty but her breath stank like that of a dog or a cat. The world started to spin and, but for the firm grip of Mab's hands on my shoulders, I would have fallen backwards off the stump.

Then, just as her warm lips pressed softly against mine, I felt a succession of searing pains in my left forearm. It was as if someone had stabbed it four times with a long sharp pin.

In agony, I lurched to my feet and, with a gasp, Mab fell away from me, backwards onto the grass. I looked at my forearm. There were four scars on it, vivid in the moonlight, and I remembered what had caused them.

Alice had once gripped my left forearm so hard that her fingernails had gone deep into my flesh. When she'd released me, there were four bright-red beads of blood where her nails had cut me.

Days later, on our way to her aunt's place in Staumin, Alice had touched the scars on my arm. And I remembered exactly what she'd said:

Put my brand on you there . . . That won't ever fade away.

I hadn't been sure what she meant and she had never really explained herself. Then again, in Priestown, we'd quarrelled and I was about to go my own way when Alice had shouted out: *You're mine. You belong to me!*

At the time I hadn't really thought that much about it. Now I began to wonder if there was more to it than I'd realized: Alice and the three girls seemed to believe that a witch could somehow make you hers for life. Whatever the truth of it, I had broken free of Mab's power and somehow it was due to Alice.

As Mab struggled angrily to her feet, I showed her the scars on my arm.

'I can't be yours for ever, Mab,' I told her, the words flying into my mouth as if by magic. 'I already belong to someone else. I belong to Alice!'

No sooner had I spoken than Beth and Jennet both fell gracefully off their tree stumps and rolled backwards down the hill again. Once more I could hear them crashing through the bushes and brambles all the way to the bottom of the hill, but this time they neither shrieked nor laughed.

When I looked at Mab, her eyes were blazing with anger.

Quickly I reached down and snatched up my rowan staff, ready to strike her if need be. Mab looked at the raised staff, flinched and took two swift steps backwards.

'You *will* belong to me one day,' she said, her lips tightening into a snarl. 'Just as sure as my name's Mab Mouldheel! And it'll happen much sooner than you think. I want you, Thomas Ward, and you'll be mine for sure when Alice is dead!'

With that she turned away, picked up both lanterns

and walked back down the slope into the trees by a different path from the one we'd used to ascend.

I was shaking all over in reaction to her words. I'd been talking to three witches from the Mouldheel clan. Mab had certainly known where to find me – Alice must have told her. So where *was* Alice? I felt sure Mab and her sisters must know.

One part of me wanted to head north back to Downham and tell the Spook what had happened. But I hadn't liked the way Mab had snarled as she'd issued her threat. Alice was surely their prisoner, in their power? They might kill her as soon as they got back. So I had no choice: I had to follow the sisters.

I'd noted the direction that Mab had taken. She'd gone south. Now I had to follow her and her sisters down the more dangerous eastern side of the hill; follow them towards the three villages that made up the three points of what Father Stocks had called the Devil's Triangle.

CHAPTER 6
THE CELLAR OF MIRRORS

I was a seventh son of a seventh son, so a witch couldn't sniff me out at a distance. That meant I could follow the three sisters safely as long as I didn't get too close. I would also have to watch out for other even more dangerous members of the Mouldheel family.

At first it was easy. I could see the glow of the lanterns and hear the three girls moving through the wood ahead of me. They were making quite a lot of noise: voices were raised and they seemed to be arguing. At one point, despite all my care, I stepped on a twig. It broke with a loud crack and I froze to the spot, afraid that they might have heard me. I needn't have worried.

They were making their own even louder noises ahead, and were completely unaware that I was following.

When we left the wood, it became more difficult. We were in the open, on a bleak slope of moorland. The moonlight increased the risk that I would be seen so I had to stay much further back, but soon I realized I had another advantage. The three girls came to a stream and followed its banks as it changed direction, before it curved back in a bow-shape and allowed them to continue on their way south. That confirmed for me that they were indeed witches. They couldn't cross running water!

But *I* could! So instead of always following behind, I could take a more direct route and, to some extent, anticipate where they were going. As they dropped down off the moor, I began to travel parallel with them, keeping to the shadows of hedgerows and trees whenever possible. This went on for some time, but the terrain gradually became rougher and more difficult, and then I saw another dark wood ahead; a thick clump of trees and bushes in a valley that ran parallel to Pendle Hill on my right.

At first I thought it would be no problem. I simply slowed down and allowed them to get ahead again, following at a safe distance as before. It was only after I'd moved into the trees that I realized that something was now very different. The three sisters were no longer talking loudly as they had been in the previous wood. In fact they weren't making any noise at all. An eerie silence prevailed, as if everything was holding its breath. There hadn't been more than a slight breeze before, but now not even a twig or a leaf was moving. Nor were there any of the rustling noises made by small creatures of the night, such as mice or hedgehogs. Either everything in the wood really was immobile, holding its breath, or the wood was empty of all life.

It was then, with a sudden shiver of horror, that I realized exactly where I was and why things were as they were. This was a small wooded valley. And another name for a small wooded valley is a dell.

I was walking through what Father Stocks had called Witch Dell! This was where all the dead witches gathered to prey on those who passed through or even skirted the wood. Lives were lost here every year. I gripped my rowan staff and kept perfectly still, listening carefully. Nothing seemed to be approaching, but there was soft loam under my feet, and decades of dank autumns had provided perfect hiding places for dead witches. One could already be close by, hidden under the leaves. Step forward and she would grab my ankle! One quick bite and she'd start sucking my blood, growing stronger by the mouthful.

I could use my rowan staff and probably manage to get myself free – that's what I told myself. I'd have to be quick. As the witch waxed stronger, my own strength would be waning. And what if I met one of the really strong witches? Father Stocks said there were two or three who roamed far beyond the dell in search of victims. I put this thought firmly from my mind.

I began to move forward slowly and carefully. As I did so, I wondered why the three sisters had now become so silent? Could it be that they were also worried about attracting the dead? Why should that be?

Weren't they all witches together? And then I remembered what Father Stocks had said about the ancient animosity between the three covens. Although there'd been some inter-marriage between the Deanes and the Malkins, the clans only ever gathered together when they had to combine their dark power. Maybe the Mouldheel sisters were afraid of meeting a dead witch from a rival family?

It was a tense, scary time; I risked being attacked at any moment. But at last, with a sigh of relief, I reached the far edge of the dell. I was very glad to be out from the shadow of those trees. Once more I was bathed in moonlight, watching the bobbing lanterns ahead of me and hearing the sisters' voices raised as if in anger. After ten minutes or so they were descending a steep slope and I could see the glow from a fire lighting up the sky ahead. I hung back for a while, then took refuge in a copse of ash and alder. It was ready for thinning and cutting and so provided a good hiding place. Moments later I was peering out from a thicket of saplings with a clear view of what was taking place.

Directly below was a row of terraced cottages – eight in all – and on the edge of the wide flagged back yard a big bonfire was blazing away, sparks dancing up into the night sky. In the near distance, amongst the trees, was another large cluster of cottages. This was probably Bareleigh, where the Mouldheel clan lived.

In all, there were about two dozen people below me, an even mixture of men and women, and most were seated on the flags or grass, eating from plates with their fingers. It seemed harmless enough – just a few friends gathered together on a warm summer's night to eat in the moonlight. Voices carried on the air mixed in with the sound of laughter.

Towards the edge of the fire a cauldron was suspended from a metal tripod, and as I watched, a woman ladled something into a bowl, then walked across and offered it to a girl seated at some distance from the others. Her head was bowed and she was staring down at the flags, but as the bowl was held out to her, she looked up and shook her head firmly three times.

It was Alice! Her hands were free but I saw a glint

of metal reflecting the firelight: her feet were bound together with a padlock and chain.

No sooner had I noticed her than the three sisters reached the yard. As they joined the gathering, everyone fell silent.

Without a word to anyone, Mab walked directly over to the fire. She seemed to spit into it and immediately it died right down. The sparks stopped dancing, the flames flickered low and the embers glowed momentarily before fading to grey, all in the space of a few moments. Lanterns still lit the scene brightly though, and at a signal from Mab, I saw one of the men walk across, lift Alice over his shoulder and carry her through the open back door into the end cottage to my left.

My heart was in my mouth. I remembered what Mab had said about me belonging to her once Alice was dead. Were they going to kill her now? Had the man taken her inside to do just that?

I was on the verge of running down the hill to the cottage to try and help her. It would have been hopeless with so many people there but I couldn't just stand by and let Alice be harmed. I waited for a few moments, anxiety gnawing away at my insides. At last I could stand it no longer, but before I could move the man reappeared alone at the door of the cottage and locked it behind him. Immediately Mab, with her two sisters walking just behind, led the gathering out through a gate and onto a track beyond the cottage which ran parallel to a stream.

I waited until everyone had disappeared into the distance, towards what looked to be the centre of Bareleigh, then descended the hill cautiously. There was a chance that someone was still inside the cottage; someone who'd been there all along. I mean, would they go off and leave Alice unguarded? It seemed very unlikely.

When I reached the door, I unlocked it with the special key Andrew had given me.

I eased the door open slowly and stepped directly into a cluttered kitchen. By the light of three black wax candles, I saw that the sink was heaped with unwashed plates and pots and the flagged floor was littered with animal bones and splattered with congealed fat and grease. As I closed the door gently behind me, my eyes darted around the room, alert for danger. It seemed deserted but I didn't move. I just leaned back against the door, the stink of rancid fat and rotting food in my nostrils, and breathed slowly to calm my nerves, listening very carefully all the while. The rest of the cottage sounded empty, but it was almost too silent. It seemed hard to believe that Alice would make no sound at all. At that thought, my heart began to hammer in my chest again and my throat tightened with fear. What if she'd already been killed? What if the man had brought her into the house for just that purpose?

The horror of that thought started me moving. I would have to check each room in turn. It was a small single-storey cottage, so there was no upstairs to investigate. The inner door opened into a tiny, cramped room; on the bed were creased dirty sheets, and another black candle flickered on the window ledge. There was no sign of Alice. Where could she be?

Beyond the bed, set into the far wall, was another

door. I turned the handle, eased it open and stepped through to find myself in the living room.

One glance told me that I wasn't alone! To my right was the hearth, where the embers of a coal fire gleamed. But directly facing me, sitting hunched at a table, was a witch with wild eyes and a mass of frizzy white hair. In her left hand was a candle stub with a flickering flame that gave off a lot of smoke. Instinctively I raised my staff as her mouth opened and she began to shout, shaking her fist towards me. But there was no sound, and instantly I realized that the witch wasn't actually in the room with me. I was looking into a large mirror. She was using it to watch from a distance.

How far off was she? Miles away or close at hand? Wherever she was, using another mirror, she might well be able to tell the Mouldheels that there was an intruder in the cottage. How long before somebody returned?

Below the mirror and to my left I could see narrow steps leading down into the darkness. There must be a cellar. Could Alice be down there?

Quickly I pulled my tinderbox and a candle stub from my breeches pockets. Moments later, ignoring the witch, who was still ranting silently in the mirror, I was on my way down the steps, candle in my right hand, staff in my left. There was a locked door at the bottom, but my key made short work of that; I eased it open and let the candle illuminate the room.

Relief washed over me as I saw Alice sitting with her back against the wall next to a heap of coal. She seemed unhurt. She looked up, opening her mouth to speak, fear etched into her face. Then she recognized me and sighed with relief.

'Oh, Tom! It's you. I thought they were coming to kill me.'

'It's all right, Alice,' I told her. 'I'll have you free in a minute.'

I knelt down, and it really was but the work of a moment to unlock the padlock with my key and ease the chains from Alice's legs. So far things were going really well. But when I helped her to her feet, she was shaking and still seemed fearful. It was then that I realized there was something odd about the cellar. It was too bright. One candle shouldn't have lit it so well.

As I came to my feet, I saw why. Fastened to each of the four walls, at about the height of my own head, was a large mirror set in an ornate, black wooden frame. The mirrors were reflecting the candle back, intensifying the light. But then, to my horror, I saw something else: in each mirror was a face staring out at me, eyes filled with spite.

Three were women – witches with wild, malevolent eyes and thick, unkempt hair – but the fourth looked like a child. And it was that fourth image that held my gaze, fixing me to the spot so that I felt unable to move. The head was small – that's why I'd assumed it was a boy – but the features were those of a man, completely bald and with a hooked nose. For a moment the image was still, frozen in time like a portrait, but as I watched, the mouth widened like an animal's jaws getting ready to savage its prey. The teeth within were razor-sharp needles.

Who or what it was I had no idea, but it scared me

badly – I *had* to get out of that cellar. All four figures were watching us. They now knew that I'd released Alice. I blew out the candle and returned it to my pocket.

'Come on, Alice,' I said, seizing her hand. 'Let's get away from here!'

With those words I began to lead her up the steps, but either she was afraid to go or was weakened in some way because, as I climbed, she seemed to drag and her hand tried to pull me back.

'What are you doing, Alice?' I demanded. 'They could be back at any moment!'

Alice shook her head. 'Ain't that easy. Did more than just chain me. Bound here, I am. Won't get much further than the yard anyway . . .'

'A spell of binding?' I asked, halting and turning to face her on the steps. I already knew the answer. Mab had said she was bound – she obviously hadn't been lying.

Alice nodded, her face desperate. 'There's a way to get me free of it but it ain't going to be easy. Not easy at all. Got a lock of my hair, they have. Twisted back on itself. It needs to be burned. That's the only way—'

'Where will it be?'

'Mab has it 'cos she cast the spell.'

'We'll talk outside,' I said, pulling Alice upwards again. 'Don't worry, I'll find a way . . .'

I tried to sound cheerful but my heart was sinking towards my boots. What hope had I of getting the lock of hair away from Mab with so many others to help her?

Somehow, by pulling and tugging, I managed to get Alice to the top of the cellar steps. The witch was no longer peering out through the mirror. Was she on her way here now? We got through the bedroom and the kitchen and reached the back door, but when I opened it, my heart sank even lower. I could hear angry voices some distance away but getting nearer by the second. We began to cross the yard to the gate that led to the track at the front of the house. Alice was really trying but she was gasping merely with the effort of walking, and beads of sweat were erupting on her brow.

Suddenly she came to a halt.

'Can't go any further!' she sobbed. 'Can't take another step!'

'I'll carry you!' I told her. 'Mab said you're bound for a hundred paces. If I can get you beyond that, maybe you'll be all right.' And without waiting for a reply I caught her by the legs and heaved her up onto my right shoulder. Gripping my staff in my left hand, I went through the open gate, crossed the track, then plunged through the fast-flowing stream to the far bank. Now I felt better. Witches couldn't cross running water so I'd put a barrier between us and pursuit. They'd have to find a different route, maybe going miles out of their way. It had given us a head start back to Downham.

It was hard carrying Alice and she kept moaning as if in pain. So I called out to her: 'Are you all right, Alice?'

Her only reply was to give another groan, but there was nothing for it but to keep moving, so I gritted my teeth and strode on, heading north, with Pendle Hill on my left. I knew I would soon reach Witch Dell, so

I moved to my right, further east, hoping to give it as wide a berth as possible. Soon I came upon another stream. Hearing no sounds of pursuit, I eased Alice from my shoulder and down onto the grass at the water's edge. To my dismay her eyes were closed. Was she asleep or unconscious?

I called her name several times but received no response. I tried shaking her gently but that did no good either. So, growing more concerned by the moment, I knelt down beside the stream, cupped my hands and filled them with cold water. Next I allowed the water to drip and then flow onto Alice's forehead. She gave a gasp and sat up straight, her eyes wild and fearful.

'It's all right, Alice. We've got away. We're safe—'

'Safe? How can we be safe? Come after us, they will. Won't be far behind.'

'No,' I told her. 'We forded the stream on the other side of the track. It's running water so they can't cross.'

Alice shook her head. 'Ain't that easy, Tom. Most

witches ain't stupid. Lots of streams flow down that big ugly hill over there,' she said, pointing towards Pendle. 'Would witches live where it was so difficult to get from place to place? They have ways and means, don't they? They've built "witch dams" in places where they're really needed. Turn a handle and pulleys lower a big wooden board down into the water, cutting off the flow from upstream. Of course, it don't take water that long to back up and flow around the board, but it's more than enough time to allow a few witches to cross. They won't be that far behind if I'm not mistaken!'

No sooner had Alice finished talking than I heard someone shout from beyond the trees to our rear. It sounded like they were on our trail all right, and closing in.

'Can you walk?' I asked.

Alice nodded. 'Think so,' she said, so I gripped her hand and helped her to her feet. 'Carried me out of range of the binding, you did. It hurt a lot but I'm almost free now. Though Mab's still got that lock of my hair. Dread to think what other mischief she could get up to using that. She has the advantage of me there all right!'

We carried on north towards Downham. At first Alice seemed to find it difficult to walk, but with every step she appeared to grow a little stronger and soon we were making reasonable progress. The trouble was, the sounds of pursuit were gradually getting closer. They were gaining on us.

As we climbed towards the edge of Downham Moor and entered a small wood, Alice suddenly put her hand on my arm and brought us to a halt.

'What is it, Alice? We've got to keep going—'

'Something ahead, Tom. There's a dead witch heading this way . . .'

I saw a hunched figure moving directly towards us through the trees, feet shuffling through last autumn's soggy leaves. It would be one of the really strong witches who were able to leave the dell and hunt for prey. The witch was heading in our direction, but she didn't seem to be moving very fast. We couldn't go back because the Mouldheels weren't too far behind, but we could move to the right or the left and give her a wide enough berth. But when I tried to lead Alice off the path, she put her hand on my arm again.

'No, Tom. It'll be all right. I know this witch. It's old Maggie Malkin. She's family. They hanged her at Caster three years ago but let us bring her home for burial. Didn't bury her though, did we? Carried her to the dell where she'd have company. And here she is now. Wonder if she'll remember me. Don't worry, Tom. This could be just what we need . . .'

I moved away from Alice and readied my staff. I didn't like the look of the dead witch one little bit. Her long dark gown was slimy and covered in patches of mould. There were leaves stuck to it – no doubt she buried herself under the trees to sleep away the day-light hours. Her eyes were open but they bulged from their sockets as if about to pop out onto her cheeks, and her neck was too long, with her head twisted round to the left. And where the moonlight dappled through the trees there was a faint silver trail behind her, the kind that a slug or snail leaves in its wake.

'Good to see you, Cousin Maggie,' Alice called out in a cheerful voice.

At that, the dead witch came to a halt. She was now no more than five paces away.

'Who speaks my name?' she croaked.

'It's me, Alice Deane. Don't you remember me, Cousin?'

'My memory ain't what it used to be,' sighed the witch. 'Come closer, child, and let me see you.'

To my horror, Alice obeyed, stepping right up to Maggie, who put her hand on her shoulder and sniffed loudly at her three times. I wouldn't have liked that hand touching me. Her long fingernails resembled the talons of a predatory bird.

'You've grown, child,' said the witch. 'So much so that I hardly recognize you. But you still smell like family and that's enough for me. But who's the stranger with you? Who's the boy?'

'It's my friend, Tom,' Alice said.

The dead witch stared hard at me and sniffed the air. Then she frowned and opened her mouth to reveal two jagged rows of blackened teeth.

'He's a strange one, that,' she said. 'Don't smell right and his shadow's too long. He's not good company for a young girl like you!'

A shaft of moonlight had pierced the trees, casting our shadows along the ground. My shadow was very long, at least twice the length of Alice's and Maggie's – something that always happens in moonlight. I never give it much thought. I've just got used to it.

'Better choose friends from your own kind,' continued the witch. 'That's what you should do. Anything else only ends in sorrow and regret. You'd be better off rid of him. Give him to me, that's a good girl. The hunt ain't gone well tonight and my tongue is bone-dry. So give me the boy . . .'

With those words the dead witch thrust out her tongue so far that, momentarily, it hung well below her chin.

'No, Maggie – need something juicier than him, you do,' Alice said. 'Ain't got much meat on his bones and his blood's too thin for your taste. No, back yonder, that's where the hunting's good tonight,' she went on, pointing back the way we'd come. 'Mouldheel blood is what you need . . .'

'Be there Mouldheels back there?' asked Maggie, raising her head and gazing through the trees while running her tongue over her lips. 'Mouldheels you say?'

'Enough to last you a week or more,' said Alice. 'Mab and her sisters and more besides. You won't go hungry tonight . . .'

Saliva began to dribble from the witch's open mouth, dripping onto the mouldy leaves at her feet. Then, without another word or even a backward glance, she set off towards the sound of the voices to our rear. She was still shuffling but her progress was far more rapid than before, while we carried on our journey, walking fast.

'Should keep 'em busy for a while,' Alice said with a grim smile. 'Dead Maggie hates the Mouldheels. Pity we can't stay and watch!'

Now that the immediate danger was over, my mind

turned to other things. I was dreading the answer but I just had to know.

'Did you find out anything about Jack and his family?' I asked Alice.

'Ain't no easy way to tell you this, Tom,' she said. 'But no point in not telling you the truth, is there?'

My heart lurched up into my mouth. 'They're not dead, are they?' I asked.

'Two days ago they were still alive,' Alice told me. 'But they won't be for long if something ain't done. Got 'em locked away in the pits under Malkin Tower. The Malkins done it. My family are in the thick of it.' She shook her head. 'Got your trunks too.'

CHAPTER 7
ALICE'S TALE

Within an hour or so we were knocking on the door of the presbytery. Both Father Stocks and the Spook had returned and at first my master was angry that I'd gone off by myself.

As we sat down at the kitchen table, I noticed that the mirror above the fireplace had been turned to the wall. It was still dark and Father Stocks had obviously taken that wise precaution against being spied on by witches.

My master made me give a detailed account of what had happened, and by the time I'd finished, Father Stocks had placed four bowls of hot chicken soup on the table. As my master clearly had no desire to face the witches just yet, it seemed we weren't fasting, so I wolfed down the soup gratefully.

Of course, although I explained how we'd had to flee the Mouldheels, I didn't mention that Alice had talked to the dead witch. I didn't think that would be the kind of thing the Spook would like to hear. To him, it would be an indication of how close Alice still was to her family and how little we could trust her.

'Well, lad,' he said, dunking a big slice of crusty bread into his steaming soup, 'though you were foolish to go off alone with that girl in the first place, all's well that ends well. But now I'd like to hear what Alice has to say,' he went on, looking at her. 'So start at the beginning and tell me everything that happened before Tom found you. Leave nothing out. The tiniest detail may be important.'

'Spent a day and a night sniffing around before the Mouldheels caught me,' Alice began. 'Long enough to find things out. Went to talk to Agnes Sowerbutts, one of my aunts, and she told me most of it. Some things are as clear as the nose on your face. Ain't too difficult to work out what's going on there. But other things are a mystery. As I told Tom, his brother Jack and his family are prisoners in the dungeons under Malkin Tower. No surprise, that. No surprise either that the Malkins done it. Tom's trunks are there too. And having real trouble with them three big ones, they are. Got the little boxes open easy enough but they can't get into the big trunks. They don't know what's in 'em either. Just that it's something well worth having—'

'How did they know about the trunks in the first place?' the Spook interrupted.

'Got themselves a "seer",' Alice said. 'Calls himself Tibb. Sees things at a distance, he does, but can't see into the trunks. Just knows they're worth opening. Knows about Tom too: sees the future and thinks Tom's a real serious threat. More dangerous even than you,' she said, nodding towards the Spook. 'Can't afford to let him grow up. Want Tom dead, the Malkins do. But first they want Tom's keys – so that they can open his mam's trunks.'

'Who *is* this so-called seer?' asked the Spook, a touch

of disdain in his voice. 'Was he born and bred in the County?'

My master didn't believe that anyone could see into the future, but I'd witnessed a few things that made me think he could be wrong. Mam wrote to me before we finally faced the Priestown Bane. She'd predicted what was likely to happen and had been proved right.

'Born in the County, after a fashion, but Tibb ain't human,' answered Alice. 'One glance at him tells you that—'

'You've seen him?' asked the Spook.

'Seen him all right, and so has Tom. We saw him in a mirror. The Mouldheels kept me prisoner in a cellar most of the time and there were mirrors in there, so they could keep an eye on me. But Tibb was too strong and used one of those Mouldheel mirrors to scry and spy for himself. He's seen that I'm here, but more importantly he knows that Tom rescued me. Ugly, he is, with sharp teeth. Small but strong and dangerous. Only got three toes on each foot too. No, he ain't human – that's for sure.'

'So where's he from? I've not heard of him before,' said my master.

'Last Halloween the Malkins called a truce with the Deanes and both covens got together to make Tibb. Put a big boar's head in a cauldron and cooked it. Boiled off all the pig flesh and brains and made it into brawn. Each member of the covens spat into it thirteen times. Then they fed it to a sow. Seven months or so later they slit open the sow's belly and out crawled Tibb. Ain't got much bigger since but he's stronger than a fully grown man.'

'Sounds more a tale of dreaming than waking,' said the Spook wryly, an edge of mockery in his voice. 'Where did you hear it? From your aunt?'

'Some of it. The rest from the Mouldheel sisters – Mab, Beth and Jennet. They caught me while I was skirting Bareleigh. But for Tom, they'd have put an end to me for sure. Tried to talk them into setting me free. Said I no longer belonged to my family. But they hurt me really bad. Made me say things I didn't want to say. Sorry, Tom, but I couldn't help myself. Told 'em about you, I did, and how you'd come to Pendle to try and rescue your family. Even told Mab where you were staying. I'm really sorry but I couldn't help myself . . .'

Tears began to glisten in Alice's eyes and I went across and put my arm around her shoulder.

'No harm done,' I said.

'One other thing you should know,' she went on, biting at her bottom lip before taking a deep breath. 'While I was a prisoner of the Mouldheels, the Deanes and Malkins came a-calling. Just a couple of each, that's all. Talked round the fire outside, they did – I was too far away to hear most of what was said, but I think they were trying to persuade Mab to help them do something. But I clearly saw Mab shake her head and send them away.'

The Spook frowned in puzzlement. 'Why would the Malkins and Deanes speak to a mere girl about something like that?' he asked.

'A lot's changed since you were last here, John,' Father Stocks observed thoughtfully. 'The Mouldheel coven is growing in power and starting to present a serious challenge to the other two. And it's a new generation that's responsible. Mab can't be much more than fourteen but she's more menacing than a witch twice that age. She's already the leader of the whole clan and the others fear her. It's said that she's an expert scryer and can read the future better than any witch has ever done before. Perhaps this Tibb is something the Malkins have bred to counter her growing power.'

'Then let's hope she doesn't change her mind and join with the other covens,' the Spook said gravely. 'Tibb sees things at a distance, you say,' he continued, directing his words towards Alice. 'Is it a type of long-sniffing?'

'Long-sniffing and scrying together, it is,' explained Alice. 'But he can't do it all the time. Needs to drink fresh human blood . . .'

A hush fell over the room. I could see that Father Stocks and the Spook were thinking about what had been said. 'Scrying' was the term witches used for prophecy. The Spook didn't believe in it but I could tell that he was disturbed by the way Tibb had found out about Mam's trunks. The more I'd heard, the worse the situation seemed. From the first time the Spook had warned me that we'd be travelling to Pendle to deal with the witches, I'd had serious misgivings. How could he possibly hope to deal with so many? And what were we going to do now that Jack and his family were prisoners in the dungeons under Malkin Tower?

'Why did they take them?' I asked. 'They'd got the trunks. Why didn't they just leave them behind?'

'Sometimes witches do things just for badness,' Alice answered. 'Might easily have killed them before leaving the farm. Capable of that, they are. But most likely they took 'em alive because they're *your* family. Need the keys, they do, and hostages are a way to put pressure on you.'

'We know where Jack, Ellie and Mary are now,' I said, my anger and impatience growing. 'What are we going to do about getting them free? How are we going to do it?'

'I think there's only one thing we can do, lad,' said the Spook. 'Get help. My plan was to spend the summer and the autumn harrying our enemies; trying to divide the clans. Now we've got to act quickly. Father Stocks has suggested something that I'm not entirely happy with, but he's convinced me that it's the only way we'll have any chance at all of saving your family.'

'There's an element of risk involved, I'll grant you that. But what other choice do we have?' asked Father Stocks. 'There are some rough elements living in those three villages, who either willingly or through fear of the covens lend them their support. Then there are the clan menfolk, of course. And even if we could somehow fight our way past them, Malkin Tower is formidable indeed. It's built of good County stone and has a moat, a drawbridge and a stout wooden door studded with iron beyond that. In effect it's a small castle.

'So, young Tom, this is what I propose. Tomorrow you and I will walk over to the big house at Read and speak to the local magistrate there. As next of kin to those who were abducted, you'll have to make a formal complaint. The magistrate's name is Roger Nowell and until about five years ago he was High Sheriff at Caster. He's an esquire, one rank below a knight, and also a good, honest man. We'll see if we can persuade him to take action.'

'Aye,' said the Spook, 'and during his period of office at Caster, not one single witch was brought to trial. As we well know, those charged are usually falsely accused anyway, but it does tell us a lot about him. You see, he doesn't believe in witchcraft. He's a rationalist. A man of common sense. For him witches simply don't exist—'

'How can he think like that when he lives in Pendle, of all places?' I asked.

'Some people have closed minds,' my master answered. 'And it's in the interests of the Pendle clans to keep his mind closed. So he's allowed to see and hear nothing that could make him the least bit suspicious.'

'But, of course, we won't be bringing any charges of witchcraft,' Father Stocks said, pulling a piece of paper from his cassock and holding it up. 'Robbery and kidnapping are what Master Nowell will understand. Here I have accounts by two witnesses who saw your brother and his family being taken through Goldshaw Booth on the way to Malkin Tower. I wrote out their testimony yesterday and they made their mark. You see, not everyone in that Devil's Triangle is in league with witches or afraid for their own skin. But I've promised them that they'll remain anonymous. Otherwise their lives wouldn't be worth a wisp of straw. But it'll be enough to get Nowell to act.'

I wasn't that happy with what was being proposed. The Spook had also expressed reservations. But something had to be done and I couldn't think of an alternative plan.

Father Stocks's cottage had four upstairs rooms so there was accommodation for three guests. We had a few hours' sleep and were up at dawn. Then, after a breakfast of cold mutton, the Spook and Alice stayed behind while I accompanied the priest south. This time we took the westerly route, travelling with Pendle Hill to our left.

'Read is south of Sabden, Tom,' the priest explained, 'but even if we were heading for Bareleigh, this would be the way I'd go. It's safer. You were lucky to get through that dell in one piece last night . . .'

I was travelling without my cloak and staff so as not to draw attention to myself. Not only was it witch country but Master Nowell didn't believe in witchcraft so he probably wouldn't have much time for spooks or their apprentices. Nor did I take any weapons that could be used against the dark. I trusted Father Stocks to get us safely to Read and back before sunset. And, as he'd explained, we'd be travelling on the safer side of the hill.

After about an hour we halted and slaked our thirst with the cold waters of a stream. After we'd drunk our fill Father Stocks pulled off his boots and socks, sat down on the bank and dangled his bare feet in the fast-flowing water.

'That feels good,' he said with a smile.

I nodded and smiled back. I sat near the bank but I didn't bother to take my own boots off. It was a pleas-ant morning: the sun was starting to take the chill from the air and there wasn't a cloud in the sky. We were in a picturesque spot and the nearby trees didn't obscure our view of Pendle Hill. Today it looked different, somehow friendlier, and its green slopes were dotted with white spots, some of them moving.

'Lots of sheep up there,' I said, nodding towards the hill. Closer by, beyond the stream, the field was also full of sheep and bleating, almost fully grown lambs, soon to be separated from their mothers. It seemed cruel, but farming was a livelihood and they'd end up at the butcher's.

'Aye,' said the priest. 'This is sheep country without a doubt. That's the wealth of Pendle up there. We produce the best mutton in the County and some make a very good living. Mind you, there's real poverty to balance it. A lot gain their bread by begging. One of the things about being a priest that gives me real satisfaction is trying to alleviate that need. In effect I become a beggar myself. I beg parishioners to put money in the collection plate. I beg for clothes and food. Then I give it to the poor. It's very worthwhile.'

'More worthwhile than being a spook, Father?' I asked.

Father Stocks smiled. 'For me, Tom, the answer must

be yes. But everyone must follow their own path . . .'

'What made you finally decide that it was better to be a priest than a spook?' I asked.

Father Stocks looked at me hard for a moment, then frowned. It seemed that he wasn't going to answer and I feared that my bluntness had offended him. When he finally spoke, he seemed to choose his words carefully.

'Perhaps it was the moment when I finally realized just how dark things were getting. I saw how hard John Gregory worked, dealing with this threat here and that danger there. Constantly risking his life, yet never managing to solve the real problem – that of the evil at the very heart of the world, which is far too big for us to cope with alone. We poor humans need the help of a higher power. We need the help of God . . .'

'So you absolutely believe in God?' I asked. 'You've no doubts?'

'Oh, yes, Tom. I believe in God and I have no doubts at all. And I also believe in the power of prayer. What's more, my vocation gives me the opportunity to help others. That's why I've become a priest.'

I nodded and smiled. It was a good enough answer from a good man. I hadn't known Father Stocks long but already I liked him and could understand why the Spook had called him a friend.

We walked on until, at last, we reached a gate; beyond it were wide verdant lawns where red deer grazed. They were planted with copses of trees, seemingly positioned to please the eye.

'Here we are,' said Father Stocks. 'This is Read Park.'

'But where's the big house?' I asked. There was no sign of a building of any kind and I wondered if it was hidden behind some trees.

'This is just the "laund", Tom – which is another name for a deer park. All this land belongs to Read Hall. It'll be a while before we reach the hall itself and the inner grounds. And it's a dwelling that befits a man who was once High Sheriff of the whole County.'

MISTRESS WURMALDE

Set in its own grounds within the laund, Read Hall was the most impressive rural dwelling I'd ever seen, more akin to a palace than the home of a country gentleman. Wide gates gave access to an even wider gravel carriageway that led straight up to the front door. From there, the gravel forked right and left, giving entry to the back of the building. The hall itself was three storeys high, with an imposing main entrance. Two ivy-covered wings extending to the front formed an open, three-walled courtyard. I regarded the expanse of mullioned windows with astonishment, wondering how many bedrooms there must be.

'Does the magistrate have a large family?' I asked,

regarding Read Hall in amazement.

'Roger Nowell's family did live with him here once,' Father Stocks replied, 'but sadly his wife died a few years ago. He has two grown-up daughters who've found themselves good husbands to the south of the County. His only son is in the army and that's where he'll stay until Master Nowell dies and the lad comes back to inherit the hall and land.'

'It must be strange to live alone in such a big house,' I observed.

'Oh, he's not exactly alone, Tom. He has servants to cook and clean and, of course, his housekeeper, Mistress Wurmalde. She's a very formidable woman who manages things very efficiently. But in some ways she's not at all what you'd expect from someone in her position. A stranger who was unaware of the true situation might take her to be the mistress of the house. I've always found her courteous and intelligent but some say she's got above herself and puts on airs and graces beyond the call of her station. She's certainly changed things in recent years. Once, when I visited Read Hall,

I knocked at the front door. But now only knights and esquires are welcomed there. We'll have to use the tradesmen's entrance at the side.'

So, rather than leading us up to that imposing front door, Father Stocks took us down the side of the house, with ornamental shrubs and trees to our right, until finally we halted before a small door. He knocked politely three times. After we'd been waiting almost a minute, he knocked again, this time more loudly. A few moments later a maid opened the door and blinked nervously into the sunlight.

Father Stocks asked to speak to Master Nowell and we were shown into a large, dark-panelled hallway. The maid scuttled away and we were left waiting there for several more minutes. The deep silence reminded me of being in church until it was broken by the sound of approaching footsteps. But instead of the gentleman that I'd expected, a woman stood before us, regarding us critically. Immediately, from what the priest had said, I knew that this was Mistress Wurmalde.

In her late thirties or thereabouts, she was tall for

a woman and carried herself proudly, shoulders back and head held high. Her abundant dark hair was swept sideways over her ears like a great lion's mane – a style that suited her well, for it displayed her strong features to good effect.

Two other attributes attracted my gaze, so that it involuntarily flicked rapidly between them: her lips and her eyes. She concentrated upon the priest and didn't look at me directly, but I could tell that her eyes were bold and piercing; I felt that had she so much as glanced at me, she would have been able to see right into my soul. As for her lips, they were so pale that they resembled those of a corpse. They were large and full, and despite their want of colour she was clearly a woman of great strength and vitality.

Yet it was her clothes that gave me the greatest surprise. I'd never seen a woman dressed in such a way. She wore a gown of the finest black silk with a white ruff at the collar, and that gown contained enough material to dress another twenty. The skirts flared at the hip to fall in a wide bell shape that touched the floor, obscuring her shoes. How many layers of silk would you need to achieve an effect like that? It must have cost a lot of money; such apparel was surely more suitable for a royal court.

'You are very welcome, Father,' she said. 'But to what do we owe the honour of your visit? And who is your companion?'

The priest gave a little bow. 'I wish to speak to Master Nowell,' he replied. 'And this is Tom Ward, a visitor to Pendle.'

For the first time Mistress Wurmalde's eyes fixed directly upon mine and I saw them widen slightly. Then her nostrils flared and she gave a short sniff in my direction. And in that contact, which lasted no more than a second at most, an ice-cold chill passed from the back of my head and down into my spine. I knew that I was in the presence of someone who dealt with the dark. I was filled with the certain conviction that the woman was a witch. And in that instant I realized that she also knew what *I* was. A moment of recognition had passed between us.

A frown began before quickly correcting itself and she smiled coldly, turning back to the priest. 'I'm sorry, Father, but that won't be possible today. Master Nowell is extremely busy. I suggest that you try again tomorrow – perhaps in the afternoon?'

Father Stocks coloured slightly, but then he straightened his back, and when he spoke, his voice was filled with determination. 'I must apologize for the interruption, Mistress Wurmalde, but I wish to speak to Master Nowell in his capacity as magistrate. The business is urgent and will not wait . . .'

Mistress Wurmalde nodded but she didn't look at all happy. 'Be so good as to wait here,' she instructed us. 'I'll see what I can do.'

We waited there in the hallway. Full of anxiety, I desperately wanted to tell Father Stocks my concerns about Mistress Wurmalde but feared that she might return at any moment. However, she sent the maid, who led us into a large study that rivalled the Spook's Chipenden library both in size and in the number of books it contained. But whereas the Spook's books came in all shapes and sizes and in a wide variety of covers, these were all richly bound in identical fine brown leather. Bound, it seemed to me, more for display than to be read.

The study was cheerful and warm, lit by a blazing log fire to our left, above which was a large mirror with an ornate gilt frame. Master Nowell was writing at his desk when we entered. It was covered in papers and was a contrast to the tidiness of the shelves. He rose to his feet and greeted us with a smile. He was a man in his early fifties, broad of shoulder and trim of waist. His face was weatherbeaten – he looked more like a farmer than a magistrate so I supposed he liked the outdoor life. He greeted Father Stocks warmly, nodded pleasantly in my direction and invited us to sit down. We pulled two chairs closer to the desk and the priest wasted no time in stating the purpose of our visit. He finished by handing Nowell the piece of paper on which he'd written down the testimonies of the two witnesses from Goldshaw Booth.

The magistrate read them quickly and looked up.

'And you say, Father, that they would swear under oath to the facts stated here?'

'Without a doubt. But we must guarantee that they remain anonymous.'

'Good,' said Nowell. 'It's about time the villains in that tower were dealt with once and for all – this may be just what we need to do it. Can you write, boy?' he asked, looking at me.

I nodded and he pushed a sheet of paper towards me. 'State the names and ages of the kidnapped, together with descriptions of the goods taken. Then sign it at the bottom . . .'

I did as he asked, then returned the paper to him. He read it quickly and stood up. 'I'll send for the constable and then we'll pay a visit to Malkin Tower. Don't worry, boy. We'll have your family safe and sound by nightfall.'

It was as we turned to leave that, out of the corner of my eye, I thought I saw something move in the mirror. I might have been mistaken but it looked like a brief flash of black silk, which vanished the very moment I looked directly at it. I wondered if Wurmalde had been spying on us.

Within the hour we were heading for Malkin Tower.

The magistrate led the way, seated high on a big roan mare. Just behind and to his left was the parish constable, a dour-faced man called Barnes, dressed in black and riding a smaller grey horse. Both were armed: Roger Nowell had a sword at his hip while the constable carried a stout stick with a whip hooked to his saddle. Father Stocks and I rode in an open cart, sharing the discomfort with the two bailiffs the constable had brought along. They sat beside us silently, nursing cudgels but not making eye-contact, and I had a strong feeling that they didn't want to be on the road to the tower. The driver of the cart was one of Nowell's servants, a man called Cobden, who nodded once to the priest and muttered 'Father', but completely ignored me.

The road was pitted and uneven and the ride gave us a good jolting so that I couldn't wait for it to end.

We could have made better time on foot by travelling across country, I thought, rather than keeping to the roads and tracks. But nobody asked my opinion so I just had to put up with it. And I'd other things to distract me from the discomfort of that cart.

My anxiety regarding Jack, Ellie and their child was building. What if they'd been moved already? Then darker thoughts rose up, even though I tried my best to thrust them to the back of my mind. What if they'd been murdered and their bodies hidden where they'd never be found? A lump suddenly came into my throat. After all, what had they done wrong? They didn't deserve that – Mary was just a child. And then there'd be a fourth life lost – Ellie's unborn baby, the son that Jack had always wanted. It was all my fault. If I hadn't been apprenticed to the Spook, none of this would have happened. The Malkins and the Deanes said they wanted me dead: it had to be something to do with the work I was training for.

Despite the presence of Magistrate Nowell and his constable, I wasn't very optimistic about our chances of getting into Malkin Tower. What if the Malkins just refused to open the door? After all, it was very thick and studded with iron – I wondered if that caused a problem for the witches, and then remembered that there were other clan members to open and close it. There was even a moat. It seemed to me that Nowell was relying upon their fear of the law and of the consequences of resisting. But he didn't know that he was dealing with real witches and I wasn't too confident in the power of a sword and a few cudgels to sort everything out.

There was also the problem of Mistress Wurmalde for me to think about. My instincts screamed out at me that she was a witch. And yet she was the housekeeper of Magistrate Nowell, the foremost representative of the law in Pendle and a man who, despite all that had happened in this area of the County, was convinced that witches did not exist. Did that disbelief result from the fact that he was himself bewitched? Was she using *glamour* and *fascination* – the witch powers the Spook had described?

145

What should I do about it? No point in telling Nowell, but I did need to tell Father Stocks and the Spook just as soon as I got the chance. I'd wanted to tell the priest before we set off for the tower but I hadn't really had the chance.

While those thoughts were whirling through my head, we climbed upwards through the village of Goldshaw Booth. The main street was deserted but lace curtains twitched as we passed. I felt certain that word of our coming would have already been carried to Malkin Tower. They would be waiting for us.

We entered Crow Wood and I saw the tower when we were still some distance away. It rose above the trees, dark and impressive like something made to withstand the assault of an army. Set within a clearing, on a slight elevation of the ground, it was oval in shape, its girth at its widest point at least twice that of the Spook's Chipenden house. The tower was three times the height of the largest of the surrounding trees and there were battlements on top, a low castellated wall for armed men to shelter behind. That meant there had to be a way up onto the roof from inside. About halfway up the wall there were also narrow windows without glass; slits in the stone through which an archer could fire.

As we entered the clearing and moved closer, I could see that the drawbridge was raised and the moat was deep and wide. The cart came to a halt, so I clambered down, eager to stretch my legs. Father Stocks and the two bailiffs followed my lead. We were all staring towards the tower but nothing was happening.

After a minute Nowell gave a sigh of impatience, rode right up to the edge of the moat and called out in a loud voice: 'Open up in the name of the law!'

For a moment there was silence but for the breathing of the horses.

Then a female voice called down from one of the arrow slits. 'Be patient while we lower the bridge. Be patient while we prepare the way . . .'

No sooner had she spoken than there was the grinding of a capstan and a clanking of chains; slowly the bridge began to descend. I could see the system clearly now. The chains were attached to the corners of the heavy wooden drawbridge and led through slits in the rock to a chamber within the tower. No doubt several people would now be employed turning the capstan to release the length of chain. Then, as the bridge jerked downwards, I saw the formidable iron-studded door that had been hidden behind it. It was at least as strong as the thick stone walls. Surely nothing could break through those stout defences.

At last the drawbridge was in position and we waited expectantly for the huge door to be opened. I began to feel nervous. How many people were in the tower? There'd be witches and their supporters, while there were only seven of us. Once we were inside, they could simply close the door behind us and we'd be sealed off from the world, prisoners ourselves.

But nothing happened and there was no sound from within the tower. Nowell turned and gestured for Constable Barnes to join him by the moat, where he gave him some instructions. The constable immediately dismounted and began to cross the drawbridge.

When he reached the door, he began to pound on the metal with his fist. At that sound, a flock of crows fluttered up from the trees behind the tower and began a raucous cawing.

There was no answer so the constable banged again. Immediately I caught a glimpse of movement on the battlements above him. A figure in black seemed to lean forward. A second later, a dark liquid showered down onto the head of the unfortunate constable and he jumped back with a curse. There was a cackle of laughter from above, followed by the sound of more laughing and jeers from within the tower.

The constable returned to his horse, rubbing his eyes. His hair was saturated and his jerkin spattered with dark stains. He remounted, shaking his head, and both he and the magistrate rode back towards us; they were talking animatedly but I couldn't make out what they were saying. They came to a halt facing us, close enough for me to get a whiff of what had been poured over Constable Barnes – the contents of a chamber pot. The smell was really bad.

'I shall ride to Colne immediately, Father,' Nowell said, his face florid with anger. 'Those who defy the law and treat it with contempt deserve the full consequences. I know the commander of the army garrison there. I think this is a task for the military.'

He started to ride away eastwards, then halted and called back over his shoulder, 'I'll stay at the barracks and be back just as soon as I can with the help we need. In the meantime, Father, tell Mistress Wurmalde that you're my guest for the night. You and the boy . . .'

With that the magistrate rode off at a canter while we climbed back up into the cart. I didn't look forward to a night spent at Read Hall. How could I sleep when a witch was in the house?

My heart was also heavy at the thought of Jack and his family having to spend another night in the dungeons below the tower. I wasn't too optimistic that the arrival of soldiers from the barracks would solve things quickly. There was still the problem of the thick stone walls and the iron-studded door.

Soon we were trundling our way back towards Read Hall. The constable rode slightly ahead and nothing much was said but for a short exchange between the two men who shared the cart with us . . .

'Constable Barnes don't look happy,' one said with the merest hint of a smile.

'If he keeps downwind, I *will* be!' replied his companion.

On our way back down through Goldshaw Booth there were more people on the main street. Some seemed to be going about their business while others lounged on corners. A few were standing in open doorways, gazing out expectantly as if waiting for us to pass through. There were a few catcalls and jeers and a rotten apple was hurled at us from behind, just missing the constable's head. He turned his horse angrily and unfurled his whip but it was impossible to identify the culprit. To more jeers, we continued down the main street and I was relieved when we were in open countryside again.

As we reached the gates of Read Hall, Constable

Barnes spoke for the first time since we'd begun our journey back. 'Well, Father, we'll leave you now. We'll meet here at the gates an hour after dawn, and back to the tower we go!'

Father Stocks and I clambered down, opened the gates and, after closing them behind us, began to walk up the carriageway between the lawns, while the constable rode away and Cobden continued in the same direction, presumably taking the two bailiffs home before returning to Read Hall. This was my chance to tell the priest about Nowell's housekeeper.

'Father, I've something to tell you about Mistress Wurmalde—'

'Oh, don't let her bother you, Tom. Her snobbery just comes from an inflated sense of pride. The fact that she looked down her nose at you is her problem, not yours. But at heart she's a good woman. None of us is perfect.'

'No, Father,' I told him, 'it's not that at all. It's far worse. She belongs to the dark. She's a malevolent witch.'

Father Stocks halted. I stopped too and he stared at

me hard. 'Are you sure about that, Tom? "Malevolent" or "Falsely Accused" – which one is it?'

'When she looked at me, I felt cold. Really cold. I sometimes feel like that when something from the dark is near—'

'Sometimes or always, Tom? Did you feel it when you went off alone with young Mab Mouldheel? If so, why did you go?'

'I *mostly* feel cold from the dead or those who are part of the dark but it's not always the case. But when it's as strong as it was with Mistress Wurmalde, then there can be no doubt about it. Not in my mind. And I'm sure she was short-sniffing me.'

'Perhaps she has a slight head cold, lad. Don't forget that I'm a seventh son of a seventh son too,' said Father Stocks, 'and I also feel this warning, this cold you're talking about. But I must tell you that I've never once felt it in the presence of Mistress Wurmalde.'

I didn't know what to say. I'd felt the warning cold for sure and seen her sniffing. Could I have been wrong?

'Look, Tom, what you tell me isn't proof, is it?' the priest continued. 'But let's be on our guard and think about it some more. See if you feel the same when you meet Mistress Wurmalde again.'

'I'd rather spend the night somewhere else,' I said. 'When Mistress Wurmalde looked at me, she realized immediately that I knew she was a witch. It's a warm enough night. I'd be happy to sleep under the stars. I'd feel a lot safer too.'

'No, Tom,' Father Stocks insisted. 'We'll sleep at Read Hall. That would be wiser. Even if you are right about Mistress Wurmalde, she's lived here undetected for several years and has a comfortable life – one that the role of housekeeper won't give her elsewhere. She won't do anything to undermine that or give herself away, so I think we'll be safe enough for one night, don't you? Am I right?'

When I nodded uncertainly, Father Stocks patted my shoulder. We continued towards the house and walked up to the side door for the second time that day. Once again the same maid answered the priest's knock.

But, to my relief, we didn't have to talk to Mistress Wurmalde again.

Upon being informed that her master had ridden to Colne to speak to the commander of the garrison there, and that we were to be guests at Read Hall, the maid went off to tell Mistress Wurmalde. She soon returned alone and showed us into the kitchen, where we were given a light supper. It was cold mutton again, but I didn't complain. Once we were alone, Father Stocks blessed the food quickly then ate heartily. I just looked at the cold meat and pushed my plate away, but it wasn't because it looked so unappetizing.

Father Stocks smiled at me across the kitchen table; he knew that I was fasting, preparing for danger from the dark.

'Eat up, Tom – you'll be safe enough tonight, I promise you,' he told me. 'We'll face the dark soon enough, but not in Magistrate Nowell's house. Witch or no witch, Mistress Wurmalde will be forced to keep her distance.'

'I'd rather play safe, Father,' I told him.

'Suit yourself, Tom. But you'll need all your strength in the morning. It's likely to be a difficult and anxious day . . .'

I didn't need reminding about it but I still declined to eat.

When the maid returned, she glanced crossly at my full plate, but rather than clearing the table she offered to show us up to our rooms.

They were adjacent and on the top storey, at the front of the east wing of the house, facing the wide gates. My room had a large mirror directly above the bed and I immediately turned it to the wall. Now, at least, no witch would be able to spy on me using that. Next I raised the sash window and peered out, drawing in gulps of the cool night air. I was determined not to sleep.

Soon it started to grow dark and somewhere far away an owl hooted. It had been a long day and it became harder and harder to stay awake. But then I heard noises. First the crack of a whip and then horses' hooves pounding gravel. The sounds seemed to be coming from the rear of the house. To my astonishment, a coach and four came round the side and continued down the carriageway towards the gates. And what a coach! I'd never seen anything like it in my life.

It was black as ebony and so highly polished that I could see the moon and stars reflected in it. The horses were also black and wore dark plumes, and as I watched, the driver cracked his whip above their backs. I couldn't be certain, but I thought it was Cobden, the man who'd driven our cart to Malkin Tower. Again, although it was difficult to be sure at that distance, it looked as if the gates had opened by themselves and then closed after the coach had gone through. There was certainly no sign of anyone in the vicinity.

And who was inside that coach? It was impossible to see through the windows because of the dark curtains behind the glass, but it was a carriage fit for a king or queen. Was Mistress Wurmalde inside? If so, where was she going and why? I was now wide awake. I felt sure she'd return before dawn.

CHAPTER 9
FOOTPRINTS

I watched for half an hour and nothing happened. The moon drifted slowly down towards the west, and at one point there was a brief but heavy shower of rain, a furious cloudburst that left copious puddles on the carriageway. But soon the raincloud floated away and the moon bathed everything in its yellow light once more. About another fifteen minutes passed and I was now struggling to keep awake, my eyes beginning to close, my head starting to nod, when suddenly I was jerked alert by the hoot of an owl somewhere in the darkness. Then I heard the distant sound of galloping horses and carriage wheels.

The coach was heading straight for the gates; just

when the lead horses seemed about to crash right into them, they opened of their own accord. This time I saw it clearly. An instant later the coach was racing towards the house, the driver cracking his whip as if his very life depended on it, only slowing the horses as they reached the fork that would bring them round to the rear of the house.

Suddenly I knew that I had to see if Mistress Wurmalde was in that coach. I *had* to be sure it was her and I had a strong feeling that I would see something vital. One of the back bedrooms would afford such a view. I assumed the servants had their own quarters, so apart from the priest and me there should be nobody on this floor. At least I hoped not.

Nevertheless, I stepped out into the corridor cautiously and listened. All I could hear was loud snores from Father Stocks's bedroom, so I walked down the short passageway opposite until I reached a row of bedroom doors. I eased open the first one and crept inside, trying to make as little sound as possible. It was empty and the curtains were drawn back, allowing a narrow silver shaft of moonlight to enter. Quickly I walked over to the window and, keeping in the shadow of the curtain, peered out. I was just in time. Below was a gravel courtyard pitted with puddles of rainwater. The coach had halted close to a flagged path that led to a door down to my right. I watched the driver climb out, and this time got a good look at his face. It *was* Cobden. He opened the carriage door wide and stepped back, giving a low bow.

Mistress Wurmalde climbed down very slowly and cautiously, as if she were afraid of falling; then she stepped carefully across the gravel and up onto the flagged path before sweeping on more swiftly towards the door, the hem of her bell-shaped skirt brushing the ground, her haughty head held high, her gaze stern and imperious. Cobden ran ahead and opened the door for her, again giving a low bow. A maid was waiting just beyond the doorway; she curtsied as Wurmalde entered. When the door closed, Cobden went back to the coach and drove it out of sight behind the stables.

I was just about to leave the window and go back

to my own room when I noticed something that sent a chill straight to my heart. Although the gravel was still waterlogged, the flagged path was quite dry and Mistress Wurmalde's footprints were clearly visible alongside those of the driver.

I stared at them, hardly able to believe what I was seeing. Her pointy wet footprints started at the end of the path and went right up to the door. But there was a set of smaller footprints between them. Three-toed animal footprints no larger than those of a very small child. But not those of a creature that walked on all fours. And in a moment of horror I understood . . .

Where she'd been I didn't know, but she hadn't returned alone. Those voluminous bell-shaped skirts had served a purpose. Tibb had been hiding beneath them. And now he was inside Read Hall.

In a panic, remembering the ugly, terrifying face in the mirror in that cellar, I turned away from the window and walked quickly back towards my room. Why had she brought him here in such a hurry? Was it something to do with me? Suddenly I realized what he wanted. Tibb was a seer. Whether or not he could see into the future, he could certainly see things at a distance better than any witch. That was how the Pendle covens had discovered the trunks in the first place. And Tibb must also know where the keys were – that I was wearing them around my neck. That's why he'd been brought to Read Hall in the night. Mistress Wurmalde couldn't risk acting against me while I was under Nowell's roof. But Tibb could!

I had to get out of the house, but I couldn't just leave without waking Father Stocks and warning him of the danger, so I went directly to his bedroom and rapped lightly on the door. He was still snoring loudly so I eased open the door and stepped into the room. The curtains were closed but a candle sent out a flickering yellow light.

Father Stocks was lying on the bed on his back; he hadn't bothered to get undressed and climb between the sheets. Having told me that we'd be safe in Read Hall, it seemed he'd chosen to ready himself for any threat that might come in the night.

I walked up to the edge of the bed and looked down at him. His mouth was wide open and the snoring was very loud, his lips wobbling each time he breathed out. I leaned forward, put my hand on his near shoulder and shook him gently. There was no response. I shook him again more urgently, then bent my head so that my mouth was very close to his left ear.

'Father Stocks,' I whispered. Then I raised my voice and called his name again.

Still he didn't respond. His face looked flushed. I put my hand on his forehead and found it to be very warm indeed. Was he ill?

Then the truth sank like lead into my stomach. The Pendle witches were notorious for their skilful use of poisons. I hadn't eaten the mutton. Father Stocks had! Some poisons were extremely toxic. A finely ground toadstool could have been sprinkled on the meat. Some toadstools could stop your heart in an instant; others took far longer to have an effect.

But surely Mistress Wurmalde wouldn't risk killing Father Stocks? Not under her own roof. She just wanted him in a deep sleep until morning to allow time for Tibb to get to me. He was here to get my keys.

But couldn't she have done that anyway, with no risk to herself? Then I understood. The maid must have reported that I'd not touched my supper. That's why she'd gone for Tibb. He would help her get the keys anyway, whether I slept or not!

The room seemed to spin. My heart racing, I strode to the door, walked along the corridor and started to descend the stairs. I had to get away from Read Hall, then back to Downham, in order to warn the Spook about the additional threat posed by Mistress Wurmalde. Where did she fit into the Pendle covens? And what was her part in their wicked schemes?

The dark, wood-panelled hallway had three doors: one led to the study, the second to the kitchen and the third to the drawing room. Tibb could be anywhere but I didn't want to meet Mistress Wurmalde either. She lived in the manner of the lady of the house and was, no doubt, used to being waited on hand and foot; she'd rarely visit the kitchen except to give orders, and nobody would be preparing food at this time of night. So without hesitation I opened the kitchen door. From there I'd be able to get out into the yard and make my escape.

Immediately I realized my mistake. Lit by a shaft of moonlight from the window, Mistress Wurmalde was standing by the table between me and the door. It was as if she'd been waiting for me and knew which route I'd take to make my escape. Had that knowledge been given to her by Tibb? I avoided her gaze and my eyes swept the room: it was gloomy and there were lots of dark corners. There was no sign of Tibb, but he was small. He could be hiding anywhere in the shadows – perhaps under the table or in a cupboard. Maybe he was still sheltering under her skirts?

'If you'd eaten your supper, you wouldn't be hungry now,' she said, her voice as cold and threatening as a sharp steel blade.

I looked at her but didn't reply. I was tensed, ready to run for it. But for all I knew, Tibb was somewhere behind me.

'That *is* why you're here now in my kitchen in the dead of night, isn't it? Or were you thinking of leaving without even a word of thanks for the hospitality you've received?'

Her voice had changed slightly. Meeting her in Father Stocks's presence, I hadn't noticed it, but now I detected a hint of a foreign accent. With a shock I realized that it was similar to that in Mam's voice.

'If I'd eaten my supper, I'd be in the same condition as Father Stocks,' I told her bluntly. 'That's the sort of hospitality I can do without.'

'Well, boy, you don't mince your words – I'll give you that. So I'll be equally blunt. We have your trunks and we need the keys. Why don't you give them to me now and save yourself a great deal of trouble and heartache?'

'The keys belong to me and so do the trunks,' I told her.

'Of course they do,' Mistress Wurmalde replied, 'and that's why we're willing to buy them from you.'

'They're not for sale—'

'Oh, I think they are. Especially when you hear the high price that we are willing to pay. In exchange for the trunks *and* the keys, we will give you the lives of your family. Otherwise . . .'

I opened my mouth to speak but no words came out. I was stunned by her offer.

'Well now, that's made you think, hasn't it?' she said, a gloating smile spreading across her face.

How could I refuse to give her the keys? She'd implied that my refusal would result in the deaths of Jack, Ellie and Mary. And yet, despite the pain in my heart, there was a very good reason to refuse. The trunks must be very important to the witch covens. They might contain something – perhaps knowledge of some sort – that could increase the threat from the dark. As Mr Gregory had said, there was more at stake here than the safety of my family. I needed time. Time to speak to my master. And there was something else here that was strange. Witches were very strong. So why didn't she just take the keys from me by force?

'I need some time to think,' I told her. 'I can't just decide now—'

'I will allow you one hour and not a moment longer,' she said. 'Return to your room and think it over. Then come back here and give me your answer.'

'No,' I protested. 'That's not enough time. I need a day. A day and a night.'

Mistress Wurmalde frowned and anger flashed into her eyes. She took a step towards me: her skirts rustled and the sound of her pointy shoes made two hard clicks on the cold flags of the kitchen. 'Time to think is a luxury that you can ill afford,' she told me. 'Have you got an imagination, boy?'

I nodded. My mouth was too dry to speak.

'Then let me paint a picture for you. Imagine a grim dungeon, dark and drear, crawling with vermin and rats. Imagine a bone-pit, redolent of the tormented dead, its stench an affront to high heaven. No daylight reaches it from the upper ground and just one small candle is allowed each day, a few hours of flickering yellow light to illuminate the horror of that place. Your brother Jack is bound to a pillar. He rants and raves; his eyes are wild, his face gaunt, his mind in hell. Some of it is our doing but most of the blame must fall to you and yours. Yes, it is your fault that he suffers.'

'How can it be *my* fault?' I asked angrily.

'Because you are your mother's son, and you have inherited the work that she has done. Both the work and the blame,' said Mistress Wurmalde.

'What do *you* know of my mother?' I demanded, stung by her words.

'We are old enemies,' she said, almost spitting the words out. 'And we come from the same land – she from the barbarous north, I from more sophisticated southern climes. And we know each other well. Many times in the past we have struggled against each other. But my chance for revenge has now arrived and I will prevail despite all that she can do. She is home now but still exerts her strength against us. You see, we could not go into the room where the trunks were stored. Entry was forbidden to us. She forbade it from afar, weaving her power into a barrier we could not cross. In retaliation we beat your brother until his blood flowed, but he was stubborn, and when that failed to move him, we threatened to hurt his woman and child. At last he did our bidding and went inside to bring forth the trunks. But the room was not kind to him. Perhaps it was because he betrayed you. You see, jealous of your inheritance, he secretly had a copy made when your own key was in his possession. Within minutes of surrendering the trunks into our keeping, his eyes rolled up into his head and he began to rant and rave. Thus his body lies in chains in a dungeon, but his mind must be in a place more terrible. Do you see the scene now? Is it becoming clearer?'

Before I could reply, Mistress Wurmalde continued, 'His wife is there, doing what little she can for him. Sometimes she bathes his brow. At other moments she tries to soothe his dementia with words. And for her it is hard, very hard, because she has deep sorrows of her own. It is bad enough that her young daughter is wasting away before her eyes and screams with night terrors. But even worse is the fact that she has lost her unborn child – the son and heir that your brother wanted so much. I very much doubt if the poor woman can take much more.

'But more can be supplied if that is what is needed to move you. There is a witch called Grimalkin, a cruel assassin that the Malkins sometimes send out against their enemies. She is skilled with weapons, particularly the long blade. She loves her principal work too well. Loves to kill and maim. But there is another skill that delights her sadistic mind. She loves to torture. Loves to inflict pain. Delights in the *snip, snip* of her scissors. Shall I place your family in her hands? It could be done with a word! So think, boy! Can you allow your family even one more hour of such torment – let alone the day and night you've demanded?'

My mind reeled. I remembered the image of the scissors that Grimalkin had carved into the oak tree as a warning. What Wurmalde had described was terrible, and it took all my strength not to rip the keys from my neck and give them to her there and then. But instead I drew in a deep breath and tried to banish what she'd summoned from my mind's eye. I'd changed a lot in my time as the Spook's apprentice. In Priestown I'd faced an evil spirit called the Bane and refused its demand for freedom. In Anglezarke I'd confronted Golgoth, one of the Old Gods, and despite my belief that in doing so I would forfeit both my life and my soul, had refused his demand that I release him from a pentacle. But this was different: now it was my family being directly threatened, and what had been described brought a lump to my throat and tears to my eyes.

Despite that, one thing had been at the core of everything my master had taught me. I served the County and my first duty was to the people who lived there. To *all* the people, not just to those I held dear.

'I still need a day and a night to think things through carefully. Give me that time or the answer is no,' I replied, trying to keep my voice firm.

Mistress Wurmalde hissed through her teeth like a cat. 'So you think to buy time, do you, hoping that by tomorrow they'll be rescued? Think again, boy! Don't delude yourself. The walls of Malkin Tower are strong indeed. You'd be a fool to place much faith in a few soldiers. Their blood will turn to water and their knees will soon begin to knock in fear. Pendle will swallow them up. It will be as if they'd never existed!'

She stood there, tall and arrogant, radiating malice and sure of her own power. I had no weapons here at my disposal; but they were available in Downham, not that many miles to the north. How would Mistress Wurmalde feel with a silver chain holding her fast, bound tight against her teeth? If I had my way, she'd find that out very soon. But for now I was defenceless. Witches are physically strong. I'd been in the grip of more than one and Mistress Wurmalde looked powerful enough to seize me and snatch the keys from me by force. I wondered again why she didn't do so. Or use Tibb to do her dirty work for her.

There was her position to keep up, as Father Stocks had told me. That would explain it in part. She would hope to keep her reputation intact whatever happened in the next few weeks or days. But could it be something more than that? Maybe she actually *couldn't* take the keys from me by force. Maybe I had to give them to her freely or in exchange for something else? Perhaps Mam wielded interdiction even from a distance, forming that barrier of power. It was a faint hope but one that I clung on to desperately.

'A day and a night,' I told Mistress Wurmalde. 'I need that time. My answer is the same—'

'Then take it!' she snapped. 'And as you prevaricate, think how your family are suffering. But you may not leave this house. I cannot allow it. Return to your room. Here you will remain until you surrender the keys.'

'If I don't go to Malkin Tower, Master Nowell will wonder what's happened . . .'

She smiled grimly. 'I'll send word that both you and Father Stocks are indisposed with a fever. Master Nowell will be too busy tomorrow to concern himself with your absence. You'll be the very least of his worries. No, you must stay here. To attempt to leave without my permission would be very dangerous. This house is guarded by something you certainly wouldn't wish to meet. You wouldn't get out alive.'

At that moment there came a sound from somewhere far off. The deep chimes of a clock reverberated through the house. It was midnight. The clock was striking twelve.

'Before this time tomorrow night, you must decide,' Wurmalde warned. 'Decide wrongly or fail to give an answer and your family will die. The choice is yours.'

CHAPTER 10
TIBB

I returned to my room and closed the door behind me. I was desperate to escape but afraid to try. All my courage seemed to have fled. Somewhere abroad within the house was Tibb, alert to my every move. I had nothing to defend myself with and suspected that I wouldn't reach an outer door before he fell upon me.

At first, without even a thought of sleeping, my worries and fears swirling endlessly inside my head, I pulled a chair to the window and peered out into the night. There, bathed in moonlight, the grounds and countryside beyond looked at peace. Occasionally, in addition to the distant snoring of Father Stocks, I could hear faint scratching sounds from out on the landing.

It could have been mice. But it could also have been Tibb on the prowl. It made me feel very nervous and uneasy.

I opened the window and looked down at the wall below. It was covered in ivy. Could I escape through the window? Would the ivy bear my weight? I reached down below the sill and clutched the plant, but when I tugged it, leaves and branches came away in my hand. No doubt it was cut back from the windows at least once a year – this would be new growth. Perhaps a little further down the stems would be thicker and woodier, the ivy's grip upon the stone wall firmer?

But it was filled with risk. Wurmalde wouldn't be able to sniff out my bid for freedom; the instant I began my descent, however, Tibb might. I'd have to climb very carefully and that would take time. The creature would be waiting for me before I reached the ground. If I fell, it would be worse . . . No, it was too risky. I let the thought seep away as images flooded in to replace it. The cruel pictures Wurmalde had placed in my mind became vivid and almost impossible to dismiss: Jack in torment; Mary screaming in fear, terrified of the dark; poor Ellie, mourning the unborn child she'd lost. The witch assassin, Grimalkin, let loose to inflict further pain. The *snip-snip* of her scissors . . .

But as the night slowly passed, my anxieties gave way to tiredness. My limbs grew heavy and I felt the need to lie down on the bed. Like Father Stocks, I didn't bother to get undressed but simply lay on my back on top of the sheets. At first I didn't want to fall asleep but soon my lids grew heavy and my eyes began to close, all my fears and concerns slowly ebbing away.

I reminded myself that Wurmalde had given me a full day and a night to reach a decision. As long as I stayed in the house, nothing would harm me. In the morning I'd be fresh and alert, able to find a way to solve all my problems. All I had to do was relax . . .

How long I slept I don't know, but some time later I was awakened suddenly by the sound of someone shouting.

'No! No! Leave me! Let me be! Get off me!'

I heard it as if in a dream. For a few moments I

didn't know where I was and stared up at the ceiling in bewilderment. It was very dark in the room – there was no longer any moonlight to see by. Only slowly did I recognize the voice as that of Father Stocks.

'Oh God! Oh God, deliver me!' he cried again, his voice filled with utter terror.

What was the matter with him? What was happening? And then I realized that someone was hurting the priest. Was it the witch or Tibb? I had no weapons and didn't know what I could do but I had to try to help him. Yet when I tried to sit up, I lacked the strength. My body felt heavy; my limbs didn't respond. What was wrong with me? I felt weak and ill.

I hadn't touched the mutton, so it couldn't be poison. Was it some sort of spell? I'd been close to Wurmalde. Too close. No doubt she'd used some sort of dark magic against me.

Then I heard Father Stocks begin to pray: 'Out of the depths I cry to thee, o Lord. Lord, hear my voice . . .'

At first the priest's voice was clearly audible and punctuated by groans and cries of pain, but gradually it became a faint murmur before fading away altogether.

There was a minute or so of silence but then I heard scratching sounds outside my bedroom door. Again I tried to sit up. It was useless, but by making a great effort I found that I could move my head a little and I turned it slightly to the right, so that I could look towards the door.

My eyes were quickly adjusting to the darkness and I could see enough to tell me that the door was very slightly ajar, hardly more than a crack. But as I watched, in fear and dismay, it slowly began to gape wider, making my heart hammer in my chest. Wider and wider it yawned, the hinges creaking as it slowly opened to its full extent. I gazed towards the deeper darkness beyond it, terrified but expectant. At any moment I would see Tibb enter the room.

I could see nothing at all, but I could hear him – claws scratching and scrabbling, biting into wood. Then I realized that the sound was above, not below me. I looked upwards just in time to see a dark shape moving across the ceiling like a spider to halt directly above my bed. Unable to move anything but my head, I started to take deep breaths, trying to slow my heartbeat. To be afraid made the dark stronger. I had to get my fear under control.

I could see the outline of the four limbs and the body but the head seemed far closer. I've always been able to see well in the dark and my eyes were continuing to adjust until I could finally make some sense of what threatened from above.

Tibb had crawled across the wooden panels of the ceiling so that his hairy back and limbs were facing away from me. But his head was hanging down backwards towards the bed, supported by a long muscular neck, so that his eyes were below his mouth; and those eyes were glowing slightly in the dark and staring directly towards my own; the mouth was wide open, revealing the sharp needle-like teeth within.

Something dripped onto my forehead then. Something slightly sticky and warm. It seemed to fall from the creature's open mouth. Twice more drops fell – one onto the pillow beside my head, the next onto my shirt front. Then Tibb spoke, his voice rasping harshly in the darkness.

'*I see your future clearly. Your life will be sad. Your master will be dead and you will be alone. It would be better if you had never been born.*'

I didn't reply but a calm was settling upon me, my fear receding fast.

'*I see a girl, soon to be a woman,*' Tibb continued. '*The girl who will share your life. She will love you, she will betray you and finally she will die for you. And it will all have been for nothing. All for nothing in the end. Your mother was cruel. What mother would bring a child into the world for such a hopeless future? What mother would ask you to do what cannot be done? She sings a goat song and places you at its centre. Remember my words when you look into the mouth of death—*'

'Don't speak about Mam like that!' I demanded angrily. 'You know nothing about her!' But I was baffled by his reference to a goat song. What was that?

Tibb's response was a snort of laughter, and another

bead of moisture fell from his mouth to soil my shirt front.

'I know nothing? How wrong you are. I know more than you. Much, much more than you. More now than you will ever know . . .'

'Then you'll know what's in the trunks,' I said softly.

Tibb gave a low growl of anger.

'You can't see that, can you?' I taunted. 'You can't see everything—'

'You will give us the keys soon, then we will see. Then we will know!'

'I'll tell you now,' I said. 'There's no need to wait for the keys—'

'Tell me! Tell me!' Tibb demanded.

Suddenly I wasn't afraid of him any more. I'd no idea at all what I was going to say, but when I spoke, the words came out of my mouth as if uttered by somebody else.

'In the trunks is your death,' I said quietly. 'In the trunks is the destruction of the Pendle covens.'

Tibb gave a great roar of anger and bafflement, and for a moment I thought he was about to hurl himself down onto me. But instead I heard the sound of claws cutting into the wooden ceiling panels and a dark shape moved above me towards the door. Moments later I was alone.

I wanted to get up and go into the next room to see if I could help Father Stocks, but I lacked the strength to do so. I struggled for long hours through the darkness but was too weak and exhausted to clamber from the bed, and I lay there in thrall to Wurmalde's power.

Only when the first dawn light illuminated the window did the enchantment fall from my limbs. I managed to sit up and looked down at the pillow. There was a bloodstain on it; two more on the front of my shirt. The blood had dripped from Tibb's open mouth. He must have been feeding . . .

Remembering the groans, cries and prayers from the next bedroom, I rushed out into the corridor. The priest's bedroom door was ajar. I opened it further and stepped inside cautiously. The heavy curtains were still closed, the candle had long since burned out and the room was in near darkness. I could see the shape of Father Stocks lying on the bed but I couldn't hear him breathing.

'Father Stocks,' I called and received a faint answering groan.

'Is that you, Tom?' he said weakly. 'Are you all right?'

'Yes, Father. What about you?'

'Open the curtains and let in some light . . .'

So I went to the window and drew back the curtains as he'd asked. The weather had certainly changed for the worse and the sky was heaped with dark clouds. When I turned back to face Father Stocks, I recoiled in horror. The pillow and top sheet were soaked in blood. I went to the side of the bed and looked down at him, full of pity for his plight.

'Help me, Tom. Help me sit up . . .'

He gripped my right arm and I pulled him forward into a sitting position. He groaned as if in pain. There were beads of sweat on his brow and he looked very pale. With my left hand I lifted the pillows and positioned them behind his back to offer support.

'Thank you, Tom. Thank you. You're a good lad,' he said, trying to smile. There was a tremor in his voice and his breathing was fast and shallow. 'Did you see that foul thing? Did it visit you in the night?' he asked.

I nodded. 'It came into my room but never touched me. It just talked, that's all.'

'God be praised for that,' said the priest. 'It talked to me too, and what a tale it told. You were right about Mistress Wurmalde – I've underestimated her. She cares little for her position in this house now. She's the power behind the Pendle clans, the one who's trying to unite them. Within a few days this whole district will belong to the Devil himself. Her days of pretending are over, it seems. She's already managed to unite the Malkins and the Deanes and believes she can persuade the Mouldheels to join them. Then, at Lammas, the three covens will combine to summon the Fiend and bring a new age of darkness to this world.

'When that foul creature finished talking, it dropped down from the ceiling onto my chest. I tried to throw it off but it fed ravenously and within moments I became as weak as a kitten. I prayed. Prayed harder than I've ever done before. I'd like to think that God answered, but in truth I think it only left me when it had drunk its fill . . .'

'You need a doctor, Father. We need to get you help—'

'No, Tom. No. It's not a doctor I need. Left alone to rest, my strength would return, but I won't get the chance. Once it's dark that beast will return to feed from me again and this time I fear I shall die. Oh, Tom!' he said, clutching at my arm, his eyes wide with fear, his whole body trembling, 'I'm afraid to die like this, alone in the darkness. I felt as if I was at the bottom of a great pit, with Satan himself pressing me down and stifling my cries so that even God couldn't hear my prayers. I'm too weak to move but you've got to get away, Tom. I need John Gregory now. Bring John here.

He'll know what to do. He's the only one who can help me now . . .'

'Don't worry, Father,' I told him. 'Try to rest. You'll be safe during the daylight hours. I'll get away just as soon as I can and I'll be back with my master long before dark.'

I returned to my room, wondering about Tibb and the threat he posed to me now. My studies had taught me certain things. Tibb was a creature of the dark, so he might have to hide away during the daylight hours. Even if he could stand daylight, he might not be as dangerous. I'd decided to risk climbing down the ivy, but not until the cart had passed the end of the carriage-way. I didn't want to be seen by Cobden, the driver; even the two bailiffs might be in the pay of Wurmalde.

After about twenty minutes I heard the sound of horses' hooves from behind the house and saw Cobden driving his cart down to the gates. They didn't open by themselves on this occasion and he had to climb down and unfasten them. Outside he was soon joined by Constable Barnes, who was followed by the two bailiffs on foot. After the men jumped up into the cart, the party set off for Malkin Tower without so much as a glance towards the house. No doubt Cobden had already been briefed on what to tell the constable and Nowell. As far as they were concerned, both Father Stocks and I were ill.

As I watched them ride away into the distance, I began to wonder about the wisdom of going back to Downham. The Spook and Alice would have expected us to return with news. By now, after a whole day and night without word of what was happening, perhaps they'd set off to investigate and might be on their way already. It really wasn't such a bad thing because both the Spook and Alice knew Pendle district well and would take the direct route to Read Hall, passing to the west of the hill; the way I'd come with Father Stocks. More than likely, I would meet them on the way.

I eased up the sash window and climbed out feet first, turning so that I was facing back towards the wall. I gripped the window ledge firmly and lowered myself to the full extent of my arms, then transferred my left hand to the ivy, pushing my fingers deep into it, reassured by the feel of thick woody stems. The ivy held my weight but I made a nervous descent, fearful of what could be waiting for me at the bottom. I took more than a few risks in my eagerness to get to the ground as quickly as possible, but moments later I was standing on the pebbles and immediately set off running down to the gates. I glanced back once or twice and was relieved to see that there were no signs of pursuit. Once beyond the grounds of Read Hall, I headed north across the laund, running hard towards Downham.

As the crow flies, the distance between Read Hall and Downham is probably no more than five or six miles, but the difficult hilly terrain meant it was actually quite a bit further. I had to get there and back by nightfall, and needed to run at least part of the way. It seemed sensible to complete the first journey as quickly as possible, thus making it easier to return at a more leisurely pace, because by then I'd be tired.

After the first two miles or so I slowed down to a fast walking pace. I was making good time and just after what I judged to be the halfway point, I allowed myself a five-minute rest and quenched my thirst with the cool water from a stream. But when I set off walking again, it seemed much harder to make progress. Fasting is a good idea when facing the dark but it doesn't help when real exertion is required and I hadn't eaten since the previous morning's breakfast of cold mutton: I felt weak and started to make heavy weather of it. Even so, I thought of poor Father Stocks and gritted my teeth, forcing myself to run another mile before settling down once more to a brisk walking pace. I was grateful for the cloud cover, which kept the heat of the sun from my head.

I kept hoping that I would meet the Spook and Alice but saw no sign of them at all. When I reached the outskirts of Downham, despite all my attempts at speed it was already mid-afternoon and I wasn't relishing the prospect of the return journey.

But when I arrived in Downham, to my dismay, the Spook wasn't there.

CHAPTER 11
THIEF AND MURDERER

Alice came out to meet me at the church gate. As I approached, I saw her welcoming smile start to fade. She'd read the expression on my face and knew there was trouble.

'You all right, Tom?'

'Is Mr Gregory here?' I asked.

'No. Your brother James arrived last night and they went off together first thing this morning.'

'What for? Did they say when they'd be back?'

'Old Gregory never tells me much, does he? Talked to James but mostly made sure I was well out of earshot. Still doesn't trust me and perhaps he never will. As for when he'll be back, he didn't say. But I'm sure he'll be back before nightfall. He just said that you were to wait here until he returned.'

'I can't do that. Father Stocks is in danger,' I told her. 'Soon after nightfall, if help doesn't reach him, he'll be dead. I came to fetch the Spook but now I'll have to go back alone and see what I can do.'

'Not alone, Tom,' Alice said. 'Where you go, I go. Tell me all about it . . .'

I kept my story brief, giving her the bare bones of the situation as we walked quickly past the church and between the gravestones towards the cottage. Alice didn't say much but she looked horrified when I told her about Tibb drinking Father Stocks's blood. At my mention of Wurmalde, a look of puzzlement flickered across her face.

When I'd finished, she gave a sigh. 'Just gets worse and worse, it does. I've something to tell you as well—'

At that moment we reached the house. 'Save it for the journey,' I told her. 'We'll talk as we walk.'

Wasting no time, I collected my rowan staff. My bag would have been an encumbrance so I left it behind, but I put a handful of salt in my right breeches pocket and iron filings in my left. In addition I tied my silver chain around my waist under my shirt. Once again, I left off my cloak: it was dangerous in Pendle to signal that you were a spook's apprentice.

Next I wrote a short note for the Spook to tell him what had happened:

Dear Mr Gregory,

Father Stocks is in great danger at Read Hall. Please follow me there just as quickly as you can. Bring James as well. We'll need all the help we can get.

Tibb has drunk Father Stocks's blood and left him weak and close to death. The creature will feed again after dark, and if I don't get back and help, he will certainly die. Beware Mistress Wurmalde, the housekeeper. She's a witch who is trying to unite all three covens. She comes from Greece and is an old enemy of Mam's.

Your apprentice, Tom

P.S. Some of Magistrate Nowell's servants seem to be working for Wurmalde. Trust nobody.

That done, I drank a cupful of water and had a nibble of cheese. I took more cheese with me for the journey, and within twenty minutes of arriving at Downham I was on the road again. But this time I wasn't alone.

At first we walked in silence, at a very fast pace, Alice just in the lead; she recognized the urgency of getting back to Read Hall before dark. After we'd covered about a third of the distance, I began to feel very tired but forced myself to keep going by imagining Tibb on the ceiling, about to drop down onto Father Stocks's chest. It was too horrible to think about – I had to get him away from Read Hall before that happened.

Nevertheless, almost without being aware of it, we did begin to slow. It was Alice. She was walking slightly behind me now, breathing heavily, and seemed to be having difficulty keeping up. I turned to see what was the matter and noticed that she looked pale and weary.

'What's wrong, Alice?' I asked her, coming to a halt. 'You don't look well . . .'

Alice fell to her knees and suddenly cried out in pain, then clutched at her throat and started to choke.

'Can't breathe properly,' she gasped. 'Feels like someone's squeezing my windpipe!'

For a moment I panicked, not knowing what I could do to help, but gradually Alice's breathing returned to normal and she sat down wearily on the grass.

'It's Mab Mouldheel up to her tricks. Using that lock of hair against me, she is. She's been doing it all day. But don't worry, it's starting to pass. Let's rest for ten minutes and I'll feel better. Besides, I've something to tell you. Something for you to think about . . .'

Still concerned about Father Stocks, I considered going on ahead and asking Alice to catch up when she felt better. But it seemed certain that we'd be back well before sunset and I was tired as well, so I told myself that ten minutes wouldn't matter. Besides, I was intrigued. What was she going to say?

We sat ourselves down on a grassy slope with our backs to the hill. No sooner had I taken the weight off my legs than Alice began.

'Been talking to Mab, I have. Wants me to pass on a message to you—'

'Mab Mouldheel? What were you doing talking to her?' I demanded.

'Wouldn't choose to speak to her, would I? Came looking for me, she did. It was this morning, not long after Old Gregory had left. I heard someone shouting my name from the other side of the wall and went out. It was Mab. She couldn't climb over to this side because the house is set in the church grounds. Holy ground, ain't it? Mab can't set foot there. Anyway, she wanted me to tell you this. She wants the trunks for herself; in return, she'll guide you into Malkin Tower and help you rescue Jack and his family.'

I looked at Alice in astonishment. 'Do you think she can do that?'

'Yes, and what's more I think she's fond of you. More than a bit keen, I'd say!'

'Don't be daft,' I said. 'She's a malevolent witch. We're natural enemies.'

'Stranger things have happened,' teased Alice.

'Anyway,' I said, quickly changing the subject, 'how would she get me inside the tower?'

'There's a tunnel. Leads straight into the dungeons.'

'But why do we need Mab to guide us, Alice? You're a Deane and also a Malkin on your mother's side. Surely *you* know where the tunnel entrance is?'

Alice shook her head. 'I've been in the tower a few times, but only above ground. Know that part well enough, but only Anne Malkin, their coven leader, knows where the actual entrance is. It's a secret passed down from generation to generation. Only one living person is ever given that knowledge! She'd only be allowed to show it to others if the whole coven was in mortal danger and they needed to get into the tower secretly and take refuge there.'

'So how does Mab know? Is this some sort of trick?

Maybe she's only pretending to know.'

'No, Tom, this is no trick. Remember that night when you saved me from the Mouldheels and we met Dead Maggie in the wood? Hungry for blood, Maggie was, and set off to meet 'em. Trouble is, there were too many and they got the better of her. Maggie was once the leader of the coven so she knows where the entrance is. Got the secret from her, they did. Don't know how, but it wouldn't have been pleasant. Wouldn't talk easily, our Maggie, so they must have hurt her pretty bad. Mab said she'd hurt me too if I didn't talk you round. Got my lock of hair, ain't she. I'm starting to feel unwell again – think she might be doing something to it now, just so I know what's what. And that's part of the bargain. Offer to give her the trunks and keys and she'll show you the entrance to the tunnel and help you rescue your family. Not only that – she'll return my lock of hair. Be more use to you when I get that back. At the moment I'm useless. Just a shadow of myself, I am.'

It seemed simple. All I had to do was surrender the trunks and I'd be given a chance to get Jack, Ellie and

Mary out – perhaps before midnight; before Wurmalde could carry out her threat. But, in a way, nothing had changed.

Alice did look ill. Somehow we had to get that lock of hair back from Mab, but not this way. I shook my head. 'I'm sorry, Alice, but I just can't do it. As I told you, Wurmalde says she'll swap Jack and his family for the keys too. But whether I give them to Wurmalde or Mab, I'd still have surrendered them to a witch. It would still help the dark and place the County in danger.'

'This way is better though, ain't it? Can you trust Wurmalde? Giving her the keys is easy – but what guarantee is there that you'll get your family back safely in return? Mab Mouldheel prides herself on always keeping her word. Once the bargain's made, she'll show us the way in person. She'll guide us through to the dungeons because the trunks will be nearby. She'll be in as much danger as us: be a terrible thing for her, to be caught by the Malkins, so she needs to get in and out safely. We'll be with her every step of the way. Not only that – if she's helping us, maybe she won't join up with the Malkins and Deanes. We'll be stopping the covens uniting and releasing the Fiend as well as rescuing your family.'

'It's still giving her the trunks though. I can't do that—'

'Let me try to talk her round. Let's see if she'll do it for just one trunk. If she agrees to that and is prepared to give me back my lock of hair before we enter the tunnel, then we're laughing, ain't we? Just one trunk can't do that much harm . . .'

'It's still one trunk too many. Mam wanted me to have them all and it must be for an important reason. The last thing she'd want is for me to give them to the dark!'

'No, Tom, the last thing she'd want is for Jack and his family to die!'

'I'm not even sure about that, Alice,' I said sadly. 'However much it hurts, there are more people than just immediate family to consider. There's the County and the world beyond that.'

'Then we'll do it your way!' Alice snapped. 'We'll

say that Mab can have the trunks in order to get to your family, but once we're inside the tower it'll be easy enough to get the better of her. Came up on me unawares, the Mouldheels did. And there were a lot of 'em. If it's just me and Mab, I'll sort her out for sure. Just see if I don't—'

'But she's got a lock of your hair, Alice. You said yourself you're not as strong as you should be.'

'I've got you, though, haven't I? Look, once we're inside the tower, the two of us can overpower Mab. Then we'll rescue your family before midnight, and once the soldiers have breached the wall we'll get your trunks back.'

I thought about it for a bit, then nodded. 'I'm not sure what other choice we have, though I doubt whether a few soldiers will be a match for the Malkins.'

'You may be right, Tom. We may need another plan for getting hold of those trunks, but for rescuing your family this is the best plan we have.'

'I know you're right,' I said, 'but I feel uncomfortable with betraying Mab like that.'

'Mab? You can't mean that! Just think what you're saying. Do you think *she* felt guilty when she was planning to kill me the other night? Or when she was trying to make you hers, or when she tortured me all day today with my hair? You're turning soft, Tom, like Old Gregory. Pretty girl smiles at you and your brain goes soft.'

'I'm just saying it isn't right to break a promise. My dad taught me that.'

'He didn't mean when you were dealing with a witch, though. Old Gregory probably wouldn't like our plan, but then he's never around when we need him these days. If he was, we wouldn't be having to rescue Father Stocks and your family all by ourselves.'

Her mention of Father Stocks reminded me again of the great danger he was in and the terrifying ordeal we were about to face at Read Hall. 'Alice,' I said, 'something else is puzzling me. Who exactly *is* Wurmalde? She claims to come from the same land as Mam but talks as if she's part of the covens. As if she speaks for them.'

203

Alice frowned. 'Never even heard of her before today . . .'

'But you were in Pendle until two years ago. Wurmalde's been in Roger Nowell's employment longer than that.'

'Nowell's a magistrate. Ain't likely I'd go near his house. Not stupid, am I? Nor any of my family either. As for his housekeeper – what would anyone know about her?'

'Well,' I said, 'she's a mystery all right, but we've delayed long enough now so let's press on towards Read. Feeling any better or shall I go on ahead at a faster pace?'

'I'll go as fast as I can. If I can't keep up, you'd best go on ahead.'

Our pace wasn't quite as fast as before but Alice did manage to keep up and we came within sight of Read Hall with over an hour of daylight still remaining. But now we had a problem – how to get inside unseen.

A creature of the dark, Tibb was not yet a threat, but there were still two risks. Wurmalde wouldn't be able to sniff out either Alice or me but she might glimpse us from a window. There were also the servants to worry about. Some might be unaware of what was going on behind the magistrate's back, but if Cobden had returned from Malkin Tower, he'd certainly pose a danger. I couldn't afford to simply walk down the wide carriageway.

'I think the best chance of getting inside unseen is to approach from the shrubbery at the side. I can use my key to enter by the tradesman's door . . .'

Alice nodded her agreement, so we circled round and approached from the west, moving through the bushes and trees until we were close to the side of the house, only ten or twenty paces from the door.

'We need to be very careful here,' I told Alice. 'I think it's probably best if I go in alone.'

'No, Tom. Ain't right. Need me, you do,' Alice said, her voice indignant. 'Two of us together have more chance.'

'Not this time, Alice. This is risky. You stay hidden, and if I get caught, at least I'll know there'll be somebody on the outside to help. If the worst came to the worst, you could come in after me.'

'Then give me your key!'

'I need it for the door—'

'Course you do! But once you get it open, throw it back onto the lawn. I'll come and pick it up once you're inside.'

'You'd better take my staff as well,' I told her. Father Stocks would still be weak and I'd have to help him down the stairs – my staff would be an encumbrance. It was still light, so I hoped I wouldn't have to face Tibb, and the chain would be enough to deal with Wurmalde. If I missed her, I still had salt and iron to fall back on.

Alice nodded but grimaced as I handed it to her. She didn't like the touch of rowan wood.

I walked cautiously forward across the grass. I halted close to the door and put my ear against the wood. I could hear nothing so I inserted the key and turned it very slowly. There was a faint click as the lock yielded. Before I opened the door, I held the key high so that

Alice could see what I was doing and threw it back towards the line of bushes. It was a good shot and it fell on the lawn, less than a pace away from where she was hiding. That done, I eased open the door very carefully and stepped inside. Once I'd closed it behind me, it locked itself shut. I waited, rooted to the spot for at least a minute, all the while listening for danger.

Reassured by the silence, I moved through the hallway to the main staircase. I paused and untied the silver chain from around my waist, coiling it about my left wrist, ready to throw. It was still daylight, so I didn't expect to meet Tibb yet, but I was more than ready for Wurmalde.

In the hallway I halted again and peered about. It seemed empty so I began to climb the stairs, pausing every time the wood gave the slightest creak. At last I reached the landing. Just ten steps would bring me to Father Stocks's room.

I crept along, opened the door and stepped inside. The heavy curtains had been drawn across the window again and it was very gloomy but I could just see the outline of the priest lying on the bed.

'Father Stocks,' I called softly.

When he didn't answer, I went to the window and pulled back the curtains, flooding the room with light. I turned and walked back towards the bed. Even before I reached it my heart had begun to beat very rapidly.

Father Stocks was dead. His mouth was wide open, unseeing eyes staring up towards the ceiling. But he hadn't died as a result of Tibb taking his blood. The handle of a dagger was protruding from his chest.

I felt upset and horrified at the same time, my mind reeling. I'd thought he would be safe enough until dark. I should never have left him alone. Had Wurmalde stabbed him? The blood on his shirt and the sheets appeared to come from the wound. Had she done it to cover up the fact that Tibb had taken his blood? But how could she hope to get away with murdering the priest?

As I was staring horrified at the body of poor Father Stocks, someone stepped into the room behind me. I turned quickly, taken by surprise. To my dismay, it was Wurmalde. She glared at me before a faint smile appeared on her face. But I'd already pulled back my left arm, readying the silver chain. I was nervous but I also felt very confident. I remembered my last training session with the Spook, when I'd hit the practice post a hundred times without missing even once.

A fraction of a second later I'd have cracked the chain and hurled it straight at the witch, but to my astonishment another figure came in through the doorway to stand at Wurmalde's shoulder, facing me, his forehead creased in a frown of displeasure. It was Master Nowell, the magistrate!

'A thief and murderer stands before you!' Wurmalde crowed, the accusation strong in her voice. 'Look at those bloodstains on his shirt and look what he holds in his left hand. That's silver, if I'm not mistaken . . .'

I stared at her, unable to speak, the words 'thief' and 'murderer' spinning around inside my head.

'Where did you get that silver chain from, boy?' Nowell demanded.

'It belongs to me,' I said, wondering what Wurmalde

had told him. 'My mam gave it to me.'

'I thought you came from a family of farmers?' he asked, the frown creasing his brow again. 'Better think again, boy, because you'll need a more convincing explanation than that. It's hardly likely that a farmer's wife would own such a valuable item.'

'It's just as I told you, Master Nowell,' Wurmalde accused. 'I heard a noise from your study and came downstairs in the dead of night to catch him red-handed. Otherwise you'd have lost even more than you have. He'd forced open the cabinet and was helping himself to your poor dead wife's jewellery. He ran off before I could seize him, fleeing into the night like the thief and murderer he is, and when I went upstairs to tell Father Stocks what had happened, I found the poor priest as you see him now – dead in his bed, a knife plunged into his heart. Now, not content with murder and thieving that silver chain from somewhere, he's sneaked back into your home to see what else he can get his hands on . . .'

What a fool I'd been. It had never crossed my mind

that Wurmalde would kill Father Stocks and then simply blame it on me. When I opened my mouth to protest, Nowell stepped forward and seized my left shoulder in a strong grip before snatching the chain from my hand.

'Don't waste your time trying to deny it!' he told me, his face livid with anger. 'Mistress Wurmalde and I watched you from the windows just now. We saw you circling the house with your accomplice. My men are outside searching the grounds – she won't get far. Before this month is out you'll both hang at Caster!'

My heart sank down into my boots. I realized now that Wurmalde had used fascination and glamour to control Nowell and he believed everything she said. No doubt she'd broken into the cabinet and stolen the jewellery herself. But it would be a waste of time for me to accuse her. I couldn't just come out with the whole truth either because Nowell didn't believe in witchcraft.

'I'm not a thief, or a murderer,' I told him. 'I came to Pendle following thieves who not only stole trunks belonging to me but kidnapped my family. That's why I'm here—'

'Oh, don't you worry about that, boy. I intend to get to the root of the whole matter. Whether there's a glimmer of truth in what you say or your whole story is a pack of lies we'll find out soon enough. Those who live in Malkin Tower have laughed at the law for far too long and this time I intend to bring them to justice. If they're your accomplices or it's a case of thief against thief, we'll find out tomorrow. There's been a whole day's delay persuading the military of the need to come here but I intend to send all within that tower to Caster in chains for questioning and you'll be going with them under armed guard! Now empty out your pockets. Let's see what else you've thieved!'

I had no choice but to obey. Instead of stolen goods, salt and iron showered down onto the floor. For a moment Nowell looked puzzled and I feared that he would then search my person and discover the keys around my neck, but Wurmalde gave him a strange smile and a vacant expression settled on his face before being succeeded by a new resolve. With a frown he marched me down into the servants' quarters and locked me in a holding cell that was used by the constable. It was a small room with a stout door, and without my special key I'd no hope at all of getting out. He kept my chain and Alice had my staff. I had nothing with which to defend myself.

As for Alice, I knew that she'd have sniffed out Nowell's men and fled the grounds before they'd got anywhere near her. That was the good news. The bad news was that it was very unlikely that she'd try to get into the house and free me tonight. It was just too dangerous. And she couldn't rescue my family without me. Time was passing, ticking towards the midnight deadline set by Wurmalde. If I didn't give her my keys by then, she would hand Jack, Ellie and Mary over to Grimalkin to be tortured. It didn't bear thinking about.

But while Alice was free, I still had some hope of rescue. If not tonight, she'd do her best tomorrow – if I was still alive when dawn came. Wurmalde might visit me in the night to make one final demand for the keys. Or worse – she might send Tibb.

A little while later, as I lay there in the darkness of the cell, I heard a key turning in the lock. Quickly I came to my feet and moved back to the far corner of the room. Dare I hope? Could it be Alice?

But to my disappointment and dismay, Wurmalde came in carrying a candle and closed the door behind her. I looked at her voluminous skirts and wondered if Tibb had entered the cell with her.

'Things may seem grim but they're not hopeless,' she said with a thin smile. 'Everything can be put to rights. All it would take is the keys to the trunks. Give me what I want and by tomorrow evening you could be on your way back home with your family—'

'Yes, and be hunted down as a murderer. I can never go home now . . .'

She shook her head. 'Within days Nowell will be dead and the whole district will be in our hands. So there'll be nobody around to accuse you. Just leave it all to me. All you have to do is give me those keys. It's as simple as that.'

It was my turn to smile. This was her best chance so far to take the keys by force. I was alone and at her mercy. That she didn't do so convinced me that she couldn't. 'That's *exactly* what I have to do, isn't it?' I asked. 'I have to *give* you the keys. You can't just take them.'

Wurmalde scowled with displeasure. 'Remember what I told you last night?' she warned. 'If you won't do it to save yourself, then at least do it for your family. Give me the keys or all three of them will die!'

At that moment, somewhere within the house, a clock started to chime. She stared at me until the final stroke of midnight.

'Well, boy? You've had the time you demanded. Now give me your answer!'

'No,' I said firmly. 'I won't give you the keys.'

'Then you know the consequences of that decision,' she said softly before leaving the cell. The key turned in the lock and I heard her walking away. Then there was only silence and darkness. I was left alone with my thoughts, and never had they been darker.

My decision had just cost my family their lives. But what else could I have done? I couldn't let the contents of Mam's trunks fall into the hands of the covens. The Spook had taught me that my duty to the County came before everything else.

It was just a year and three months or so since I'd been happily working with my dad back on the farm. At the time, the work had seemed boring but now I'd have given anything to be back there again with Dad still alive, Mam at home, and Jack and Ellie safe.

At that moment I wished that I'd never seen the Spook and never become his apprentice. I sat in the cell and wept.

CHAPTER 12
THE ARMY ARRIVES

When the cell was next unlocked, Constable Barnes came into the room carrying a wooden board. It was edged with metal and had two holes in it to put my hands through. I'd once seen a man placed in the stocks and a similar device had been used to clamp his wrists, holding him to the spot while a crowd pelted him with rotten fruit.

'Hold out your hands!' Barnes commanded.

As I obeyed, he opened the hinged board and then closed the two halves over my wrists and locked it with a key, which he then placed in his breeches pocket. The board was heavy and clamped my wrists tightly so that there was no chance of pulling my hands free.

'Make the slightest attempt to escape and you'll go in leg-irons as well. Do I make myself clear?' the constable demanded aggressively, his face close to mine.

I nodded miserably, feeling close to despair.

'We'll be meeting Master Nowell at the tower. Once we've battered through the walls you'll be taken to Caster to hang with the rest. Though to my mind, hanging's too good for a priest killer!'

Barnes gripped me by the shoulder and pushed me out into the corridor, where Cobden had been lurking just out of sight, a heavy cudgel in his hand. No doubt he'd been hoping I'd try to run for it. The two men led me out through a rear door to where the cart was waiting. The constable's bailiffs were already sitting in the back and they both stared at me hard. One spat on my shirt front as I struggled to climb aboard.

Five minutes later we were through the main gates of Read Hall and heading for Goldshaw Booth and Malkin Tower beyond.

When we reached the tower, Nowell wasn't alone. With

him were five mounted soldiers wearing jackets of County red that, even before we reached the clearing, made them highly visible. As our cart trundled towards them, one rider dismounted and began to walk around the tower, peering up at the stone edifice as if it were the most fascinating thing in the world.

Cobden brought the cart to a halt close to the horsemen.

'This is Captain Horrocks,' Nowell told Barnes, nodding towards a stocky man with a ruddy complexion and a small neat black moustache.

'Good morning to you, Constable,' said Horrocks, then turned his gaze towards me. 'Well, is this the boy Master Nowell's been telling me about?'

'This is the lad,' Barnes said. 'And others like him are inside that tower.'

'Don't you fear,' said Captain Horrocks. 'We'll soon breach that wall. The cannon will be here at any moment. It's the biggest gun in the County and it'll make short work of the business! We'll soon call those scoundrels to account.'

That said, the captain wheeled his horse round and led his men in a slow circuit of Malkin Tower. The magistrate and Barnes followed.

The following hours passed slowly. I was sick to my heart and close to despair. I had failed to rescue my family and had to accept that they were probably being tortured or were dead inside that tower. There was no hope of Alice reaching me now, and soon I'd be on my way to Caster with any who managed to survive the bombardment of the tower. What hope did I have of a fair trial then?

Late in the morning a huge cannon arrived, pulled by a team of six big shire horses. It was a long cylindrical barrel supported on a gun-carriage with two large wooden wheels rimmed with metal. The gun was brought into position quite close to our cart and soon the soldiers had unhitched the horses and led them some distance away back amongst the trees. Next they began to attend to the gun, using a lever and ratchet to raise the cannon's mouth higher and higher until they were satisfied. Then they put their shoulders to the wheels and positioned the carriage so that the barrel was pointing more directly towards the tower.

Barnes rode back towards us. 'Get the boy down and take the cart back to where the others are,' he instructed Cobden. 'The captain says the horses are too near. The noise of the gun will drive 'em mad with fright.'

The two bailiffs dragged me down and made me sit on the grass while Cobden took the horses and cart and followed Barnes to join the others.

Soon another cart arrived, this one loaded with cannonballs, two big tubs of water and a great heap of small canvas bags of gunpowder. All the gunners, bar the sergeant in charge, took off their red jackets, rolled up their sleeves and set to unloading the cart, piling the ammunition carefully to form neat pyramids on either side of the gun. When the first tub of water was lifted down, the bailiff to my right joked, 'Thirsty work, is it, lads?'

'This is to clean and cool the cannon!' one of the gunners called back, giving him a withering look. 'It's an eighteen-pounder, this, and without the water it'd soon overheat and explode. You wouldn't want that to happen, now would you? Not with you sitting so close!'

The bailiff exchanged a look with his companion. Neither of them seemed at ease.

The unloading completed, that cart was also taken back into the trees, and soon after that Captain Horrocks and Nowell rode close by, heading in the same direction.

'When you're ready, Sergeant!' Horrocks called down to the gunners as he cantered past. 'Just fire at will. But take this chance to sharpen up your skills. Make every shot count. As likely as not, we'll soon be up against a much more dangerous foe . . .'

As the two men rode out of earshot, the bailiff, undaunted by his previous exchange with the gunner, couldn't resist speaking up again. 'Dangerous foe?' he asked. 'What did he mean by that?'

'That's not really any of your business,' the sergeant said with a swagger. 'But since you ask, there's talk of an invasion south of the County. Chances are we'll have a more serious battle to fight than this little siege.

But not a word to anyone or I'll cut your throat and feed you to the crows.' The sergeant turned away again. 'Right, lads. Load up! Let's show the captain what we can do!'

A gunner lifted one of the canvas bags and pushed it into the mouth of the cannon while his companion used a long rod to ram it down deep into the barrel. Another picked up a cannonball from the nearest pile and rolled it down into the barrel, ready for firing.

The sergeant turned our way again and spoke to the bailiff on my left, the one who'd kept silent. 'Ever heard a big gun like this go off?' he asked.

The bailiff shook his head.

'Well, it's loud enough to burst your eardrums. You need to cover them like this!' he instructed, clapping his hands over his ears. 'But if I were you, I'd walk back about a hundred paces or so. The lad won't be able to cover his ears, will he?' He looked at my wrists, still clamped apart by the wooden board.

'Bit o' noise won't matter much to this lad. Not where he's going. Murdered a priest, he did, and he'll hang before the month's out.'

'Well, in that case it won't do no harm to give him a small dose of Hell to be going on with!' said the sergeant, staring at me with open disgust as he strutted back to the cannon and gave the order to fire. One of the soldiers lit a reed fuse protruding from the top of the gun and then stood well clear with his companions. As it burned lower, the gunners covered their ears and the two bailiffs followed suit.

The noise of the cannon going off was like a thunderclap right next to me. The gun carriage jerked back about four paces and the shot hurtled through the air towards the tower, howling like a banshee. It fell into the moat, throwing up a spout of water as a great flock of crows soared out of the trees in the distance. A cloud of smoke hung in the air about the cannon, and as the gunners went to work again, it was like watching them through a November fog.

First they adjusted the elevation, then they cleaned the inside of the barrel with rods and sponges, which they kept dipping into the tubs of water. Eventually they fired again. This time the thunderclap felt even louder, but strangely I no longer heard the flight of the shot through the air. Nor did I hear it strike Malkin Tower. But I did see it hit the wall low down, throwing up splinters to shower back into the moat.

How long this went on I couldn't say. At one point the bailiffs had a short conversation. I could see their lips moving but I couldn't hear a word they were saying. The sound of the gun had deafened me. I just hoped it wouldn't be permanent. Smoke hung all around us now and I had an acrid taste at the back of my throat. The pauses between firing grew longer and longer as the gunners spent more time using sponges on the barrel, which was no doubt starting to overheat.

At last the bailiffs must have grown weary of being so close to the gun. They dragged me to my feet and walked me back a hundred paces, as the sergeant had advised. After that it wasn't so bad and gradually, in the delays between firing, I realized that my hearing was coming back. I could hear the howl of the shot through the air and the crack of the iron ball striking the stones of Malkin Tower. The gunners knew their job all right – each shot struck approximately the same point on the wall, but as yet I could see no evidence that it was being breached. Then there was another delay. They ran out of cannonballs and the wagon bringing a fresh supply didn't arrive until late in the afternoon. By then I was thirsty and asked one of the bailiffs for a drink of the water they were swigging from a stone jug brought by one of the soldiers.

'Aye, help yourself, lad,' he laughed. Of course, I couldn't lift the jug, and when I knelt down close to it, intending to lick beads of water from its neck, he simply moved it out of reach and warned me to sit back down or he'd give me a thumping.

By sunset my mouth and throat were parched. Nowell had already ridden back in the direction of Read Hall. The failing light had halted work for the day and, leaving one young gunner on duty guarding the cannon, the others made a fire back amongst the trees and were soon busy cooking supper. Captain Horrocks had also ridden off, no doubt to find a comfortable bed for the night, but the horsemen had remained to share the supper.

The bailiffs dragged me back into the trees but we sat with Barnes and Cobden, some distance away from the soldiers' cooking fire. The bailiffs set to making a fire of their own but there was nothing to cook on it. After a while one of the soldiers came across and asked if we were hungry.

'We'd be very grateful if you could spare us a bite,' Barnes said. 'Thought it would all be over by now and I'd be back at Read tucking into my supper.'

'That tower's going to take a bit longer than we thought,' the soldier replied. 'But don't you worry, we're getting there. Up close you can see the cracks. We'll breach it afore noon tomorrow and then we'll see some fun.'

Soon Barnes, Cobden and the bailiffs were tucking into platefuls of rabbit stew. With knowing winks they set a plate down on the grass in front of me.

'Tuck in, boy,' Cobden invited, but when I tried to kneel and bring my mouth down close to the plate, it was snatched up and the contents thrown into the fire.

They all laughed, thinking it a great joke, and I sat there, hungry and thirsty, watching it splutter and burn while they ate. It was getting darker and the cloud had gradually thickened towards sunset. I hadn't much hope of sneaking away because they'd decided to take turns watching me and the soldiers would have their own sentry posted anyway.

Half an hour later Cobden was on guard while the others slept. Barnes was snoring loudly with his mouth wide open. The two bailiffs had nodded off the moment they stretched themselves out on the grass.

I didn't even bother trying to sleep. The board fastened to my wrists was tight and starting to hurt and my head was churning with all the things that had happened – my encounters with Wurmalde and Tibb and my failure to save poor Father Stocks. Cobden had no intention of allowing me to drop off anyway.

'If I have to stay awake, then so shall you, boy!' he snarled, kicking my legs to drive the point home.

After a while, though, it seemed to me that he was

having trouble staying awake himself. He kept yawning and pacing about before coming across to give me another kick. It was a long uncomfortable night but then, about an hour or so before dawn, Cobden sat down on the grass with a glazed expression in his eyes; his head would nod before jerking back to wakefulness, and each time, he glared at me as if it were entirely my fault. After this had happened four or five times his head dropped onto his chest and he began to snore gently.

I looked across towards the soldiers' campfire. They were some distance away so I couldn't be absolutely certain, but none of them seemed to be moving. I realized that this was the one chance I might get to escape, but I waited a few more minutes to make sure that Cobden was fast asleep.

At last, very slowly, I stood up, afraid to make the slightest noise. But as soon as I was on my feet, to my dismay, I glimpsed something moving in the trees. It was some distance away but something grey or white seemed to flicker. Then I saw another movement a little further to the left. Now I was certain, so I crouched down low. I was right. Figures were moving towards me through the trees to the south. Could it be more soldiers? Reinforcements? But they didn't march like soldiers. They seemed to glide silently, like ghosts. It was almost as if they were floating.

I had to get away before they arrived. The board clamping my wrists would affect my balance and make running difficult, but far from impossible. I was about to take a chance when I glimpsed another movement and looked back to see that I was completely surrounded. Shadowy figures were converging on us from all points of the compass. They were nearer now, and I could see that they were clad in black, grey or white gowns – women with glittering eyes and wild, unkempt hair.

They were almost certainly witches, but from which coven? The Malkins were supposed to be inside the tower. Could it be the Deanes? Had there been moonlight, I'd have noticed their weapons earlier. It was only as they moved closer to the fire that I realized that each witch was carrying a long blade in her left hand and something else – as yet unidentifiable – in her right.

Had they come to murder us in our sleep? With that dark thought, I realized that I couldn't just run off into the trees and leave my captors to their fates. They'd treated me badly but they didn't deserve to die like this. Constable Barnes wasn't working directly for Wurmalde and probably just thought he was doing his duty. If I woke them up, there was still a chance that, in the confusion, I'd be able to escape.

So I nudged Cobden with my foot. When there was no response, I kicked him harder, but again to no avail. Even when I bent and shouted his name right into his ear, he just carried on snoring gently. I tried the same with Barnes, with no more success. At that moment the truth struck me . . .

They'd been poisoned! Just like poor Father Stocks had been at Read Hall. Again, I was all right because I'd eaten nothing. There must have been something in the rabbit stew. How it had got there I didn't know, but now it was too late because the nearest witch was no more than fifteen paces away.

I tensed, ready to run for it, choosing a space to my right; a gap between the trees which was not blocked by a witch. Then a voice called out to me, one that I recognized. It was the voice of Mab Mouldheel.

'No need to be scared, Tom. No need to run. Here to help you, we are. We've come to bargain . . .'

I turned to watch Mab walk up to the sleeping Cobden. She knelt and lowered her blade towards him.

'No!' I protested, horrified by what she was about to do. Now, for the first time, I could see what she was holding in her other hand. It was a small metal cup with a long stem – a chalice to collect the blood. The Mouldheels were witches who used blood-magic. They were going to take what they needed.

'We're not going to kill 'em, Tom!' Mab said, giving me a grim smile. 'Don't you worry yourself. We just want a little of their blood – that's all.'

'No, Mab! Spill just one drop of blood and there'll be no bargain between us. No deal at all . . .'

Mab hesitated and looked up at me in astonishment. 'What are they to you, Tom? They hurt you, didn't they? And would have taken you to Caster and hanged you without a second thought. And this one belongs to Wurmalde!' she said, spitting down at Cobden.

'I mean it, Mab!' I said, looking over at the other witches, who were gathering to listen. A second group was moving towards the soldiers' camp, blades at the ready. 'I might be prepared to do a deal, but spill one drop of blood and I'll never agree. Call them off. Tell them to stop!'

Mab stood up, her eyes sullen. Finally she nodded. 'All right, Tom, just for you.' At that, the other Mouldheels turned their backs on the soldiers and slowly returned to join us.

It struck me now that the men at my feet could be dying anyway because of the effects of the poison. Witches are skilled at both poisons and antidotes, so there might still be time to save them.

'There's something else,' I told Mab. 'You've poisoned these men with that stew. Give them the

233

antidote before it's too late . . .'

Mab shook her head. 'We put it in the water, not the stew, but it's not going to kill 'em,' she said. 'We just wanted them asleep while we took some of their blood. They'll wake up with bad heads tomorrow – that's all. I need these lads to be on their mettle in the morning. Need them to keep up the good work and blast a hole in that tower! Now follow me, Tom. Alice is waiting back yonder.'

'Alice is with you?' I asked in surprise. Mab had said the same thing when she'd lured me from Father Stocks's house. Then, her intention had been to kill Alice.

'Course she is, Tom. Been negotiating, we have. Lots to do before dawn – if we want to rescue that family of yours.'

'They're dead, Mab,' I said sadly, my eyes starting to brim with tears. 'We're too late.'

'Says who?'

'Wurmalde was going to have it done if I didn't give her the keys by midnight.'

'Don't trust *her*, Tom,' Mab said dismissively. 'They're still alive. Seen 'em, I have, with my mirror. They're not in a good way, admittedly, so we mustn't waste any time. But you've got a second chance, Tom. I'm here to help.'

She turned and led the way back through the trees. That day my thoughts had been at a very low ebb. It had hardly seemed possible that I might even save myself, never mind my family. But now I was free and suddenly filled with new hope and optimism. There really *was* a chance that Jack, Ellie and Mary were still alive; perhaps we'd be able to bargain with Mab and get her to show us the entrance to the tunnel that led to the dungeons below Malkin Tower.

CHAPTER 13
THE SEPULCHRE

Alice was waiting at the edge of Crow Wood. Lit by the pre-dawn light, she was sitting on a rotten log, my staff at her feet. Facing her, with watchful, distrustful eyes, were Mab's sisters, the twins Beth and Jennet.

As I approached, Alice stood up. 'You all right, Tom?' she asked anxiously. 'Here – let me get that cruel thing off you . . .'

She pulled my special key from the pocket of her dress and in moments had unlocked the board, hinged it open and thrown it to the ground. I stood there rubbing the circulation back into my wrists, relieved to be free of it.

'Wurmalde killed poor Father Stocks and blamed me,' I told her. 'They were taking me off to Caster to hang—'

'Well, they ain't taking you anywhere now. You're free, Tom—' Alice said.

'Thanks to me,' Mab interrupted, giving me a sly smile. 'It was me, not Alice, who helped you. Just remember that.'

'Yes – thank you,' I said. 'I appreciate you setting me free.'

'Free so we can bargain,' said Mab. 'So let's get on with it . . .'

Alice tutted. 'I've told her what's what, Tom,' she said, 'but she won't give me back my lock of hair. One trunk ain't enough for her either.'

'Don't trust you, Alice Deane – no further than I can spit!' Mab said, turning down the corners of her mouth. 'Two of you and only one of me, so I'm holding onto that lock o' hair until this is over. Soon as I get what I want, you can have it back. But one trunk won't do. Give me the keys to all three and it's a bargain. In exchange I'll get you safely to the dungeons under yonder tower. With me to help we can save the lives of your family. If I don't go with you, they'll die for sure.'

Mab looked really determined and I sensed that I wasn't going to get Alice's lock of hair back until she had the keys. Which meant that, in the tunnel, Alice would still be in Mab's power and unable to help me overcome her. I'd have to do it myself.

My dad had taught me that a bargain was a bargain and that it was wrong to go back on your word. Now I was planning to do just that and I found it hard. Moreover, even though she'd done it for her own ends, Mab had just rescued me, which meant that I was no longer a prisoner about to be taken to Caster and hanged. I owed her something for that, but now I was about to betray her. I felt guilty on both counts but knew I had no choice. I had to deceive Mab because lives depended on it. I'd no intention of giving her even one of the trunks, but I had to be crafty.

'You can have two trunks, Mab. Two and no more. That's my best offer . . .'

She shook her head firmly.

I sighed and stared at my feet, pretending to be thinking deeply about the situation. After almost a full minute I looked her straight in the eye. 'My family's lives are in danger so I've no choice, have I? All right – you can have all three trunks.'

A grin split Mab's face from ear to ear. 'The keys then and it's a bargain,' she said, holding out her hand.

It was my turn to shake my head. 'If I give you the keys now, what guarantee have I got that you'll guide us to the dungeons? It's no different to you being out-numbered in the tunnel, is it?' I said, gesturing towards the other witches, who were watching and listening to every word. 'Once we rescue my family you can have the keys. Not a moment sooner.'

Mab turned her back on me, perhaps so that I couldn't see her eyes or read the expression on her face. I felt certain she would cheat me if she could.

At last she turned back to face me. 'That's a bargain then,' she agreed. 'But this is going to be difficult. We'll need all our wits about us to get into that tower alive! We'll have to work together.'

As we prepared to set off, I picked up my staff.

Mab frowned. 'You don't need that nasty stick,' she said. 'Best leave it behind.'

I knew she didn't like rowan wood and regarded it as a weapon that I could use against her, but I shook my head firmly. 'My staff comes with me or the bargain's off!' I told her.

Alice and I followed Mab in a slow widdershins curve, an anti-clockwise circuit of the tower. Soon we had left Crow Wood behind but still kept the same approximate distance from Malkin Tower, which was always visible to our left against the brightening sky.

In the distance, on our right, the vast bulk of Pendle Hill was also visible and suddenly I thought I saw a light flare right on the summit so I halted and stared towards it. Mab and Alice followed the direction of my gaze. As we watched, the light flickered before burning steadily so that it was visible for miles around.

'Looks like someone's lit a fire right on top of the hill,' I said.

There were special hills throughout the County where beacons were sometimes lit, the signal passing from hilltop to hilltop much faster than a messenger on horseback could ride. Some of them even took the name 'Beacon Fell' like the one to the west of Chipenden.

Mab glanced towards me, gave a mysterious smile, then turned away and continued the journey. I shrugged at Alice and we followed at her heels. The signal must be for somebody, I thought. I wondered if it was something to do with the witch clans.

After about fifteen minutes Mab pointed ahead. 'Yonder's where the entrance is!'

We were approaching what my dad would have called a 'neglected wood'. You see, most woods are 'coppiced' every few years or so, which means that some of the saplings are hacked down and taken for firewood. This also helps the wood by creating light and space for the remaining trees to develop so that both humans and trees benefit. But here, amongst the mature trees of this wood – oak, yew and ash – was a dense tangled thicket of saplings. The area hadn't been touched for many a long year and it made me wonder why.

Then, as we reached the edge, I suddenly glimpsed tombstones amongst the undergrowth and realized that the trees and vegetation concealed an abandoned graveyard.

At first glance it looked impenetrable, but a narrow path led into the thicket and Mab plunged in without a backward glance. That surprised me because I knew she couldn't set foot on holy ground. It must have been deconsecrated, probably by a bishop, and was no longer a holy place.

I followed Mab, with Alice close at my heels, and within moments I glimpsed some sort of ruin to our left, covered with moss and lichen. Only two walls were standing and the tallest section came no higher than my shoulder.

'What's that?' I asked.

'All that's left of the old church,' Mab called back

over her shoulder. 'Most of the graves were dug up and the bones taken elsewhere and reburied. The ones they could find, anyway . . .'

Right at the heart of the thicket we reached a clearing, which was scattered with tombstones. Some had fallen flat, others leaned at precarious angles, and there were holes in the ground where the coffins had been dug up and removed. They hadn't bothered to fill in the graves again and now they were hollows filled with weeds and nettles. And there, amongst the tombstones, was a small stone building. A young sycamore tree had grown right through the roof, splitting the stones, its branches forming a leafy canopy. The walls were covered with ivy and the building had no windows, just a rotting wooden door.

'What's that?' I asked. It was far too small to be a chapel.

'It's a sepulc—' began Alice.

'He asked *me*,' interrupted Mab. 'It's a sepulchre, Tom. A grave-house above ground, once built for a family with more money than sense. Six shelves, it has,

243

and each one is still a resting place for dead bones . . .'

'The bones are still there?' I asked, not sure which girl to look at. 'Why didn't they move them with the rest?'

'The family didn't want their dead disturbed,' Mab said, walking towards the door of the sepulchre. 'But they've been disturbed already and will be again.'

She gripped the handle and slowly eased open the door. It was already dark in the shade of the sycamore, but beyond that door was absolute blackness. I didn't have a candle stub and tinderbox with me but Mab reached into the left pocket of her gown and pulled out a candle of her own. It was made from black wax, and as I watched, the wick suddenly sprouted a flame.

'Be able to see what we're doing now,' she said, smiling wickedly.

Holding the candle aloft, Mab led the way into the sepulchre, the flame illuminating the slabs of stone – the shelves which held the remains of the dead. I saw what Mab meant by saying the dead had been disturbed. Some of the bones had been dislodged from the shelves and were scattered on the floor.

Once inside, she stepped back and closed the door behind us, the flame flickering in the draught so that the eye-sockets of the nearest skull were animated by shadows, the dead bones seeming to twitch with unnatural life.

No sooner was the door closed than I experienced a sudden chill and heard a faint groan from the far corner of the sepulchre. Was it a ghost or a ghast?

'Nothing to worry about there,' Mab said, walking towards that ominous sound. 'It's only Dead Maggie and she's not going anywhere now . . .'

The dead witch was in the corner, leaning back against the damp wall. Rusty metal rings clamped her ankles, each connected by a chain to another ring bolted into the stone flags. The metal was iron, so no wonder she was suffering. Maggie was trapped all right.

'Is that a Deane I smell?' she whimpered, her voice quivering with pain.

'Sorry to see you in such a state, Maggie,' Alice said, stepping towards her. 'It's me, Alice Deane—'

'Oh! Help me, child!' Maggie begged. 'My mouth be drier than my bones be sore. I can't abide these shackles. Free me from this torment!'

'Can't help you, Maggie,' Alice replied, stepping even closer. 'Wish I could but there's a Mouldheel here. Has a lock of my hair, she has, so I can't do nothing.'

'Then come closer, child,' Maggie croaked.

Obediently Alice bent close and the dead witch whispered something into her ear.

'No whispering! No secrets here! Keep clear o' Maggie,' Mab warned.

Immediately Alice moved away, but I knew her well enough to read a subtle change in her expression: Maggie had whispered something of importance; something that might just help us against Mab.

'Right!' Mab continued. 'Let's get on with it. Follow me. It's a tight squeeze . . .'

She knelt down and crawled across the lowest bone-shelf to her left, disturbing the skeleton that lay upon it. Within moments all I could see was her bare feet before they disappeared from view like the rest of her. She'd taken the candle and the inside of the sepulchre was plunged into darkness.

So, gripping my staff, I crawled onto the cold stone slab, following her into the narrow space between it and the shelf above, feeling the bones under my body as I dragged myself across. Beyond the shelf, the fingers of my right hand clutched soft earth and, seeing a flicker of light ahead, I pulled myself head first into a shallow tunnel where Mab was waiting. She was on all fours – the roof was too low for her to stand.

Alice had already told me that the only way my trunks would ever leave Malkin Tower was through the big iron-studded wooden door, the same way they'd got inside, and one glimpse at that confined space confirmed this. So what did Mab hope to achieve? Even if she did reach the trunks, it would be impossible to bring them out this way.

I faced the same problem, but at least I might be able to rescue my family. And as long as I didn't give away the keys, no witch would be able to open the trunks.

Once Alice had joined us in the tunnel, Mab wasted

no time and crawled away on her hands and knees while we followed as best we could. I'd come across a few tunnels since becoming the Spook's apprentice but never one so tight and claustrophobic as this. It had no supports at all and I had to force myself not to think about the great weight of earth above us. If the tunnel collapsed, we'd be trapped down here in the darkness: we might be crushed quickly; we might suffer a slow, terrifying death by suffocation.

I lost all track of time. We seemed to be crawling along for an eternity, but at last we emerged into a earthen chamber large enough for us to stand up. For a moment I thought we were directly underneath the tower but then I saw another tunnel straight ahead. Unlike the one we'd just crawled through, this was big enough to walk upright in and had stout wooden props supporting the roof.

'Well,' Mab said, 'this is as far as I've been. Don't smell good, this tunnel . . .'

So saying, she leaned in and sniffed loudly three times. I wondered how good she was at it. The Spook had once told me that the ability varied from witch to witch. After one quick sniff she turned away and gave a shudder of horror. 'Something wet and dead down there,' she said. 'Don't fancy that tunnel at all!'

'Don't be soft, girl!' Alice sneered. 'Let me sniff the tunnel out too. Two noses are better than one – ain't that so?'

'Right – but be quick about it,' Mab agreed, eyeing the tunnel nervously.

Alice wasted no time. One quick sniff and she smiled. 'Nothing much to worry about down there. Wet and dead we can handle. Tom's got his rowan staff. Should be enough to keep it at bay. So off you go, Mab. You lead the way! That's if you ain't too scared. Thought you Mouldheels were supposed to be made of sterner stuff!'

For a moment Mab glared at Alice and curled her lip, but then she led the way into the tunnel. I gripped my rowan staff tightly. Something told me that I would need it.

CHAPTER 14
THE WIGHT

I f the guardian of the tunnel was wet and dead,
then it was probably a 'wight' and there'd certainly
be water in the tunnel. I'd read about wights in the
Spook's Bestiary: they were rare in the County but very
dangerous. They were created by witches, who bound
the soul of a drowned sailor to his dead body by dark
magic. The body didn't decay but became bloated and
tremendously strong. They were usually blind, their
eyes eaten by fishes, but had acute hearing and could
locate a victim on dry land while still submerged.

As I was about to follow Mab, Alice gestured with
her hand, signalling that I should stay back and allow
her to go first. I could tell that she was planning some-

thing but I didn't know what. So I let her go ahead and just hoped she knew what she was doing.

We seemed to be walking for ages, but at last we began to slow before coming to a halt.

'Don't like this,' Mab called back. 'There's water ahead. Smells bad. Don't look safe at all . . .'

I squeezed forward next to Alice so that we could see over Mab's shoulder. I'd expected to see running water – maybe a stream or underground river that she couldn't cross. Instead the tunnel widened out to form an oval cave, which contained a small lake. The water almost reached the sides of the cave, but to the left was a narrow muddy path, sloping down towards the water. It looked very slippery.

The lake worried me. It was murky, the colour of mud, and there were ripples on the surface; something that you'd expect on water agitated by wind. But we were underground and the air was still and calm. I also had a feeling that the lake was very deep. Was something nasty lurking under the surface? I remembered what Mab had sniffed out – 'something wet and dead'.

Was it a wight, as I suspected?

'Ain't got all night, Mab,' Alice called out cheerfully. 'Don't like the look of it much myself so the sooner we're past it the better!'

Looking more than a little nervous, Mab transferred the black candle to her right hand and stepped out onto the muddy path. She'd only taken a couple of steps when her bare feet began to slide. She almost lost her balance and had to put out her left hand to steady herself against the wall. The candle flickered and almost went out.

'Easy does it, girl!' Alice said, the mockery strong in her voice. 'Ain't a good idea to fall in there. Need a good pair of shoes, you do. Wouldn't like the feel o' that slimy mud between my toes. Make your feet stink worse than ever!'

Mab turned back towards us and her lip curled in anger once again. She was just about to give Alice a good earful when something happened that made my heart lurch right up into my mouth.

Faster than I could blink, a big hand, pale, bloated

and bloodless, came straight up out of the water and grasped Mab's right ankle. Immediately she lost her footing and, squealing like a piglet, fell sideways onto the mud, the lower half of her body splashing down into the water. She began to scream in terror, and as I watched, she started to slide further down into the lake. Alice was between us or I'd have held out my staff for Mab to grasp. To allow the wight to take her was too horrible.

Mab was still holding onto the candle but she was flailing her arms about and it looked sure to be plunged into the water at any second. If it went out, we'd be in the dark, unable to see where the threat was coming from. As if she'd read my thoughts, lithe as a cat, Alice leaped forward and snatched the candle from Mab's hand, then stood back and watched her slowly being dragged under.

'Save her, Alice!' I cried out. 'Nobody deserves to die like that . . .'

Alice looked reluctant, but then, with a shrug, she leaned forward, grasped Mab by the hair and started to pull her back.

At that, Mab screamed even louder – it now became a painful tug of war. Something beneath the surface was trying to drag her under; Alice was resisting and trying to pull her back. Mab must have felt like she was being torn in half.

'Jab it with your stick, Tom!' Alice shouted. 'Give it a good poke and make it let go!'

I stepped onto the muddy path next to her and aimed the point of my staff towards the water, looking for a target. The water was churning with mud now, big waves lapping at the edge of path, and I couldn't see a thing. All I could do was aim at a point somewhere just below where Mab's feet should be. I jabbed hard two or three times. It made no difference, and I was aware that Alice was losing the battle: the water was almost up to Mab's armpits.

I tried again. Still no luck. Then, on my eighth or maybe ninth attempt, I made contact with something. The water heaved and suddenly Mab was free and Alice was dragging her back up onto the path.

'Right, Tom, we ain't finished yet. Here, take the candle. Stand by with your staff in case it comes again!'

I accepted the candle and held it as high as I could so that it illuminated the whole surface of the murky lake. In my left hand was my rowan staff, ready to jab at the wight.

Alice suddenly got Mab in an arm-lock and, with her left hand still knotted in her hair, forced her into a kneeling position and pushed her head down until it was almost touching the water.

'Give me what's mine!' she shouted into Mab's left ear. 'Do it quick or that thing down there will rip your nose off!'

For a moment Mab struggled, but then the water began to heave as if something big were swimming up towards the surface.

'Take it! Take it!' she cried out, fear and panic in her voice. 'It's round my neck!'

Alice released Mab from the arm-lock and, still gripping her by the hair, used her free hand to tug something out from inside the neckband of her dress. It was a piece of string. Alice bit through it with her teeth, pulled it from Mab's neck and held it out towards me.

'Burn it!' she shouted.

As I held the candle under it, I saw that the string was knotted about a twist of hair; the lock of hair from Alice's head that placed her in Mab's power. The candle-flame ignited the string and it flared up with a *whoosh*. There was a faint smell of burning hair and then Alice allowed the charred remains to fall into the water.

That done, she tugged Mab to her feet, gripped her arm and pushed her along the path towards the far side of the lake. I followed cautiously, trying not to slip, eyeing the water fearfully. As I watched, something big floated up towards the surface. In the shadows, close to the far wall, a huge head emerged, the hair knotted and tangled on top but billowing out beside it. The face was white and swollen, the eyes empty black sockets, and as the nose emerged, it sniffed loudly like a blood-hound seeking its prey.

But moments later we had reached the safety of the

far tunnel and the immediate danger was over. Mab looked wet and bedraggled, all her former confidence gone. But since we'd arrived in Pendle, I'd never seen Alice look happier.

'We need to thank Dead Maggie for that!' Alice said, giving me a wide grin. 'Whispered what I needed to know. A wight, that was, and easy enough to sniff out. Always guards that path. Trained it well, they did. Wouldn't touch anyone with Malkin blood in their veins. I'm a Deane by name but I'm a Malkin half through. That's why I made you walk further back, Tom. Mab here was in the biggest danger.'

'It's not nice to be tricked!' Mab said. 'Still, I'm not complaining too much. Just as long as I get my trunks.'

'Got my lock of hair back, so I'm not complaining either,' Alice said with a smirk. 'And if you want those trunks, first we need to find Tom's family, safe and sound. So no tricks – that's if you know what's good for you!'

'I won't be tricking Tom,' said Mab. 'Happen he

just saved my life, jabbing that wight like that. I won't forget that in a hurry.'

'*Oooo, happen he saved my life,*' mimicked Alice. 'Happen I did too, not that you'd notice,' and she got a new fierce grip on Mab's hair and forced her ahead along the tunnel.

I felt sorry for Mab. There seemed no need to treat her so roughly, and I said as much to Alice.

She let go of Mab's hair reluctantly and was just about to answer me back when we were both distracted. Another thirty or so paces had brought us to a wooden door set in stone. It seemed that we'd reached an entrance to Malkin Tower.

There was a latch with a lock underneath. I gave Alice the candle to hold and she pulled Mab to one side while I grasped the latch and lifted it slowly, trying not to make any noise. But when I pulled, the door resisted. It was locked – though that was no problem when the Spook's brother Andrew was a locksmith. Alice gripped the candle in her teeth and held out my special key. I took it from her, inserted it into the key hole, turned it, and had the satisfaction of feeling the lock yield.

'Ready?' I whispered, handing the key back to Alice. She nodded.

'And please, no more bickering girls. Just keep the noise down until I've found my family and we're out of here,' I said.

'And I've got my trunks,' added Mab – but Alice and I ignored her, and I lifted the latch again, slowly opening the door.

Inside it was jet-black but there was a strong stench of rot and decay that made me heave. The air was tainted with death.

Alice wrinkled her nose in disgust and brought the candle to the open door. Ahead of us was a passageway with cell doors on either side. Each had an inspection hatch of iron bars about head height. In the distance was what looked like a much larger room with no door. Would my family be in one of those cells?

'You watch Mab,' I told Alice. 'Give me the candle and I'll check each cell . . .'

At the first cell I held the candle close to the bars in the door. It seemed to be empty. The second had an occupant, a skeleton covered in cobwebs and dressed in ragged breeches and a threadbare shirt, its legs and arms fastened to a wall by chains. How had the prisoner died? Had he simply been abandoned and left to starve? I felt a sudden chill, and as I watched, a narrow column of light appeared over the skeleton and an anguished face began to form above it.

The face grimaced and tried to speak, but instead of words, all I could hear was a wail of torment. The prisoner was dead but didn't know it, and was still trapped in that cell, suffering just as badly as he had in his final days. I would have liked to help, but other things were more urgent. How many more ghosts were there down here that also needed release? It could take hours and hours to talk to each tormented spirit and persuade them to cross over to the other side.

Using the candle, I checked each cell. It seemed that none of them had been used for a long time. There were sixteen in all, and seven of them contained bones.

When I reached the end of the passageway, I listened very carefully. All I could hear was the faint dripping of water, so I turned and beckoned Alice forward. I waited until she brought Mab to my shoulder, then nervously stepped out into the room at the end. The candlelight couldn't reach into all the dark corners of that vast space. Water dripped onto the flags from above and the air felt dank and chilly.

At first glance it appeared to be deserted. It was a large circular chamber, with another passageway radiating from it, identical to the one I'd already examined. Additionally, stone steps curved upwards around the wall of the chamber to a trapdoor in the ceiling, which would give access to the floor above. Five huge cylindrical pillars supported that high ceiling, each bristling with chains and manacles. I also noted a brazier full of cold ashes and a heavy wooden table with an assortment of metal pincers and other instruments.

'This is where they torture their enemies,' Alice said, her voice echoing in the silence. Then she spat onto the flags. 'Ain't good to be born into a family like this . . .'

'Aye,' said Mab. 'Maybe Tom should choose his friends more carefully. If it's a witch you want for a friend, Tom, there's better families to choose one from.'

'I ain't a witch,' said Alice and she tugged at Mab's hair hard enough to make her squeal.

'Stop it,' I hissed. 'Do you want them to know we're here?'

The girls looked shame-faced and stopped their quarrelling. I looked about me and shuddered at the thought of what must have occurred in this chamber; wave after wave of coldness slipped down my spine. Many of the dead who'd suffered were still trapped here.

First there was the other passageway to search. I'd already looked into sixteen cells but I had to search them all; one of these others might contain my family. From what I'd already seen of the dungeons, I now feared the worst. But I had to know.

'I need to check each of the cells,' I told Alice. 'It'll take a little while but it's got to be done . . .'

Alice nodded. 'Course you do, Tom. But seeing as there's only one candle, we'll stay close.'

No sooner had Alice spoken than there was the sound of coarse laughter from above – a man's voice, raucous and rough, followed by a shrill feminine peal of mirth which ended in a cackle. We froze. It seemed to be coming from just above the trapdoor. Were the Malkins coming down into the dungeons?

But to my astonishment Mab broke our nervous silence, not even bothering to keep her voice low. 'Don't worry none,' she said. 'They don't come down here, not now – and that's a promise. Scryed it, I did. You're wasting your time, Tom. It's up yonder that we'll find your family.' She gesticulated upwards.

'Why should we listen to you?' hissed Alice. 'Scrying indeed! Didn't scry that wight, did you?'

I just ignored their bickering. Alice had told me that Mab always kept her word. Maybe she was right, but I had to see for myself and it seemed obvious to me that there were witches on the floor above. So, with a heavy heart, I began a systematic search of the second passageway, still on edge at the thought that the trap-door above might open at any minute and the Malkins rush down the steps to seize us.

Many of the cells contained bones, but apart from the occasional rat, nothing seemed to be alive down there. I was relieved when it was over, but then I eyed the steps, wondering what was on the next floor.

Alice glanced at the candle, then looked at me sadly, shaking her head. 'Don't like to tell you this, Tom, but it has to be said. Won't be easy to escape back down the tunnel in the dark, will it? You ain't going to be safe passing that wight. We need to leave soon, before the candle gutters out.'

Alice was right. The candle had burned low. Soon we'd be plunged into darkness. But I couldn't leave yet.

'I'd just like to check the floor above. One look and we'll be on our way.'

'Then do it quickly, Tom,' Alice said. 'Prisoners were sometimes kept up there and questioned. If that failed, they were brought down here to be tortured and left to rot.'

'You should have searched up there when I told you,' Mab said. 'That way we wouldn't have wasted so much time.'

Ignoring her again, I set off towards the steps. Alice followed, still keeping a tight hold on Mab, although she'd let go of her hair and was gripping her arm. At the top of the steps I reached up and tried the trapdoor. It wasn't locked but I took a deep breath before I began to lift it very slowly, listening carefully for any hint of danger. What if the witches were lying in wait above? What if they grabbed me as soon as the trapdoor was open?

Only when it was fully open did I poke my head out into the space above, raising the candle slowly to illuminate the darkness. It seemed empty of life. Not even a rat moved upon the damp flags. The inside of the tower rose above me, a hollow cylinder with a spiral of narrow steps rising widdershins against the curve of the stone wall. At intervals there were wooden cell doors. The air was damp and there were wet patches and streaks of green slime on the wall; water was drip-

dripping from above to splash the flags to my left. Even the section of the tower above me was still probably underground. I climbed up through the trapdoor and moved towards the steps, beckoning Alice to follow.

'Be patient with me, Alice. I'll be as quick as I can. I'll just run up and check each door. If they're not there, we'll get out while we still can . . .'

'Come this far, we have,' said Alice, her voice echoing up into the vast space above. 'We might as well go all the way. These are the last of the cells anyway. Next floor is above ground – the living quarters and where they keep their stores. You go and see. I'll stay here and keep an eye on Mab.'

But before I could move there was a sudden distant crash, followed by a deep rumble that seemed to shake the walls and the flags beneath my feet.

'Sounds like they're firing at the tower again,' Alice said.

'Already?' I asked, astonished that the soldiers were back to their work so soon.

'Started soon after first light,' Mab said. 'Bit earlier

than we wanted. Could have done with some more time, but that's your fault, Tom. If you'd let me take their blood, they'd have slept until later.'

'Never mind her, Tom,' Alice said. 'All mouth, ain't she? Go on up the steps. Sooner we're out of here the better!'

I didn't need any further encouragement and set off right away. But despite the need for haste, I didn't run. The steps were narrow and the higher I went, the more daunting the stairwell to my left became. I reached the first cell and peered in through the hatch of bars. Nothing. Before I reached the second there was another crash, followed by a rumble and a vibration that ran down the steps from above; the gun had been fired at the tower again.

The second cell was also empty but then, at the third door, I heard a sound. It was a child crying in the dark. Could it be little Mary?

'Ellie! Ellie!' I called. 'Is that you? It's me, Tom . . .'

The child stopped crying and someone moved inside the cell. There was a rustle of skirts and the sound of shoes crossing the flags towards the cell door. Then there was a face against the grille. I held up my candle but for a moment didn't recognize her. The hair was wild, the face painfully thin, the eyes sore and red-rimmed with tears. But there was no doubt. No doubt at all.

It was Ellie.

CHAPTER 15
LIKE LITHE CATS

'Oh! Tom! Is that you? Is that really you?' Ellie cried, tears starting to pour down her face.

'Don't you worry, Ellie,' I told her. 'I'll soon have you out of there and you'll be on your way home . . .'

'Tom, I wish it were so easy,' she said, sobs making her shoulders shake as tears ran down into her open mouth. But I'd already turned away and was beckoning Alice to come up the steps.

She climbed fast, pushing Mab ahead of her, and wasted no time in opening the cell door. As I entered, illuminating the cell with the candle, Mary ran to her mother, who scooped her up in her arms. Ellie looked at me with wide hopeful eyes but then stepped back uncertainly as Alice and Mab came into the cell after me.

Then I noticed Jack. There was no bed in the cell, just a heap of dirty straw in the far corner, and my brother lay on it. His eyes were wide open and he seemed to be staring at the ceiling. He wasn't blinking.

'Jack! Jack!' I called, walking over to where he lay. 'Are you all right?'

But of course he wasn't all right and I knew that the moment I saw him. He made no response to my voice at all. His body was in the cell but his mind was surely elsewhere.

'Jack doesn't speak. He doesn't recognize me or Mary at all,' Ellie said. 'He even struggles to swallow, and all I can do is wet his lips. He's been like this ever since we left the farm . . .'

Ellie's voice failed as she was overcome with emotion again, and I could only stare at her helplessly. I felt like I should comfort her in some way, but she was my brother's wife and I'd only ever hugged her a couple of times: the first was at the celebration just after they'd got married; the second was when I'd left home just after Ellie had been terrified by the visit of the witch, Mother Malkin. Something had changed between us from that moment. I remembered her parting words as she warned me never to visit the farm during the hours of darkness:

You might bring back something bad with you and we can't risk anything happening to our family.

And it had all come true. Ellie's worst fears had been realized. The Pendle witches had raided the farm because of the trunks that Mam had left me.

It was Alice who did what I should have attempted. Still gripping Mab by the arm, she moved closer to Ellie and stroked her shoulder lightly. 'Be all right, now,' she said softly. 'It's just as Tom says. We can get out of here. Soon have you home again, don't you fear.'

But Ellie suddenly flinched away. 'Keep away from me and my child!' she shouted, her face twisted in fury. 'You're the one that started it all! Keep away, you evil little witch! Do you think that I can ever go back home now? We'll never be safe there. How can I take my

271

child back? They know where we are now! They can find us anytime they want!'

Alice looked sad but she didn't reply, simply stepped back to my side. 'Ain't going to be easy getting Jack down those steps, Tom, but the sooner we try the better.'

I glanced around the cell. It was a dismal sight, damp and cold, with slimy water trickling down the far wall. It wasn't quite as bad as the picture painted by Wurmalde, but to have been plucked from the safety of their farm and brought to this was terrible. But something even worse than that had damaged Jack.

Was it because he'd gone into Mam's room? She'd warned me how dangerous it was. Even the Spook couldn't enter there unharmed. Not only that: Jack had copied my key – otherwise he wouldn't have been able to open the door when the witches demanded it. Was he in some way paying the price for that too? But surely Mam wouldn't want Jack to suffer like this?

'Can you do anything to help Jack?' I asked Alice. She was good with potions and usually carried a small pouch with a selection of plants and herbs.

Alice looked at me doubtfully. 'Got some stuff with me – won't be able to boil it up though, so it won't be half as effective. Ain't sure it'll work anyway. Not if it's your mam's room that's hurt him . . .'

'I don't want her touching Jack anyway,' Ellie said, looking in disgust at Alice. 'Just you keep her away from him, Tom. That's the least you can do!'

'Alice can help. She really can,' I told Ellie. 'Mam trusted her . . .'

Mab tutted as though she had doubts about Alice's skills but I ignored her, and Alice simply glared at her. Then Alice pulled the small leather pouch of herbs from her pocket. 'Any water?' she asked Ellie.

At first I thought that Ellie wouldn't reply but then she seemed to see sense. 'There's a small bowl on the floor over there but it's got precious little in it.'

'Watch her!' Alice told me, nodding towards Mab, who merely shrugged. Where could she go anyway? Up towards the Malkins? Or down towards the tunnels? Mab had no chance at all alone in the dark and she knew it.

Alice went over to the bowl of water, unfastened the pouch and removed a small section of leaf, which she doused in the water, holding it there to soak. I heard the sound of cannonballs hitting the tower once more before she finally went over to Jack, opened his mouth and pushed the fragment of leaf inside.

'He could choke!' Ellie exclaimed.

Alice shook her head. 'Too small and soft now for that. Fall apart in his mouth, it will. Don't think it'll help much but I've done my best. Candle will go out soon and then we'll be in real trouble.'

I looked at the flickering candle stub. It wouldn't last more than a few minutes at the most. 'We're going to have to try and carry Jack. You take his legs, Alice,' I suggested, moving round to try and lift him by the arms.

But I'd been optimistic about the candle. At that very moment it guttered out.

It was very dark in the cell and for a moment nobody

moved or spoke. Then Mary began to cry and I heard Ellie whispering to her.

'It's still not hopeless,' I said. 'I can see pretty well in the dark. So I'll take the lead and carry Jack down with Alice, as I said. It'll be hard, but we can do it.'

'Makes sense, that,' Alice agreed. 'Let's do it now. No use wasting any more time.'

I'd tried to sound confident but the steps were steep, with a sheer drop beyond into the stairwell. Even if we got down safely, the wight still guarded the tunnel and it would be very difficult to carry Jack safely past it. It was better than just waiting here for the Malkins to come down and cut our throats, but it didn't offer much hope.

It was then that Mab spoke in the darkness. I'd forgotten all about her for a moment. 'No,' she said. 'All we have to do is wait. The gunners will breach the walls soon and the Malkins will come down the steps and make their escape along the tunnels. Once they've gone, we can go up and get out through the hole blasted in the tower wall.'

For a moment I didn't reply, but then the hair on the back of my neck stood up. Had Mab foreseen this? Was this the way she planned to get the trunks out of the tower? Through the breached walls? Whatever the truth of it, what she'd just said made sense. The first part of her idea might work, but I couldn't see how she hoped to evade the soldiers and get the trunks out. And if we went up the steps, I at least would end up in Caster Castle, where I'd be hanged for a crime I hadn't committed.

'It might be better to follow the Malkins down as they make their escape,' I suggested.

'Trust me!' Mab said. 'It's safer to go up than be trapped in the tunnels with the Malkins. We'll get your family to safety and I'll get the trunks, so we'll both win.'

The more I thought about it, the better her plan seemed. Ellie, Jack and Mary were certainly better in the hands of soldiers than of witches. Nowell had said that everyone caught inside the tower would be sent to Caster for trial. But surely they would realize immediately that Jack and his family were the victims. My story would be borne out. If necessary our neighbour, Mr Wilkinson, could be summoned to give evidence. He'd seen what had happened.

For Alice it might not be so easy. She was from Pendle and had Malkin blood in her veins. There was a danger that the only one of that family sent to trial would be Alice. And as for myself, I knew what to expect. I would go to Caster too, accused of the murder of poor Father Stocks. My heart sank at the prospect. I had no witness of my own, and Nowell would believe whatever Wurmalde told him.

But at least the trunks would be seized by the military, not the witches, and eventually my family would be free to return home. For myself, I tried not to think of a future much beyond that.

Mary was crying again and Ellie was trying to reassure her, difficult though it was in the darkness, with fear heavy in the damp air.

'I think Mab's right, Ellie,' I said, trying to sound optimistic. 'The tower's under attack by soldiers. They were brought in by the local magistrate to rescue you from the Malkins. Mab's idea could just work. All we have to do is be patient.'

Intermittently cannonballs continued to pound the tower. Nobody spoke in the darkness but occasionally Jack gave a faint groan. After a while the child stopped crying and just gave the odd whimper.

'We're just wasting time,' Alice said impatiently. 'Let's go down now, back through the tunnel, before the Malkins come.'

'That's stupid!' Mab retorted. 'In the dark? Carrying Jack and with a small child to mind? All right *you* talking – the wight won't be after *you*. Look, I've told you already that I've scryed this. Don't you Deanes ever listen? Seen it all. We're all going up to safety and I'm going to get my trunks.'

Alice gave a snort of derision but didn't bother continuing the argument. We both knew that, whatever happened, Mab wasn't going to get her trunks.

It must have been half an hour before the gun finally

stopped firing. Before I could mention the fact, Mab spoke.

'They'll be through the wall now,' she said. 'It's happening just as I said. Soon the Malkins will come running down the steps. If they come in here, we'll need to fight for our lives . . .'

Out of consideration for Ellie's fear for her husband and child, I would have kept that quiet. But Mab was blunt. Some of the Malkins might be ordered to kill their prisoners. If so, I wondered how many they would send. At least we had surprise on our side. There were more of us in the cell than they expected.

'Mab's right,' I said. 'Lock the cell from the inside, Alice. That'll keep the element of surprise.'

Alice hissed through her teeth in annoyance at my support of Mab, but a moment later I listened to her turn the key in the lock and I gripped my staff tightly. Immediately afterwards, somewhere outside the cell, I heard a door opening, followed by a distant murmur of voices. Then I heard footsteps on stone. Somebody was coming down – and not just one person: several.

There were voices and also heavy boots and the click of pointy shoes echoing across the stairwell.

Nobody spoke in the cell. We all knew the danger we were in. Were they coming for Jack, Ellie and Mary, or simply making their escape? We'd no chance at all against so many, but even though it seemed hopeless, I wouldn't give in without a fight.

The footsteps drew nearer and moments later, through the hatch of bars, I glimpsed candlelight and shadowed heads bobbing from right to left past the cell door as the witches and clan supporters made their escape. I heard them reach the bottom of the steps and start to climb down through the hatch, perhaps two dozen or more of them. Suddenly it was silent and I hardly dared to hope that they'd gone. Maybe in their haste to escape they'd forgotten their prisoners completely?

'In a moment two of 'em will come back up,' Mab whispered. 'We need to be ready!'

It was then that I heard a female voice in the distance. I couldn't make out the words but the tone was unmistakable, the cold voice filled with cruelty. My heart sank as someone began to climb towards us, retracing their steps.

As they approached the door, close by, in the darkness of the cell, someone sniffed loudly. 'Two of them, that's all,' said Alice, who had just sniffed out a confirmation of what Mab had predicted.

In reply, Mab's voice cut through the darkness. 'Two it is,' she said, 'and one's only a man. I'll soon sort him . . .'

Two sets of footsteps drew nearer: the click of pointy shoes and the thud of heavy boots. A key was inserted into the lock and beyond the bars a woman spoke.

'Leave the child to me,' she said. 'She's mine . . .'

As the door opened, I lifted my staff, ready to defend Ellie and her family. The man was holding a lantern in his right hand and a dagger in his left – one with a long, cruel blade. At his shoulder stood a witch with a thin hard mouth and eyes like black buttons stitched unevenly into her forehead.

They had no time to register surprise. No time to take a breath. Before they could react, before I could even take a step forward, Mab and Alice attacked. They pounced like lithe cats, claws outstretched, leaping towards startled birds pecking for worms. But these weren't birds and they couldn't fly. They retreated and suddenly disappeared off the steps, screaming as they fell. The sound of them hitting the ground below made me shudder.

The lantern had fallen in the doorway and the candle within was still alight. Mab picked it up and held it over the steps, looking down into the stairwell.

'Got a bit o' light to see by now,' she said. 'That should make things easier.'

When she turned back towards us, she was smiling and her eyes were cruel. 'They won't be a bother now. Nothing so good as a dead Malkin,' she said with a glance at Alice. 'Time to go up the steps . . .'

By contrast, I could see that Alice was shaking, and she crossed her arms over her stomach tightly, as if she were about to be sick.

From above there came a new sound, grinding and metallic.

'The soldier boys are inside now,' Mab said. 'That'll be the sound o' the drawbridge being lowered. Time to go up, Tom—'

'I still say we should go down and follow the Malkins,' Alice said firmly.

'No, Alice. We'll go up. I feel that's the right thing to do,' I told her.

'Why take her side, Tom? Why let her twist you round her little finger?' Alice protested.

'Come on, Alice! I'm not taking sides. I'm trusting my instincts like my master always says. Help me, please,' I pleaded. 'Help me carry Jack up the steps . . .'

For a moment I thought she wasn't going to respond, but then she came back into the cell to help. As she bent to lift Jack, I could see that her hands were shaking.

'Carry my staff, Ellie,' I said, holding it out towards her. 'I might need it later.'

Ellie looked afraid and was probably in shock, her mind reeling from what had just happened. But, still carrying her child, she accepted my staff, gripping it firmly in her left hand. I heaved Jack up by the shoul-

283

ders and Alice took his legs. He was a dead weight and it was bad enough having to lift him, never mind carry him up the steps. We struggled along, with Ellie following behind. It was back-breaking work and we had to rest every twenty steps or so. Mab was getting further and further ahead, the light from the lantern growing dimmer.

'Mab!' I called up after her. 'Slow down. We can't keep up!'

She ignored me, not even bothering to look back. I was afraid that she would go up to the floor above, leaving us alone in the dark on those dangerous narrow steps. But my fears proved unfounded. The witches had locked the upper hatch behind them, no doubt hoping to delay their pursuers. Mab was sitting there below it, grim-faced, waiting for Alice to use my key to unlock it. However, she was still first through and we followed as best we could. Only after we'd pulled Jack up and lowered him carefully to the floor did I have time to look about me.

We were in a long room with a low roof; in one corner

there were sacks of potatoes piled right up to the ceiling, with a mound of turnips close by. Above another heap, this time of carrots, salted hams hung from the ceiling on great hooks. The room wasn't dark and we no longer needed the lantern. A shaft of daylight lit the far end, where Mab was standing with her back to us. I walked towards her, with Alice at my shoulder.

Mab was standing in front of an open door. She was gazing with fascination at something on the floor. Something that had been left behind in this storeroom.

There were the three large trunks that the witches had stolen from me. Mab had reached them at last – but she still didn't have the keys.

CHAPTER
16
MAM'S TRUNKS

I looked up beyond the trunks and through the open doorway into broad daylight and silence. The air was full of dust motes, but where were the soldiers?

'It's too quiet out there,' I said.

Alice nodded. 'Let's go and see,' she suggested.

Together we walked through into a large room, the cluttered living quarters of the Malkins. There were dirty sheets and sacks on the floor for sleeping on, and against the walls were piles of animal bones and the remains of old meals. But some of the food was fresh; broken plates and uneaten food littered the flags. It looked as if the wall had been breached while the Malkins were still eating breakfast and they'd fled, leaving everything behind.

The ceiling was far above, with more steps spiralling up the inside of the tower. There was a smell of cooking smoke, but that masked the medley of stenches beneath it: unwashed bodies; rotting food; too many people living closely together for too long. Stones from the wall had tumbled down in a heap, crushing a table and scattering cooking pots and cutlery, and through that breach I could glimpse the trees of Crow Wood.

The gap was narrow but just wide enough to admit a man. Soldiers had obviously been inside because the huge door was flung back and the drawbridge had been lowered. And there, in the distance, far beyond the moat, I could see them – soldiers in red coats, scurrying about like ants. They were hitching the gun carriage to the shire horses, preparing to move off, it seemed. But why hadn't they pursued the Malkins? It would have been easy enough for them to smash through the hatch and get down into the levels below. Why hadn't they finished the job after going to so much trouble? And where was Master Nowell, the magistrate?

I heard a noise behind me, the slap of bare feet against cold flags, and turned to see that Mab had come into the room. She was smiling triumphantly.

'Couldn't have been better! Didn't just poison the water so we could free you,' she crowed, looking directly at me. 'Had another reason. We didn't want those gunners to see the Pendle beacon last night. Needed 'em to go to work this morning and blast a hole in the tower so that we could get the trunks out. And word must have come from the barracks at Colne summoning 'em back. Well, we've done with 'em now, so the soldier boys can rush off to war and get themselves killed.'

'War?' I demanded. 'What war? What do you mean?'

'A war that'll change everything!' Mab crowed. 'An invader's crossed the sea and landed far to the south. But although it's a great distance away, all the counties will have to band together and play their part. I saw it all! I saw the beacons sending their message from county to county, ordering the soldiers back to barracks, the fire seeming to leap from hilltop to hilltop. Saw the war coming. Scryed it all, I did. But it was all about timing in the end. Better than Tibb, I am.'

'Oh, stop your crowing!' said Alice, trying to deflate her. 'You can't see everything. You're not half as clever as you think you are. You can't see what's in Tom's boxes and you couldn't see the way into the tower. That's why you had to torture poor Maggie. Didn't see the wight coming either!'

'Didn't do too badly though, did I? But you're right, I could do even better. It all depends on the ritual. Depends on the night it's done. Depends whose blood I drink,' Mab said slyly. 'Tom's little niece would do the trick. Give me her blood at Lammas and I could see it all. All I want to see. Now give me the keys to those trunks and I'll let you go.'

Sickened by what she'd just said, I raised my staff. I would have brought it crashing down on her head, but she just smiled at me as bold as brass and pointed through the big wooden door. My gaze followed her finger and there, beyond the drawbridge, I saw something that made my heart plummet into my boots.

The soldiers in red coats had gone. There were no shire horses. No gun carriage. Instead there were figures walking out of the trees and crossing the tussocky grass towards us. Others were much closer to the drawbridge – women in long gowns carrying blades. Mab had planned it all down to the tiniest detail.

The Malkins had fled down the tunnels. The soldiers had gone off to war, leaving the job unfinished. And now the Mouldheels were coming for the trunks. Mab had always intended to get them out of the tower this way. She had scryed well enough to win. The plan Alice and I had hatched was hopeless. Mab had outwitted us and we couldn't get the better of her now. I felt sick to my stomach. Ellie and Jack would be prisoners again – and the threat to their child was real. The cruel expression on Mab's face told me that.

'Think about it, Tom,' she continued. 'You owe me. I could have waited in the woods with the others, couldn't I? Just waited in safety for the soldiers to leave, just as I knew they would. Instead, I risked my life getting you into the tower so you could save your family. I saw what was going to happen. That the Malkins would have cut their throats as they escaped. I saw it as plain as the nose on your face; saw them coming into the cell with their blades. And I helped you save them. But I didn't just do it for nothing. You know what we agreed. So you owe me plenty. We have a bargain and I hold you to it! I always keep my word and I expect you to do the same!'

'You're too clever for your own good!' Alice said, suddenly seizing Mab by the upper arm. 'But it ain't over yet. Not by a long way. Come on, Tom. We've got the lantern. We can escape back down the tunnels!'

So saying, she forced Mab back into the storeroom and I followed at her heels, the possibilities whirling inside my head. The Malkins would still be down there but they would be heading for the sepulchre entrance and might be well away by the time we reached it. It gave us half a chance. Better than staying here, at the mercy of the Mouldheels.

Ellie was on her knees beside Jack, who was breathing heavily, his eyes closed. Mary was clutching at her mother's skirts, close to tears.

'Quick, Ellie, you'll have to help me,' I said softly. 'There's more danger ahead. We need to go back down the tunnels as fast as we can. You'll have to help me carry Jack.'

Ellie looked up at me, her expression a mixture of anguish and bewilderment. 'We can't move him again, Tom. Not down there. It's too much to ask. He's too ill – he won't be able to stand it—'

'We've got to, Ellie. We've no choice.'

Mab started to laugh but Alice pulled her hair sharply.

As I moved to grasp Jack under the arms, Ellie shook her head and fell across his chest, using the weight of her body to prevent me from trying to lift him. Desperate, I considered telling her about the threat to her daughter. It was the only thing I could think of to get her moving.

But I said nothing. It was already too late. The Mouldheels were already coming into the room – a dozen of them at least, amongst them Mab's sisters, Beth and Jennet. The group formed a circle about us, staring at us with cold, pitiless eyes, ready to use their blades.

Alice looked at me, her own eyes full of despair. I shrugged hopelessly and she released Mab.

'I should kill you now,' Mab said to Alice, almost spitting the words out. 'But a bargain's a bargain. Once the trunks are open you can leave with the rest. Now, Tom, it's up to you . . .'

I shook my head. 'I won't do it, Mab,' I said. 'The trunks belong to me.'

Mab leaned forward, grabbed Mary by the arm and dragged her away from her mother. Beth threw her a knife and she caught it expertly and held it towards the child's throat. As the little girl began to cry, her face filled with anguish, Ellie ran at Mab but didn't manage more than two steps before she was flung to the floor and pinned there, a knee in her back.

'Give me the keys or I'll take the child's life now!' Mab commanded.

I lifted my staff, measuring the distance between us. But I knew I couldn't strike quickly enough. And what if I did? The others would be on me in seconds.

'Give them the keys, Tom!' screamed Ellie. 'For pity's sake don't let them hurt her!'

I had a duty to the County, and because of that responsibility I'd already risked the lives of Ellie's family by refusing before. But this was too much. Mary was now screaming hysterically, more upset by the plight of her mother than by the threat from the knife. Mab was going to kill her while I watched, and I couldn't bear it. I let the staff fall from my hands. I bowed my head, sick with despair.

'Don't hurt her, Mab,' I pleaded. 'Please don't hurt her. Don't hurt any of them. Let them all go and I'll give you the keys . . .'

Alice, Ellie and Mary were taken out of the tower and escorted towards the distant trees; two of the witches carried Jack between them like a sack of potatoes. After I'd agreed to surrender the keys, Alice hadn't spoken again. Her face was a blank. I'd no idea what she was thinking.

'They'll stay under guard in the wood,' Mab said. 'They can go free when the trunks are open and not a moment before. But you're not going anywhere. You're staying here, Tom. And we'll be cosy without Alice – that Malkin/Deane cross-breed – getting in our way. Well then, give me the keys and let's get started . . .'

I didn't argue. I felt helpless. The whole situation was a nightmare that I couldn't find my way out of. I'd let down the County, the Spook and my mam. With a heavy heart I pulled the keys from my neck and gave them to her. She walked across to the trunks and I followed, standing meekly at her side. Only Beth and Jennet had stayed in the room with us, but more armed Mouldheels were just outside, guarding the door.

'Which one should I open first?' Mab asked, smiling at me sideways.

I shrugged.

'Three trunks and three of us,' Beth called out from behind. 'That's one each. You choose quick, Mab, then we can open ours. My turn next.'

'Why should I go last?' Jennet complained.

'Don't worry,' Beth replied. 'If I choose wrong, you might get the best.'

'No!' Mab hissed, whirling to face her sisters. 'All three trunks belong to me. If you're lucky, I might give you a gift each. Now, be quiet and don't spoil it for me. I've worked hard to get these.'

The twins flinched away from Mab's hostile gaze and she turned her attention back to the trunks. Suddenly she knelt and inserted one of the three small keys into the lock of the central trunk. She wriggled the key about but it wouldn't turn, and with a frown of annoyance she tried another trunk. When that also failed to unlock, Jennet giggled.

'Third time should do it, sister!' she taunted. 'Not your lucky day, is it?'

When even the third trunk failed to yield to the key, Mab came to her feet and faced me, her eyes blazing with anger. 'These the right keys?' she demanded. 'If this is a trick, you'll be more than sorry!'

'Try one of the other keys,' I suggested.

Mab did so, but the result was the same. 'Think I'm stupid?' she shouted; then her expression became cruel and she turned to Jennet. 'Go and bring the child here!'

'No,' I said. 'Please don't do that, Mab. Try the other key. Maybe that'll work . . .'

By now I was anxious and my palms began to sweat. It had been bad enough surrendering the keys in the first place. But if they wouldn't open the trunks, I knew that Mab's revenge would be terrible and that she'd start by hurting the child. What was wrong? I wondered if the trunks would only open if *I* held the key. Could that be possible?

Mab knelt again and tried the third key. The first two trunks again failed to open but, to my relief, the third gave a click and the key finally turned. She looked up with a smile of triumph and then slowly lifted the heavy wooden lid.

The trunk was full, but of what exactly it was not possible to see yet. A large piece of white material was neatly folded on top. Mab lifted it up, and as it unfurled, I saw that it was a dress. Suddenly I realized it was a wedding dress. Was it Mam's? It seemed likely. Why else would she keep it in her trunk?

'Too big for me, this is!' Mab said with a smirk, holding it up against her body, the hem trailing on the floor. 'What d'you think, Tom? Look rather fetching, don't I?'

She was holding the dress the wrong way round, the back facing towards me, and with a gasp I made out the line of buttons running from neck to hem. I'd no time to count them but I saw enough to suspect that they were made of bone. The last time I'd seen buttons like those they were on a dress worn by Meg Skelton, the lamia witch who'd lived with the Spook at Anglezarke. Was my mother's wedding gown fastened by bones like a lamia witch's dress?

Mab threw the dress towards Jennet. 'Gift for you, Jennet!' she called. 'You'll grow into it one day! Just have to be patient, that's all.'

Jennet caught it, screwing up her face in disgust.

'Don't want this old dress! You have it, Beth,' she said, passing it to her twin.

By now Mab had pulled a second item from the trunk. It was another garment. Again she held it against her body, trying it for size, even though it was evidently a man's shirt.

Instantly I guessed what it was: Dad's shirt – the one he'd used to shield Mam's body from the fierce rays of the sun when he'd found her bound to a rock with a silver chain – the chain that had been in my possession until Nowell had taken it from me. She'd saved the shirt in memory of what he'd done.

'This musty old shirt's your gift, Beth!' Mab called, throwing it towards her sister with a mocking laugh.

Of course, it was better than Mary being hurt, but it pained me to see Mam's things treated in that disrespectful way. Mam's life was in this trunk, and I'd wanted to sift through her things at my leisure rather than watching Mab paw them. And Tibb believed there was something of great importance here. Something that Mab might discover at any moment.

Mab now turned her attention back to the trunk, her eyes ranging greedily over its contents. There were jars and sealed bottles, each one labelled. Were they medicinal potions? Could there be something in there that might help Jack? Then there were lots of books of different sizes, all of them bound in leather. Some looked like diaries and I wondered if Mam had written them. One especially large volume drew my eye and made me want to pick it up. Could it be a record of her life with Dad on the farm? Or even an account of her life *before* they met?

There were also three large canvas bags tied at the neck with string. Mab lifted out one of these, and as she set it down on the floor, I heard the distinct clink of coins. Her eyes widened and she hastily untied the string and plunged her hand into the bag. When she brought it out again, there was a glint of gold: her hand was full of guineas.

'Must be a fortune here!' Mab said, her eyes almost bulging from their sockets with greed.

Quickly she checked the remaining two bags; they

too were full of gold coins – enough money to buy Jack's farm many times over. I'd never have guessed that Mam had so much money left.

'That's one bag each!' Beth exclaimed.

This time Mab didn't contradict her sister. Her eyes had returned to the trunk. 'Money's good to have,' she said, 'but I'd bet my life that there's something even better in here. Wonder if it's those books? Could be lots of knowledge here – spells and things. Wurmalde wanted these trunks badly. She wanted your mam's power. So there's got to be something in here well worth having!'

She chose the largest of the books, the one that had intrigued me, and pulled it from the trunk, but when she opened it at a random page, she began to frown. As she flicked through, the frown became deeper.

'It's all in a foreign language!' she exclaimed. 'Can't make head nor tail of it. Can you read this, Tom?' she demanded, thrusting the book towards me.

I knew before I looked that it wouldn't be in Latin because that was a language many witches were familiar with. It was Mam's book and, quite naturally, it was in her own language – Greek. The language she'd taught me from a very early age.

'No,' I said, trying to sound convincing. 'Can't make any sense of it at all . . .'

But at that moment a small envelope fell out of the pages and spun to the floor. Mab stooped and picked it up, holding it out for me to see before tearing it open.

To my youngest son, Thomas J. Ward

She screwed up the envelope and tossed it away before unfolding the letter. She frowned again and held it out towards me.

'It's not good enough, Tom,' she said with a sneer. 'Getting into bad ways, you are. First you won't keep to a bargain and now you're telling lies. Thought better of you. This letter's written in the same language as the book. Why would a mother write to her son in a language he didn't understand? Better tell me what it says. Otherwise the others won't be going anywhere –

except to their graves!'

I accepted the letter and began to read, the words as clear to me as if they were written in my own language.

Dear Tom,

This trunk was intended to be the first to yield to the keys.

The other trunks can be opened only in moonlight and only by your own hand. Within them my sisters sleep, and only the kiss of the moon can restore them to wakefulness. Do not fear them. They will know that you are of my blood and will watch over you, if necessary. giving their lives so that you may live.

Soon the dark made flesh will walk

the earth once more. But you are my own hopes made flesh and, whatever the cost in the short term, you have the will and strength to triumph in the end.

Just be true to your conscience and follow your instincts. I hope that one day we will meet again, but whatever happens, remember that I will always be proud of you.

Mam

CHAPTER 17
MOONLIGHT

'Well! What does it say?' Mab demanded.

I hesitated but I was thinking fast. Mam's sisters? What sort of sisters slept in trunks like these? And how long had they been there? Since Mam came to the County and married Dad all those years ago? She must have brought her sisters back with her from Greece!

And I'd seen something very much like this before, back in Anglezarke. Lamias. There were two kinds of lamia witches – the domestic and the feral. The first category had been like Meg Skelton, the Spook's true love: identical to a human woman but for a line of green and yellow scales running the length of her back. The second type were like Meg's sister, Marcia: they scuttled about on four limbs, were covered in scales and drank blood. Some could even fly short distances. Could it be that Mam was a lamia, domestic and benign? After all, Greece was the homeland of Meg and Marcia too. The feral Marcia had been returned home in a coffin so as not to terrify the other passengers on the boat – the Spook had used a potion to make her sleep on the journey. He'd used the same potion to make Meg sleep for months at a time.

Then I remembered how Mam used to go up to her special room once a month. She went alone and I never asked what she did there. Had she been talking to her sisters then putting them back to sleep in some way? I felt pretty sure that they must be feral lamias. Perhaps the two of them together would be a match for Mab and the other Mouldheels.

'Come on, I'm waiting!' Mab snapped. 'My patience is running out fast.'

'It says that the other trunks can only be opened in moonlight and that *I* must turn the key.'

'Does it say what's inside?'

'No hint at all, Mab,' I lied. 'But it must be something special and more valuable than what we've already found in this trunk. Otherwise they wouldn't be more difficult to get into.'

Mab looked at me suspiciously so I kept talking to distract her. 'What happened to the other smaller boxes that were in Mam's room?' I demanded. There had been lots of other boxes, all taken by the witches who'd raided the farm.

'Oh, them . . . Heard they were full of rubbish – cheap brooches and ornaments, that's all. The Malkins shared 'em out amongst their clan.'

I shook my head sadly. 'That's not right. They belonged to me. I had a right to see them.'

'Just feel lucky that you're still alive,' Mab said.

'Will you let Alice and my family go now?' I pressed her.

'I'll think about it . . .'

'Jack's ill – he must have help. They need a horse and cart to get him to a doctor as quickly as possible. If he dies, I'll never open the trunks for you. Come on, Mab, keep your word. You've already got one trunk and I'll open the other two tonight, as soon as the moon comes up. Please.'

Mab stared hard into my eyes for a moment, then turned to her sisters. 'Go and tell the others to let them go.'

Jennet and Beth hesitated.

'He needs that cart, Mab. He can't walk,' I persisted.

Mab nodded. 'Then he shall have it. Just see that you keep your word. Go on, jump to it!' she snapped, turning to her sisters. 'And tell 'em to hurry those masons up!'

'Masons?' I asked as Beth and Jennet left to do their sister's bidding.

'Masons to fix the wall. The Malkins are finished here. This tower belongs to us now. Times have changed. We rule Pendle now!'

Within an hour a team of four masons had arrived and set to, repairing the wall. The men seemed nervous and were clearly working under duress. They obviously wanted to get the job over and done with as quickly as possible and displayed great strength, energy and dexterity in heaving the heavy stones back into position.

Others from the clan went down the steps under orders to secure the lower regions of the tower. They were soon back, reporting that, as expected, the Malkins had left the lower dungeons and escaped through the tunnel. Mab gave orders for guards to stay down there on watch. When the Malkins found out that the soldiers had left the vicinity, they might try to return.

Before nightfall the breach in the wall had been repaired, but Mab had one more job for the masons. She made them carry the two heavy locked trunks up the narrow steps and onto the battlements above. That done, they left hurriedly and the drawbridge was lowered, sealing us within the tower.

In addition to Mab and her sisters there were another ten witches, who made up the numbers of the coven. But there were also four older women, whose job was to cook and carry for the rest. They made a thin potato and carrot soup, and despite the fact that the members of a witch clan had made it, I accepted a plateful. But fearing poison or some potion that would place me under Mab's control, I checked that it was ladled from the same cooking pot as everyone else's. When they had started, I dunked bread into it and began to eat.

After supper I would have liked to start sorting through Mam's trunk but Mab would have none of it and ordered me to keep away. 'You'll get your fill of them trunks before you're finished,' she told me. 'Months it's going to take you, to translate all those books . . .'

Soon after sunset, carrying a lantern, Mab led me up towards the battlements, Beth and Jennet at my heels. At the top of the steps we passed into another room with a wooden floor, in which the mechanism for controlling the drawbridge was housed. It consisted of a large wooden capstan wheel with a system of wooden cogs and gears and a ratchet attached to a chain. Turning the wheel would wrap the chain around it and raise the bridge.

Beyond that we emerged onto the flagged battlements, which provided a good view on all sides. Pendle Hill rose high above the trees of Crow Wood and, because of the meadowland between the tower and the edge of those encircling trees, nobody could approach unseen. The gunners had gone off to war and now the tower was in the hands of the Mouldheels, theoretically unassailable. But then I glanced towards the trunks. Little did they know what waited within.

As it grew dark, the lantern seemed to grow brighter. I knew that the moon would already be above the horizon, but there was a stiff breeze from the west, driving low rainclouds across the sky. It might be some time before moonlight fell upon the trunks, if at all.

'Looks like rain, Mab,' I told her. 'Might have to wait until tomorrow night.'

Mab sniffed the air and shook her head. 'Moon'll show its face soon enough,' she said. 'Until then, we'll wait up here.'

I stared out into the darkness, listening to the distant

whine of the wind through the trees, thinking of all that had happened in the few days since we'd reached Pendle. Where was the Spook now? And what could he hope to do against the power of the witch clans? Poor Father Stocks was dead, and my master couldn't hope to shift the Mouldheels from Malkin Tower alone, never mind deal with the others – especially the Malkins. And he didn't even know yet about the existence of Wurmalde, who was a real puzzle. How did she fit into the complex society of the Pendle witches? She'd talked about taking revenge on Mam, but what exactly was she trying to achieve in Pendle?

I glanced at Mab, who was staring up at the night sky. 'You've done well, Mab,' I flattered her, hoping to get her talking so that I could learn more about what we faced. 'You've beaten the Malkins. And even with the help of the Deanes they'll never be able to get you out of this tower. It's yours for ever now.'

'It's been a long time coming,' Mab agreed, looking at me a little suspiciously. 'But I saw my chance and I made it happen. With your help, Tom. We're a good team, me and you, don't you think?'

I wasn't sure what she was driving at. Surely she couldn't be taking a shine to me. Not me, a Spook's apprentice. No, it had to be fascination and glamour she was trying to use on me. I decided to ignore her and change the subject.

'What do you know of Wurmalde?' I asked.

'Wurmalde!' Mab said, spitting onto the flags. 'She's nothing but an incomer. A meddler, she is, and the first who'll get bad things happening to her. I'll sort her.'

'But why would she come here when she's not from one of the clans? What does she want?'

'She's a loner. Don't come from a good witch clan herself so attaches herself to others. And for some reason she wants to be in this county and to raise the power of the dark – to strike out at you and your mam, I think. She's mentioned your mam; really seems to hate her for some reason.'

'I think they knew each other back in Greece,' I said.

'Your mam a witch?' Mab asked me directly.

'Of course not,' I said, but I wasn't convincing myself,

let alone Mab. Powers, potions, bone buttons and now two feral lamia 'sisters'. I was starting to believe deep down that my mother was indeed a lamia witch – a benign, domesticated one, but a witch nonetheless.

'You sure about that?' asked Mab. 'Just seems to me that Wurmalde's pretty interested in the power of your mam's trunks, and your mam seems to have been very clever at stopping anyone getting into them. How could she do that if she wasn't a witch?'

I ignored her.

'Don't worry,' Mab teased. 'Nothing to be ashamed of, being related to a witch.'

'My mother's not a witch,' I protested.

'So you say, dearie,' she said, making it obvious she didn't believe a word of it. 'Well, whatever your mam is, she's Wurmalde's enemy, and Wurmalde wants the three covens to join together at Lammas to raise Old Nick and destroy you and all your mother's hopes, I think. But don't fret, the Mouldheels won't be part of it, not us. No, not despite all her attempts to persuade us. We've left 'em to their folly. Going too far, it is,' she said, shaking her head furiously. 'Too much of a risk.'

Mab fell silent but now I was really curious. I wanted to know what she meant about 'going too far'.

'A risk? What do you mean by that?' I asked.

It was Beth who answered for her sister. 'Because once you done that, there's no going back and he's in the world to stay. And you might not be able to control him. That's the big risk you take. Once Old Nick gets back into the world, there's no end to the mischief he might do. Got a mind of his own, Nick has. Lose control of him and he could make us suffer too.'

'But don't the Malkins and Deanes know that?' I asked.

'Of course they do!' Mab snapped. 'That's why they want us to join 'em. First of all, if three clans work together there's more chance of raising Old Nick in the first place. Then, if it's successful, with three covens working together we might be able to keep him in check. But it's still a risk, and the others are fools to be taken in by Wurmalde's promises of increased power and darkness. And why should I work with them anyway? As I said, the Mouldheels are the power in Pendle now, so let the others go to the Devil!'

For a moment there was silence as we both stared into the darkness, until suddenly the moon came out from behind a cloud. It was a thin crescent, a waning moon with horns facing towards the west. The light was pale but it shone on the trunks, casting their shadows across the battlements.

Mab held out the keys and pointed to the nearer trunk. 'Keep your promise, Tom,' she said softly. 'You won't regret it. We could have a good life here – you and me.'

She smiled at me and her eyes glittered like stars, her hair gleaming with an unearthly silver light. It was only moonlight, I knew that, but for a moment she was radiant. Although I understood exactly what she was trying to do, I could still feel the power she was exerting. Glamour and fascination were being used against me: Mab was trying to bind me to her will. Not only did she want me to open the trunks; she wanted me to do it willingly and happily.

I smiled back and accepted the keys. Her efforts were wasted. I was already both willing and happy to open the two trunks. And she was about to get the biggest surprise of her life.

Apart from the largest key, the one that opened the door to my room back at the farm, they appeared identical. But the second one I tried opened the lock with a click. I took a deep breath and slowly raised the lid. Inside the trunk, folded back upon itself, was something large. It was wrapped in a piece of sail-cloth and bound with string. Instinctively I placed my hand on the upper surface, expecting to feel movement, but then I remembered that the creature within would sleep until touched by the light of the moon.

'There's something big in here, Mab,' I said. 'I'll need a hand to lift it out. But I'll open the other trunk first and see what's inside that . . .'

Whether Mab agreed or not, I was already trying to open the second trunk. If they were indeed feral lamias, then one would surely be enough to see off the Mouldheels. But I wanted them both awake to make absolutely sure. I raised the second lid . . .

'Same thing here, Mab. Let's lift them both out.'

Mab didn't look too sure but Beth leaned forward eagerly and we heaved the long heavy bundle from the trunk and placed it on the flags. Stretched out, it was about one and a half times the length of my own body. Jennet, not to be outdone, helped me with the second trunk. That completed, I smiled up at Mab.

'Cut through the string, Jennet,' I said.

Jennet pulled her knife from her belt and obliged, and I started to unwrap the sail-cloth. I'd almost finished when disaster struck!

The moon went behind a cloud.

Mab brought the lantern across and held it at my shoulder. My heart sank, my confidence evaporating. I hesitated, hoping that the moon would come out again. Would the Mouldheels know what a lamia was? They might have heard of them, but hopefully, as lamia witches weren't native to the County, they wouldn't have seen one in the feral state. But if they did guess correctly, the two dormant creatures would be at the three sisters' mercy. Once they'd used their blades, the kiss of the moon would come too late.

'Hurry up, Tom!' Mab ordered impatiently. 'Let's see what we have here . . .'

When I didn't move, she reached down and snatched back the cloth, immediately giving a little gasp.

'What's this then? Never seen anything like this before!' she exclaimed.

I'd been face to face with Marcia, Meg Skelton's feral sister. I remembered well her cruel face, white and bloated, with red blood dribbling from her chin. I also remembered her long greasy hair, scaly back and four limbs ending in sharp claws. This creature was larger than Marcia. I was pretty sure that it was a feral lamia, but not the kind that just scuttled about on the ground. This was the other type, which I'd never seen before. The one that could fly short distances. It had black feathered wings folded across its back and also short feathers on its upper body.

Additionally there were four limbs: the heavier lower two had sharp, deadly claws; but, by contrast, the upper limbs were much more like human arms, with delicate hands, and nails hardly longer than a woman's. The creature was stretched out face-down but its head was turned towards us so that half the face was visible. The visible eye was closed but wasn't as heavy-lidded as Marcia's. In fact, it seemed to me that the face was attractive, with a kind of wild beauty, though there was more than a hint of cruelty about the mouth; the lower body of the creature was covered in black scales, each one coming to a fine point like a hair, the whole effect making me think of an insect.

As I said, the black wings were folded across the back, and where they met was a hint of something lighter beneath. I suspected that, like some insects, the lamia had double wings. Four wings in all, the lighter pair beneath protected by the heavier defensive armour of the outer two.

Mab sniffed loudly three times. 'Dead, it looks. Dry and dead. But it don't smell that way. Something odd here. A mystery. Are they just in a deep sleep?'

'There must be a reason for this, Mab,' I said, desperate to buy time. 'It's a puzzle to me too. No doubt we'll find the answers in those books we found in the other chest. But it's my guess that the other one is the same. That they're both familiars. Think how useful it would be to have something like this doing your bidding! Not a bad exchange for just surrendering a little of your blood . . .'

'Wouldn't like to think how much blood this thing here would expect,' Mab said, looking at me doubtfully and moving the lantern back a little way so the creature's face was in shadow once more. 'Put 'em back in the trunks,' she said, looking at her sisters. 'Hurry up, Beth. And you help her, Jennet. They're horrible things and I don't like the look of 'em one bit. Feel much better once they're safely back under lock and key.'

Obediently Beth seized the edge of the canvas, no doubt intending to wrap up the creature before putting it back in the trunk. But at that moment the moon came out, and instantly the lamia's visible eye opened wide.

It seemed to look straight at me before giving a sort of shudder and coming up slowly onto its four limbs.

The twins squealed in fear and ran back towards the hatch. Mab merely stepped away cautiously, pulling the blade from her belt and holding it at the ready.

The lamia's head turned towards me so that I could see both its eyes. Then it sniffed very loudly before turning back towards the three sisters. By now, Beth was already scrambling through the hatch, Jennet close behind. The creature shook itself very deliberately, like a dog ridding itself of water droplets after emerging from a river, then glared towards Mab.

'You didn't see this, Mab, did you?' I shouted.

'You knew, didn't you?' she accused. 'You read what was in the trunks but didn't tell me! How could you, Tom? How could you do it? How could you betray me?'

'I opened the trunks. I kept my word and I hope you like what you see,' I said quietly, trying to control my anger. How could she accuse me of betraying her when I'd been forced to do her bidding? I began to tremble, remembering how she'd held the knife against Mary's throat, and suddenly my words came out in a rush of anger.

'All three trunks belong to me! That's the truth and you know it. And now you've lost the trunks and lost control of this tower too. You didn't rule Pendle for long,' I jibed, hearing my own voice ugly with mockery. Instantly I regretted having rubbed salt into the wound. There was no need to speak like that. Dad wouldn't have liked it.

The lamia took a step towards Mab and she took two hurried steps backwards. 'You'll be sorry for this,' she threatened, her voice low but filled with venom. 'I actually cared about you, and now you've let me down! So you give me no choice! No choice at all. We *will* join up with the other clans and do what Wurmalde wants. She wants you dead. Wants to hurt your mam and thwart her plans. Wants to stop you becoming a spook. And now I'm going to help her! See how you like it when Old Nick hunts you down! See how you feel when we send him after you!'

The lamia advanced again, its movements slow and deliberate, and panic animated Mab's face. She gave a scream of terror and dropped both blade and lantern before scrambling down through the hatch after her sisters.

Wasting no time, I walked forward, picked up the fallen blade and used it to cut the string that bound the other long bundle before quickly unwrapping the sail-cloth to allow moonlight to fall upon the creature within. Moments later both lamias were fully alert. They looked at me searchingly but I couldn't read the expression in their eyes. I was suddenly very nervous, my mouth becoming dry. What if they didn't know me? What if Mam was wrong?

Could these really be my aunts? Mam's sisters? I remembered my Aunt Martha, on Dad's side, a kindly old lady with red cheeks and a ready smile. She was dead now but I recalled her with fondness. These creatures couldn't be more different! And yes, I had to admit it: this meant that Mam must be a lamia too.

What had happened? Could Mam's sisters have stayed feral while she slowly shape-shifted into the domestic form, benign and kind? She'd been human in shape when Dad first met her. He'd been a sailor, his ship calling at a port in Greece. When he'd found her bound with a silver chain, her hand had also been nailed to the rock. Who'd done that and why? Did it have something to do with Wurmalde?

Afterwards Mam'd taken Dad back with her to a house with a walled garden. They'd lived there happily for a while, but some nights Mam's two sisters had come to visit. Then I realized that my first guess was wrong. Dad had said they were tall, fierce-looking women. They'd seemed angry with him. He thought that was why Mam had insisted that they leave Greece and make their home in the County – to get away from her sisters.

However, unknown to him, they must have been placed in those trunks when they were still domestic. Then they must have slowly shape-shifted back to the feral because they'd been deprived of human contact, dormant for years and years. It all seemed to point to that. I remembered something else that Mam had once said to me:

None of us are either all good or all bad – we're all some-

where in between – but there comes a moment in each life when we take an important step, either towards the light or towards the dark . . . maybe it's because of a special person we meet. Because of what your dad did for me I stepped in the right direction and that's why I'm here today.

Had Mam perhaps not always been good? Had meeting Dad changed her? As my mind whirled with those thoughts, the two lamias turned away and headed for the open hatch, dropping through it in turn. I followed more slowly, first picking up the lantern that Mab had discarded. I climbed down into the wooden room that housed the device for lowering the drawbridge and looked through the second hatch into the vast living area below.

The air was full of screams but they were coming from the storeroom into which the Mouldheels had fled; they were no doubt trying to escape by climbing through the other hatch into the first section of the tower below ground. I began to descend the spiral of steps towards the floor.

By the time I reached ground level, the screams and

shouts were distant, fading away by the second. But there was a trail of blood that led from one of the tables near the wall into the storeroom. I wondered which of the witches was the victim and walked towards the door slowly, reluctant to face what I might find there.

However, I saw that the storeroom was already empty. I walked across and peered down through the hatch. It was dark, but in the distance I could see the bobbing lights of lanterns against the walls as the Mouldheels fled down the spiral steps, and the vast space echoed with faint screams. I lifted my own lantern and peered down. The trail of blood continued beyond the hatch. The eye of a lamia glittered, reflecting back the light. She was dragging something down the steps. It was a body. I couldn't see the face – just legs and bare feet slowly receding downwards.

The Mouldheels belonged to the dark but I felt sorry for the dead victim below. And I didn't feel good about betraying Mab, even though I'd done it for the sake of the County. But what if she was right? What if she did escape the lamias and unite with the other clans to spite me? Had I just put myself, my family and all the County in even greater danger?

I closed the hatch and turned away, sickened. I would have locked it if I could but Alice still had my special key. I trusted Mam. I knew that I'd nothing to fear from the lamias. They were family, and I had their blood in my veins. But I still didn't want them near me. I wasn't ready to face who I was just yet.

CHAPTER 18
JAMES THE BLACKSMITH

It was a long night. I tried to sleep, hoping to blot out for a while everything that had happened, but it was useless, and finally I went back up onto the battlements and waited for the sun to come up.

It seemed to me that I was safe enough in the tower. The drawbridge was up, the breach in the wall had been repaired and the two lamias would prevent either the Mouldheels or the Malkins coming back through the tunnels and up into the tower. But I needed to know how Jack was.

If only I could bring him and his family into the safety of the tower . . . And one of the potions in the first trunk might well be able to help him. I wanted to see the Spook too – to warn him about Wurmalde and tell him everything that had happened; but even more urgently I had to talk to Alice. She knew where I was, and if news reached her about what had happened, she might come back to the tower. She would be able to look through the potions and perhaps work out which one to use. It was dangerous out there and my courage was faint, but I knew that if Alice hadn't come to the tower the next day, then I would have to go and look for her.

The sun came up and climbed into a sky which was clear, without even a hint of cloud. The morning wore on, but apart from the crows and the occasional distant glimpse of deer or rabbits, the clearing between the trees and the tower was empty of life. In a way, as the rhyme says, I was 'king of the castle'. But it meant nothing. I was lonely and afraid and I didn't see how life would ever get back to normal. Would Magistrate Nowell eventually come back and demand that I surrender? If I refused, would he bring the constable and lay siege to the tower again?

By the afternoon my appetite had returned and I went down into the living area again. The fire was still smouldering so I stoked up the embers and started to bake jacket potatoes for my breakfast. I ate them straight from the fire, too hot to hold for more than a second at a time. I burned my mouth a little but they were delicious and the pain was worth it. It made me realize how little I'd eaten since arriving in Pendle.

I found my rowan staff in a corner and sat for a while holding it across my knee. Somehow it made me feel better. I thought of the silver chain that had been confiscated by Nowell. I wanted it back – I needed it for my work. But at least Mam's trunks were back in my possession. I still felt weary and afraid but decided that, after nightfall, I'd have to set off and find Alice or the Spook. Under cover of darkness I'd have more chance of evading capture – either by witches or the constable and his men. I wouldn't be able to use the drawbridge: once I'd let it down and left the tower there'd be nobody there to raise it again and any of the witches could easily get in. So I'd have to leave by the tunnel and risk an encounter with the wight. That decided, I pushed some more spuds into the fire for my supper and went up to the battlements to spy out the lie of the land.

I waited and watched, gathering my courage as the sun sank towards the horizon. After about half an hour or so I glimpsed a movement in the trees. Three people emerged from the wood and began to walk towards the drawbridge. My heart leaped with hope. One was the Spook, clearly identifiable from his staff and cloak. He was carrying two bags and walked purposefully, a gait that I could always recognize from a distance.

The person to his left was Alice – there was no doubt about that – but at first I didn't recognize his other companion, who was carrying something over his shoulder. He was a big man, and as he drew closer, I felt there was something familiar about his gait too; the way his shoulders rolled as he strode out. Then, suddenly, I recognized him.

It was my brother James!

I hadn't seen James for almost three years and he'd

changed a lot. As he approached, I could see that the blacksmith's trade had put muscle on him and he was broader at the shoulder. His hair had receded from his forehead somewhat but his face glowed with health and he looked in his prime. And he was carrying a huge blacksmith's hammer.

I waved furiously from the tower. Alice saw me first and waved back. I saw her say something to James and he immediately grinned and waved as well. But the Spook just continued walking, his face grim. At last the three of them halted in front of the moat, facing the raised drawbridge.

'Come on, lad!' the Spook shouted up, gesturing impatiently with his staff. 'Don't dawdle. We haven't got all day! Get that bridge down and let us in!'

It proved easier said than done. The good news was that the heavy capstan, which seemed designed for two to operate, not just one, had a ratchet system. That meant that as I turned it, releasing the chains, the weight of the bridge didn't spin the wheel more than an eighth of a turn at a time before the ratchet stopped the cog turning. Otherwise it would have whirled out of control, breaking my arms or worse.

Lowering the drawbridge was only half the battle. Next I had to open the big rusty iron-studded door. But as soon as I'd drawn back the heavy bolts, it began to grind on its hinges. Moments later James heaved it wide open, threw down his hammer and got his arms around me, squeezing me so hard that I thought my ribs might break.

'It's good to see you, Tom! It's really good. I wondered if I'd ever see any of you again,' he said, holding me at arm's length and giving me a huge grin. James had broken his nose badly in a farm accident and it was now squashed back against his face, giving him a roguish appearance. It was a face with 'character', as Dad used to say, and never had I been more happy to see it.

'There'll be time for talk later,' said the Spook, entering the tower, Alice at his heels. 'But first things first, James. Get that door closed and bolted and raise that bridge. Then we can afford to relax for a bit. Well, what have we here . . . ?'

He paused to glance down at the trail of blood that led into the storeroom and raised his eyebrows.

'It's Mouldheel blood. Mam's sisters were in two of the trunks,' I said. 'They're feral lamias . . .'

The Spook nodded but didn't look too surprised. Had he known all along? I began to wonder.

'Well, word came to us that the Mouldheels had fled down the tunnels soon after the Malkins, but we didn't know why,' he said. 'So this explains it. Where are the lamias now?'

'Down below,' I said, gesturing with my thumb.

James had closed the big wooden door and thrust home the bolts. 'Mechanism for the bridge up there, Tom?' he asked, gesturing upwards.

'Through the trapdoor and on the left,' I said and, giving me a quick smile, James ran up the steps two at a time.

'You all right, Tom?' enquired Alice. 'Got help for Jack then came here as soon as we could.'

'I feel better now you three are here but I've had a

few scary moments, to say the least. How is Jack?'

'Safe enough for now. He and Ellie and Mary are in good hands. Did my bit too, just in case. Brewed him up something else, I did. Still unconscious, but his breathing's much better and there's colour in his cheeks now. Physically, he seems much stronger.'

'Where is he? At Downham?'

'No, Tom. It was too far to take him and I wanted to get back here and see if I could help you. Jack's at Roughlee with one of my aunts—'

I looked at Alice with dismay and astonishment. Roughlee was the Deane village. 'A Deane! You've left my family with a Deane?'

I looked across at my master but he just raised his eyebrows.

'Aunt Agnes isn't like the rest,' said Alice. 'She ain't all bad. Always got on well, we have. Her second name's Sowerbutts and she once lived in Whalley, but when her husband died, she came back to Roughlee. She keeps to herself. Her cottage is on the outskirts of the village and none of the others will even know your family's there. Trust me, Tom. It was the best I could do. It'll be all right.'

I wasn't happy, but as Alice concluded, there came the sound of the capstan turning and the bridge being raised. We waited in silence until James came down the steps again.

'We've a lot to say to each other so let's settle ourselves down,' said the Spook. 'Over there by the fire looks as good a place as any . . .'

He helped himself to a chair and pulled it up close to the flames. James did likewise but Alice and I sat down on the floor on the other side of the fire.

'Wouldn't mind one o' those spuds, Tom,' said Alice. 'Ain't smelled anything that good for days!'

'Those'll be ready soon and I'll do a few more . . .'

'I've sampled your cooking before so I'm not sure that's such a good idea,' said the Spook dryly, making his customary jibe. But despite that, I knew he'd enjoy a baked potato, even if he suffered a few singed fingers. So I went into the storeroom and came back with an armful of spuds and began to push them into the

337

embers of the fire with a stick.

'While you've been getting yourself into serious trouble, I've been busy myself,' said the Spook. 'I have my own way of sniffing things out and there are always one or two folk who aren't afraid to speak up and tell the truth.

'It seems that since last Halloween, emissaries of the Deanes have been slowly moving in on Downham village to plant their evil and terrorize the good folk. Most villagers were too terrified to warn Father Stocks who, apart from the thefts from the graveyard, had no idea that things had deteriorated so far. Fear is a terrible thing. Who can blame them when their children are threatened? When their sheep waste away before their eyes and their livelihood's in jeopardy? By the end of the summer the whole place would have belonged to that witch clan. As you know, lad, I like to work alone – apart from my apprentice, that is – but this wasn't the time for it.

'I tried to rouse the menfolk to action but I was making heavy weather of it. As you know, most people fear our trade and the villagers were too nervous even to open their doors to me. But then your brother James arrived and, after first talking man to man with Matt Finley, the Downham blacksmith, he was able to make them realize the grave danger to themselves and their families. Finally some of the village men gathered in support. I'll spare you the details but we cleared out the Deanes, root and branch, and they won't be coming back for a long time, if at all!'

I glanced at Alice but she showed no reaction to all this talk of the Deanes.

'As a result of all that,' continued my master, 'I got your note very late, lad. Too late to help. We set off for Read and met up with Alice, who'd been waiting for us on the outskirts of the laund. Together we travelled here to Crow Wood. Poor Father Stocks,' he said, shaking his head sadly. 'He was a good apprentice and a loyal friend to me. He didn't deserve to die like that . . .'

'I'm sorry, Mr Gregory,' I said. 'There was nothing I could do to save him. Tibb took his blood but then

Wurmalde killed him with a knife—' The memory of Father Stocks lying murdered on the bed returned so vividly that I almost choked on my words. 'She acts like the mistress of the house – she controls Master Nowell as well. She blamed me for the murder; he believes everything she tells him and was going to send me off to Caster to hang as soon as the tower was breached. He'll be after me again. And who's going to believe me?' I asked, getting more frightened by the second at the thought that I might still be taken off to Caster Castle.

'Calm yourself, lad. Hanging's the least of your worries! Word has it that Master Nowell and Constable Barnes have both gone missing. I suspect that neither will be in any condition to press charges.'

Suddenly I remembered what the housekeeper had said to me in the cell at Read Hall: 'Wurmalde told me that Nowell would be dead within days and that the whole district would be in their hands.'

'The first might well be true,' said the Spook, 'but not the second. This land of ours may be at war but we've a battle or two of our own to fight yet. It's not over by any means – not while I've breath still left in my body. We're probably already too late to save the magistrate but we can still deal with Wurmalde – whoever she is . . .'

'She's an old enemy of Mam's, as I told you in my letter,' I said. 'She's the driving force behind what they're going to attempt at Lammas. She wants to destroy all the good that Mam's fought for. She wants to kill me, prevent me from being a spook and then plunge the County into darkness. That's why she wanted Mam's trunks. She probably thinks they contain the source of Mam's power. And it's her idea to raise the Fiend. Mab had refused to join with the other clans, but just before the lamias chased her and her clan from the tower, she got angry and said that she was going to join with the Malkins and Deanes; that she was going to help Wurmalde.'

The Spook scratched at his beard thoughtfully. 'Looks like we've paid a high price for driving them from this tower. Keeping the clans apart is our main objective so these trunks have cost us dear. It seems to me that Wurmalde is the key to all this. Once we settle with her, there's half a chance the whole scheme will just fall apart. The witch clans have always been at each other's throats. With her gone it'll be back to normal. It's just three days to Lammas so we've little time to waste. We need to carry the fight to her. We'll strike where and when she least expects it.

'Then, win or lose, we'll turn our attention to the witches' sabbath and try to halt the ceremony. James finally convinced the villagers at Downham that the futures of their families depended on them helping us, so they promised to lend a hand. They were feeling brave at the time, fresh from driving out the Deanes, but a few days have passed since then and reflecting on the danger might have lessened their commitment – though I'm sure some will keep their promise. Well, lad,' said the Spook, staring into the embers and rubbing his hands, 'where are those baked potatoes? I'm as ravenous as a wolf so I might as well risk one after all!'

The new ones weren't ready yet but I used a stick to drag one I'd cooked for myself out of the embers. I picked it up and quickly tossed it towards my master. He caught it deftly and I tried not to smile too much as he started passing it from hand to hand to stop his fingers burning.

And despite all the bad things that had happened, I could afford to grin. I'd already had more than one piece of good news. Ellie and her child were safe and Jack, if not recovered, seemed to be improving. And perhaps I wouldn't be taken to Caster after all.

But there was something I hadn't told the Spook. Not believing in prophecy, he would only have been annoyed. Mam had said in her letter that the dark made flesh would soon walk the earth. By that she meant the Fiend. Mam had been right before. If she was right this time, then we would fail to break up the Lammas Sabbath, leaving the Devil loosed into the world.

It soon grew dark outside and as we ate, bathed in the light and warmth of the fire, I felt better than I had for days. At least Mam had balanced her dark words

343

with optimism. I couldn't understand how I'd find the strength to stand up to the Devil, but I had to trust in what she believed.

After about an hour it was decided that we should get some rest; with everything that had happened and the excitement of seeing James, Alice and the Spook again, I knew I wouldn't be able to sleep, so I volunteered to keep watch. In any case it was better that I was alert in case the two lamias came sniffing around. I was confident that James and I wouldn't be on the menu but I wasn't so sure about the others. At first I'd intended to tell James that they were his aunts, but the longer I thought about it, the less it seemed like a good idea. Despite over a year's training to be a spook, I still found it hard to deal with the idea that the two creatures were actually Mam's sisters. It would be much harder for James to cope with. So, on reflection, unless it proved absolutely necessary, I decided to keep it from him.

The Spook and Alice were soon fast asleep but after a while James stood up, put a finger to his lips and pointed away from the fire towards the far wall, where Mam's trunk was. I followed him over.

'I can't sleep, Tom,' he said. 'I just wondered if you'd like to talk for a while?'

'Of course I would, James. It's really good to see you. I'm just sorry things are this way. I keep thinking it's my fault,' I told him. 'Being apprenticed to a spook just seems to attract trouble. Ellie and Jack had been worried all along that something like this might happen—'

James shook his head. 'There's more to it than that, Tom. A lot more. Mam wanted you to take on that job. She wanted it more than anything else in the world. That's what she told me at Dad's funeral. And something else. She pulled me to one side and said that evil was growing in the world and that we'd have to fight it. She asked me, if the time came, to move back to the farm and give my support to Jack and his family. And I agreed.'

'You mean live there?' I asked.

James nodded. 'Why not? I've no real ties at Ormskirk.

There was a girl I grew fond of, but it came to nothing in the end. She married a local farmer last year and I was hurt for a while, but you have to move on. I could give Jack a bit of a hand with the farm when things are busy. I even thought we could build a forge behind the barn.'

'You'd get some work but not enough to live on,' I told him. 'There are *two* smiths working from Topley now. Everyone goes to them.'

'Thought I might try brewing some ale on the side as well. That's how Dad's farm got its original name.'

That was true enough. Once, long before Mam bought it for Dad, it had been called 'Brewer's Farm' and had supplied ale to the local farms and villages.

'But you don't know anything about brewing!' I protested.

'No, but I know good ale when I taste it!' James countered with a grin. 'I could learn, couldn't I? Who knows what can be achieved when you set your mind to it! What is it, Tom? You don't look that happy at the idea of me coming home to live. Is it that?'

'It's not that, James. It just worries me, that's all. The Pendle witches know where the farm is now. Whatever we do here, it won't be over. It'll never be over. I just don't want to see another brother hurt.'

'Well, it's what Mam wanted and I'm going to do it. I think the time she spoke of has already come; if there is some sort of enduring threat, then I think I should stand by my brother and his family. Anyways, it might be quite a while before Jack fully regains his strength. It's my duty – that's the way I see it, so my mind's made up.'

I nodded and smiled. I knew all about duty and I knew what my brother meant.

James pointed down at Mam's trunk. 'What have you found in there? Was it worth all the trouble?' he asked.

'I think so, James. The story of Mam's life is some-where inside this trunk – but it might take some time to work it all out. And there might just be something very powerful; something that we could use to fight the dark. It's got lots of her books in it – some look like

347

diaries; accounts from when we were children. There's money as well. Would you like to take a look?'

'Oh, yes, please, Tom, I'd really like that,' James said eagerly, so I lifted the lid.

As he stared at the contents of the trunk with wide eyes, I lifted out one of the bags of money and untied the string before pulling out a handful of guineas.

'There's a fortune there, Tom!' he gasped. 'Has that money been in the house all these years?'

'Must have been. And those two other bags are full of the same,' I replied. 'We should split it seven ways – it belongs to all Mam's sons, not just me. Your share could pay for the cost of a forge and keep the wolf from your door until you've got established.'

'That's very generous of you, Tom,' James said, looking doubtful and shaking his head, 'but if that's what Mam had wanted, she'd have shared it amongst us herself. No, the fact that it's in the trunk, together with all the other things that'll be useful to you in your trade, means you might need it for something else. Something more important . . .'

I hadn't thought of that. There was a reason for everything Mam did. It needed thinking about some more.

James picked up the largest of the leather-bound books, the one that had attracted my eye when I first opened the trunk. He opened it at a page close to the front.

'What's this?' he asked, looking puzzled. 'It looks like Mam's handwriting but I can't make moss nor sand of it. It's in a foreign language . . .'

'It's Mam's language, Greek,' I told him.

'Of course, Tom. I wasn't thinking. But she taught *you* the language, didn't she? I wonder why she didn't teach me?' For a moment he looked sad but then his face brightened. 'I expect it was because of the trade she wanted you to follow, Tom. She had a good reason for everything and always did things for the best. I don't suppose you could read a little of the book to me? Would you mind? Just a few words . . .'

So saying, he handed me the book, still open at the original page that he'd chosen at random. I glanced at it quickly. 'It's Mam's diary, James,' I told him before reading aloud, translating from the top:

> 'Yesterday I gave birth to a fine healthy son. We will call him James, a good County name and his father's choice. But my own secret name for him shall be Hephaestus, named after the god of the forge. For I see its light in his eyes just as I see the hammer in his hand. I have never been happier. How I wish I could be a mother with young children for ever. How sad it is that they must grow up and do what must be done.'

I stopped reading and James looked at me in astonishment. 'And I became a blacksmith!' he exclaimed. 'It's almost as if she chose that for me from birth . . .'

'Maybe she did, James. Dad arranged your apprenticeship but maybe Mam chose your trade. That's certainly what happened in my case.'

There was something else that I didn't bother to mention. But perhaps, in time, James would realize it for himself. It was the way he had picked the page that referred directly to his birth and name. It was almost as if Mam had reached out from afar and made him choose that page. This was the book that had attracted me too; the book from which the letter had fallen, telling me what I needed to know about the contents of the other two trunks.

If that was the case, it made me realize just how powerful Mam was. She'd prevented the witches from opening the trunks and now they were in our hands and protected by her lamia sisters. Thinking that made me more optimistic. The dangers ahead were great, but with a mam like mine behind me and my master at my side, maybe things would all work out in the end.

CHAPTER 19
AGNES SOWERBUTTS

In the morning Alice cooked us a good breakfast, making the best of the ingredients available. I helped her by cleaning out the pots and pans and peeling and chopping potatoes, carrots and turnips. We boiled one of the hams as well, after Alice had sniffed it carefully to make sure that it hadn't been poisoned.

'Make the most of this, lad,' the Spook told me as I tucked into the steaming stew. 'It's the last big meal we'll be eating for some time. After this we'll be fasting and getting ready to deal with the dark!'

My master hadn't yet outlined his plans for the day but I was more concerned about something that had kept me awake for much of the night.

'I'm worried about my family,' I told him. 'Can't we go to Roughlee and bring them back here? There might be something in Mam's trunk that we can use to cure Jack . . .'

The Spook nodded thoughtfully. 'Aye, that sounds like a good idea. Best to get them out of Deane territory. It'll be dangerous, but with the girl to guide you I'm sure you'll manage all right.'

'It'll be fine, Tom,' Alice agreed. 'Don't worry, they're all right – we'll get 'em back here safe and sound in a couple of hours. And I'm sure there'll be something in the trunk to help your brother.'

'And while you're doing that,' said the Spook, 'James and I will pay another visit to Downham. Time's getting short and it seems to me that it would be wise to rally some of the village men and get them back here to the refuge of the tower. We'd be better placed to strike when the need arises. And on our way there we'll be on the lookout for Wurmalde and young Mab. The first needs binding and putting out of harm's way. The second should have calmed down a bit by now and might just listen to reason.'

353

* * *

After breakfast I took a clean shirt from my bag and discarded the bloodstained one, glad to be rid of it at last, with the terrible memories it evoked of poor Father Stocks's death. Less than an hour later we were on our way. With nobody to raise the drawbridge after we'd left, we had to use the tunnel. The Spook took the lead carrying one lantern; Alice brought up the rear, lighting the steps from behind with another. As we descended, everything was silent and deserted and I noticed that the bodies of the witch and her male companion had been removed from the foot of the stairwell. But once through the lower trapdoor I sensed a presence. The lanterns revealed nothing and the only sound was the echo of our footsteps. But the circular hall was large and there were lots of dark shadows beyond the pillars; as we left the steps, the hair on the back of my neck began to rise.

'What have we here?' asked the Spook, pointing at the furthest of the pillars.

He walked towards it, his staff at the ready, lantern

raised. I was at his shoulder, my own staff in my left hand, Alice and James close at my heels.

At the foot of the pillar was a wooden bucket and something was dripping into it steadily. Another step forward and I saw that it contained blood and that it was slowly being filled as we watched.

Looking up, I saw that there were chains hanging from the darkness of the ceiling far above; chains that had no doubt been used to bind prisoners while they were tortured or left to die of starvation. Now those chains had been put to another use. Attached to them at intervals, all the way up into the dark, were small animals: rats, weasels, rabbits, stoats and the odd squirrel or two. Some were fastened by their tails, others by their legs, but all hung head downwards. They had been killed and their blood was dripping into the bucket. It reminded me of a gamekeeper's gibbet: dead animals nailed to a fence both as a warning and a display of kills made.

'It's a grim sight,' the Spook said, shaking his head. 'But we must be grateful for small mercies. There could be people hanging there . . .'

'Why have the lamias done that? What's it for?' I asked.

The Spook shook his head. 'When I find out, lad, I'll write it up in my notebook. This is new to me. I've never dealt with this type of winged lamia before so we've a lot to learn. It could be that it's just a way of collecting blood together from a lot of small animals to make it amount to a more satisfying meal. Or it could be something that only makes sense to a feral lamia. Year by year our store of knowledge grows, but we must think ahead, lad, and not always expect immediate answers. Perhaps one day you'll finally get a chance to read your mam's notebooks and find the answer there. Anyway, let's move on. We've no time to waste.'

When he had finished speaking, there came a slight scratching noise from somewhere above. I looked up nervously and heard a click as the Spook released the blade from its recess in his staff. As we watched, a dark shape scuttled down the pillar towards the arc of light cast by the lanterns. It was one of the feral lamias.

The creature had climbed downwards head first. Its wings were folded across its back and its body was in shadow. Only its head was clearly illuminated. The Spook angled his blade towards the lamia and James stepped forward and raised his huge hammer, ready to strike. The lamia responded by opening its mouth wide and hissing, giving us a glimpse of razor-sharp white teeth.

I put down my staff and touched the Spook and James lightly on the shoulder. 'It'll be all right. It won't hurt me,' I said, stepping between them and moving closer to the lamia.

Mam said the creatures would protect me, even at the cost of their own lives, and I felt that James was safe too. It was the Spook and Alice that I was worried about. I didn't want it to attack them. Neither did I want anyone to kill it in self-defence.

'Take care, Tom,' Alice pleaded from behind. 'Don't like the look of it. Dangerous, ugly thing, it is. Don't trust it, please . . .'

'Aye, the girl's right. Be on your guard, lad. Don't get too close,' warned the Spook.

Despite their warnings I took another step nearer. There were scratch marks on the stone pillar made by the creature's sharp talons. Its eyes were staring straight into my own.

'It's all right,' I told the lamia, keeping my voice calm. 'These people are my friends. Please don't hurt them. Just guard them as you would guard me, allowing them to come and go freely as they wish.' Then I smiled.

For a moment or two there was no response, but then the cruel eyes widened a fraction and the lips parted slightly. It was more of a grimace than a smile. Then, from beneath its body, one of the forelimbs was raised towards me, the nails less than a hand-span from my face. I thought it was going to touch me but, quite definitely, the lamia dipped its head in agreement and, still keeping its eyes locked upon mine, scuttled backwards up the pillar to be lost in darkness.

I heard James let out a big sigh of relief behind me.

'Wouldn't want to be in your line of work for any-thing!' he exclaimed.

'I don't blame you for that, James,' said the Spook, 'but somebody's got to do it. Anyway, let's press on . . .'

Alice took the lead now, holding her lantern high, and went into the passageway between the cells. On either side were the unquiet dead. I could sense their anguish, hear their pleading voices. James, not being a seventh son of a seventh son, would be spared that, but I was eager to move on quickly into the tunnel and leave all that pain behind me. However, before we reached the wooden door that led to the outer tunnel, the Spook rested his hand upon my shoulder and came to a halt.

'This is terrible, lad,' he said softly. 'There are spirits in torment here. More trapped together in one place than I've ever encountered before. I can't just leave them like this—'

'Spirits? What spirits?' James asked, looking around nervously.

'It's just the spirits of those who died here,' I told him. 'They're nothing to worry about but they're in pain and need releasing.'

'Aye,' said the Spook, 'and it's my duty to deal with them now. I'm afraid it's going to take me some time. Look, James, you press on to Downham. You don't need me. In fact you might find it easier to rally the villagers if I'm not there. Stay overnight and bring as many back here as you can tomorrow. Don't try to use the tunnel – I don't think it'll do much for the villagers' courage to pass through this dungeon. Come straight up to the tower and we'll lower the drawbridge. And another thing – I wouldn't mention the death of poor Father Stocks just yet. It'll be a real blow to the village, not good for their morale. And as for you two' – he looked at Alice and me in turn – 'get yourselves off to Roughlee and bring Jack, Ellie and the child back here to safety. I hope to see you again in a few hours at the most.'

It seemed to be for the best, so we left the Spook with a lantern as he prepared for the long task of sending the tormented dead of Malkin Tower towards the light. Then we set off along the tunnel, Alice in the lead and James close behind me.

Soon we came to the lake and Alice stepped forward warily, holding her lantern high. A sudden stench of rotting assailed my nostrils. I felt uneasy. The water had been agitated on my previous visit but this time it was still and calm, reflecting back the glowing lantern and Alice's head and shoulders like a mirror. Then I saw why.

The wight no longer guarded the tunnel. Several pieces of it were floating in the water. The head was close to the far wall. A huge arm was on the nearside bank, the thick bloodless fingers resting on the muddy path as if attempting to claw their way out of the lake.

Alice pointed down at the path. There were footprints on it – but they weren't human. They'd been made by one of the feral lamias.

'It cleared the way for you, Tom,' said Alice. 'And unless I'm very much mistaken we won't have any witches to worry about either.'

Alice was probably right, but as we skirted the lake, my feeling of unease returned. The wight was clearly destroyed but I had a strange feeling that I was being watched.

We quickly went past the lake, stepping over the bloated fingers, and continued on our way until we reached the earthen chamber. After standing there for a few moments, listening for danger, we moved on into the final low section of tunnel, which forced us down onto our hands and knees. Crawling forward, we found it hard going, but at last we dragged ourselves through onto the bone-shelf and into the sepulchre. As I clambered out, Alice was dusting herself down. She held the lantern aloft and I glanced across at the empty leg irons in the corner. Dead Maggie was gone, probably freed by her family as they made their escape.

We extinguished the lantern and Alice left it just inside the door of the sepulchre against future need. Outside, we said a quick farewell to James, who headed north towards Downham. Moments later Alice and I were making our way through the trees towards

Roughlee, a strong wind bending the saplings, the smell of imminent summer rain strong in the air.

For a while we walked in silence. The sky grew darker, it began to rain and I was becoming increasingly uneasy. Although I generally trusted Alice's judgement, the more I thought about it, the more it seemed the height of folly to have left my family with one of the Deanes.

'This aunt of yours – are you sure she's to be trusted?' I asked. 'It must be quite a few years since you last met her. She might have changed a lot since then. Maybe she's fallen under the influence of the rest of her family?'

'Ain't nothing to worry about, Tom, I promise you. Agnes Sowerbutts never practised as a witch until her husband died. And now she's what people hereabouts call "wise". She helps people and keeps her distance from the rest of the Deane clan.'

I felt better on hearing that. It seemed that Agnes was what the Spook would have termed 'benign' and used her power to help others. When we came within sight of her house, things looked even more promising. It was an isolated, one-storey farm cottage at the foot of a slope, on the edge of a narrow track; to the south-west, at least a mile away, chimney smoke from the village rose through the trees.

'You wait here, Tom,' Alice suggested. 'I'll just go down and see if everything's all right.'

I watched Alice descend the hill. By now the dark clouds were pressing lower and the rain increasing in force – so I pulled up the hood of my cloak. The door to the cottage opened before Alice reached it and she spoke to someone who remained out of sight in the porch. Then she turned and beckoned me down the incline. When I reached the door, she'd already gone inside, but then a voice called to me from the cottage.

'Get yourself inside out of the rain and close the door!'

I did as I was told. It was a woman's voice, a little gruff but also filled with a mixture of kindness and authority. A few paces brought me into a cramped living room with a small fire burning in the grate and a kettle close to boiling on the hob. There was also a rocking chair and a table upon which stood a single unlit candle – which, I noted with interest and some relief, was made of beeswax rather than the black wax favoured by malevolent witches.

The room was cheerful – somehow filled with more light than the tiny front window should have allowed. There were lots of cupboards and row upon row of wooden shelves laden with all manner of jars and odd-shaped containers. Each bore a label on which was written a word or words in Latin. Without doubt I was in the presence of a healer.

Alice was drying her hair with a towel. Agnes Sowerbutts, standing next to her, only came up to her niece's shoulder but was as wide as she was tall, with a warm smile that welcomed me into her home.

'It's good to meet you, Tommy,' she said, handing me another towel. 'Dry yourself before you catch cold. Alice has told me a lot about you.'

I nodded, thanked her for the towel and made

myself smile back out of politeness. I didn't really like being called 'Tommy' but it hardly seemed worth complaining. I dried my face, concerned that there was no sign of Ellie, Jack and Mary.

'Where are my family?' I asked. 'Are they all right?'

Agnes walked closer and patted my arm in reassurance. 'Your family are safe in the next room, Tommy. They're sleeping peacefully. Would you like to see them?'

I nodded, and she opened a door and ushered me into a room which contained a large double bed. There were three figures lying on their backs atop the covers – Jack and Ellie, with the child between them. Their eyes were closed and for a moment a chill ran down my spine and I feared the worst. I couldn't even hear them breathing.

'Ain't nothing to worry about, Tom,' Alice said, coming into the bedroom behind me. 'Agnes has given 'em a strong potion. Sent all three into a deep sleep so they can regain their strength.'

'Not been able to cure your brother, sad to say,'

Agnes said, shaking her head. 'But he is stronger now, and should be able to walk when he wakes. Can't do nothing about his mind though. It's in a fair old muddle. Doesn't know whether he's coming or going, does poor Jack.'

'He'll be all right, Tom,' Alice said, coming across and squeezing my hand in reassurance. 'Soon as we get back I'll sift through your mam's trunk. Certain to be something in there to sort him out.'

Alice meant well but it still didn't make me feel much better. I began to wonder if my brother would ever make a full recovery. We went back into the living room and Agnes boiled us up a fortifying herb drink. It tasted bitter but she assured me that it would do us good and build up our strength for whatever lay ahead. She told me that my family would wake naturally within the next hour and they should be strong enough to walk back to Malkin Tower.

'Anything new to tell us?' Alice asked, taking a sip of her drink.

'Family don't tell me much,' Agnes said. 'They don't

bother me and I don't bother them but I can see things for myself. There's been a lot of activity these past few days. They're getting ready for Lammas. More Malkins visited yesterday than I've seen in a month o' Sundays. Been Mouldheels here too – a thing I've never known in my lifetime.'

Alice suddenly laughed, a slight edge of mockery in her voice. 'Bet they didn't all walk by your window, so how come you know all this?'

Agnes coloured slightly. At first I thought she'd taken offence but I soon realized that it was embarrassment. 'Old woman like me needs some excitement, don't she? No fun in looking out of my window onto fields of bleating sheep and windswept trees. What I do is the next best thing to gossip. Keeps me from being too lonely.'

Alice smiled at me and squeezed my arm affectionately. 'Likes to use a mirror, Aunt Agnes does, so she can see what's going on in the world. Would you do it for us now, Aunt?' She turned her smile towards the old lady. 'Important, it is. We need to see what the

Mouldheels are up to. Best of all, we'd like to see Mab Mouldheel. Could you find her for us?'

For a moment Agnes didn't reply, but then she gave a little nod and went across to the far corner of the room. There, she rummaged around in a cupboard and pulled out a mirror. It wasn't very large, not much more than twelve inches tall by six or so wide, but it was framed in brass and set on a heavy base. She placed the mirror on the table and positioned the candle just to her left. Then she drew up a chair and sat facing the mirror.

'Close the curtains, Alice!' Agnes commanded, reaching towards the candle.

Alice did as she was bid and the heavy curtains plunged the room into gloom. The moment Agnes's hand closed about the candle, it flared into life. I trusted Alice's judgement but I suddenly started to suspect that Agnes was a little more than just a healer. A wise woman didn't use mirrors and candles. The Spook wouldn't have been happy, but then again, Alice often did things he didn't approve of. I just hoped that, like Alice, Agnes always used her powers for good rather than to serve the dark.

For a moment there was a silence in which I could hear only the rain pattering hard against the window. Then, as Agnes began to mutter under her breath, Alice and I stood behind her so that we could look over her shoulders into the mirror, which began to cloud almost immediately.

Alice's right hand gripped my left. 'Good with mirrors, is Agnes,' she whispered into my ear. 'Even give the Mouldheels a run for their money!'

A sequence of images drifted across the mirror: the inside of a cluttered cottage; an old woman sitting hunched in a chair stroking a black cat on her knee; what looked like the altar of a ruined chapel. Then the mirror grew dark and Agnes began to rock from side to side, the words tumbling from her lips faster and faster, the sweat beginning to ooze from her brow.

The mirror brightened a little, but now all we could see was wild racing clouds and then what looked like branches thrashing in the wind. It seemed odd. How was she doing it? Where was the other mirror?

We seemed to be looking upwards from the ground. Then two people appeared. They were distorted, and immense. It was like an ant's-eye view, looking up at giants. One figure was barefooted; the other wore a long gown. Even before the image sharpened and I could see their faces, I knew who they were.

Mab was talking animatedly to Wurmalde, who was resting her hand on her shoulder. Mab stopped speaking and they both smiled and nodded. Suddenly the image began to shift. It was as if a dark cloud were moving across from the left of the picture, and I realized that our vantage point had been obscured by the edge of Wurmalde's skirts. Then I glimpsed one of the witch's pointy shoes and then, next to it, a bare foot, three-toed with sharp, cruel nails. She was hiding Tibb under her skirts again.

The image faded and the mirror grew dark but we'd seen enough. It looked like the Mouldheels were about to join the other two clans. Agnes blew out the candle and came wearily to her feet. After opening the curtains, she turned and shook her head. 'That evil little

371

beastie gives me the shivers,' she said. 'World would be a better place without it.'

'Without Wurmalde too,' Alice said.

'How did you do that?' I asked Agnes. 'I thought there had to be two mirrors . . .'

'Depends how strong the witch is,' replied Alice, answering for her aunt. 'Water will do just as well. It can be in a basin, or if it's really calm, even a pond will do. Aunt Agnes was really clever and skilful: Wurmalde and Mab were standing on the edge of a big puddle, so she used that.'

At those words a shiver ran down my spine, and in my mind's eye I saw that dark underground lake again, with the pieces of the wight floating motionless, the surface like glass. And I remembered my sense of unease.

'I felt a chill when we passed the underground lake,' I said. 'As if I was being stared at. Could someone have been using it like a mirror to see us pass by?'

Agnes nodded and her eyes became thoughtful. 'That's possible, Tommy. And if that's so, they'll know you've left the safety of the tower and will be lying in wait when you go back.'

'So let's go the other way then,' I suggested. 'The Spook's still inside Malkin Tower so he could lower the drawbridge for us. We can go straight through the wood towards it. They won't expect that.'

'Could try that,' Alice said doubtfully. 'But they could be waiting in Crow Wood too, and we'll have to shout for the Spook to let us in. Still, we might have a better chance there. Specially if we go round the long way and approach from the north.'

'There's another problem though,' I said. 'The Spook will be busy for hours dealing with the dead down in the dungeons. So he wouldn't hear us. We'll have to wait before we go back. Wait until after dark . . .'

'You're more than welcome to stay here until then,' Agnes said. 'How would you like some broth to warm your insides? Your family will be hungry when they awake. I'll make some for us all.'

As Agnes prepared the food, there was a faint cry from the next room. Little Mary had woken up. Almost immediately I heard Ellie soothing her, so I rapped lightly on the door and went in. Ellie was comforting her child and Jack sat on the edge of the bed near the door with his head in his hands. He didn't even look up when I came in.

'Are you feeling better, Ellie?' I asked. 'And how's Jack?'

Ellie gave me a little smile. 'Lots better, thanks, and Jack seems stronger too. He hasn't spoken yet, but look at him – he's well enough to sit up. That's a big improvement.'

Jack was still in the same position and hadn't acknowledged me, but I tried to be cheerful because I didn't want to alarm Ellie. 'That's great news,' I told her. 'Anyway, we're going to get you back to Malkin Tower for safety.'

At my words, alarm flickered onto her face.

'It's not that bad,' I told her, trying to be reassuring. 'It's in our hands now and perfectly safe.'

'I hoped never to see that grim place again,' she said.

'It's for the best, Ellie. You'll be safe there until we can get you home to the farm. Before you know it, everything will be back to normal.'

'I'd like to think so, Tom, but the truth is I haven't much hope. All I ever wanted was to be a good wife to Jack and have my own family to love. But what's happened has spoiled everything. I don't see things ever getting back to how they were. I'll just have to put a brave face on it for poor little Mary's sake.'

At that moment Jack came to his feet and shuffled towards me, a puzzled expression on his face.

'Great to see you on your feet, Jack!' I said, holding out my arms to greet him. The old Jack would have gripped me in a bear-hug and almost crushed my ribs in his exuberance, but my brother was far from being recovered. He halted about three paces away and his mouth just opened and closed a few times; then he shook his head in bewilderment. He seemed steady enough on his feet but words had deserted him. I just hoped that Alice would be able to find something in Mam's trunk to help him.

* * *

Soon after sunset we thanked Agnes Sowerbutts and were on our way, the rain having eased to a light drizzle.

Alice and I were walking ahead leading the way but our pace wasn't very fast. The rain finally stopped altogether, but there was thick cloud and it was very dark, which at least made it harder for anyone lying in wait to spot us. Little Mary was nervous and kept clinging to her mother, who had to keep stopping to comfort her. Jack just ambled along as if he'd all the time in the world, but he stumbled into things and at one point tripped over a log, making enough noise to alert every witch in Pendle.

Our plan was to keep to the east, passing Crow Wood far to the right. The first part went well, but as we curved round to approach the tower directly from the north, I started to become increasingly uneasy. I could sense something out there in the dark. At first I hoped my imagination was playing tricks, but the clouds were being ripped and torn by the wind and starting to fragment, the sky growing lighter by the minute. Then the moon found a gap in the clouds and the whole area was lit with a faint silver light. When I glanced back over my shoulder, I could actually see figures in the distance before a large cloud once more plunged us into darkness.

'They're behind us, Alice, and getting nearer,' I told her, keeping my voice low so as not to alarm the others.

'Witches. Lots of 'em!' Alice agreed. 'Some of their menfolk too.'

We'd entered the trees of Crow Wood and were moving towards a fast-flowing stream, closing on it with every step. I could hear the rush and hiss of water boiling over rocks.

'We'll be safe if we can just get across!' I shouted.

Luckily the bank was low and I steadied Ellie as she hastened across, carrying Mary. The water hardly reached our knees but the rocks were very slippery underfoot. Jack made heavy weather of it and fell twice, the second time close to the far edge, but he dragged himself up onto the muddy bank without complaining.

We'd all reached the far side and I was relieved that the immediate danger was over. The witches would never be able to cross. But at that moment the moon came out again briefly and I saw something that filled me with dismay. Twenty or so yards to our right was a witch dam, a heavy wooden board suspended above the water. Supported by ropes that ran across pulleys to handles on either side of the stream, the board was fitted between two grooved posts that would guide it into position as it was lowered.

We'd gained a little time but it wouldn't be enough. It would take our enemies just a few moments to lower the dam into position and stop the flow of water. Once across, they'd catch us long before we reached the tower.

'There's a way to stop 'em, Tom!' Alice yelled. 'It's not hopeless. Follow me!'

She ran towards the witch dam. Flickering moonlight lit the scene briefly and Alice pointed to the water underneath the board. I could see what appeared to be a thick dark line running directly from bank to bank.

'It's a groove, Tom,' Alice shouted. 'Clan menfolk move the stones away and cut a trench in the bed of the stream. Then they line it with wood. It makes a tight seal so that the water can't get through. If we can put some of the stones back, they won't be able to lower it fully.'

It was worth a try and I followed Alice down the bank into the water. In theory it was easy. All we had to do was find a few stones and put them in the trench. In practice it was very difficult. It was dark and the first time I plunged my arms down past my elbows into the cold water, my fingers couldn't get a grip on anything. The first stone I found was deeply embedded and wouldn't budge. The second was smaller but still too heavy to lift and my fingers kept losing their grip.

At the third attempt I found a stone just a little bigger than my fist. Alice was ahead of me and had already put two stones into place close to our side of the bank.

'There, Tom! Place it close to mine. Won't take too many . . .'

By now I could hear hoarse breathing and the rapid

379

slap of feet against the damp ground. After a further struggle I found another stone – this was twice the size of my first – and I splashed it down towards the trench, positioning my shoulder against the lower edge of the raised board to help me aim in the darkness. But our pursuers were very close now. When the moon came out again, I glimpsed the burly figure of a man reaching for the handle.

I found another stone and just managed to drop it into the trench when I heard the wheel turning: the board began to rumble downwards. I was going to search again but Alice gripped my arm.

'Come on, Tom. That'll do! Won't be able to make a seal and the water will still flow . . .'

So I followed Alice back up onto the bank; we ran to where Jack, Ellie and Mary were waiting and led them off through the trees. Had we done enough? Was Alice right?

Ellie was exhausted by now and stumbled along at a snail's pace, still clutching her daughter. We needed to move faster. Much faster.

'Give Mary to me,' Alice insisted, holding out her arms for the child.

For a moment I thought that Ellie would refuse, but she nodded her thanks and handed over the child. With the rumble of the board growing fainter behind us, we kept going until we reached the clearing. The tower was ahead. We were almost safe.

As we came within shouting distance of the tower, my hopes soared: I heard a grinding noise from within, and as I watched, the moon came out again and, with a clanking of chains, the drawbridge began to descend. Worried by our late return, the Spook must have been watching from the battlements and seen our approach.

But as we reached the very edge of the moat, I heard a guttural shout behind us. I glanced back towards the trees and my hopes sank faster than the last stone I'd dropped into the trench. There were shadowy figures sprinting over the grass towards us. The witches must have crossed the stream after all.

'We should have used more stones,' I said bitterly.

'No, Tom, we did enough,' Alice said, handing Mary back to Ellie. 'Ain't witches but it's almost as bad. Clan menfolk, they are.'

There were at least half a dozen of them rushing towards us, angry men with wild eyes, brandishing long knives, blades glittering silver in the moonlight. But the drawbridge was down now and we backed onto it, Alice and I taking up a defensive position on its very edge, keeping the others between us and the big iron-studded door. The Spook would be descending the steps now, just as fast as he was able. But our enemies were almost on us.

I could hear my master drawing back the heavy bolts, but would he be in time? Ellie gave a cry behind me and then I heard the sound of the big door grinding on its hinges. I raised my staff to defend myself, hoping to deflect the blade that was arcing towards my head. But someone else was beside me now. It was the Spook, and out of the corner of my eye I saw his staff spear forward towards my assailant. The man screamed and fell sideways into the moat with a tremendous splash.

'Get inside!' shouted the Spook. 'Get inside, all of you!'

He was standing his ground as two others ran towards us, shoulder to shoulder. I didn't want to leave him to face them alone but he pushed me so hard towards the door that I stumbled and almost fell. Just then the moon went behind a cloud and we were plunged into darkness again. Without thinking, I obeyed, reaching the door at Alice's heels. There was another cry of pain and I glanced back. Someone seemed to fall and there was another splash. Was it the Spook? Had they knocked him into the water? Then a shadowy figure was running towards the door, but even before I'd raised my staff to defend myself, I saw that it was my master.

He stumbled inside, cursed, threw down his staff and put his shoulder to the door. Alice and I helped him, and we just managed to get it closed before something heavy crashed against it. The Spook slammed the bolts home. Our enemies were too late.

'Up the steps and raise that drawbridge!' the Spook

commanded. 'Both of you! Look sharp!'

Alice and I ran up the steps, and together we began to turn the capstan. Down below we could hear angry shouts and metallic crashes as our enemies hammered uselessly against the door. It was hard work but, our shoulders straining against the resistance of the wheel, we continued to turn the capstan and bit by bit the bridge was raised. Just before it was fully up against the door, the banging outside ceased and we heard distant splashes as our enemies jumped into the moat. It was either that or be crushed between the heavy wooden bridge and the huge door.

After that we were safe. Safe for a while at least. The Spook, Alice and I discussed what had happened, while Ellie tried to make Mary and Jack comfortable. We were all weary, and before an hour had passed we were settling down for the night, once again sleeping on the floor, wrapped in dirty blankets. I was exhausted and soon fell into a dreamless sleep, but I awoke during the night to hear someone sobbing nearby. It sounded like Ellie.

'You all right, Ellie?' I called out softly into the darkness.

Almost immediately the crying ceased but she didn't reply. After that it took me a long while to get back to sleep. I began to wonder what tomorrow would bring. We were running out of time. In two days it would be Lammas. We had lost a day bringing Jack back to the tower so I was sure the Spook's priority tomorrow had to be settling with Wurmalde. If we didn't find her and stop the witches, then the dark made flesh would be walking amongst us and it wouldn't just be Ellie crying herself to sleep at night.

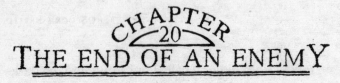

CHAPTER 20
THE END OF AN ENEMY

When we awoke, the Spook would allow me only
water and a nibble of County cheese. I was
right. We were off to deal with Wurmalde once and for
all. She wouldn't sniff us out but there was a chance
that Tibb might. In that case we could be walking into
a trap, but we had to take that chance.

Even before we reached Read Hall there'd be danger.
Witches would almost certainly be watching the tower
from the edge of the clearing, and at the first sound of
the drawbridge coming down they'd attack: once again
we'd have to use the tunnel. But of course, they'd be
using a mirror to watch the underground lake so they'd
know we'd left the tower. They might even be lying

in wait in the thickets of the old graveyard, ready to ambush us. Yet despite the risks, the Spook was determined to strike at Wurmalde, whom he considered to be the dark heart of the threat to the County.

He pulled a whetstone from his bag and there was a click as he released the blade from its recess in the end of his staff and began to sharpen it.

'Well, lad,' he said gruffly. 'We have a job to do. We must bind Wurmalde and place her where she can do no more harm. And if anyone gets in our way . . .'

He paused, testing the sharpness of the blade with his finger, and when he looked at me, his eyes were hard and fierce; then he glared at Alice.

'You stay here, girl, and look after Jack. Reckon you'll be strong enough to lower the drawbridge when James gets back with the villagers?'

'If Tom managed it, so can I,' she said with a cheeky smile, 'and in the meantime I'll see if I can find anything in that trunk to help Jack.'

Down in the dungeons beneath the tower there was a

change in the atmosphere; a change for the better. The Spook had done his work: the dead had left their bones behind and were now at peace.

Of the two lamias there was no sign. I held my candle aloft to reveal that the dead animals were still fixed to the chains but their desiccated bodies no longer dripped blood. We walked on into the tunnel warily and reached the small lake, where the pieces of the wight still floated. The surface of the water was like glass and again I had a strong sensation of being watched. The only thing that had changed was the stench, which was now stronger than ever. Both the Spook and I covered our mouths and noses with our hands and tried not to breathe until we'd passed beyond the fetid water.

Finally we had to crawl, the Spook still in the lead and muttering under his breath. It was hard going but at last we dragged ourselves through into the sepulchre. As I clambered out, the Spook was brushing the dust and mould from his cloak.

'My old bones didn't take too kindly to that,' he

complained. 'It'll be good to get out into the fresh air.'

'They had a dead witch shackled here,' I told the Spook, pointing to the leg irons in the corner. 'Her name was Maggie and she was once the Malkins' coven leader. The Mouldheels tortured her to find the tunnel entrance. Now she's free again . . .'

'How strong was she?' the Spook asked.

'Not like Old Mother Malkin, but strong enough. She travelled miles from Witch Dell to hunt.'

'Whatever happens in the next few days, there'll still be years of work ahead of us before Pendle is finally cleared,' the Spook said, shaking his head wearily.

I blew out the candle and placed it next to the lantern that Alice had left behind on our last visit.

'Bring that lantern, just in case, lad,' commanded the Spook. 'We might have to search Read Hall's cellars.'

As we made our way cautiously through the thickets of the abandoned graveyard, rainclouds were gathering overhead, a strong wind blowing from the west. We hadn't taken more than two dozen paces before we saw that witches had indeed been waiting in ambush. There were three of them, all dead. The surrounding grass was splattered with blood, the bodies covered in flies. Unlike the Spook, I didn't get too close, but even from a distance it appeared to be the work of the lamias. Once again, it seemed, they'd cleared the way.

Just over an hour later we were approaching Read Hall. I wasn't keen to re-enter a house where Tibb had terrorized me and Wurmalde had accused me of mur- der – and where, no doubt, poor Father Stocks's body was still lying atop the sheets, the knife in his chest; but it had to be done.

We were walking into danger without a doubt. Both Tibb and the formidable Wurmalde might be lying in wait; not to mention servants and possibly other witches from the clans. But as we drew closer, it soon became clear that something was badly wrong. The front door was opening and closing in the wind.

'Well, lad,' the Spook said, 'as they've left it open for us, we might as well use it!'

We made our way to the front door and entered. I

was about to close the door behind us when my master put his hand on my shoulder and shook his head. We kept perfectly still and listened very carefully. Apart from the noise of the door and the whine of the wind outside, the house was silent. The Spook looked up the staircase.

'We'll let the door carry on banging,' he whispered into my ear. 'To change even the slightest thing could alert anyone inside. It's too quiet so I suspect the servants have fled the house. We'll start by searching the downstairs rooms.'

The dining room was empty; it looked as if nobody had been in the kitchen for days – there were unwashed dishes in the sink and a smell of rotting food. Despite the morning light, Read Hall was gloomy and there were dark corners where anything could have been lurking. I kept thinking of Tibb. Was the creature still somewhere here?

The last room we came to was the study. As soon as we entered, I could smell death. A body was lying face down between the bookshelves.

'Light the lantern,' the Spook commanded. 'Let's take a closer look . . .'

It was clear that the corpse was Nowell. His shirt was in tatters, almost ripped from his back, and it was matted with dried blood, with more leading from the body towards the far door, which was open. There were also books scattered around him. The Spook glanced up at the top shelf, from where they'd clearly fallen, before kneeling down and rolling the dead magistrate onto his back. The eyes were wide open, the face twisted in terror.

'It looks like Tibb killed him,' the Spook said, gazing up at the highest shelf again. 'No doubt it was up there and dropped down onto his shoulders as he walked beneath. The creature might still be in the house,' he added, pointing to the trail.

He opened the door. Beyond it the blood trail led down narrow stone steps into the darkness. My master went down, his staff at the ready, while I followed close behind, holding the lantern high. We found ourselves at the entrance to a small cellar. Along the right-hand wall were well-stocked wine racks. The stone floor was clean and tidy and the trail of dried blood led to the far corner, where Tibb lay face down.

He was even smaller than I remembered when he'd gazed down at me from the ceiling – hardly larger than a medium-sized dog. His legs were tucked underneath the thick black fur of his body, which was caked with dried blood. But small as he was, I knew that Tibb was incredibly strong. Father Stocks had been unable to fight him off and Nowell had been murdered by him. Both victims had still been in the prime of life.

The Spook approached Tibb cautiously and I heard a click as he released the blade from its recess in the end of his staff. At the sound Tibb stretched out his arms, unsheathed his claws and lifted his head, turning its left side upwards to face us. It was the head that sent a particular chill of horror down my spine. It was completely hairless and smooth and the eyes were cold, like those of a dead fish, the open mouth revealing thin needle-like teeth. For a moment I expected Tibb to leap at the Spook, but instead the creature gave a groan of anguish.

'*You've arrived too late,*' Tibb said. '*My mistress has abandoned me, leaving me to die. So many things I've seen. So many. But not my own death. That's the last thing that any of us see!*'

'Aye,' said the Spook, readying his blade. 'I hold your death in my hands . . .'

But Tibb just laughed bitterly. '*No,*' he hissed. '*I'm dying even as you speak. My mistress never told me just how short my life would be. Nine short weeks in all. That's all I've had. How can that be right? Nine weeks from birth to old age and death. Now I lack even the strength to raise my body from this cold floor. So save your strength, old man. You need it for yourself. Precious little time remains to you either. But the boy who stands at your side may carry on your doomed work. That's if he lives beyond the new moon —*'

'Where is Wurmalde now?' demanded the Spook.

'*Gone! Gone! Gone to a place where you will never find her. Not until it's too late. Soon my mistress will summon the Fiend through the dark portal into this world. For two days he will do her bidding. That done, he will choose his own path. Do you know what task she has set? What price*' *the Fiend must pay for what my mistress gives him?'*

The Spook sighed wearily but didn't bother to reply. I saw his hands twitch on the staff. He was readying himself to slay the creature.

'The death of this boy is the task. He must die because he is his mother's son. The son of our enemy. Once, in a distant land, she was an immortal like my mistress and wielded dark power. But she faltered. Despite many warnings, she reached towards the light. So she was bound to a rock and left to die; left there to be destroyed by the sun, the very symbol of the light she wished to serve. But, by mischance, a human saved her. A fool freed her from her chains—'

'My dad was no fool!' I interrupted. 'He was good and kind and couldn't bear to see her suffer. He wouldn't have allowed *anybody* to suffer like that.'

'Better for you, boy, had he passed on by. For then you would never have been born. Never have lived your short futile life! But do you think that merely by being rescued she was changed for ever? Far from it! For a while she was in torment, not knowing which way to go, dithering between darkness and light. Old habits die hard, and gradually the

*dark drew her back. So she was given a second chance and
commanded to slay her rescuer, but she prayed, disobeyed
and turned to the light once more. Those who serve the light
are hard upon themselves. To make up for what she had
done, she gave herself a cruel penance – she surrendered her
immortality. But that was only half of it. She chose to give
her youth, the best part of her pitifully short life, to her
rescuer. She gave herself to a mortal man, a common sailor,
and chose to bear him seven sons.'*

'Seven sons who loved her!' I cried. 'She was happy.
She was content—'

*'Happy! Happy? Do you think happiness comes so easily?
Imagine what it must have been like for one who was once so
high to serve a mortal man and his brood, the stench of the
farmyard ever in her nostrils. To share his bed while his flesh
withered with age. To deal with the tedium of the everyday
routine. She regretted it, but at last his death has freed her,
ending her self-inflicted penance, and now she has returned
to her own land.'*

'No,' I said. 'It wasn't like that at all! She loved
my dad—'

'*Love,*' sneered Tibb. '*Love is a delusion that binds mortals to their fates. And now your mother has risked all in a bid to destroy what my mistress holds dear. She wants to destroy the darkness and she has fashioned you as her weapon. So you must never be allowed to grow up into a man. We must put an end to you.*'

'Aye,' said the Spook, raising his staff, 'and now it's time to put an end to you—'

'*Have mercy,*' pleaded Tibb. '*I need a little more time. Let me die in peace—*'

'What mercy did you show to Master Nowell?' demanded the Spook. 'So what you gave to him, I'll give to you . . .'

I turned away as the Spook stabbed downwards. Tibb gave a short scream that transmuted itself into the squealing of a pig. There was a brief snuffling and then silence. Still not looking at the creature, I followed my master up the steps and back into the study.

'Nowell's body will have to stay unburied for a while,' the Spook said, shaking his head sadly. 'No doubt poor Father Stocks is still upstairs, and maybe

397

we'll never find out what happened to Constable Barnes. As for Wurmalde, from what that creature just said she could be anywhere and we haven't time to just search blindly. We've still got the witch covens to deal with, so let's start by getting back to the tower. James should return soon with the men from Downham. We can't deal with the witches alone. We need to raise a small army and get ourselves organized. Time's running short.'

The Spook paused by Nowell's desk. It wasn't locked and he started to search the drawers. Within moments he held up my silver chain.

'Here you are, lad,' he said, throwing it towards me. 'No doubt you'll be needing this before very long.'

We left Read Hall and set off in a heavy downpour for Malkin Tower, the things that Tibb had said going round and round inside my head.

Wet and bedraggled, we made the journey through the tunnels without mishap; then, as we prepared to climb the spiral steps up into the tower, I turned to the Spook, wanting to get a few things off my chest.

'Do you think what Tibb said was true?' I asked.

'Which bits are you referring to, lad?' asked the Spook gruffly. 'The creature belonged to the dark and that makes *anything* it said dubious, to say the least. As you well know, the dark deceives whenever it is to its advantage to do so. It said it was dying, but how could I be sure that was the case? That's why I had to kill it there and then. It might have seemed cruel but it was my duty. I had no choice.'

'I mean the bit about my Mam once being like Wurmalde – being an immortal? As mam's sisters are lamias, I thought she'd be the same.'

'No doubt she is, lad. But what does being an immortal actually mean? This world itself will end one day. Maybe even the stars themselves will go out. No, I don't believe that anything lives for ever in this world, and nothing with any sense would want to. But lamias live a very long time. In their human form they may seem to age, but once feral again they become young once more. They could have many lifetimes in human shape and start out each time looking like a young woman. One day we may find out what that creature meant. Maybe it lied. Maybe it didn't. As your mam said, the answers are in those trunks and one day, if all goes well, you'll maybe get a chance to look through them properly.'

'But what about the Fiend coming through the portal? What is a portal anyway?'

'It's a sort of invisible gate. A weakness between this world and the places where creatures such as the Fiend dwell. Using dark magic the witches will try to open it and allow the Fiend through. We'll just have to do our best to put a stop to it,' said the Spook, his voice echoing up the steps. 'We need to break up the Lammas sabbath and halt the ritual. Of course, that's much easier said than done. But, even if we fail, your mother's made provision. That's why she left you that room—'

'But would I have time to get there if the Fiend's been ordered to hunt me down and kill me? It's a long way home . . .'

'Things loosed into the world often take time to gather their wits and gain power. Remember how the Priestown Bane was disorientated for a while? Once freed into the wider world, it was weakened at first and grew in power slowly. Well, I suspect this so-called 'Fiend' may have the same problem. You'd get some time – how much, it's impossible to say. But if I do give the word, get yourself home just as soon as you can and take refuge in that room of yours.'

'There was something else Tibb said that bothers me,' I said. 'Something he said when I saw him for the first time. He said that Mam was singing a goat song and I was at its centre. What could that mean?'

'You should have been able to work that out for yourself, lad. In your mam's tongue the word "tragos" means goat. And "oide" means ode or story. So a goat song is a tragedy. That's where we get the word from. And if you're at its centre, Tibb is saying that your life will be tragic – wasted and doomed to failure. But it's best to look on the bright side and take all that with a pinch of salt. Each day we make decisions that shape our lives. I still can't accept the idea that anything can be preordained. No matter how powerful the dark becomes, we have to believe that, somehow, we'll defeat it. Look up there, lad! What do you see?'

'Steps leading to the upper part of the tower . . .'

'Aye, lad, steps – and a lot of them! But we're going to climb them, aren't we? Weary as my old bones are, we're going to climb every one of those steps until we reach the upper floor and the waiting light. And that's what life's all about. So come on! Let's get on with it!'

So saying, the Spook led the way up the spiral steps and I followed at his heels. Up towards the light.

CHAPTER 21
BACK TO DOWNHAM

There was good news waiting for us back in the tower. Alice had found something that she really thought might finally cure Jack.

'Sent him into another deep sleep, it has,' she explained. 'But this potion heals the mind rather than the body. It was all there in one of your mam's notebooks – how to mix it; how much of each herb to use. Everything. And all the ingredients were inside the trunk, each one labelled.'

'I can't thank you enough,' Ellie said, smiling at Alice warmly.

'Ain't me you need to thank – it's Tom's mam. Take years to learn all there is in that trunk,' Alice continued.

'Compared to this, Bony Lizzie knew nothing.'

Jack continued to sleep until late in the afternoon and we were feeling really optimistic that, before long, it would be the old Jack who woke. But then we got the bad news.

James returned. But he returned alone. The Downham villagers were too afraid to help.

'I tried my best,' James said wearily, 'but there was nothing more that I could do. Their courage has deserted them. Even Matt Finley, the blacksmith, refused to leave Downham.'

The Spook shook his head sadly. 'Well, if they won't come to us, then we'll just have to go to them. But I'm not optimistic, James. You got through to them last time and I felt confident that you'd be able to do it again. But we'll have to try. Tomorrow night is the Lammas sabbath and we must disrupt it at all costs. No doubt Wurmalde will be with the other witches, and I think that's going to be my best chance of finding and binding her.'

So, soon after dark, we prepared to return to Downham. We were leaving Ellie, Jack and Mary behind in the tower, where they'd be safe.

'Well,' said the Spook, looking at James, Alice and me in turn, 'I wish there were an easier way. But it's got to be done. I just hope we all come safely through what lies ahead. Whatever happens, one thing is in our favour. This tower is now in our hands and the trunks and their contents are safe. So at least we've achieved that.'

My master was right. The lamias controlled Malkin Tower now. With luck I'd soon be able to return and look through Mam's trunks properly. But first – hopefully with the help of the Downham villagers – we had to face the witch clans and break up their sabbath before the ritual could be carried out.

So we left the tower using the tunnels once more. As we walked north, the wind was blustering in from the west and there was a chill in the air. At Downham we spent the remainder of the night in Father Stocks's cottage, grabbing a few hours' sleep while we could.

Up before dawn to catch the men before their working day began, we wasted no time in calling at each house in the village, desperately trying to rally an army. I accompanied Alice, dealing with the outlying cottages and nearest farms, while the Spook and James concentrated on its heart.

We arrived at the first cottage just in time to find its occupant stepping out into the grey dawn light. He was a farm labourer, gnarled and grumpy, rubbing sleep out of his bleary eyes with the prospect of a long hard day's work ahead. Even before we spoke, I could tell that he'd give us short shrift.

'There's a meeting at dusk in the church,' I told him. 'All the menfolk of the village are invited. It's to plan how we can deal with the threat from the witches. We've got to sort them tonight . . .'

Alice's pointy shoes didn't help. The man's eyes flicked suspiciously from them to my cloak and staff. I could tell that he didn't like the look of either of us.

'And who's calling this meeting?' he demanded.

I thought quickly. I could use James's name. Most of

them would know him by now, but they'd also rejected his recent plea. The man seemed nervous enough already and if I mentioned the Spook, I'd probably scare him off altogether. The lie slipped from my lips even before I could think.

'Father Stocks . . .'

The man nodded in acknowledgement of the name. 'I'll do my best to be there. Can't promise though – I've a busy day ahead.' With that he slammed the door shut, turned on his heels and set off up the hill.

I turned to Alice and shook my head. 'I feel bad about lying,' I told her.

'Ain't no use thinking that way,' she told me. 'Did the right thing for sure. If the priest were still alive, he *would* be calling the meeting. What's the difference? We're just calling it for him, that's all.'

I nodded uncertainly, but from that moment the pattern was set and on each subsequent occasion I used Father Stocks's name. It was difficult to judge how many were likely to attend the meeting but I wasn't optimistic. The truth was, some didn't even bother to answer their doors, others muttered their excuses, while one old man went into a rage:

'What's your sort doing in our village? That's what I want to know,' he said, spitting towards Alice's shoes. 'We've been hag-ridden enough in the past but it'll happen no more! Get ye gone from my sight, little witch!'

Alice took it calmly and we simply turned and went on our way. The Spook and James had had little more success than us. My brother said that it all depended on the blacksmith. He'd seemed in two minds, but if he did decide in favour of action, then many of the others would follow his lead. When I told the Spook about my lie, he made no comment, simply nodding in acknowledgement.

The remainder of the day was spent in anxious waiting. Time was running short. Would the villagers turn up in sufficient numbers to give us a chance? If they did, would we be able to persuade them to act? Then again, would we have enough time to race to Pendle Hill and disrupt the Lammas rituals? While these thoughts were whirling through my head, I suddenly remembered something else: 3 August, two days after Lammas, was my birthday.

I remembered the celebrations we used to have back at the farm. When one of our family had a birthday, Mam would always bake a special cake. I'd travelled a long way from such happy times. How could I even think beyond the danger we would face when dark fell? It seemed useless to hope for too much from this life. Such happiness belonged to my brief time as a child and now that was over.

As the sun went down, we waited patiently in the narrow church with its single aisle. We'd helped ourselves to candles from the tiny sacristy and placed these on the altar and in the metal candlesticks on either side of the doorway.

Long before the first villager came nervously into the church and took a seat near the back, the sky had darkened to the hue of Horshaw coal. This first visitor was an oldish man who walked with a limp – one better

409

suited to resting his weary bones by the fireside than venturing up onto Pendle Hill to fight a battle that was fraught with peril. Others followed, either singly or in pairs, but even after almost half an hour had passed there were no more than a dozen. Each man removed his cap on entering. Two of the boldest nodded towards James, but without exception all kept their eyes averted from the Spook. I could sense their extreme nervousness. The men had frightened faces, some visibly shivering despite the mildness of the air, and looked ready to flee rather than fight. It seemed to me that at the first sign of a witch they'd scatter and run.

But then, when all seemed lost, there was a murmur of voices from outside in the darkness and a big man dressed in a leather jerkin walked into the church at the head of at least another two dozen villagers. I guessed that this was Matt Finley, the blacksmith. Out of respect for the sanctity of the church, he removed his hat, and as he took his place in the front pew, he nodded to James and the Spook in turn. We'd been standing to the left of the small altar, close to the wall, but when the newcomers had all taken their seats, the Spook signalled to my brother, who stepped forward and positioned himself facing the aisle.

'We really appreciate that you've all taken the time and trouble to listen to us tonight,' James began. 'The last thing we want is for you to place yourselves in danger but we do desperately need your help and wouldn't ask if it were possible to do what's required by ourselves. A terrible evil threatens us all. Before midnight there'll be witches up on Pendle Hill. Witches who plan to loose a great mischief into the world. We need to stop them.'

'If I'm not mistaken, there are witches up on yonder hill already,' said the blacksmith. 'They've just lit a beacon that can be seen for miles!'

At these words, concern tightened the Spook's face; he shook his head and stepped forward to stand beside James. 'There's serious work to do tonight, lads,' he said. 'Time is short. That beacon up yonder signals that they've already begun their foul work. It gives notice of the threat to you, your families and all that you hold dear. The witches think they own the whole land now. No longer content to cower in remote dells, they flaunt their evil from the very top of Pendle Hill! If we don't stop them, darkness will fall upon this land. None of us will be safe – neither the strong nor the weak; neither adult nor child. No more will we sleep easy in our beds. The whole world will become a place of danger, plague and famine, and the Fiend himself will walk the lanes and byways of the County, while witches rule the earth and prey upon your children. We must make this land safe!'

'*Our* village is safe now!' snapped the blacksmith. 'And we've fought hard to make it that way. Not only that: if needs be, we'd fight again to keep it this way. But why should we risk our lives to do the work that's the duty of others? Where are the men of Roughlee, Bareleigh and Goldshaw Booth? Why don't *they* drive out the canker that's in their midst? Why is it up to us?'

'Because the good men left in those villages are too few,' replied the Spook. 'The dark has bitten too deep there and the resulting wounds have festered. Those who hate the dark might once have fought and won. Now the witch clans rule and good folk have mostly gone elsewhere – or died in the dungeons beneath Malkin Tower. So this is your chance now – maybe the last you'll ever have – to fight the dark.'

The Spook paused and a silence fell. I could see that many gathered there were thinking carefully about what he'd just said. It was then that a voice growled angrily from the back. 'Where's Father Stocks? I thought *he*'d called the meeting. That's the only reason I came!'

It was the farm labourer from that first cottage I'd called at with Alice. The first man I'd lied to. There was a muttering from the back of the church. It seemed that others felt the same way.

'We weren't going to tell you this, lest it drained away the last dregs of your courage,' said the Spook. 'But now it has to be said. A good friend of this village has died at the hands of the witch, who's the chief insti-gator of all this trouble. A friend who's done more than anyone to keep you and your families safe. I speak of

Father Stocks, your parish priest. And now I speak in his name, asking for your help.'

At the mention of Father Stocks, all the candles in the church flickered together and almost went out. The door closed, yet there was no wind; no earthly explanation for it. Gasps were heard from the congregation and Finley, the blacksmith, put his head in his hands as if in prayer. I shivered, but the moment passed and the candles burned steadily once more. The Spook waited a few seconds to allow the shocking news to sink in before continuing.

'So I'm begging you now. If you won't do it for yourselves, do it for poor Father Stocks. Repay the debt that you owe a man who gave his life fighting the dark. The witch, who slew him in cold blood when he lay helpless, is called Wurmalde, a witch who covets even the bones of your beloved dead. A witch who, given half a chance, would drink the blood of your children. So fight for them and for your children's children. Do it now! Fight while you still can. Before it's too late. Either that or end up like the poor folk in the villages to the south . . .'

Matt Finley, the blacksmith, looked up and stared hard at the Spook. 'What do you want us to do?' he asked.

'Witches can sniff out approaching danger and they'll know we're coming,' replied the Spook, locking eyes with the blacksmith, 'so there's no need for stealth. Once we move in, make as much noise as you like. In fact the more the better! You see, they're not always that precise when it comes to numbers. There are enough of you to make the threat serious, but we need to make it appear even larger than it is. They won't know how many of us there are and we can work that to our advantage. As well as weapons we'll need torches.'

'What will we face up there? How many?' demanded Finley. 'Most men here have families to support. We need to know what our chances are of getting back in one piece.'

'As for numbers, I can't be sure,' admitted the Spook. 'There'll be at least two or three for every one of us, but

415

that's not a worry because there's a good chance most of you won't even need to strike a blow. My intention is to disrupt what they're attempting and drive them off the hill to the west. In the confusion I'll deal with Wurmalde and their evil schemes will come to nothing.

'I suggest you split yourselves into five groups of six or so; each group to take up a different position on the eastern slope. James here will climb a little higher up and light his torch. That'll be the signal for you to light yours. That done, move up the hill steadily and swing round towards the beacon. One more thing – don't bunch. Each group should spread out some way – for all they know there might be others without torches walking amongst you. As I said, they'll just sense the threat, not the details of what they face.

'So that's the plan. If you've anything to say, say it now. Don't be afraid to ask.'

Someone spoke up immediately from the back of the group: it was the old man who'd been the first to enter the church. 'Mr Gregory, will we be in danger of attack from . . .' he asked nervously. He didn't complete his sentence and when the Spook looked directly at him, the man simply gestured upwards and uttered one further word: 'Broomsticks?'

The Spook didn't smile, although I knew that in other circumstances he might easily have started roaring with laughter. 'No,' he said. 'I've been following my trade for more years than I care to remember but in all that time I can honestly say that I've never seen a witch fly on a broomstick. It's a very common superstition but it simply isn't true.

'Now it's my duty to inform you of the dangers if the worst should happen. Beware of their blades. They'd cut your heart out as soon as look at you and most have great strength – much more than your average man. So beware of that. Don't let them get close. If necessary, use your clubs and sticks in defence.

'Oh, and one more thing. Don't look into their eyes. A witch can get you in her power with a glance; don't listen to a word she says, either. And remember, there might well be some male clan members to face. If so, be equally on your guard. They learn a lot from the women they associate with. They won't fight fair and can get up to all sorts of tricks. But as I said, most likely it won't even come to a pitched battle. Anything else?'

Nobody spoke but Matt Finley shook his head for all of them. He looked as grim-faced and resigned as the rest. They didn't want to face the witches but accepted that for the sake of their families they had no real alternative.

'Well,' said the Spook, 'we've little time to waste. They're up on yonder hill earlier than I expected. But whatever's done is done, so now let's make sure they don't do anything worse. God be with you all.'

In response, some of the villagers crossed themselves; others bowed their heads. The Spook had never really made it clear whether or not he believed in God. If he did, it wasn't the God prescribed by Church doctrine. Nevertheless, it was exactly the right thing to say, and within moments the groups were leaving the church to go and collect their makeshift weapons and torches.

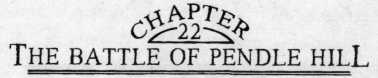

CHAPTER 22
THE BATTLE OF PENDLE HILL

Outside the church it smelled like rain again, and in the distance I heard a faint rumble of thunder. A storm was on its way.

We raced south into the lee of the hill. Time was short and the minutes were ticking away to midnight. I kept glancing up uneasily towards the summit, where the beacon lit the night sky over the hill, the glow reflecting back from the low clouds.

All who'd assembled in the church were with us but not all were equally fit. By the time we'd crossed the stream to reach Fell Hollow, the place the Spook had appointed for our final gathering prior to the attack on the hill, our party was strung out over more than half a mile and more precious time was lost. But even the less fit were valuable. They could carry torches and help to swell the size of the army visible to the witches.

Although frustrated by the delay, as our band gathered in the hollow, I suddenly felt more optimistic. There were thirty or more men prepared to do battle with the witches on the hill. My brother James and Matt Finley carried huge hammers; others were armed with clubs; a few had staffs and all were carrying unlit torches. It was a better response than the Spook had expected.

At last it was time to attack and, as agreed, the villagers spread out in groups along the eastern slope of Pendle, ready for the ascent. When this was finally accomplished, the Spook turned to face my brother.

'Well, James, you know what you have to do. As you climb, keep your distance from us three: they won't be able to sniff us out – for, as you know, Tom and I are both seventh sons of seventh sons and long-sniffing doesn't work on us, and Alice has witch blood from both sides of her family so that should serve her just as well. They won't get a hint until we're in really close, and by then it'll be too late. We'll move to the south-east of the hill and climb up from there directly towards the fire. With a bit of luck, and making the best use of the confusion, I'll bind Wurmalde and bring her back down while the rest flee.'

James nodded. 'Whatever you say, Mr Gregory. Anyways, I'll be off. So good luck to the three of you. And take care, Tom. I'll be thinking of you . . .'

With that, he gave us a wave and set off at a brisk pace up the hill, moving away from us diagonally, his big hammer across his shoulder. I felt nervous, and not only for myself. This was a very dangerous situation. The Spook had told the villagers that the witches would probably flee from the hill as soon as they attacked – he had to do that. If he gave them the full range of possibilities, they'd probably be too scared to help. It was his duty to use all possible means to stop the Lammas sabbath before something from the dark was released into the County.

But things could go badly. The witches might well

stand and fight. We weren't just facing covens of thir-teen; the clans were also there, to witness what was about to happen. There might be more than a hundred people on the hill; if it came to a pitched battle, we'd be greatly outnumbered. I was worried about the Spook and Alice. James too. I already had one brother who was seriously hurt. I didn't want something bad hap-pening to James as well.

'Well then,' said the Spook, 'let's get ourselves as close as possible to that fire. We want to be ready when the attack starts. And whereas I want the others to draw attention to themselves, we must be as quiet as church mice. We need the element of surprise.'

So saying, he led the way south before gradually beginning a direct ascent towards the beacon. I fol-lowed close behind him, glad of my staff, Alice at my own heels. The climb was steep and the grass coarse, with big tussocks and treacherous, uneven ground. It was dark now and it would be easy to twist an ankle. The Spook had told me that the plateau atop the hill was just as bad. A lot of rain fell on Pendle and there were bogs aplenty. But there was also one thing to our advantage – heather.

It grew in profusion as we neared the summit and gave us some cover. The Spook put his hand on my shoulder and pressed, signalling that I should drop to my knees. I continued to follow him upwards, now crawling through the heather, the wet ground soon soaking the knees of my breeches, while ahead of me the sky grew red, until I could actually see the sparks from the huge fire rising up to soar over us, blasted by the prevailing westerly wind.

At last the Spook came to a halt and waved me forward. I crawled until I was kneeling alongside him, Alice taking up a position on my right. We were facing the fire, and what I saw dashed such hopes as I'd had: I no longer had any illusions that we were going to destroy the power of the Pendle covens. Despite the Spook's avowed intention in coming here, I knew now that it just wasn't possible. There were too many of them and the threat they posed was too great. To our right there had to be two hundred or more people in an arc facing towards the fire, all of them either witches or part of the clans. And they were armed to the teeth. The women had knives at their belts, some brandishing them wildly so that the blades reflected the firelight; the men had long sticks with knives or barbarous hooks lashed to the end.

There, beyond the fire, facing towards the gathering, and with four other witches at her side – one of them Mab Mouldheel – was the tall, threatening figure of Wurmalde. She was addressing the clans, moving her arms dramatically to emphasize what she was saying. I could just about hear her voice, carried by the wind, but was too far away to make out the actual words.

There seemed to be little happening in the way of rituals. To one side of the main gathering, sheep were roasting on spits and I could even see casks of ale. It looked like they were planning some sort of celebration.

'I can see Mab, but who are the three others with Wurmalde?' I asked, keeping my voice low – though there was little chance that I could be heard: the wind was blowing towards us and the witches were crying out in response to Wurmalde, some shrieking loud enough to wake the long-time dead.

It was Alice who answered. 'One on the right is Anne Malkin, coven leader. Next to her is Old Florence, who governs the Deanes. Getting on in years, she is, and little threat to us tonight. They must have carried her up the hill. The third is Grimalkin, the assassin . . .'

At the name Grimalkin I felt the hairs on the back of my neck move. She was the cruel killer whom Wurmalde had threatened to use against Jack and his family; the one who marked the boundaries of Pendle with her warning sign.

Suddenly Wurmalde stopped speaking, and after a few moments' silence the witches surged towards the casks of ale and spits of roasting sheep. If the celebrations were beginning, then did it mean the ritual had already been completed?

It was as if the Spook had read my mind. 'I don't like the look of this at all,' he said. 'I'm afraid we've arrived too late . . .'

Soon the clans were celebrating with abandon, quaffing ale and wolfing down roasted mutton while I could only watch in dismay, my heart sinking lower and lower. Had the Fiend already come through the portal? If so, he would be gathering strength. Soon he would be coming for me.

As I watched, something happened to silence the celebrations. A lone witch ran towards the fire from the north-east. She must have been placed on the summit to keep watch. Whatever she said to the gathering, all the witches suddenly became less boisterous; some turned their backs on the fire and faced north or east. Some even seemed to be looking in our direction, and even though everything I'd been taught told me that they couldn't sniff us out from that distance, I became very nervous.

When I glanced down and to my right, I could see the torches moving up the hill. The Spook had planned things well. The villagers were spread out in groups, with the groups themselves not too close together, which gave the illusion that an army was climbing

Pendle. But would the witches fall for that? By now the clans were definitely alarmed. Sentinels kept running back from their positions on the summit to report to the gathering.

After a while the clans began to shrink back behind the fire and a few were even beginning to slip away to the west, as if trying to lose themselves in the darkness beyond the firelight. But then it all went wrong . . .

Once the villagers reached the summit and moved onto the plateau towards the witches, it became increasingly apparent that they were pitifully few in number. You could see their advance becoming slower and slower as they saw the armed horde they faced. Now the witches began to jeer and yell, brandishing their weapons while moving purposefully forwards. It looked as if all was lost. I wondered what the Spook would do now. It was hopeless but I couldn't see him remaining hidden here in the shadows while the villagers were slaughtered. In a moment he'd lead me and Alice forward to join the fray.

By now the villagers had come to a halt, standing in

a thin, uncertain line. They looked ready to turn and flee at any moment. But then I heard a man shouting what sounded like orders and, to my astonishment, someone burst from the line and ran directly towards the waiting witches. It was a big man brandishing a huge hammer. At first I thought it was Matt Finley, the Downham blacksmith, but then I recognized him beyond all doubt. It was James! He was running flat out, water splashing up each time his boots landed on the soggy ground; the spray glistening orange and red in the firelight so that he seemed to be running through fire – either that or his boots themselves flickered flames into the darkness.

Now, rather than remaining in a thin line, the villagers bunched up tightly behind him and followed him, most running forward at full pelt. As if by chance, or maybe some dormant battle instinct, moments before reaching their enemies, they somehow achieved the shape of a wedge, which drove hard into the massed witches, splitting the group almost into two halves before being brought to a standstill by the sheer weight of their numbers. James was the point of that wedge, and now I could see his hammer rising and falling and hear shrieks and shouts as the witches fought back and battle was joined.

I feared for James. How long could he survive, pressed hard by so many opponents? But before I could dwell on my fear, the Spook touched my shoulder.

'Right, lad, follow me. This is our chance. But you stay here, girl,' he commanded Alice. 'If things go badly, you of all people wouldn't want to fall into their hands!'

So saying, the Spook stood up and began to run towards the other side of the fire. I followed close at his heels and Alice, ignoring his warning, was at my right shoulder. And then we had a stroke of luck. Grimalkin, the assassin, went to join the fray, and now only four witches were standing to the rear of the fire – just Wurmalde, Mab, Old Florence and Anne Malkin.

We were closing on them fast when they finally saw the threat. It was close, so very close. Within moments the Spook would have cast his chain over Wurmalde and carried her off down the hill while I tried to hold off any pursuit. But it was not to be. Wurmalde shrieked out a command and some witches nearest to the fire turned their backs on the battle and rushed forward, quickly moving between us and our quarry.

The Spook never paused. Still running at full tilt, he downed the first witch with a sideways swing of his staff. The next opponent was a big bear of a man, wielding an enormous cudgel, but this time the Spook used the point of his staff. The blade flashed and the man went down. But now the Spook was gradually being brought to a halt as witches and their supporters pressed in on us from every side. I started swinging my own staff desperately, but hope was leaving me fast. There were simply too many of them.

Two witches faced me: one gripped the end of my staff and held it tightly, her face grimacing with the pain of holding the rowan wood; the second, her expression filled with cruel intent, raised her knife and I saw the long serrated blade arcing down towards my chest. I brought up my right arm to try and fend off the blow even though I knew I was already too late.

But her blade failed to strike home. I glimpsed a dark shape above me and felt a sudden wind, something passing so close above that it almost touched my head, and the witch with the blade screamed as she was lifted clean off her feet and hurled away from me. She fell onto the edge of the fire, throwing up a shower of sparks.

I looked up and saw spread wings – another lamia gliding down towards me with death in its ferocious eyes; in that instant the lightning flashed directly above so that those wings became translucent and I could see the network of veins within. Sharp claws slashed and the feet hooked into the second witch, dragging her hand away from my staff. Then the wings were still no more; faster and faster they beat, becoming a blur, as sharp claws lifted and tore before hurling her away.

People were running then. Not towards us; they were fleeing, holding their arms high to ward off the terror that fell upon them from out of the darkness. Ahead, I glimpsed the Spook. He was running hard towards the south-western edge of the plateau. He was chasing Wurmalde. I glanced around, looking for Alice, but could see no sign of her. Witches were scattering in every direction and cries of pain and terror filled the air.

So I followed the Spook. After all, Wurmalde was the key to all this; the one who had brought the covens together. He might need my help. I still had my staff and my chain. If anything went wrong, I might still be able to bind the witch.

As we ran, the heavens opened and a deluge began, the rain driving in hard from the west. We soon slowed down: the slope was steep and slippery with the rain. I kept losing my balance and falling. Most of the time I struggled downwards in darkness, but then, in the far distance, I saw two small specks of light. Even when lightning flashed there was no sign of Wurmalde; the Spook was getting further and further ahead despite all my efforts to keep up. But finally, after what seemed like an endless desperate and difficult descent, the incline became less steep and, in a flash of sheet lightning, I saw the witch some way ahead of the Spook.

Far beyond her, waiting on a narrow track, was her black coach. The specks of light I'd seen were the two lanterns, one on either side of the driver, who was twisting round in his seat, staring back up the hill towards us.

Now that the ground had levelled out somewhat, the speed of the chase increased dramatically. The Spook was still way ahead of me, his cloak billowing behind him as he ran. His legs seemed to be flying across the grass and I was struggling to keep up. Now, with every stride, he was gaining on the witch as she ran desperately towards the coach. Cobden looked back at her briefly but made no attempt to get down and assist her. Now he was staring up at the low clouds boiling overhead and his whip was raised, ready to drive the horses forward.

As she grasped the handle and pulled open the door, Wurmalde almost fell, but a moment later she was inside. The Spook had now reached the coach and was actually reaching for the handle and raising his staff when Cobden cracked his whip in the air to send the team of horses plunging forward. His whip cracked again, its tip making cruel contact with the animals' backs; whinnying with pain and fear, they accelerated away while the Spook came to a halt, baffled.

'She's got away!' he said, shaking his head in frustration as I came to his side. 'So near. We almost had her! Now she's free to work her evil again!'

But the Spook was wrong. There was another flash of sheet lightning directly above, and out of that light dropped a dark shape. It swooped low over the coach and seemed to strike Cobden from behind. He thrust up an arm to defend himself but had already lost his balance. He fell forward onto the horses, then slipped between them. The hooves trampled him momentarily before the wheels ran over him. I heard the beginning of a scream but it was drowned out by the thunder.

Driverless, the horses plunged on, carrying Wurmalde's coach faster and faster down the steep track. Illuminated by another brilliant flash of lightning, the dark shape plunged downwards again to land

heavily on the roof of the coach, and in the succeeding
darkness I heard its claws begin to rip into the roof
before the sound was drowned by thunder once more.
I'd seen that coach by moonlight and knew it was con-
structed from heavy, strong wood. But now, again lit
by lightning, it seemed to splinter and collapse like an
eggshell. Moments later the lamia took to the air again,
but this time its flight was more ponderous. Round and
round it spiralled, slowly gaining height as, dragged by
the terrified horses, the wreck of the carriage continued
down the hill, rocking violently from side to side, as if
about to overturn at any moment.

I'd been close to the eighteen-pounder – the County
cannon that had fired upon Malkin Tower with such a
tremendous roar – but that was nothing compared to
the way the elements behaved now. Flash after flash
filled the heavens while forked lightning rent the sky
over the hill. It was as if this was God's cannon, explosion after explosion hurling down wrath upon the
witches of Pendle.

I looked up and saw the lamia carrying Wurmalde,

its insectoid wings whirring desperately as, buffeted by the wind, it strove to gain height. Now it began to move back towards the hill.

'Gore Rock!' cried the Spook, his voice just audible above the tumult of the elements.

For a moment I didn't know what he meant, but then the lamia released Wurmalde and I heard her scream as she fell through the turbulent air. I didn't hear her hit the rock because the sound was drowned out by thunder but I knew what had happened. Shuddering at the thought of what we would find, I followed the Spook towards the sacrificial boulder.

'Stay here, lad,' he commanded, going forward to investigate.

I didn't need telling twice and waited there shivering until he returned to my side.

'So much for immortality!' he said grimly. 'She won't bother us again. It's over at last.'

But it wasn't, and I feared the worst. It was only when we met some of the others coming down the hill that the truth was confirmed. Alice was among them but she was limping badly.

'Are you all right?' I asked her.

'Ain't nothing to worry about, Tom. Just twisted my ankle running on the slope, that's all . . .'

Then I realized that there was no sign of James, and even before she spoke again I knew by her face that something terrible had occurred.

'Is it James?' I asked, horrified at the thought that something had happened to my brother.

Alice shook her head. 'No, Tom. James is all right. Nothing worse than a few cuts and bruises. He's helping to carry some of the injured off the hill. It's you, Tom. You're in terrible danger. Tried to catch Mab, I did, but she got away. But not before she boasted that they'd won; that they'd already carried out the ritual on Gore Rock as the sun went down. I believe her, Tom. So we were already too late when we climbed the hill.' Alice's face was twisted with anguish. 'Old Nick's crawled through the portal. He's in the world already and you're the one he'll be coming for. Run, Tom! Run – please. Back to the farm! Back to your mam's room – before it's too late.'

The Spook nodded. 'The girl's right. That's all you can do now. There's no refuge safe enough for you here. And those two lamias will have no chance at all against what's coming. I don't know how long you've got – it'll take the Fiend some time to adjust to this world and gather strength. Just how long before he comes after you, I wouldn't like to guess. Here,' he said. 'Take my staff. Use the blade if you have to! Use it against anyone or anything that gets in your way! We'll follow on after you as quickly as we can. Just as soon as we've sorted things out a bit here. And once in your mam's room, stay there until it's safe.'

'How will I know when it is safe?' I asked.

'Trust your instincts, lad, and you'll know when it's safe. In any case, don't you remember what that foul creature told us? Creatures of the dark often lie, but I suspect that Tibb *was* telling the truth about the limits of the power the witches have over the Fiend. For just two days he'll be in the power of the covens, bound to their will. Survive that long and he'll no doubt have mischief of his own to carry out on the third day and will leave you alone. Now get you gone before it's too late!'

So we swapped staffs, and without a backward glance I set off at a run. Mam had been proved right. The dark made flesh would now walk the earth. I was scared and I was desperate, but I kept my pace steady because it was a long way back to Jack's farm.

CHAPTER
23
BLOOD MOON

I moved west, trying to get as far away from the hill as possible. The witches had fled the summit and there was a risk that I might encounter one or more of them at any point.

I couldn't wait to be clear of the Pendle district altogether. The storm was dying down and moving away to the east; now the flashes of lightning were more distant, the gaps between these and the subsequent rumbles of thunder growing. Darkness was both friend and enemy: friend because it aided my swift, secret passage across witch country; enemy because out of it at any second might emerge the Fiend, the Devil himself.

A dark wood lay in my path and I paused, listening carefully before I moved on into the trees. The wind had died down completely and everything was very still. Not a leaf moved. All was silent. But it didn't feel right. My instincts warned me of danger waiting within. I turned and decided to make a detour round the outside of the wood, avoiding meeting danger head on. But it didn't help. Whatever it was came looking for me.

A dark shape stepped out from behind the trunk of an ancient oak and moved into my path. Trembling, I lifted the Spook's staff and pressed the secret lever so that, with a click, the blade emerged from its recess.

It was very dark beneath the tree but the figure that confronted me and the pale glimmer of the face – most of all the bare feet – were familiar to me. Even before she spoke, I knew that it was Mab Mouldheel.

'I've come to say goodbye,' she said softly. 'You could've been mine, Tom, and then none of this would have happened. You'd have been safe with me, not running for your life like this. Together we could've sorted

441

the Malkins once and for all. Now it's too late. Soon you'll be dead. You've got a few hours at the most. That's all that's left to you now.'

'You don't see everything!' I said angrily. 'So get out of my way before—'

I raised the staff towards her but Mab just laughed. 'I've seen where you're going now. It wasn't too hard to see that. Think your mam's room's going to save you, do you? Well, don't be so sure about that! Nothing stops Old Nick. His will be done, on earth as it is in Hell. The world belonged to him in the old days and now it's his once more and he'll do what he wants with it. King o' the world, he is, and nothing stands in his way.'

'How could you do it?' I asked angrily. 'How could you be part of that madness? You told me yourself that the Fiend can't be controlled. He'll control you and threaten the whole world. What you've done is insane. I can't understand why you'd do it!'

'Why? Why?' shouted Mab. 'Don't you *know* why? I cared about you, Tom. Really cared. I *loved* you!'

I was stunned by her use of the word 'love'. For a

moment we both fell silent. But then Mab's torrent of words continued:

'I trusted you. Then you betrayed me. But now we're finished for ever and I don't care what happens to you. Even if you escape Old Nick, it's odds on that you'll never get home anyway. You'll be dead long before then. The Malkins aren't taking any chances. Want you dead real bad: to make doubly sure, they've set Grimalkin on you. She's after you now and not too far behind. If you're lucky, she'll kill you quickly and there won't be too much pain. Best turn round, go back towards her and get it over with, because if you make it hard for her, then she'll make it hard for you. She'll kill you slowly and painfully!'

I took a deep breath and shook my head. 'You'd better hope that you're right, Mab,' I said. 'If I survive, you're going to be very sorry. One day I'll come back to Pendle for you. Specially for you. And you'll spend the rest of your life in a pit eating worms!'

I ran straight at her and Mab flinched to one side as I sped past. I was no longer conserving my strength now.

I was running hard through the darkness. Running for my life, imagining Grimalkin closing in on me with every stride I took.

At times I was forced to rest. Running made my throat hot and dry and I had to stop occasionally to slake my thirst from streams. I couldn't afford to halt for long because Grimalkin would be running too. They said that she was strong and tireless. My knowledge of the County wouldn't help me too much either. No advantage in taking short cuts. Grimalkin was County too – and a skilled assassin, able to track me whichever obscure path I chose.

Soon I had another problem. Things started to feel very wrong. Since becoming the Spook's apprentice I'd often been scared, and mostly with good reason. I had two very good reasons now: my pursuit by Grimalkin and the threat conjured up by Wurmalde and the three covens. But it was more than that. I can only describe it as a sense of foreboding and anxiety. The feeling that usually only comes in nightmares: an extreme dread, a mortal fear. One moment the world was the way it had always been; the next, it had changed for ever.

It was as if something had entered my world as I ran towards Jack's farm – something as yet invisible – and I knew that nothing would ever be the same again.

That was my first warning that things were terribly wrong. The second was to do with time. Night or day, I've always known what time it is. Give or take a minute or so, I can easily tell the time by the position of the sun or the stars. Even without them though, I always just know. But as I ran, what my head told me didn't match what I could see. It should have been dawn but the sun hadn't come up.

When I looked towards the eastern horizon, there wasn't even the faintest glimmer of light. There were no clouds now – the wind had torn them to tatters and wafted them east. But when I looked up, there were no stars either. No stars at all. It just wasn't possible. At least, not possible in the world as it had once been.

But there was one object very low in the sky: the moon – which shouldn't have been visible. The final

445

stage of the waning moon is a very thin crescent with its horns pointing from left to right. I'd seen that yesterday before the storm struck Pendle. Now the moon should have been totally dark. Invisible. Yet there was a full moon very low on the eastern horizon. A moon that didn't shine with its normal silvery light. The moon was blood-red.

There was no wind either. Not a leaf moved. Everything was utterly still and silent. It was as if the whole world was holding its breath and I was the only living, breathing, moving creature on its surface. It was summer but it suddenly became very cold. My breath steamed in the freezing air and the grass at my feet whitened with hoar frost. Hoar frost in August!

So I ran on towards Jack's farm, the only sound that of my boots beating a rhythmical tattoo on the hardening earth.

I seemed to be running for an eternity but at last I saw Hangman's Hill ahead of me. Beyond it was the farm. Soon I was jogging up into the trees that shrouded its upper reaches. I was so close now; so close to the refuge that Mam had prepared. But the moon was red – so red, bathing everything it its lurid, baleful light. And the hanging men were there. The ghasts. The remnants of those who had been hanged long ago during the civil war that had torn the whole land asunder, dividing the County, ripping families apart, setting brother against brother.

I'd seen the ghasts before. The Spook had made me confront them as we set off from the farm in the first minutes of my apprenticeship. As a young lad I'd heard them from my bedroom. They were a fact; they scared the farm dogs, keeping them from the pastures immediately below. But even when I'd confronted them with the Spook, they had never seemed so vivid, never so real. Now they groaned and choked as they slowly turned, suspended from the creaking branches. And their eyes seemed to be staring towards me in accusation – eyes that seemed to be saying that it was somehow my fault; that I was to blame for them hanging there.

But they were just ghasts, I told myself, remembering one of the very first things the Spook had taught me. They *weren't* ghosts – lingering sentient spirits, bound to the scene of their death. They were just fragments, memories remaining while their spirits had passed on – hopefully to a better place. Still they stared hard at me and their gaze chilled me to the bone. And then there was a sudden alarming sound: someone was running up the hill towards me, feet thundering on the hard, frozen ground!

Grimalkin, the witch assassin, was behind me and she was closing in for the kill.

CHAPTER
24
DESPAIR

The witch was chasing me through the dark wood, getting nearer and nearer by the second.

I was running as fast as I was able, weaving desperately, with branches whipping into my face. Twice I ducked aside as cold dead fingers brushed my forehead. Ghast fingers. The fingers of the hanging men.

Ghasts were mostly phantasms – images without substance. But fear gave them strength and solidity, and I was terrified: terrified of the assassin; terrified of the death that chased me through the wood. And my terror was feeding the dark.

I was tired and my strength was failing but I drove myself harder and harder towards the summit of

Hangman's Hill. Once I'd reached it, a faint hope quivered within me. Downhill, the going was easier. Beyond the trees was the fence that bordered the northern pasture of the farm. Climb over that fence and it wasn't more than half a mile or so to the farmyard and the back door of the house. Then up the stairs. Turn the key to Mam's room. Get inside. Lock it behind me. Do that and I'd be safe! But would I have time for *any* of that?

Grimalkin might pull me back as I climbed over the fence. She could catch me crossing the pasture. Or the yard. Then I would have to wait while I unlocked the door. I imagined my trembling fingers trying to insert the key into the lock as she ran up the stairs behind me.

But would I even reach the fence? She was getting nearer now. Much nearer. I could hear her feet pounding down the slope towards me. *Better to turn and fight,* said a voice inside my head. *Better to face her now than be cut down from behind.* But what chance did I have against a trained and experienced assassin? What hope against the strength and speed of a witch whose talent was murder?

In my right hand I gripped the Spook's staff; in my left was my silver chain, coiled about my wrist ready for throwing. I ran on, the blood moon flickering its baleful light through the leaf canopy to my left. I'd almost reached the edge of Hangman's Wood but the witch assassin was very close now. I could hear the pad-pad of her feet and the swish-wish of her breath.

As I ran beyond the final tree, the farm fence directly ahead, the witch sprinted towards me from the right, a dagger in each hand, the long blades reflecting the moon's red light. I staggered to my left and cracked the chain to send it hurtling towards her. But all my training proved useless. I was weary, terrified and on the verge of despair. The chain fell harmlessly onto the grass. So, exhausted, I finally turned to face the witch.

It was over and I knew it. All I had now was the Spook's staff but I barely had the strength to lift it. My heart was hammering, my breath rasping and the world seemed to spin about me.

Now I could see Grimalkin for the first time. She wore a short black smock tied at her waist but her skirt was divided and strapped tightly to each thigh to aid running. Her body was criss-crossed with narrow leather straps to which sheaths were bound, each holding a weapon: blades of different lengths; sharp hooks; small implements like shears . . .

Suddenly I remembered what the Spook had pointed out carved on the oak tree soon after we'd entered Pendle. They weren't shears. They were sharp scissors, used to cut flesh and bone! And around the witch's neck was a necklace of bones. Some I recognized as human – fingers and toes – and thumb bones hung from each earlobe: trophies from those she'd slain.

She was powerful and also beautiful in a strange sort of way, and looking at her made my teeth tingle. But her lips were painted black, and when she opened her mouth in a travesty of a smile, I saw that her teeth had been filed to points. And at that moment I recalled Tibb's words . . .

I was looking into the mouth of death.

'You're a disappointment,' Grimalkin said, leaning back against the trunk of the final tree and pointing her daggers downwards so that the long blades crossed against her knees. 'I've heard so much about you, and despite your youth I hoped for more. Now I see that you're just a child and hardly worthy of my skills. It's a pity I can't wait until you become a man.'

'Then let me go, please,' I begged, seeing just a faint glimmer of hope in what she said. 'They told me that you like a kill to be difficult. So why *don't* you wait? When I'm older, we'll meet again. Then I'd be able to put up a fight. Let me live!'

'I do what must be done,' she said, shaking her head, genuine sadness in her eyes. 'I wish it were otherwise but . . .'

She shrugged and allowed the blade to fall from her right hand and bury itself in the soft earth at her feet. Then she held her right arm wide as if offering an embrace. 'Come here, child. Rest your head against my bosom and close your eyes. I will make it swift. There will be a brief moment of pain – hardly more

453

than a mother's kiss against your throat – and then your struggle against this life will be over. Trust me. I will give you peace at last . . .'

I nodded, lowered my head and approached her, my heart racing. As I took the second step towards her waiting embrace, tears suddenly flowed down my cheeks and I heard her give a deep sigh. But in completing that step, I flicked the Spook's staff from my right hand to my left. And with all the speed and strength that I could muster I drove it hard towards her so that the blade went straight through her left shoulder, pinning her to the trunk of the tree.

She uttered no sound at all. The pain must have been terrible but her only reaction was a slight tightening of the lips. I released the staff, leaving it still quivering in the wood, then turned to run. The blade had gone deep into the tree and the staff itself was rowan. She would find it difficult and painful to free herself. Now I had a chance to reach the safety of Mam's room.

I'd only taken two steps when something made me turn and look back towards the witch. She had reached across with her right hand and taken the blade from her left and now, with incredible speed and force, she hurled the knife straight at my head.

I watched it spinning towards me, its blade reflecting the red light of the moon. End over end it came. I could have tried to duck or even step to one side, but neither movement would have saved me from the speed and force of that blade.

What I did was not done consciously. I had no time to think. I made no decision. Some other part of me acted. I simply concentrated, my whole self focused on that spinning blade until time seemed to slow.

I reached up and plucked it out of the air, my fingers closing about the wooden handle. Then I cast it away from me onto the grass. Moments later I was climbing the fence and running across the field towards the farm.

The farmyard was still and silent. The animals were being cared for by our neighbour, Mr Wilkinson, so that wasn't alarming in itself. It was just that I felt very

455

uneasy. A sudden fearful thought pushed itself into my head.

What if the Fiend were already here? What if he were already inside the darkness of the farmhouse? Lurking inside one of the downstairs rooms, ready to follow me up the stairs and pounce as I tried to unlock the door of Mam's room?

Thrusting the thought aside, I ran past the site of the burned barn and across the yard towards the house. I glanced at the wall, which should have been covered in a profusion of red roses. Mam's roses. But they were dead, blackened and withered on their stems. And there was no Mam waiting to greet me inside. No Dad. This had been my home but now it looked more like a house from a nightmare.

At the back door I paused for a moment to listen. Silence. So I went in and ran up the stairs two at a time until I faced the door to Mam's room. Then I pulled the keys from my neck and, with shaking fingers, inserted the largest one into the lock. Once inside, I locked the door behind me and leaned back against it, breathing deeply. I gazed around at the empty room with its bare floorboards. The air here was much warmer than outside. I felt the mildness of a summer's night. I was safe. Or was I?

Could even Mam's room protect me from the Devil himself? Hardly had I began to wonder about that when I remembered again something that Mam had said:

If you're brave and your soul is pure and good, this room is a redoubt, a fortress against the dark . . .

Well, I was as brave as I could manage under the circumstances. I was afraid, true, but who wouldn't be? No, it was the bit about my soul being pure and good that worried me now. I felt that I'd changed for the worse. Bit by bit, the need to survive had made me betray the way that I'd been brought up. Dad had taught me that I should keep my word, but I'd never for one moment intended to keep my bargain with Mab. It had been for a good reason, but nevertheless I'd deceived her. And the strange thing was that Mab, a witch who belonged to the dark, always kept her word.

And then there was Grimalkin. She had a code of honour but I'd beaten her with guile; with sly deceit. Was that why the tears had gushed from my eyes as I'd pretended to step towards her deadly embrace? Those tears had come as a complete surprise to me. An emotion had welled up inside and I'd had no control over it. Those tears had probably put Grimalkin further off her guard: she'd assumed I was crying in fear.

Had they in fact been tears of shame? Tears because I knew I'd fallen so far short of the behaviour that Dad had expected of me? If my soul was no longer pure and good, then the room might not protect me, and my lies had merely put off the moment of my destruction.

I walked across to the window and peered out. It overlooked the farmyard, and in the light of the blood moon I could see the blackened foundations of the barn, the empty pig and cattle pens, and the north pasture reaching to the foot of Hangman's Hill. Nothing moved.

I paced back towards the centre of the room, growing increasingly nervous. Would I see the Devil approach?

And if so, what form would he take? Or would he simply materialize out of the empty air? No sooner had that scary thought entered my head than I heard terrifying noises from outside – loud booms and bangs, thuds against the walls – and the house actually began to shake. Was it the Fiend? Was he trying to break into the house? Smash through the stones?

It certainly sounded as if something were battering at the walls. Next, powerful rhythmical thumps came from above. Something heavy was pounding on the roof and I could hear slates falling down into the yard. There were fearful bellowing and snorting sounds too, like those of an angry bull. But when I rushed to the window again, there was nothing to be seen. Nothing at all.

As suddenly as they had started, the sounds ceased, and in the deep silence that followed, the house itself seemed to be holding its breath. Then there were more noises, but from within the house; from down in the kitchen. The smash and crash of cups and saucers. The clatter of cutlery on stone flags. Someone was throwing crockery hard onto the floor; emptying drawers of kitchen utensils. Moments later that ceased too, but into the brief silence intruded a new noise – that of a rocking chair. I could hear it clearly, creaking as its wooden runners made rhythmic contact with the flags.

For a moment my heart leaped. I'd heard that sound so many times as a child: the familiar noise of Mam rocking in her chair. She was back! Mam had come back to save me and now everything would be all right again!

I should have had more faith; realized that she wouldn't leave me to face this horror alone. I reached for the key, actually intending to unlock the door and go downstairs. But I remembered just in time that Mam's chair had been smashed to pieces by the witches who'd raided the house. The crockery had already been broken too, the knives and forks scattered on the flags. They were just sounds, re-created to lure me from the safety of the room.

That sinister rocking faded and ceased. The next sound was much nearer. Something was climbing the stairs. It wasn't the thump of heavy boots. It sounded more like a large animal. I could hear its panting breath, the pad, pad of heavy paws on the wooden stairs and then a low, angry growl.

Moments later claws started scratching at the bottom of the door. At first it was exploratory and half-hearted, like a farm dog lured by the appetizing smell of cooking, but remembering its place in the scheme of things and trying to get into a kitchen without doing too much damage. But then the clawing became more rapid and frantic, as if the wood were being ripped to shreds.

Next I had a sense of something huge; something far larger than a dog. A sudden stench of death and rot assailed my senses and, filled with alarm, I backed away from the door just as something thudded against it heavily. The door began to groan and buckle as if a great weight were being pressed against it. For a moment I thought it would shatter or be flung open but then the pressure eased and all I could hear was the panting breath.

After a while even that faded away and I began to

have more faith in the room and what Mam had done to protect me. Slowly I started to believe that I was safe and that not even the Devil himself could reach me here. Eventually my fear receded, to be replaced by weariness.

I was close to exhaustion now, hardly able to keep my eyes open, so I stretched myself out on the hard wooden boards. Despite the discomfort, I fell almost immediately into a very deep sleep. How long I slept for it was impossible to say, but when I got up, nothing had changed. I walked over to the window and gazed out over the same bleak scene. Nothing moved. It was a nightmare vision of timelessness. But then I realized that I was wrong. There had been one change. The ground was even whiter, the frost covering thicker and more extensive. Would the blood moon ever set? Would the sun ever shine again?

Within the room there was still the mild warmth of a County summer's night, but gradually, even as I watched, frost started to form on the outside of the window until it became white and opaque.

I walked across and placed my hand against it. The air around me was balmy, but the cold of the window bit into my skin instantly. I breathed hard onto the glass until a small circle of visibility formed, allowing me a narrow view of the same dismal outer scene.

Was I trapped in some sort of earthly hell? Had the arrival of the Fiend done more damage than the Spook had expected, creating a timeless frozen domain over which he would rule for ever? Would it ever be safe to leave Mam's room?

I felt defeated and weary and my mouth was parched, for I'd brought no water with me! What a fool I'd been! I should have thought of that and prepared myself better. To stay in Mam's refuge for any significant length of time, I needed water and provisions. Things had happened so quickly though. From the time I'd entered Pendle with the Spook it had been one threat after another; danger after danger. What chance had there been?

For a while I paced the floor. Backwards and forwards from wall to wall. There was nothing else to do. Backwards and forwards, my boots thumping on the wooden boards. As I paced, I started to develop a severe headache. I didn't usually get headaches but this one was really bad. It was as if a great weight were pressing down on the top of my head and it throbbed with every frantic beat of my heart.

How long could I go on like this? Even if time was actually passing, it wasn't like anything I'd experienced before. With that I had a sudden dark thought . . .

Mam had protected the room and the Fiend couldn't get in. But that didn't stop what he could do *outside* the room. He had changed the world – or at least changed the world that I could see from the window. Everything outside this room – the farm, the house, the trees, people and animals – was in his grip. Would I ever be able to leave the room again? Maybe the world would only return to normal once I went outside?

Dark thoughts started to slip into my mind, despite all my efforts to keep them out. What was the use of anything? We were born, we lived a few years, grew old and then died. What was the point of it all? All those people in the County and the wide world beyond, living their short little lives before going to the grave. What was it all for? My dad was dead. He'd worked hard all his life but the journey of his life had had only one destination: the grave. That's where we were all heading. Into the grave. Into the soil, to be eaten by worms. Poor Billy Bradley had been the Spook's apprentice before me. He'd had his fingers bitten off by a boggart and had died of shock and loss of blood. And where was he now? In a grave. Not even in a churchyard. He was buried outside because the Church considered him no better than a malevolent witch. That would be my fate too. A grave in unhallowed ground.

And poor Father Stocks hadn't even been buried yet. He was still lying dead in bed at Read Hall, his body rotting on the sheets. All his life he'd struggled to do right, just like my dad. Better to get it over with now, I thought. Better to leave Mam's room. Once I was dead it would be finished with. There wouldn't be anything to worry about any more. No pain, no more heartache.

Anything was better than being imprisoned in this

room until I died of thirst or starvation. Better to go outside now and be done with it . . .

I was actually walking towards the door and reaching for the key when I sensed a sudden coldness; a warning: something that didn't belong in this world was close by. In the corner of the room furthest from the door and the window, a shimmering column of light began to form.

I backed away. Was it a ghost or something from the dark? I saw walking boots materialize first, then a black cassock. It was a priest! The head formed quickly, the face looking towards me uncertainly. It was the ghost of Father Stocks!

Or was it? I shivered again. I'd met things that could shape-shift. What if this was the Fiend, taking on the form of Father Stocks in order to deceive me? I fought to steady my breathing. Mam had said that nothing evil could enter here. I had to believe that. It was all I had left. So whatever the apparition was, it had to be good, not evil.

'I'm sorry, Father!' I cried. 'Sorry that I didn't return

in time to save you. I did my best and got back before dark fell, but it was already too late . . .'

Father Stocks nodded sadly. *'You did all you could, Tom. All you possibly could. But now I'm lost and afraid. I've been wandering in a grey fog for what seems like an eternity. Once I thought I saw a faint glimmer of light ahead but it faded and died away. And I keep hearing voices, Tom. The voices of children calling my name. Oh, Tom! I think they're the voices of the children I never had, my unborn children calling out to me. I should have been a real father, Tom. Not a priest. And now it's too late.'*

'But why are you here, Father? Why have you come here to visit me? Are you here to help?'

The ghost shook its head and looked bewildered. *'I just found myself here, Tom, that's all. I didn't choose to be here. Perhaps somebody sent me. But why I don't know.'*

'You lived a good life, Father,' I told him, stepping closer and starting to feel sorry for him. 'You made a difference to lots of people and you fought the dark. What more could you do? So just go back. Go and look after yourself and forget me! Leave me – go back and search for the light.'

'I can't, Tom. I don't know how. I've tried to pray but now my mind's just full of darkness and despair. I tried to fight the dark but didn't do it very well. I should have seen what Wurmalde was long ago. I let her blind me with glamour and fascination. Nowell suffered the same. But I should have known better. I failed as a priest, and all my training as a spook came to nothing. My life's been a complete waste. It was all for nothing!'

The plight of poor Father Stocks finally made me forget my own fears. He was in torment and I had to help. I remembered how the Spook usually dealt with troubled ghosts that couldn't move on. If giving them a good talking to had no effect, he would ask them to consider their own lives. To focus on a happy memory. A memory that usually freed them from the chains binding them to this world.

'Listen to me, Father. You were a spook as well as a priest. So remember now what John Gregory taught you. All you have to do is think about a happy memory and concentrate on that. So think now! Think carefully.

Concentrate! What was your happiest moment on this earth?'

The anguished face of the dead priest shimmered and almost faded away, but then it came back into sharp focus and looked very thoughtful.

'*One morning I woke up and looked about me. I was lying on a bed and the sun was shining through the window and dust motes were dancing in that broad beam of sunlight, glittering like a thousand angels. But for a moment I could remember nothing. I didn't know who I was. I didn't know where I was. I couldn't even remember my own name. I had no worries, no cares. I was just a point of consciousness. It was as if I was free of the burden of life. Free of all that I'd been and done. I was nobody but I was everybody at the same time. And I was happy and content.*'

'And that's exactly what you are now,' I told him, seizing on the idea he'd just put forward. 'You're nobody and you're everybody. And you've already found the light . . .'

Father Stocks's mouth opened in astonishment; then a slow smile spread across his face, a smile of joy and understanding. His ghost slowly faded away and I smiled too; my first smile for a long time. I'd just sent my first ghost into the light.

And, speaking of light, Mam's room was suddenly full of it! As Father Stocks faded away, a bright shaft of sunlight fell through the window, and it too was full of gleaming dust motes, just as the dead priest had described.

I took a deep breath. It seemed to me that I'd been very low. The Fiend hadn't been able to enter the room but somehow he'd reached into my mind so that I would despair, open the door and go out to him. Just in time the ghost of Father Stocks had appeared and I'd forgotten my own pain. My ordeal was over. I knew instinctively that it was safe, at last, to leave the room.

I walked over to the window. The blood moon had gone. The nightmare was over. Suddenly my awareness of the passage of time returned. Two days must have passed since the arrival of the Fiend through the portal, so it was now the third day of August. Today was my birthday. I was fourteen.

The sky was blue, the grass green and there wasn't a trace of frost anywhere. It had all been a trick, an illusion to draw me from the room to my destruction.

Then I saw two people walking side by side down Hangman's Hill towards the farm. One of them was limping, and even from a distance, I recognized them: it was the Spook and Alice. My master was carrying two bags and two staffs. But then I saw that something on the hill above them had changed.

A dark vertical shadow, like a scar, now divided the wood.

CHAPTER 25
A NEW ORDER

I unlocked the door, left the house and gazed about me at a scene of devastation. The chimney stack had collapsed onto the roof and most of the windows had been smashed. Roof tiles were scattered about the yard, fence posts had been uprooted and Mam's rose stems had been torn from the wall. The Fiend had probably done that in frustration at not being able to get into her room.

But the destruction didn't end there. I gazed up at Hangman's Hill and realized just what that dark scar was. A wide path had been cut through the wood, the trees flattened. It looked as if the Fiend had felled them as he descended to attack the house. Felled them as easily as a scythe cuts a swathe of grass. What strength and power that suggested! Even so, Mam's room had withstood the attack.

But it was over now. The air was still and the birds were singing. I walked across the yard and headed towards Hangman's Hill, meeting the Spook and Alice at the open gate of the north pasture. Alice limped forward and put her arms round me and gave me a big hug.

'Oh, Tom! I'm so glad to see you. I hardly dared hope that you'd survive . . .'

'I'm sorry we couldn't do more, lad,' said the Spook. 'You were on your own from the moment you ran for the farm and there was nothing that anybody could have done to help. Once here, we watched from the hill but it was too risky to get any closer. By the time we arrived, the Fiend had conjured up a dark cloud, which had settled right over the house and yard, obscuring them from view, and we could hear him within it, battering, bellowing and doing his worst. It was bad having to keep our distance and do nothing to help, but

473

I put my trust in that mother of yours, hoping that what she'd done to the room would be enough to keep you safe. And it looks like that trust was well-founded.'

'But he's in the world now, isn't he?' I asked, hoping that the Spook might contradict me.

Shattering my last hope, he just nodded grimly in silent confirmation. 'Aye, he's here all right. You can feel it. Something's changed. It's like the first chill in the autumn air. A warning of winter. A new order of things has begun. As Father Stocks once said, the Fiend is the dark made flesh, but Wurmalde and the witches could only control him for two days. They sent him after you, but now that's over and he'll be making his own plans. He's no longer bound to their will, and hopefully he'll forget you for a while. But now nobody in the County is safe. The power of the dark will grow even faster and we'll all have our work cut out to keep it at bay. Our trade was dangerous before, but what we face now doesn't bear thinking about, lad!'

I pointed up at the scar that divided Hangman's Wood. 'Is there damage like that elsewhere?' I asked.

'Aye, lad, there is – but just along the direct path from Pendle Hill to here. Crops have been flattened, along with a good many trees and the odd building or two. No doubt lives have been lost, but once here the Fiend concentrated on trying to get at you; the County was spared what could have been far worse.'

'So we failed,' I said sadly. 'A force that can do that is far too strong for anybody to face. How big is he? Is he some sort of giant?'

'According to the old books, he can take any shape he wants and make himself large or small,' the Spook replied. 'But most of the time he looks just like a man. Somebody you wouldn't give a second glance. And he doesn't always use brute strength; he often gets his way by cunning. How much of that is true, only time will tell. But cheer up, lad. Where there's a will there's a way. We'll find the means to deal with him one day. Wurmalde is dead; without her the witch clans will soon be at each other's throats again. And we've struck a mighty blow at the Malkins. That tower's theirs no longer. Those two lamias seem to have made it their home. That means your trunks are safe and we've got an even better place to operate from when we visit Pendle again—'

'What? We're going back now?' I asked wearily. The thought of that was almost too much to bear.

'No, it's back to Chipenden now for a well-earned rest. But we'll go back one day. Either next year or the one after. The job's not finished yet. And there's a lot of hard practice ahead for you now. Had you got Grimalkin with the chain, there'd have been no need to use my staff, would there?'

I was too tired to argue so I just nodded.

'Still, you escaped with your life, lad, which wasn't too bad under the circumstances. By the time we reached the tree, which was just beyond the edge of the path cut by the Fiend, she'd freed herself and was long gone, but her blood was still on it. She'd thrown down my staff and couldn't have touched the chain even if she'd wanted to. It's back safe and sound in your bag for now. But that's another enemy you've made for yourself – one more reason to be on your guard!'

I wasn't too bothered about Grimalkin. One day I'd face her again, but it would be when I was older; when she could gain more satisfaction from killing me. But the idea of something as powerful as the Fiend terrified me. It made me really worried about the future – my own and that of the whole County.

'While I was in Mam's room, Father Stocks's ghost paid me a visit,' I told the Spook. 'We talked and I was able to send him towards the light.'

'Well done, lad. Father Stocks will be missed in the County, and I've lost a friend. Sending him to the light is something you can be proud of. There are things in this job that can give a lot of satisfaction, and giving peace to the unquiet dead is one of them.'

'Are James and Jack all right?' I asked.

'As far as we know,' the Spook replied. 'We went back to Downham with the villagers first, helping to carry back their wounded. Then we picked up our bags and came straight here while James headed for Malkin Tower. He was going to bring Jack and his family here – that is, if your brother was fit enough to travel.'

'Then couldn't the three of us stay here for a few days until they arrive?' I asked. 'We could clean up the place a bit. Make things a bit easier for them.'

'I suppose you're right, lad. So be it. We'll stay here and get things sorted.'

So that's what we did. The three of us mucked in and cleared the mess from the rooms and brought a glazier up from the village to fix the windows. I climbed up onto the roof and did what I could with the chimney stack, managing to fix it well enough to allow the smoke to rise freely. It would do until we could get a mason to carry out a proper repair. After a few hours of hard work we had the place clean and tidy, and by nightfall we'd eaten a good meal and had a welcoming fire blazing in the kitchen.

Of course, things would never be back to normal, but we just had to make the best of it. And I wondered if Ellie would be brave enough to live here at the farm again. She might just decide to take her child somewhere safer. After all, the witches knew where it was;

one day they might come here seeking revenge. I knew that a lot would depend on how well Jack recovered. If James did stay and work here, that might bolster Ellie's courage.

The Spook dozed in front of the fire while Alice and I went outside and sat on the step, staring up at the stars. For a while we didn't speak. I was the one who broke the silence.

'It's my birthday today,' I told Alice. 'I'm fourteen now . . .'

'Be a man soon then,' she said, giving me a mocking smile. 'Bit scrawny though, ain't you? You'll need feeding up a bit before then. Need a bit more inside you than that crumbly old cheese.'

I smiled back at her, and then I remembered what Tibb had said to me after Father Stocks's blood had dribbled from his mouth onto my shirt:

I see a girl, soon to be a woman. The girl who will share your life. She will love you, she will betray you, and finally she will die for you.

Did he mean Mab? She'd shocked me by saying she

loved me. I'd betrayed her but she'd also betrayed me by summoning the Fiend to hunt me down. Or did he mean Alice? If so, that prophecy was terrible. Could it possibly come true? I didn't like to think about it and it certainly wasn't something to tell Alice, who believed that the future *could* be foretold. Better to say nothing. It would only make her unhappy.

But there was something else that made me feel a little uneasy. At first I was going to let it go, but a question kept buzzing around inside my head until I just *had* to ask it out loud.

'When I was with Mab and her sisters, something happened that made me think about something you once did. Mab seemed to believe she could own me in some sense – make me belong to her. But when she tried, I felt a pain on my left forearm, in the place where you once jabbed your fingernails into me. You said that you'd put your brand on me. That worries me, Alice. We put brands on cattle and sheep to show ownership. Is that what you've done to me? Have you used dark magic to control me in some way?'

Alice didn't speak for quite a while. When she did, it was to ask me a question. 'Just before you got the pain, what was Mab doing?'

'She was kissing me—'

'What did you let her do *that* for?' Alice asked sharply.

'I didn't have much choice,' I replied. 'My staff rolled out of my hand and I couldn't move.'

'Good job I *did* put my brand on you then. Otherwise you'd have been hers completely. Given her the keys without blinking an eye, you would.'

'So she couldn't own me because you already did?'

Alice nodded. 'Ain't as bad as you make it sound. You should be grateful. What I've done means no witch can ever control you like that. It's my mark, see. My brand. It warns them off. Apart from that it don't mean much though. Not if you don't want it to. Don't have to sit next to me. Move if you want. Do you want to go?'

I shook my head. 'I'm happy sitting here next to you.'

'And I'm happy here sitting next to you. So we're

both happy. What can be wrong with that?'

'Nothing. But don't ever tell the Spook though, or he'll send you away again.'

We didn't speak for a while, but then Alice reached across and got hold of my hand. Her left hand holding mine. I couldn't believe how nice it was to sit there holding hands with her like that. It was even better than the other time on the way to her aunt's at Staumin.

'What are you using?' I asked. 'Fascination or glamour?'

'Both,' she said, giving me a wicked smile.

Once more, I've written most of this from memory, just using my notebook when necessary.

I'm back in Chipenden with Alice and the Spook and it's autumn again. The leaves are starting to fall and the nights are drawing in.

At the farm things are going well. Jack's able to talk again, and although he's still not back to what he was, he's improving steadily and expected to make a full recovery. James kept his promise and is living at the farm as well. He's built a forge next to the new barn and the work is starting to pick up. Not only that – he really does intend to go ahead and start brewing and selling ale, so the farm will live up to its original name once more.

I know that Ellie isn't completely happy though. She's afraid that the witches might pay another visit, but she does feel better now that both Jack and his brother are around.

The arrival of the Fiend means that everything's changed and become more dangerous. Once or twice, when we've talked about it, I think I've seen a flicker of fear on the Spook's face. Things are certainly getting darker.

The news from down south isn't good. It seems that the war is going badly and new recruits are needed to replace those who've fallen in battle. A press gang of soldiers is doing the rounds of the County, forcing young lads into the army against their will. The Spook is concerned that it might happen to me. He says that he usually sends each apprentice to work with another spook for six months or so – that way they see a different master at work and gain valuable experience. So, at the first sign of trouble, he's thinking of placing me with Arkwright, who works beyond Caster. He doesn't think the press gang will go that far north.

The trouble is, Alice wouldn't be able to go with me. But I'll just have to do as I'm told. He's the Spook and I'm only the apprentice. And everything that he does is for the best.

Thomas J. Ward

Mouldheels and Maggots

Born into the Pendle witch clans, I was – my mother a Malkin, my father a Deane. But though I was raised there, the last place in the world I'd ever want to visit is Pendle. The clans fight each other and I've a lot of enemies there – mostly Mouldheels. Lots of spite, there is. Lots of hatred. Vendettas that've lasted centuries. Fall into the hands of enemies there and they'll take your bones and drink your blood. Even so, I went back. I went back alone. I did it for Tom Ward. Did it all for him.

Because Tom's the only person in this whole world I really care about – he's my best friend. Ain't like me, Tom. He belongs to the light and he's apprenticed to a spook named John Gregory.

We'd travelled from Chipenden to visit the farm where Tom was born and grew up. He wanted to see inside the boxes that his mam had left him. Must say I wanted to see inside them too. Curious, I was. Very curious and just dying to know all their secrets. But when we got there, the boxes were gone. Stolen. The barn had been burned to the ground, the farmhouse ransacked and Tom's family kidnapped. Didn't take me long to sniff out that witches had done it. That they'd taken Tom's brother, Jack, his wife, Ellie, and their little child, Mary. The trail led towards Pendle and Tom was desperate to set off after them then and there. But I talked him out of it.

I mean, how long would a spook's apprentice survive alone in the shadow of that brooding hill? Seventh son of a seventh son, he is. Love his bones, they would. Cut 'em out just before dawn. Ain't any bones better than Tom's – that's for sure.

So I travelled on alone while Tom went back to Chipenden to tell the Spook what had happened. Went east to Pendle. Told you I'd enemies there – and that's true – but I got friends too, though precious few. And the best friend I got in that hag-ridden place is my aunt, Agnes Sowerbutts. Got a soft spot for Agnes, I have. She'd have brought me up but for Bony Lizzie.

I remember the night that Lizzie came for me. I like to think I was upset but I don't remember crying. My mam and dad had been cold and dead in the earth for three days and I still hadn't managed to shed a single tear. Wasn't for want of trying. I tried to remember the good times, I really did. And there were a few, even though they fought like cat and dog and clouted me even harder than they hit each other. I mean, you should be upset, shouldn't you? It's your own mam and dad and they've just died so you should be able to squeeze out one tear at least.

There was a bad storm that night, forks of lightning sizzling across the sky and crashes of thunder shaking the walls of the cottage and rattling the pots and pans. But that was nowt compared to what Lizzie did. There was a hammering at the door fit to wake the rotting dead, and when Agnes drew back the bolt, Bony Lizzie strode into the room, her black hair matted with rain, water streaming from her cape onto the stone flags. Agnes was scared but she stood her ground, placing herself between me and Lizzie.

'Leave the girl alone!' Agnes said calmly, trying to be brave. 'Her home is with me now. She'll be well looked after, don't you worry.'

Lizzie's first response was a sneer. They say there's a family resemblance. That I'm the spitting image of her. But I could never have twisted my face the way she did that night. It was enough to turn the milk sour or send the cat shrieking up the chimney as if the Devil himself was reaching for its tail.

'The girl belongs to me, Sowerbutts,' Lizzie said, her voice cold and quiet, filled with malice. 'We share the same dark blood. I can teach her what she has to know. I'm the one she needs.'

'Alice needn't be a witch like you!' Agnes retorted. 'Her mam and dad weren't witches so why should she follow your dark path? Leave her be. Leave the girl with me and get about your business.'

'She's the blood of a witch inside her and that's enough!' Lizzie hissed angrily. 'You're just an outsider and not fit to raise the girl.'

It wasn't true. Agnes was a Deane all right but she'd married a good man from Whalley. An ironmonger. When he died, she'd returned to Roughlee, where the Deane witch clan made its home.

'I'm her aunt and I'll be a mother to her now,' Agnes retorted. She still spoke bravely but her face was white and I could see her plump chin wobbling, her hands fluttering and trembling with fear.

Next thing, Lizzie stamped her left foot. It was as easy as that. In the twinkling of an eye, the fire died in the grate, the candles flickered and went out and the whole room became instantly dark, cold and terrifying. I heard Agnes scream with fear and then I was screaming myself and desperate to get out. I would have run through the door, jumped through a window or even scrabbled my way up the chimney. I'd have done anything, just to escape.

I did get out, but with Lizzie at my side. She just seized me by the wrist and dragged me into the night. It was no use trying to resist. She was too strong and she held me tight, her nails digging into my skin. I belonged to her now and there was no way she was ever going to let me go. And that night she began my training as a witch. It was the start of all my troubles.

I'd only seen Agnes once since that awful night but I knew I'd be welcome at her house now as I returned to Pendle. In fact, no sooner had I walked down through the darkness of the trees than her door opened wide and she stood there, her smile brighter than the beeswax candles that illuminated her rooms. Uses a mirror for scrying, Agnes does, and she'd seen me coming.

'Come in, Alice, girl, and warm your bones!' she called out in her gruff but kindly voice. 'It's good to see you again. Just sit yourself down by the fire and I'll boil you up some tasty broth.'

While Agnes busied herself, I sat in her rocking chair facing the warm fire, my eyes drawn upwards to the rows of shelves that I remembered so well. She was a healer and the shelves were full of pots and jars. There were also leather pouches tied with string containing the blends of herbs and potions she used to practise her craft.

Soon I was sipping delicious hot broth while my aunt seated herself on a stool by the fire. It was a long time before she spoke. 'What brings you to Pendle again, girl?' she asked cautiously. 'Is Lizzie nearby?'

I shook my head. 'No, Agnes. Ain't you heard? No need to worry yourself about Lizzie. Trapped in a pit in Old Gregory's garden at Chipenden, she is. Stay there till she rots! Best place for her . . .'

So I explained how I'd befriended Tom Ward and was now staying at the Spook's Chipenden house, helping to make copies of the precious books in his library. I told her about the theft of Tom's boxes and the kidnapping of his family – Jack, Ellie and their young child.

'Thought you might like to help me, Aunt. I've no clue where they've been taken and I don't know where else to turn. Thought you might scry 'em for me with your special mirror . . .'

Without a word, Agnes went and fetched her scrying mirror from the cupboard. It was small but set in a brass frame with a heavy base. Then she blew out all her candles but one, which she set just to the left of it. Soon she was muttering incantations under her breath and the glass flickered to brightness. She was searching for Tom's family. Images began to form . . .

I glimpsed a dark stone wall. Curved, it was. We were looking up at it. Not much doubt, was there? We were looking at Malkin Tower. Agnes was using the surface of the moat to see it. Water's as good as a mirror if you're skilled like Agnes. Quickly a new image flashed across the mirror: the arched ceiling of a dark, dank dungeon with dripping water. Then a weary pain-racked face filled the glass, eyes closed. It was El-lie!

Her hands reached towards us and I realized that we were peering up at her from a bowl of water. The image distorted and fragmented. She was dabbing water onto her face. Then the mirror darkened and Agnes gave a sigh and turned towards me.

'Was that Ellie, girl?'

I nodded.

'Just used the mirror to be sure,' Agnes said. 'But I suspected the Malkins from the start. You've no chance of getting them out of that tower alive. Best get yourself away from Pendle, girl. It's more dangerous than it's ever been. Go while you're still able to breathe!'

I spent the rest of the night with Agnes. We chatted about old times and she told me what had been happening more recently. How the Mouldheels were growing in strength and had a new coven leader – a girl witch called Mab. Apparently this Mab could peer into the future so well that, to counteract her power, the Malkins and Deanes had called a truce and created an evil creature called Tibb, using dark magic. Tibb was a seer and could also see things at a distance. Agnes reckoned that was how they'd found Tom's boxes.

*

I spent the night in Agnes's back room, and at dawn I headed for Malkin Tower. Knew I couldn't do much on my own but I thought I might as well just sniff around a bit before pushing on to the church at Downham, where I'd meet up with Tom and Old Gregory. Might find out something useful. It was worth a try. But then, as I circled through Crow Wood, skirting Bareleigh to the north, the sun dappling the tree trunks, I saw a girl ahead, sitting on a stump. Staring at me, she was. Sniffed her out right away and knew she was a witch.

As I got nearer, her feet told me more. Barefooted, so she had to be a Mouldheel. Last of the three main clans to settle in Pendle, they were. Before that they were nomads. Called 'stink-feet' by some and, later, 'mouldy-heels'.

She didn't look much older than me and was certainly no bigger. So why should I run? I kept walking towards her, ready to fight if necessary. She had pale hair that hung down beyond her shoulders, and green eyes. Her clothes were in tatters too. No pride in their appearance, the Mouldheels. She was one of them all right.

I halted about five paces away and tried to stare her out but she wouldn't look away. 'Shouldn't have come here, Alice Deane,' she warned, a faint smile on her face. 'You'll never leave Pendle alive . . .'

How did she know who I was? I gave her a dirty look and spat at her feet. 'Haven't met before, have we? Know that for sure 'cos I'd have remembered your ugly face!'

'Scried you in a mirror. Knew who you were the moment you crossed into Pendle. Don't you know who I am?'

'Don't really care who you are, girl,' I told her. 'You look nowt and you are nowt!'

'Well, you should care who I am 'cos you'll have good cause to remember me. My name's Mab. Mab Mouldheel . . .'

It was the girl Agnes had told me about, the new leader of the Mouldheels. I wasn't impressed, I can tell you, so there wasn't much point in wasting words. Mab was supposed to be a seer. Good at seeing the future. But she didn't see what hit her.

I went straight for Mab, gave her a good slapping in the face and grabbed a handful of her hair. She fell sideways off the log and we rolled over and over. Couple of seconds and I knew I was stronger than she was. I was just getting the better of her when there were shouts in the distance. More Mouldheels! Lots of 'em!

Struggled to get away then, I did, but Mab hung onto my clothes and hair. Almost tore myself free but she held me fast. Then rapid footsteps. Somebody running hard towards us. Next, something hit me really hard on the side of the head and everything went dark.

I woke up with a thumping headache to find myself sitting in a meadow, my back against a dry-stone wall. My hands were free but my legs were chained together. I wasn't in Crow Wood any longer. Cottages in the near distance looked like Bareleigh, the Mouldheel village. The sun was high in the sky. Had to be almost noon.

'She's awake!' someone called out, and I turned my

head to see three girls walking barefoot towards me through the long grass. One of them was Mab; the other two looked like twins. They had thin faces with hooked noses and narrow, mean mouths.

The three girls sat down in the grass opposite me, Mab in the middle. 'Meet my twin sisters, Alice Deane,' Mab called out. 'This is Jennet and this is Beth. Both younger than me but older than you.'

I looked at Jennet. She was eating something from the palm of her left hand. White, soft, squishy, wriggling things that didn't like sunlight. They were maggots!

'Want one o' these?' Jennet asked, holding her hand out towards the other two girls.

Mab declined with a curt shake of her head but Beth popped a couple into her mouth and began to chew. 'Good, these,' she said with a crooked smile.

'Should be!' Jennet mumbled, stuffing her own mouth full of writhing maggots. 'Got 'em from a dead cat. Black one, it was, too. Black-cat maggots are always the tastiest.'

'Well, sisters,' Mab said, squinting straight into my face. 'What should we do with this ugly Deane? Roast her over hot coals or tie her to a tree and let the crows peck out her eyes?'

'Best we cover her with leeches,' said Beth. 'Once they're plump and squishy with blood we can eat 'em! Nothing quite so juicy as a bloated leech.'

'Prefer sheep-ticks,' Jennet said. 'But they're hard work collecting.'

'Ain't a Deane any longer,' I interrupted, directing my words at Mab. 'Finished with my family, I have. Could be on your side if you'd have me. Sick of the Deanes. Sick of the Malkins too.'

'Who you trying to fool?' Mab sneered. 'Wasn't born yesterday, was I? You'd better talk now and tell us why you're here. What brings you back to Pendle?'

'Supposed to be a seer, ain't you?' I laughed. 'Wouldn't have to ask questions if you knew your craft!'

Shouldn't have laughed like that. Mab was livid. Tried to fight 'em off but my legs were bound and it was three against one. The twins held me down while Mab pulled out a blade and cut off a lock of my hair. I began to tremble then. Knew I was in her power now all right. Using dark magic, they could hurt me real bad. They took me back to the row of cottages where Mab and her sisters lived. Got me down into a cellar and started to work on me.

The first time they questioned me it wasn't that bad. Mab slapped me a few times. Getting her own back, she was, for the pasting I'd given her in the woods. I said nowt anyway. And didn't cry out. Wouldn't give 'em the satisfaction.

After that they left me alone in the dark for an hour or so. There were four mirrors in that cellar, one on each wall. Despite the dark, out of the corners of my eyes I kept glimpsing things. Witches spying on me. Making sure I wasn't trying to get away.

When Mab and her sisters came down the steps the second time, they meant business. Mab had my lock of hair. Kept stroking it, she did, and muttering dark spells. Then the pains started. Pins and needles in my feet for starters. Next bad cramps in my stomach. But the worst thing of all was when I started to choke. It was just like cold invisible hands squeezing my throat. Couldn't breathe, could I? An hour of that and I told 'em everything they wanted to know. No hope of escape either. Even if I could have got free of the padlock and chain, they'd put a bind on me – a spell that meant I couldn't go more than fifty paces from that cellar. Hopeless, it was.

Told 'em about Tom and the Spook staying at Downham presbytery. Told 'em why we'd come to Pendle – to rescue Tom's family and get back his boxes.

'That's all I need, Alice Deane!' Mab gloated. 'I'm off to Downham now to lure Tom back here. I'll tell him you asked me to bring him. He'll follow me for sure then. We'll have his bones before the night's over!'

I really hadn't wanted to do it. Last person in the world I'd hurt is Tom; I felt really bad giving his whereabouts away. Putting him in danger like that. And I was afraid that Mab's plan to lure Tom here might just work. She set off for Downham right away, taking her sisters with her.

After that it was all up with me. Said they were going to take both my bones and my blood just before dawn. Left me down in the cellar for a couple of hours, then some others from their clan took me out into the yard, where a big cauldron was bubbling, and made me sit on the ground nearby. Lots of other Mouldheels there – they all came across and gathered round me. Thought they were going to hit me but they just stared down at me, their mouths thin, hard lines. Women and men, there were – not all witches – but every last one of 'em a clan member and sworn enemy of a Malkin or a Deane.

Someone shouted that the food was ready so they left me alone then. But they didn't eat from the pot. Two big baskets full of roasted chicken were brought out and they filled their plates and went and sat in small groups, leaving me be. Started laughing and chatting amongst themselves then. Nobody offered me any chicken but I was too scared and anxious to eat anyway.

An old woman was stirring the pot. She came across and sneered down at me. 'Pain's coming your way, girl!' she gloated. 'Lots and lots of pain. It hurts a lot when they take your bones. No matter how sharp the knife, it's still agony. Brewed you up a broth, though. I'll fetch you some now . . .'

So saying, she went back to that bubbling pot and ladled out some broth into a bowl. Came back and offered it to me. 'Sip that, girl. Laced with special herbs, it is. It'll take away some of the pain – not all of it, but it might just make it bearable.'

I shook my head. Maybe she meant it kindly but most likely not. Didn't like the smell wafting up from the bowl she was holding under my nose. Some believe that the more it hurts when they take your bones, the more powerful the dark magic, so it could have been a broth to make me hurt more. I couldn't take a chance. I shook my head a second time and she shuffled away, grumbling and muttering under her breath.

Soon after that, Mab and her two sisters came down the hill. I was relieved that Tom wasn't with them. Mab looked angry so something must have gone wrong. Went right up to the fire, Mab did, and spat into it. Flames died down right away. Then, on Mab's orders, one of the Mouldheel men picked me up and carried me back down to the cellar and left me alone.

I waited to die. Thought then of all I'd lost. I'd never see Tom Ward again. That hurt me most of all. Didn't seem fair. Tears came to my eyes and I sobbed deep in my throat. I'd assumed that we'd have years together; that I'd be with him until he'd finished his apprenticeship with Old Gregory and then some more. Couldn't believe it was all over.

I was scared too. Really scared. I thought of the knife, the pain and dying in agony. It started to get really cold in that cellar. Witches kept glancing down at me from the mirrors on the walls. And then something else appeared in a mirror that was even more scary. I saw the ugliest of faces. Looked like a child but it had no hair at all and a grown man's features with really sharp needle-like teeth. What was it? And then, suddenly, I knew. It had to be Tibb, the creature that the Malkins and

Deanes had made. It seemed to be looking straight at me, laughing and leering, till I turned away in fear and let a few tears come.

I heard boots coming down the steps and my heart began to race, my whole body trembling with fear. Then the door opened and somebody was standing there holding a candle. But it wasn't a Mouldheel with a sharp knife.

It was Tom Ward. He'd come to rescue me. From a clan of witches, I am, and don't deserve to be Tom's friend. But I'd do anything for him. Anything at all. Even die for him if necessary.

Alice Deane

The Journal of
THOMAS J. WARD

COVERNS AND CLANS

A <u>Covern</u> means thirteen witches gathered to use
dark magic. Larger family of witches called a <u>Clan</u>. It
includes men, women, and children who don't directly
practise witchcraft.

HISTORY OF PENDLE CLANS

Malkins, Deanes, and Mouldheels are the three main
clans in Pendle. Malkins first witches to make home
in Pendle. Oldest and most powerful group. Original
tower was owned by local landowner. Malkins drove
him out. Used curses, poison, and abduction of his
eldest son. Henceforth became known as Malkin Tower.
Extended the building. Mainly downward. Earth
mounds east of Crow Wood contain soil excavated
from deeper dungeons. Some of the mortar is brown
because mixed with human blood and powdered bone.
Not all Malkins live in tower. Most now live in village
of Goldshaw Booth.

Deanes came later, from beyond sea to west. Big battles in Crow Wood. Lots of buried bones. Failed to capture Malkin Tower. Made their home in village of Roughlee. Very proud people. Easily take insults. Imagine grievances and can become spiteful. Still dream of making tower their own.

Mouldhills last to arrive. These witches formerly nomadic and went barefooted. Others called them "stink feet" or "mouldy heels," hence present name. Gradually infiltrated village of Bareleigh and made it their home. The three main witch villages quite close together. Sometimes known as **Devil's Triangle**. There are other smaller Pendle witch clans but smaller and less powerful: Hewitts, Ogdens, Nutters, and Preesalls. Also some incomer witches but these mostly shunned.

POWER OF WITCH CLANS

Clans very powerful and dangerous. Spook says best example of why they should be feared happened seventy years ago. Witch Finder called Wilkinson arrived in Pendle to deal with clans once and for all. Brought two priests, three wardens, and thirty special constables. All armed.

Made base in Downham. Started to arrest suspected witches in Devil's Triangle. Swam over thirty. Three drowned. One died of fever afterwards. Five floated and were tried. All five found guilty and hanged. Wilkinson began second phase. More arrests.

In meantime witches collected their dead. Buried them under loam in Witch Dell. Travelling back to Downham after dark, Wilkinson tricked into passing through dell. Half his party slaughtered by dead witches. Bodies recovered later. All drained of blood. Thumb bones missing.

Made hasty retreat from district but Malkins used powerful curse. Within thirteen months every last one dead, including Wilkinson. Some died in accidents. Others just vanished from face of earth. Probably victim of witch assassins. Wilkinson's death particularly horrible. Nose and fingers fell off. Ears turned black and withered away. Tried to hang himself. Failed when rope broke. Mad with pain, drowned himself in pond. So witch clans' revenge was total.

WITCH ASSASSINS

Each clan employs at least one witch assassin – role to seek out and destroy enemies. Some no better than poisoners but Malkins' assassin formidable. Successor chosen by challenge and mortal combat.

Previous assassin was Kernolde the Strangler who mostly used rope to kill but sometimes traps and pits full of spikes. Hung victims by their thumbs.

Defeated by Grimalkin who slew Kernolde in Crow Wood. Birds pecked her bones clean. Grimalkin's favourite weapons – long blades. Skilled blacksmith. Forges her own weapons. Very fast and strong. Has code of honour. Never wins using trickery. Likes opponent to be a dangerous challenge. Has dark side. Sometimes uses torture.

Snips flesh and bone. Carves above sign on trees to mark territory or warn others away. All fear snip-snip of her terrible scissors.

PRESENT SITUATION

Deanes and Malkins getting closer. Starting to unite.
Mouldheels much more mysterious. As well as blood
and bone magic they're skilled with mirrors, sometimes using them for scrying, which means foretelling
the future (Spook doesn't believe in this). Mouldheels
mostly keep distance from other two clans so far but
new danger is that someone is trying to unite all three.
Very dangerous that. Together could do great evil.

WITCHES' SABBATH

These are celebratory feasts where covens gather at
midnight.

Candlemas (February 2). Witches make their own
black candles. Tallow wax always mixed with human
blood. Many contain poisonous herbs too. Some
candles have specific purpose. Can make victims fall
helpless into deep sleep. Or become in thrall to a
witch. Also can make time seem to pass more quickly
or slowly than it really does.

Walpurgis Night (April 30). Sabbath when novitiates
are assigned to the witches who'll train them. Blood

rituals. Spells of binding. Attempts to control trainees and take away free will. Not all survive. Blood of the slain used to anoint the successful.

Lammas (August 1). Most propitious Sabbath for opening portal to the dark. This is when attempts made to contact the Fiend or summon him to our world. Needs at least combined strength of three covens to attempt this safely.

Halloween (October 31). Celebrates coming of dark winter months. Witch feast when ghosts most receptive to interrogation. Forced to answer questions and some can prophesy. Witches usually wear masks at this Sabbath. Even when main clans celebrate separately, spies will infiltrate. If detected spies slain, their blood and bone taken for dark magic.

BLOOD AND BONE MAGIC

Spook told me more about these. Witch who uses
Blood Magic mostly takes it just before the full
moon. Children preferred but adults and animal blood
acceptable if thirst great enough. Water witches use it
mainly for sustenance but Pendle witches always
to accumulate power. Also increases strength and
agility. Longevity too. Used in rituals to summon
spirits and slay enemies at a distance. Mouldheels use
it to enhance scrying ability.

Witches who use **Bone Magic** prefer freshly taken
bones. Must be from a person killed just before dawn.
Nothing wasted. Those bones not used immediately
buried for future use – but not as powerful. When
needed (could be years later) witch sniffs them out
like a dog. Washes them in milk before use. All bones
useful but thumb bones are most sought after. Can be
used to summon the dead.

PROPHECIES

Will any of them come true? They worry me a lot.

"He'll be the best apprentice you've ever had and he'll also be your last."

Mam wrote that in letter to the Spook. Nice if I could be his best ever apprentice but sad because of the Spook. Means his job and maybe his life are coming to an end.

"You will die in a dark place, far underground with no friend at your side!"

That prophecy part of curse against Spook. Made by three Pendle clans. I thought it might happen in Priestown but he survived. Still worries me. We spend lots of time underground!

"I see a girl, soon to be a woman. The girl who will share your life. She will love you, she will betray you, and finally she will die for you."

This prophecy made by Tibb. Didn't mention girl's name. Could it be Alice? This is one that scares me most. Couldn't bear to lose Alice.

Thomas Ward's apprenticeship
continues in ...

BOOK FIVE: THE SPOOK'S MISTAKE

OUT NOW IN PAPERBACK

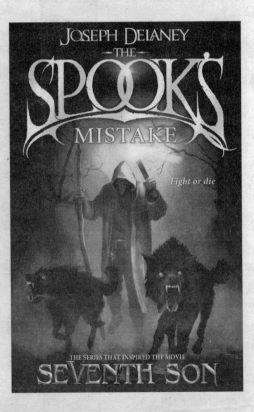

Or start reading right now!
Also available in ebook and audio download